A MOMENT IN TIME

Andrianna stepped back to get a better view of her nude figure. It was the body of a beautiful young woman—firm, full, and desirable . . . and *desiring*. That was the rub. She wanted him, and he had tired of her before he had even had her. *Or had he?*

She had to find out, and not tomorrow. She had to do it this very night. She had spent a life of denial. Tonight she would not be denied. She rushed out of the bathroom, grabbed for her cape and wrapped it against her nakedness. If he wasn't in his cabin, she would comb the ship until she found him.

She flung her door open wide, prepared to rush out into the night, only to find him there, breathing as hard as she was, his eyes blazing with a fierce light. . . .

TILL THE END OF TIME

JUNE FLAUM SINGER

ZEBRA BOOKS
KENSINGTON PUBLISHING CORP.

For my youngest daughter, Valerie,
truly a woman of value and valor

This book is a work of fiction. Names, characters, places, and incidents are used fictitiously. This work of fiction does not purport to be a factual record of real events or real people. The actions and motivations of the characters named after real people are entirely fictional and should not be considered real or factual.

ZEBRA BOOKS

are published by

Kensington Publishing Corp.
475 Park Avenue South
New York, NY 10016

Copyright © 1990 by Jungo, Inc. Published by arrangement with Contemporary Books, Inc.

First Zebra Books printing: March, 1992

Printed in the United States of America

ACKNOWLEDGMENTS

My thanks to Dr. Jordan Crovatin and Kaylee Davis for their generosity in sharing their expertise with me, and to my editor, Nancy Coffey, for her inspired but gentle guidance and unerring eye. It has been a joy. And as always, my thanks to Joe for the best of everything.

CONTENTS

Prologue

Los Angeles
1990

February 14

Standing at her bedroom window to look out at the golden day, breathing in the sweet morning air drifting in on a tiny breeze, she was so lost in reverie she didn't sense his presence until he was directly behind her. Then she could feel his lips on her nape and his warm body moving against hers.

She pressed back against him, and for several moments she didn't move, barely breathing as she felt the familiar electrifying sensations coursing through her. Then he spun her around and she reached up to draw his face down to hers so that she could brush her lips across his again and again, touch his skin, smooth his hair, desperate to embrace *all* of him and be so embraced in return.

They followed ritual, he stroking her here, she caressing him there, doing each and every lovely thing lovers had done for centuries but believing it was all fresh and new and a wonder. Then, when the demand for the final gratification could no longer be denied, the waiting no longer tolerable, he picked her up and carried her to the bed.

After he left her, she lingered in bed languorously, immersed in the lovely afterglow she was reluctant to surrender. And she thought as she had before, but only after being with *him,* that sex before sundown — and, on this day, before breakfast — was something very special and, as her mother before her had testified, a golden surprise, moments stolen from eternity . . .

She stirred, her eyelids fluttered open, and she knew she wasn't lying in her big, velvety bed with its lacy pillows, satiny sheets, and downy comforter. Then, when she realized exactly what kind of bed she *was* lying in and that she was hooked up to all kinds of tubes, she knew where she was and what was happening to her. She was in a hospital. And maybe she was dying . . .

"Oh, God, not yet. I'm not ready to die!" she cried out.

It wasn't so much that she was afraid. It was that, for the first time, life was so incredibly sweet and she wasn't ready. She herself wasn't ready, and neither was he.

And then she said it again, softly, a plea: "Please, God, not yet. Not now . . ."

She felt a cool hand on her forehead and through a haze saw several people — nurses, doctors in white coats — moving about, consulting one another.

They are so busy, and I am so tired . . .

"Where am I?" she asked the nurse, who began to adjust one of her various attachments.

The young woman smiled at her sweetly. "Don't you worry. You're going to be fine."

"Which hospital am I in?" she persisted.

"Cedars-Sinai."

"Cedars-Sinai? Are you sure? That doesn't seem right."

"Oh? Why not?" the nurse asked, humoring her.

"Because I've visited friends here, and there's always been a view."

Maybe it was only Cedars' best rooms that had the view of the picture-pretty Hollywood Hills, she thought. But wouldn't *she* — *his* wife — have one of the very best rooms? A suite on the eighth floor? A room with a view?

"But I can't see out," she whimpered childishly. "There aren't any windows in this room!"

"That's because you're in ICU. But before you know it you'll have a lovely room, one with our very best view."

ICU! The Intensive Care Unit. Of course! Where else would they put her? She'd been warned. Oh yes, she'd been warned that her situation was precarious. And she had gone ahead anyway. But not heedlessly. It had been a calculated risk. It was for him. It was the least to which he was entitled.

"What day is it?" she asked the nurse.

"It's Wednesday, the fourteenth. Saint Valentine's Day. Maybe someone will bring you a present. Wouldn't that be nice?"

"Are you *sure* it's Valentine's Day?"

"Yes. Sure."

"Today is a very special day," she told the nurse.

"Of course it is."

But she could tell the nurse didn't *really* understand. Didn't know that it was the *big* day. It was the day *he* crossed over a very important line. The line that separated the mere millionaire from the billionaire. And though she *was* supposed to get a very special present today — he had told her so, and unlike her, he never lied — she knew that now there would be no more gifts from him. When he found out that she was in the hospital and why, he would never forgive her. And of course his special present to her didn't really matter. What mattered was her present to him.

"You mustn't tell him that I'm here," she whispered urgently. "He's going to be very angry."

"No," the nurse soothed. "No one's going to be angry with you."

"Oh, he will! And he has every right to be."

In truth she had never seen him *really* angry. Certainly not with her. But this time he would be. This time he would be

11

so furious he would damn her soul for all eternity . . . just as Heathcliff had damned Cathy's.

"Now, we need to know who your doctor is," the nurse said, bending over her. "It's very important. Then we'll get him right over here and everything will be fine."

"No, he'll be angry too. Who brought me here?"

"I'm not sure, but someone said it was your housekeeper who called 911."

"Oh, that's good," she said with relief. "I wouldn't want *him* disturbed. Today's too important a day. He can't be disturbed today."

"You don't want to disturb your doctor? Is that it? Believe me, he will *want* to be called. And he won't be angry, I promise you."

"No, not the doctor! Heathcliff!" She thrashed about in agitation.

She doesn't understand! I have to make her understand!

"You can't disturb *Heathcliff!* And he *will* be angry! He'll be so angry he will curse me! He'll throw himself across the bed and cry bitterly. And then he'll damn my soul for all eternity. He'll say, 'Catherine Earnshaw, may your soul never rest in peace for as long as I live, because *you* are my soul, and I cannot live without my soul.' "

The nurse sighed and stroked her hand. "No, dear. No one will curse you, believe me. Now just close your eyes and try to get some rest, okay?"

Obediently she closed her eyes. It was too much of an effort to keep them open. Too hard even to speak . . .

She heard someone—a man's voice—ask the nurse, "Did you get the name of her doctor out of her?"

No, she didn't! I can't tell anybody that! It's a secret!

"I'm afraid not, Doctor. I'm afraid she's out of it. She's really rambling. She said someone called Heathcliff was going to be very angry with her. That he was going to curse her. That he was going to throw himself across her bed and say, 'Catherine Earnshaw, I damn your soul for all eternity!' But

12

that isn't her name, is it, Doctor Hale? Catherine Earn-shaw?"

"Hardly." The voice was dry and sad at the same time. "Heathcliff and Catherine Earnshaw are characters out of a novel, Miss Peters. Tragic lovers."

"But, Doctor, she thinks she *is* Cathy!"

"Yes . . . but it's not uncommon for someone in her condition to slip in and out, to lose touch with reality."

"Oh, Doctor, are we going to be able to—?" The words caught in the young woman's throat.

"Maybe—if we ever find out who her doctor is. If we can figure out in time what the hell is really wrong with her in the first place . . . Damn! I can't believe they'd bring in a woman like this, rich as hell and in this condition, and no one in that goddamn house of hers knows who her doctor is! It doesn't make sense."

And then she heard another man—another doctor?—speak. "They've finally located her husband."

Oh, no! He can't be bothered today! He mustn't be!

She wanted to cry out in protest, but her voice failed her.

"He called from his car to say he's on his way."

"And in the meantime did anyone find out from him who her doctor is?" That was Dr. Hale's voice again, and it was harsh with frustration. "Didn't anyone tell him that we *have* to have her medical records? That it's crucial?"

"I don't know. I didn't speak with him. But I'm sure the situation was explained to him—that we had to get hold of those records. Well, he should be here before long, and then we'll—"

"Before long? Well, let's just pray that he makes it before the lady slips into a coma she won't come out of. This situation is intolerable! Here we are in one of the best-equipped hospitals in the world with the wife of a man who's one of the *Forbes* Four Hundred, she's in a life-and-death crisis, and *we're* forced to work in the dark without a medical history. Unbelievable!"

Oh no, Doctor, not unbelievable at all. Secrets have been the mainstay of my life . . .

But now it was all coming apart. All her secrets exposed to the cruel, hard light of day. Would he be angrier at the secrets and the lies or that he'd been disturbed today of all days—the day the dream of his life was to become reality?

Though it was silent now, the room vibrated with tension. She forced her eyelids open by sheer will to see all of them looking at her. Her own gaze traveled from face to face, and she saw a different expression on each one. Sorrow. Desperation. Pity. Even rage. That face filled with rage had to be Dr. Hale's, she thought.

The eyelids fluttered shut again. She couldn't bear to see these emotions exposed so nakedly.

"Oh, it's so sad. And she's so beautiful . . ." Nurse Peters said, as if she were already mourning her passing.

Then, just before she slipped into unconsciousness once more, she heard the second doctor say softly, "Well, this is a first for me. I never had a billionaire's wife as a patient before."

"Is he *really* a billionaire?" the nurse asked.

"If he isn't, he's the closest thing to it." That was the second doctor's voice again.

It was Dr. Hale who said huskily, "But the problem is I'm not at all sure even a billionaire's money can save her . . ."

When she opened her eyes once again, it took her a few seconds to reorient herself—to realize once more where she was and what she was doing there. And then she did remember, and the chilling fear coursed through her again. How much time had passed? Was it still St. Valentine's Day? Had *he* come? Had he already come and gone, filled with disappointment? Or had he simply come and gone, cutting his losses coolly and quickly like the good businessman he was?

She remembered his once having said, "If you realize a deal's gone sour, you don't fool around trying to sweeten the pot, throwing good money after bad. You get out fast."

Wasn't she the deal gone sour? As sour as it got?

Or had it been as she had first imagined? He standing

14

over her, consumed with rage, damning her soul for all eternity?

And then she saw him. He was standing in the doorway. And, God help her, he *did* look full of rage, scowling as she had never seen him scowl. Even Heathcliff couldn't have done it better! But there was something else — though his face was livid with fury, he was crying!

Before she knew him, she'd scorned the past — thinking about it was a waste of time — and hadn't even considered the future, uncertain as it was. Before she had fallen in love with him, she'd clung only to an imperfect present, believing it was all she had or could ever hope for. And then she had met him and dared to dream of a future — of love, of golden surprises, of sex in the afternoon . . .

Has he come to damn me or only to say good-bye?

He approached her bed, and despite the tears and the wrath, never had he appeared so beautiful to her. Not even that first time. Oh, she would never forget that day, the first time she saw Jonathan West . . .

Part One

The QE2
November 9-13, 1988

One

She would always remember the first time she saw Jonathan West as if it were a movie unfolding before her eyes in dazzling wide-screen color. It was autumn, a very cold day, and she was about to board the *QE2* departing Southampton to arrive in New York five days later.

She was down on the quay looking up as Dwight Rumson, who had escorted her to the ship in his limousine, was making a last-ditch effort to change her mind about going to New York. Just as she had anticipated he would. Like all wealthy men, Dwight did not give up easily.

He wanted her to marry him and swore that he was passionately in love with her.

He was standing very close now, pressing, urging her to get back in the car, telling her that they could just drive away and let the ship leave without her. For him it was that simple. But he was wrong. It was neither simple nor possible.

But she listened attentively to his every word. She owed him that much. He had been a good friend and very kind. But then, when she saw the tall, blond stranger on deck looking down at her, she felt a faint, nearly imperceptible quickening of her pulse and was startled by it. It had been a long, long time since she had experienced that particular sensation.

She looked away, then back up again, then quickly away

19

once more, missing Dwight's last remark. But Dwight didn't miss a thing. "What is it?" he demanded irritably.

"What is what?"

He said reproachfully, "You weren't listening, Andy."

She hated when he called her Andy.

"Of course I was listening."

She smiled at him sweetly, determined not to look at the handsome stranger again. After all, there'd never been a lack of handsome strangers in her life. As for Dwight, there'd never been a shortage of his kind either.

"I think I'd better board now, Dwight. Are you coming up? You don't have to, you know. Maybe it would be better if we just said good-bye here."

Actually she had been ready to move on for months now. She had already overstayed if not her welcome, then at least her leave in London. She had allowed Dwight's attentions to become a too-comforting habit, let herself grow too dependent on the security of his adoring and stable presence just as she had before . . . with other men, in other places.

Besides, despite what Dwight *thought* he wanted, by staying she would only give him false hope. He didn't understand that marriage to him, or to anyone else for that matter, was not a viable option for her. Not even if she were madly, crazily, recklessly in love with him, which she wasn't.

Oh, she loved him in her fashion, and she would certainly miss him. But *in* love? She was well past that stage in life when one succumbed to deep passion. A woman past thirty-five had no business being *crazy in love.* That was for the very young or for those still impossibly starry-eyed.

And then, as Dwight took her arm, gripping it too tightly as if trying to hold on to her by force, she looked up again and found that the disconcertingly handsome man on deck was looking down at her as if mesmerized.

There was no mistaking him for anything but an American. Was it the way he held himself? she wondered. Big shoulders squared back like a football hero. Was it his size? Or was it that easy self-assurance that Americans seemed to wear like a suit of clothing?

Or, for that matter, *was* it the clothes he was wearing that identified him as an American? He wasn't wearing an overcoat or even a raincoat even though the day was foggy and cold, especially here on the water. American men loved to appear heroic about the cold and the damp. And his suit was definitely not the meticulously tailored Savile Row banker's pin-striped number Dwight wore under his fitted cashmere topcoat, nor was it country squire tweed or that terribly stylish latest something from the Italian designers. There was something essentially mainstream United States about his look—nice, neat, current enough but decidedly not high style. Still she had the feeling—a feeling rare to her—that the man inside the suit was someone very high style indeed. She found that feeling vaguely unsettling.

And the way he was staring down at her! Bloody cheeky!

Even with the distance separating them she could sense the intensity of his gaze. Not the casual interest of the correct Englishman or the blatantly sexual stare of the Continental. No, his gaze was more—she groped for the right words—frankly curious and curiously forthright. Just plain interested. Very *much* interested.

And she felt foolish. A very attractive, very vital young man was doing nothing more extraordinary than looking at her with interest, and she was making a big thing of it!

More fool you, she chided herself. Still, she was very much conscious of his continued observation as she and Dwight moved up the gangplank, followed by the chauffeur carrying her many small pieces of luggage while she herself carried the matching jewelry case.

She glanced down at her jewelry case. That and the other pieces of her luggage, including the trunks already delivered to her stateroom, probably told more about her than anything else at that precise moment. More than Dwight with his arm around her waist, more than the liveried chauffeur and the shiny black limousine in which they'd arrived, more than the fact that she was booked into one of the *Queen's* most costly suites.

The luggage of burnished burgundy glove-soft leather was

a bon voyage present from Dwight, her English millionaire, just as the set of matched Vuitton she had left America with nearly thirty years before to start life anew on foreign soil had been a gift of another millionaire, her mother's beloved, Andrew Wyatt.

Maybe that was the reason millionaires had played such a large part in her life, she mused, a predilection for them being passed on in the genes like a fondness for reading . . . or even a killing disease.

But then it wasn't *exactly* the same predilection. Her mother, Elena, had loved Andrew Wyatt so, maybe more than life itself, while she herself merely *liked* her own millionaires—or, at most, loved them as she loved Dwight Rumson.

Even now the luggage brought it all back—that long-ago time when she, a frightened little girl with big eyes and dark braids hanging down her back, had left California's sunny wine country for a strange new land, with a new name and a new identity, long before assuming new identities and the names to go with them became a lifelong habit. Long before she'd become one of those mysterious cosmopolitan women who wander from resort to city to countryside, ever moving from place to place in search of something achingly elusive, more citizen of the world than of any particular nation, with no corner of the landscape to call home.

"Where are you from?"

Her usual answer: "London," or "Paris," or "Zurich." Perhaps "Rome."

"You were born there?"

Sometimes she said yes and let it go at that. Other times she replied, "I'm an English citizen [or French or Swiss or whatever], but I was actually born in Italy [or in South Africa, Malaysia, or Sweden]. My father was in foreign service, you understand."

That was when she chose to mention a father. Every now and then she claimed to have been orphaned early on and sent to live with her father's brother, who was the one in foreign service.

As for her unaccented English: "I've always gone to either American or English schools, no matter where I lived, don't you know?" Which was one of the few statements about her past that came reasonably close to the truth.

When occasionally asked in a straightforward manner, "Who are you?" she had a poem by Emily Dickinson at the ready.

"I'm Nobody! Who are you?
Are you — Nobody — too?
Then there's a pair of us!
Don't tell! they'd advertise — you know!"

This always delivered in a charmingly self-deprecating fashion and accompanied by a bright self-mocking smile, but it fooled no one. All were convinced that, if nothing else, she was definitely a Somebody.

Mysterious? Absolutely. But wasn't that a requisite for any seductive, incredibly attractive woman of the world?

Rich? Who could really tell? She *looked* rich, *acted* rich, *dressed* rich, and her jewelry collection could only be described as fabulous.

Famous? Not so anyone would notice, fame and mystery being qualities severely at odds. Still, there was something about her that made people think she might be . . . or had been — a vague feeling, as elusive as she herself.

However, certain facts were self-evident and incontestable. She was beautiful, elegant, and to be seen only in the very best places with the most impeccably eligible men. And no matter what else she was or wasn't, she was definitely a world-class act.

She was well aware that no matter where she went there would always be *some* conjecture about her. But the one thing no one actually guessed was that what she really was was a woman on the run, trying to escape not only the past but the future as well.

* * *

When Jonathan West first noticed the tall, slender woman sheathed in a to-the-ankle fur down on the quay, he was standing well apart from the other voyagers already on board who were caught up in the festive spirit of embarking on an ocean crossing, talking excitedly to one another and waving madly at those left on shore. He'd been taking advantage of this free block of time—for him a rare commodity—by jotting down thoughts and observations in a small leather-bound notebook that he always kept with him, a practice that had served him well over the years.

But then, catching sight of her, his pen paused in midair. She *had* to be the most striking woman he'd ever seen . . .

First there was her hair. Long and inky black, caught in the stiff breeze coming off the water, it blew back from her forehead like a stormy cloud. And there was the way she carried herself. Regally. Her back impressively erect, her long neck lifted up and out from her shoulders so that her head was held high with her chin tipped up slightly, as if she were fully aware of who she was and damn proud of it.

But then he took note of the opulent fur coat that disclosed little of her proportions or her legs, which he nevertheless assumed were superb. The coat was obviously expensive, although he had no idea whether it was mink or sable, and it wasn't its worth that he found arresting. Rather it was the way she clutched it tightly about her, not wearing it merely for warmth or flaunting it as a fashion statement but as if using it as protective covering, to shield her from an oppressive and alien world.

Fancying himself an astute student of body language, Jonathan West found this most intriguing. More than intriguing; as fascinating as the woman herself. Then his gaze moved to the distinguished older man who was talking so rapidly and, from the look of it, most intensely, standing so close that he was almost on top of her, and he recognized him. He'd seen his picture in the financial pages often enough. The man was Dwight Rumson, the eminent British

24

financier and one of Europe's wealthiest men. And now Jonathan was more intrigued than ever. Intrigued by and *jealous* both of Rumson's standing in the world's financial community and of his obviously intimate relationship with this beautiful woman.

Then Jonathan wondered if *beautiful* was an adequate enough description. Many women were beautiful, especially in his home base of Los Angeles, where physical beauty was commonplace. Perhaps *stunning* was the word he was searching for, but was one word sufficient to describe this exquisite and exotic creature?

Once Dwight Rumson and the woman were on deck, Jonathan moved nearer to the couple inch by inch, eager to better scrutinize her each and every feature and, not incidentally, to eavesdrop on their conversation. He wanted to determine the exact status of their relationship, to affirm his hope that Rumson was on board *only* to see her off. That would give *him* five days at sea with her.

He moved another few inches sideways until he was less than a yard away from them, close enough now to see that the upturned collar of her coat highlighted a face both delicate and strong, and he wondered at that apparent contradiction. *Could* a face—the woman herself—be delicate and strong at the same time?

Now he could see hollowed curves formed by prominent cheekbones, a firm, clean sweep of chin line, a generous mouth. Her nose was straight, neither too long nor too short. A *patrician* nose, he decided, and her eyes were large and elongated.

He wished he could make sure of their exact color, but the angle at which she held her head made that determination difficult, so he pretended to drop his notebook and then, bending to retrieve it, managed to maneuver himself into a position where he could look directly and boldly into her eyes.

And then, just before shadowed lids dropped to cover

25

them from view, he saw eyes the color of amber, and he inhaled sharply. He was not a man who believed in psychic visions or things occult, yet he had *known* somehow before he looked into them that her eyes would be exactly that color—yellow-orange, like a cat's—just as if he had gazed into them in some other lifetime.

He thought of how at the very last moment, just as he'd been about to leave for Heathrow to catch his flight on the *Concorde,* he'd learned, strictly by chance, that the *QE2* was departing for New York that very same day with first-class accommodations still available—one of its top-graded, split-level penthouse suites appropriately called the Queen Elizabeth among them—and in a matter of seconds he had decided to change his plans, something he almost never did.

He tried to rationalize the compulsive decision, telling himself that he could use the few days at sea to relax. But relaxing was another thing he rarely did, something he really didn't relish. Doing business was practically the only thing he really savored—it was his vocation and his avocation, his favorite sport, his *raison d'être.*

When he couldn't convince himself that he had changed his plans for the purpose of enforced relaxation, he told himself he was doing it for the experience of traveling on a great ship since it might prove useful in the future. He *was* thinking of expanding the scope of his operations. Real estate, his first love and the foundation of his success, was beginning to get, well, boring. And though there was certainly satisfaction in the fact that his acquisitions got ever grander, transforming yet another fading grande dame of a hotel into a glittering debutante of hotels was losing its luster. A hotel is a hotel is a hotel, he thought. But a shipping line was—could be—another story. There was something dashingly romantic about the sea. And should a shipping line suddenly be up for grabs, to have already observed and experienced its operation was to be forearmed.

Now he wondered whether it really had been mere chance that had put him aboard the *Queen.* Chance? Luck? An eye to the future? Or had some unknown and unseen force been

26

at play here, putting him on this particular ship on this particular crossing to bring him together with the woman with the glowing amber eyes?

Fate? Kismet? Preordained destiny? Did it really matter? The fact was that he was here and she was here, and all things were possible.

For him all things had always been possible. As a matter of record, when asked, as he frequently was, to what he attributed his fantastic success at a mere thirty-five—a *wunderkind* of the financial world—his standard answer, accompanied by his disarming movie star smile, was: "Believe in yourself, listen to your gut, and don't waste time worrying about the other guy." Often he would add after an appropriate pause, "If you spend your whole life checking your back for knives, you'll never even see what's ahead."

Now his gut told him it was very possible that by the time they docked in New York he and this woman of mystery would be involved in a fateful relationship.

Of course, if she's Rumson's wife—

But, somehow, he didn't think so. He probed his mental files. *Was* Dwight Rumson married? Even if he had ever known this, he couldn't remember now.

His mistress, then? Didn't men like Rumson—older, powerful, movers and shakers—always have mistresses?

Does she fit the mold of mistress? Possibly. He didn't know all that much about them. Was there any particular kind of woman who became a rich man's mistress? Younger? Older? Sophisticated and worldly as opposed to fresh and dewy-eyed? If the latter was the case, would she be discarded when the dew was off the rose? As far as he was concerned, this woman was ageless, her appeal a throwback to women of legend—Helen of Troy, Cleopatra, Napoléon's Josephine—an enchantress no sane man would ever discard.

Well, mistress or wife, he wasn't going to be deterred. He simply wasn't in the habit. Chuckling to himself, he recalled what Harley Thompson, West Coast real estate magnate and his constant nemesis, had said in a *Fortune* interview when asked to comment on Jonathan's "checking your back" quote:

27

"That guy could have a dozen stilettos sticking out of his back, and he'd still be smiling, holding out his hand to shake the hand of *his* next victim. *Then* he'd go to the hospital. . . ." He'd had the quote blown up and mounted, and it had resided on his office wall for the last three years.

Very much conscious of the American's rather obvious efforts to position himself so close to her and Dwight, she was amused, flattered, exhilarated, and irritated all at the same time. She even knew *why* she was irritated: it was because she *was* exhilarated and irked with herself for being so. She had no business being aroused by and attracted to this too-young, too-attractive American.

Still, when he looked into her eyes and she back into his startlingly bright blue ones, for a second there—before she lowered her lids to shut him out—she saw an image reflected in his eyes, the image of a woman who frightened her—a rashly foolish woman, a dangerously reckless woman . . . a woman capable of falling in love.

She kept smiling at Dwight, but she wished he would leave so that she could go to her stateroom. She needed to get away from this American with his too-intrusive eyes and too-audacious manner. And she was tired. Very tired.

But Dwight still wasn't ready to disembark, not having quite finished his long good-bye.

"You'll write? You'll call?" he implored.

"Of course."

"You do know that I love you?"

"I know, Dwight. No one's ever been kinder."

"Kinder!" Rumson cried, disparaging the word. "I want you to marry me, and you tell me I'm kind."

"But Dwight, I told you in the very beginning that marriage was out of the question, that it was impossible."

Jonathan felt a rush of elation. He even gloated. *Any fool can see that she and Rumson are an impossible twosome.*

Rumson seized her hand. "But you never really told me *why!* If one doesn't give reasons, then nothing makes sense."

28

Jonathan heard the banker sigh. "I thought that I could make you love me!"

Her smile was bittersweet. "But I do love you."

Rumson shook his head morosely. "Not enough. Not in the right way."

Jonathan noted with satisfaction that she didn't dispute his words.

There was a second warning from the ship's horn for those not sailing to disembark.

"Don't be surprised if I show up in the States sooner than you think," Rumson warned.

And don't you be surprised if you show up and the lady's already spoken for!

"That would be wonderful, Dwight. As soon as I'm settled in I'll let you know where I am."

"I'm not giving up, you know. I'll change your mind yet: I'll never give up until you belong to me."

Until you belong to me! What arrogance! Then, realizing that he himself was being arrogant—the arrogance of the young as opposed to the arrogance of the superrich—Jonathan reproved himself for a second. Then he shrugged. It was the way things were. Someday there'd be some young man breathing down his own neck, being arrogant about his youth . . .

There was a final kiss—impassioned on Rumson's part, merely affectionate on hers. Good, Jonathan thought, waiting impatiently for Rumson to depart.

He watched her go to the railing to wave to Rumson below, to blow him a kiss. But the moment Rumson stepped into his limousine she moved away from the rail and unthinkingly wrapped her fur coat even more tightly about her. Did she feel suddenly bereft, vulnerable without her billionaire? Was she having second thoughts, or was it something else entirely?

It was quite possible that he was reading far too much into the gesture, yet Jonathan didn't think so. If he were a director filming a movie in which a supposedly sophisticated, self-confident heroine suddenly found herself friendless in a threatening situation — a woman in crisis — it was exactly the type of gesture he would have her use. Like a woman who must cross a border to find at the last minute that officials posted there are demanding passports, documents — and she is a woman without papers . . .

But the moment passed, and she straightened her shoulders and threw her head back, sending the long mane of dark hair into lovely motion, appearing once again regal and impervious.

He took a step toward her, but as he did so she looked him full in the face, her eyes impenetrable yet at the same time sending him a message: *Stop!* Then she turned on her heel, spoke to a ship's officer, and walked off briskly.

Jonathan West was not dismayed. Rather he felt the blood roaring in his veins, sending adrenaline coursing through his body. There was nothing he loved more dearly than a challenge. It was at least half the fun, and the fun had just begun. But first things first, and that meant finding out the lady's name, which, of course, was as simple as approaching the ship's officer.

He found out not only her name but the name of her suite — the Queen Anne on Signal Deck — which meant that they were neighbors.

He rolled her name over his tongue. It was a beautiful name, he thought, and completely compatible with its owner. He couldn't imagine a name suiting a woman more. And as he stood at the rail watching the shore fade from view, he repeated the name over and over again, whispering it on the wind. Andrianna DeArte . . . Andrianna DeArte . . . Andrianna DeArte . . .

It was a romantic name, a heroine's name right out of a storybook, a modern fairy tale, just as she herself was. And all his life, ever since he had been a young boy in sunny middle-class San Diego, he had dreamed of a storybook princess all his own — almost as much as he had dreamed of being a millionaire.

Then, abruptly, he knew he *had* to know more about her.

Placing a direct call to his office in Los Angeles via the ship's satellite phone system, he gave her name to his executive secretary and demanded a quick profile. Figuring that he should have an answer in a couple of hours, he went in search of one of the lounges on board to sit out the wait.

Working on his second Glenfiddich at the piano bar in the Queen's Yacht Club, which was one more drink than he customarily consumed at any one time, he had an answer sooner than he had anticipated. It seemed, his secretary reported, that the only information that had been quickly available on the lady in question was that she was an actress — a minor one — who had for the last two or three years been living in London, where she had appeared in a couple of minor stage productions, and that she was the constant companion of Dwight Rumson, a prominent figure in Britain's financial community and a candidate for knighthood.

"I already know that!" he said irritably. "What else? Where did she live before England? Is she married? Divorced? What's her history?"

But it seemed that this information hadn't been readily available. Did he wish an in-depth investigation initiated?

Jonathan was perplexed. How could there be so few data available on a woman who was obviously a beauty of world renown, the companion of a world-class player the likes of Rumson? It didn't make sense. If anything, the little kernel of information deepened the mystery more than it enlightened.

Frustrated, he barked that someone either wasn't doing his job or had the wrong woman. In any case he certainly *did* want an in-depth investigation initiated immediately, and he wanted the answers by morning. On that note he hung up the phone and finished off his drink. By tomorrow he'd have the whole story, he thought, not imagining for a moment that what seemed to him a simple task for any competent investigator posed a much more complex problem.

But then he had no idea that the woman in question changed her country of residence as often as some women replaced their good leather handbags. Or, for that matter, her name. There was no way he could have known that Andrianna DeArte had also been, in turn, Ann Sommer, Anna della Rosa, and other variations on the theme such as Andrea de Sommer and Annabel DeRosa after she had started out life as Andrianna Duarte in northern California's beautiful, peaceful, eternally green Napa Valley.

Two

She was only seven then and knew nothing of death. Still, although no one — not the visiting nurse or the doctor or even her beloved Rosa — had said a word to her, she sensed that her beautiful mother was dying.

Then, when her mother's friend — so tall and straight and who, to her child's eye, always appeared so stern and unsmiling — arrived in his long black car, she was certain of it.

For as long as she could remember the man with the eyes like blue marbles and hair the color of the tan crayon in her extra-big box of crayons had *never* come to visit at their nice white house, set at some distance from a cluster of much shabbier houses, more than once a month or, at the very most, twice. And now, only two days after his last visit, he was back again, and this time he didn't seem as stern as usual. This time he even smiled at her. And this time, unlike all the other times, there were no presents for her.

Usually the second his driver, Ralph, held the door open for him he would step out of the car with a present for her in hand and immediately give it to her without a word, a kiss, or even a pat on her dark hair. But the presents were always beautifully gift-wrapped — pink foil with fuchsia satin ribbon

33

or perhaps yellow paper as bright as buttercups with silk flowers tucked into an orange bow. Once the present was a dress so perfect and exquisite that her mother almost cried. "Oh, Andy," she had said, hugging her friend, "this has to be the most beautiful dress I've ever seen!" And then her mother had turned to Andrianna, her flecked yellow eyes large with excitement. "Isn't it the most beautiful dress you've ever seen, sweetie?"

What little girl wouldn't love a royal blue velvet dress studded with tiny seed pearls, a great big lace collar, and a long, flouncy skirt? It was a dress fit for a princess, and she moved her head up and down in mute agreement.

But then, when Elena gently prodded her, "What do you *say*, darling?" she remembered what she'd been taught to say and said it: "Thank you, sir."

At the same time, however, she was vaguely conscious that Rosa, who lived with them and loved them and did all the household chores since Elena was "delicate" and had to rest a lot, was muttering under her breath as she stood watching. "And where will she wear such a dress? To visit with the queen? Or maybe to have tea with you and your fancy wife in your big beautiful house, Mr. Rich Man?"

It was then that she sensed that Rosa, who always seemed to know *everything*, didn't like the man her mother called Andy—didn't like him and didn't trust him no matter how many presents he handed out. This came as a surprise. She had thought that anyone who gave so many pretty presents had to be *nice*—wonderful—even if he didn't smile very much.

Each time Andy came to visit, Ralph the chauffeur took her and Rosa for a long ride in the shiny black car, up and down the roads of the countryside, sometimes to another town to have an ice cream sundae, occasionally to a country fair or festival. And she, despite Rosa's rumblings and mumblings, was always excited to be riding in the beautiful car—to bounce up and down on the butter-soft leather seat, to feel

34

the burnished wood of the paneling, satin to the touch, to sniff the aroma of the perfect vivid pink roses sitting in silver and green glass bud vases on either side of the luxurious interior.

"Isn't this a wonderful car?" Andrianna would ask Rosa each time they went for a ride even though Rosa would usually answer only in sour grumbles. "Of course it's wonderful. Why wouldn't it be? It's a millionaire's car!" Or "A millionaire can buy just about anything! *If* he wants to . . ."

And when she said she thought millionaires had to be very wonderful and nice, Rosa merely grunted that they were nice only if they spent their money on the right things — things like a good name.

Most of these remarks went straight over Andrianna's head, but one thing sank in — she came to think of her mother's friend as "the millionaire."

Years later she would come to know that the millionaire's car was a Rolls-Royce, and that the car's green and silver bud vases also bore a celebrated name — Tiffany. By that time she also knew that the full name of the man her mother called Andy was Andrew Wyatt, of *the* San Francisco Wyatts, and that in northern California the Wyatt name was as special as the name Duarte was not. And certainly not when it was also one's mother's maiden name.

And by this time, all grown up, she also knew the value of what wise old Rosa had referred to as a *good* name, whether it was Rolls-Royce, Tiffany . . . or Wyatt.

As for the name Andrianna being the feminine form of Andrew, she didn't need to grow up to figure that one out. She'd done *that* long before.

Growing up, there'd be other things she would come to understand — when a certain day would suddenly be remembered, a certain afternoon suddenly recalled . . . when the meaning of certain words and conversations that had been incomprehensible to her when she first heard them would suddenly become crystal-clear. Rosa's bitter complaints, her dire forecasts for the future, and in turn, Elena's vague, distracted, defensive answers, her distraught yet always optimistic replies . . .

One conversation came to mind in particularly vivid recall—one that took place immediately after Mr. Wyatt's penultimate visit . . .

As soon as she and Rosa returned from their ride in the Rolls that afternoon, Andrew Wyatt barely took the time to throw a hasty good-bye over his shoulder before stepping into his car to take his leave. Elena explained to Rosa with an entreating, apologetic smile that he had a very important appointment in San Francisco.

"And what did Mr. Rich Man have to say for himself this nice, sunny afternoon, Elena? Did he, by chance, say that he was going to give you-know-who his good name? Or that he was going to provide for her future?"

The beautiful Elena sighed wearily. "We didn't talk about it today."

"And why not? Tell me," Rosa demanded, her voice rising. "Was what you were doing so much more important than talking about the future of—?"

She broke off when Elena, casting a desperate glance in Andrianna's direction, sank weakly into a chair and cried, "Rosa, please! Not now! Later. Please, try to understand!" Her eyes were beseeching. "He loves me—both of us—truly he does. And I *will* do it! I will talk to him! When the time is right. But today . . . the time went so fast. I don't know. Before I knew it, you two were back and the time was gone. You know how it is . . ."

"No," Rosa said flatly. "I *don't* know how it is. All I know is that you have to do something before it's too late! Elena, you're running out of time!"

But then, looking at Elena, so vulnerable, so frail in her lacy rose and silver negligee, the dark, dark hair pulled back from her face so tightly, the skin stretched so thinly over the fine bones, the older woman didn't have the heart to persist.

Making a feeble attempt at humor to atone for upsetting Elena once again and forgetting for the moment that Andrianna was in the room, Rosa threw her short arms up in the air and exclaimed in mock fun, "That's what comes of sex in the afternoon. I always said no good can come of making love before the sun goes down. Haven't I told you that repeatedly, Elena? That it's just the wrong time of the day?"

"Oh, Rosa!" Elena cried, grateful for the welcome reprieve, getting up from her chair to rain kisses on the troubled but now determinedly cheerful face—furrowed forehead, wrinkled brown cheeks, compressed lips forced into a smile. "Don't you know? Sex—love—in the afternoon is *golden* . . . like a wonderful surprise! Minutes stolen from eternity!"

Her mother's words had made no more sense to her than Andrianna's own conversations with Rosa along the same lines ever did. She knew about surprises, but *sex* . . . love . . . in the afternoon? She knew what love was—what she and her mother and Rosa felt for each other—but she didn't know what sex was. As for minutes stolen from eternity, she didn't understand the meaning of the word *eternity,* much less how long it lasted.

She was about to ask her mother what *exactly* was a wonderful surprise, but then Elena began to have difficulty breathing and had to be put to bed.

Thinking only that Elena needed to rest for a few hours as she so often did, Andrianna, eager to help Rosa make her mother more comfortable, was the one who plumped up the pillows, forgetting all the questions she'd wanted to ask.

That evening Andrianna waited for her mother to feel better, to get up and sing or dance around the house as she did when she was feeling very happy. But she waited in vain.

The next morning she waited again, this time for Elena to rise from her bed and go over to the window to look out and cry, "Oh, what a glorious day!" And then, after breakfast, maybe they would go out into the sunshine to tend to the garden. The fragrant roses that they grew in many beautiful colors—pink, crimson, yellow, white, orchid, and peach—

37

were her mother's favorites.

But when the bright and sparkling day came and went without Elena getting up, with Dr. Hernandez coming and going the whole day through, the dreadful suspicion that her mother was *never* going to get up again began to take root in Andrianna's mind and grew until it was confirmed by Andy's unscheduled appearance, and then she was terrified.

But only seconds later she changed her mind. She remembered what Rosa had said about millionaires—that they could buy . . . do . . . just about anything they wanted!

Then, when she and Rosa were immediately sent for a ride in the limousine, she was convinced. *When they came back from their ride, her mother would be as good as new!*

She'd be sitting up and smiling at them. She'd be laughing and looking as beautiful as they had ever seen her. The millionaire was going to do it!

When Ralph, his usually impassive face grim, finally brought them back to the house and held the car door open, Andrianna burst out to rush past him, unable to wait another second to see her mother sitting up and holding out her arms to her.

But as she raced into the house and then into her mother's bedroom, she saw that her mother was lying perfectly still, her eyes closed, her hands folded on the pure white sheet. And then Andrianna saw him—the millionaire—sitting in a chair pulled up to the bed and doing *nothing*, nothing at all, just sitting there with his face in his hands.

Terrified, she turned to Rosa, who was right behind her, but Rosa wasn't looking at her. Rosa was staring at Elena, lying so still, and then Rosa was tearing at her own hair with wild fingers, running over to where her mother lay, to kneel there, weeping at the foot of the bed.

Andrianna's eyes suddenly felt like hot coals burning in her head and her legs like twin rocks, so leaden she couldn't move them. Her mouth fell open, her bottom lip hung loose, as a scream from deep down within her struggled to come out but could not. It was stuck there in her throat, choking her, and the only sound to emerge was a ghastly gagging noise.

Rosa, who in her grief had forgotten Andrianna for the moment, turned, still kneeling, and held out her arms to her. And Dr. Hernandez came over to lay a hand on her shoulder. "She'll be all right," he told Rosa. "All she needs is a little time. Naturally this is a traumatic experience for the child, a—"

And then the scream emerged, high and terrible and piercing, and it filled all the corners of the room, followed by a series of low, haunting cries.

The doctor bent down to her then, and Rosa stumbled to her feet to rush over to her to wrap her arms about her. But Andrianna tore herself loose from them to spring like a baby tiger at Andrew Wyatt, who sat locked in his private world.

She was all over him at once, beating at him with her clenched fists, kicking at him with scrawny legs, tearing at his hair with frenzied fingers.

Andrew Wyatt tried to catch her flailing hands, to still the kicking of her feet, to fend off the fingernails that raked his cheeks into a pattern of red-streaked scratches, but she fought back so ferociously that the doctor and Rosa had to pull her off him.

Then, finally, she broke down and sobbed like any heartbroken child. She'd been so sure that he had come to save her mother—a millionaire, a white knight, his steed a long black car.

But she *was* only seven then, and it was all a confused jumble to her. Still, she was old enough to be instinctively frightened when she and Rosa returned to the pretty white house after her mother's burial to find Andrew Wyatt, who had not attended the funeral, waiting for them.

And she was old enough to think of eavesdropping on the conversation between Rosa and him when she was sent out of the room so that they could talk. And then, when she heard their voices—Rosa's high and loud and Mr. Wyatt's soft and hushed—she was wise enough to know that in the

39

end whose voice was louder wouldn't matter for much. In the end the millionaire would have his way and Rosa would have no say.

"You don't have anything to worry about, Rosa. I assured Elena that you'd be provided for, and you will be. You can live in this house for as long—well, as long as you wish, and you'll receive a monthly check. We'll call it a pension."

"But I don't care about the house or your pension," Rosa cried. "It's her . . . the child . . . Andrianna. You don't want her, and I do. I love her. I'll take care of her like she was my own. It's what Elena would want—"

"No. I know you mean well and that you love Andrianna, but it's *not* what Elena wanted," he said firmly. "I promised her that—"

Rosa made a spitting noise. "What did you promise Elena? That you would love her baby, that you would give her *your* name, take her into *your* home, *your* family?" The elderly woman laughed bitterly.

"Come now, Rosa, you know I can't do that . . . that it's impossible. Elena understood that. She always understood that, and I never made any false promises. What I did promise her was that I would take care of Andrianna, see to it that she had a good home, a proper background, and an education, and that's exactly what I intend to do. I'm just as concerned with Andrianna's welfare—her happiness—as you are."

"No!" Rosa screamed hoarsely. "You don't care about her happiness! How can she be happy without love, a real family?"

"I see that you don't understand, Rosa. She is *going* to have a real family—a proper family and a proper name—just as I promised Elena. Now that was what you always wanted for her too, wasn't it? I would think you'd be pleased."

And then his voice dropped so low Andrianna couldn't hear what he said next. All she heard was Rosa weeping.

40

They were at the airport in San Francisco, Rosa hugging Andrianna to her tightly while the expressionless Eva Hadley, who was to accompany Andrianna on her flight, stood to one side, giving the two a few minutes alone to make their good-byes.

"Please, Rosa, you *have* to come with me," Andrianna whispered, terrified of being separated from the one person she knew loved her.

"I can't," Rosa wept.

"But why not?"

"I told you why, my love. You're going off to start a new life—a good life with a wonderful family." Rosa tried to smile through her tears.

"But I don't want to!" Andrianna wailed. "I don't want a new family! I don't want to go away! I'd rather stay with you, Rosa. Please, Rosa, please! Why can't I stay with you?"

"Because Mr. Wyatt says so," Rosa said in desperation as the announcement came over the loudspeaker that flight 1020—her baby's flight—was now boarding.

"But why do we have to listen to him?"

"We just have to," Rosa mumbled as Miss Hadley, smiling brightly, came over to take Andrianna by the hand. "Time to go, I'm afraid," she said briskly. "Give Rosa a last kiss and come along."

Rosa's arms dropped to her side helplessly, letting go. She fell back a couple of steps, giving Andrianna a little push. "Go!"

"Why, Rosa, why?" Andrianna sobbed over her shoulder as she was borne along by the determined Eva Hadley.

But Rosa, her face buried in a large handkerchief, shoulders drooping, only turned away.

Eva Hadley accepted a glass of champagne from the pretty blond stewardess.

"And what would you like, honey?" the young woman asked Andrianna, who, quiet now, wiped at the dried tears

41

on her cheeks with the back of her hand. "Orange juice? Ginger ale?"

When Andrianna didn't answer, she asked, "How about a Coke?"

When Andrianna still didn't answer, Eva Hadley answered for her, saying cheerfully, "I guess Ann doesn't want anything right now. Perhaps later . . ."

"Okay, Ann. If you change your mind, be sure to let me know, you hear?" the stewardess offered kindly, moving on.

Andrianna looked at her traveling companion with big, indignant eyes. "My name's not Ann. It's Andrianna! Andrianna Duarte!"

"No, dear, I'm afraid it's not. It's Ann Sommer now," Eva said decisively.

"You're a liar!"

"You must *not* use words like *liar*, Ann, and you must *never* raise your voice. The Sommers are not the sort of people who will look kindly on that sort of behavior. Now, can you read?"

"The Sommers? Who are they? And of course I can read! Don't you know anything? I'm almost eight years old, and I'm going into the third grade in the fall."

"Good. Then look at this." She took a small booklet from her handbag. "This is called a passport. When you leave one country and go to another, you must have one of these. Now this is *your* passport. See? There's *your* picture."

Andrianna was amazed to see that Eva Hadley was right. It *was* a picture of her, even though she couldn't remember when it had been taken.

"And since you're such a big girl and know how to read, you tell me what name you see there."

Andrianna didn't say the name aloud, but she read it without difficulty. The name on the passport with her picture in it was Ann Sommer!

Three

Jonathan was finishing his second scotch when it occurred to him that he should see about his reservation for dinner if he wanted to make sure he and Andrianna DeArte were seated at the same table in the Queens Grill, the restaurant that accommodated those passengers occupying the ship's deluxe suites. Luckily there was only one seating, which simplified matters.

"This is Jonathan West," he said into the phone as he waved the bartender away. "Just checking. When Miss DeArte made her table reservation for dinner this evening, did she remember to mention that we're to be seated together?"

"Miss DeArte? One moment, sir . . . No, I'm afraid not. It appears that Miss DeArte hasn't made *any* table reservation as yet, but of course that isn't a problem. We'll be sure to seat you both at the same table."

With that settled, Jonathan went shopping. Formal dress was required in the grill, and he was unprepared, having expected to stay only one night in London, and all he had packed before leaving Los Angeles was a clean shirt and a change of underwear.

Fortunately there was a Harrods on board, and he found a dinner jacket that fit him perfectly without additional tailoring and a tux that, requiring only minimal alteration, would be ready the next day, compliments of the shop's custom tailor. Then, after selecting the obvious basic necessities he'd need for the five days at sea, which included a heavy leather jacket, he thought of the shipboard activities he and Andrianna might participate in together and selected swimming trunks, a terry robe, a couple of cashmere sweaters and a heavy cabled one, as well as some sweats for early morning runs around the deck. Did Andrianna run? he wondered. Or did she prefer to stroll?

Shopping completed, Jonathan found himself with something he rarely had to deal with—hours to kill. How did a confirmed workaholic spend suddenly available time? Well, he *was* there to observe the shipboard experience, so he might as well get on with it . . . see what this floating palace had to offer.

He began with the *Queen*'s Golden Door Spa at Sea, took a whirl at the electronic golf course, then worked out in the gym, followed by a swim and a massage. Finally he visited the barbershop for a shave and a trim he really didn't need. Then he settled down with the stack of contracts and memos in his briefcase. But he found it difficult to concentrate and was relieved when it was finally time to dress for dinner.

Resplendent in his white dinner jacket, black tie, Jonathan was one of the first to take his seat in the dining room so that he'd be able to catch sight of Andrianna the moment she made her appearance, so that he, rather than the dining room's maître d', would be the one to hold her chair out for her. But then he sat, oblivious to the luxurious appointments of the dining room—the rich sycamore paneling, the striking Italian tile, the prints by Erté gracing the walls, the tables laden with the Haviland china and Baccarat crystal—for what seemed to him an endless chunk of time. While he politely but cursorily acknowledged the other diners seated at his table, his eyes remained fixed on the entrance to the room.

Then, while he partook indifferently of lobster pâté, Jonathan decided that apparently Ms. DeArte was one of those women who enjoyed making late and therefore dramatic appearances. Or maybe it was only that at the last minute, for some reason or other, she had decided to change her gown. But while her absence dulled his enjoyment of the wild mushroom soup and arugula salad set before him, it only whetted his appetite for that moment when she would finally appear before his starved eyes.

But then, as his entrée was being served, a roast duckling Meursault, and she still hadn't arrived, Jonathan, gloomily dispirited, was forced to conclude that she wasn't going to appear at all. He finished quickly and got up to leave, murmuring apologies to the other guests. As he strode out of the dining room, all three women at the table followed him with wistful eyes, their male companions eyeing him with mingled resentment and envy.

He spent the remainder of the evening in the Players Club. Moving peripatetically from baccarat to blackjack to roulette, he played automatically, won consistently, and collected his winnings absentmindedly. At one point he thought he spotted Andrianna at another table and started to dash off without stuffing his money into his pocket. A petite brunette caught his arm, fluttered long eyelashes, and said coyly, "If Monsieur cannot think of a way to spend his money . . . ?"

Jonathan looked down at her, displayed his dazzling white smile, at once charming and ingratiating, and said, "But I'm sure you'll think of something," as he gallantly swept the pile to her side of the table. Then he was off before she could make any further suggestions.

But Ms. DeArte was nowhere to be seen. Frustrated, he pulled a chair up to the blackjack table. "No luck tonight?" queried a silver blonde draped in blue silk.

"Actually, I've done quite well." Jonathan grinned.

"How much have you won?"

"I don't know exactly," he confessed somewhat sheepishly.

"Really?" She raised an eyebrow, not quite believing him.

"Really," he said.

It was true. When he was only playing games as he was

45

tonight, the money was of no importance — only the winning was. Winning was always a serious business.

It had always been so for him, even when it hadn't been a real competition and no prize was at stake at all. Even as a little boy at the beach playing with other little boys, when the contest was nothing more than seeing who could keep his head under water the longest, he had striven to be the best. Sometimes he had thought his lungs would burst, but he never came up for air until he knew that all the others already had.

"Perhaps we could count it together . . ." the blonde suggested archly. "Then you would know for sure —"

"Thanks, but I think I'll call it a night."

At any other time, in any other place, he might have taken her up on her offer. She was certainly attractive enough — the pale blond hair thick and glossy, the lips soft and inviting, the eyes a clear, vivid blue. He could find no fault with those huge eyes, staring frankly at him now, beckoning . . .

Then he realized what was missing, what was wrong. The lady's eyes were fine — they were simply the wrong color.

Still brooding about the woman with the amber eyes and all the possible reasons she had chosen not to dine in public, he decided to return to his stateroom and his stack of contracts. If he wasn't able to concentrate, he could, he reflected dryly, always take advantage of the stateroom-accessible audio and video library the *Queen* touted as one of her many attractions. Hell, he might even take a turn in the Jacuzzi, another of the purported highlights of his luxury suite.

As he approached his cabin door, he saw a fur-clad figure half-obscured by the all-encompassing fog leaning over the rail and looking out at a black sea. Still, he instantly recognized her, and as was crooned in a song popular when he was a boy — a song that hadn't made sense to him at the time since he had always been of a realistic bent of mind — his heart stood still.

Without stopping to think he started to stride toward her.

46

But before he could take a second step, she hugged the fur coat to her, huddling into it as if seeking to disappear into its depths before she appeared to vanish into the fog, taking the few steps necessary to enter her suite. Now he realized that her suite—the Queen Anne—was the one next to his own, and he felt a rush of pleasure. She was only a wall away . . .

Stripping himself of his clothes in record-breaking time and getting into bed, Jonathan visualized her undressing, taking off each article of clothing slowly, piece by piece—first the fur coat, now the dress, now the clinging slip that followed every line of her magnificent body, now the gossamer underthings, undoing the fastenings of a lacy garter belt, fingertips lingering on silken thighs, now sensuously drawing her stockings down the long length of what he was sure were extraordinary legs, perhaps looking into the mirror at her own image as she did so, maybe smiling, pleased with her own loveliness, taking satisfaction in the perfection of her body, even touching herself or sinuously stroking a satiny nightgown into place over full breasts and round hips. Or maybe, he thought, she didn't wear a nightgown at all . . .

Was she in bed now? he wondered as he felt the heat of desire as he had never felt it before, touching his erection, thinking of bringing himself to climax but abandoning the idea as rapidly as it had evolved.

He wouldn't settle for that, he thought. He wouldn't compromise the exquisite lovemaking they were ultimately going to share—he was sure of it!—with an empty act. Impatient as he was and suddenly terribly lonely just thinking of her, he knew that he had to wait for the real thing. It would be only a matter of time, he promised himself. *Tomorrow . . . and if not tomorrow, then the next day . . .*

Abruptly Jonathan sat up and snapped the light on as he reached for the telephone.

It took an endless few minutes to get through to his secretary.

"Yes, sir," Patti answered crisply. "I will have that report for you in—"

"Forget it," Jonathan told her. "That's why I'm calling. I want you to cancel the investigation on Andrianna DeArte."

"Yes, sir! Forgotten, Mr. West. And while I have you on the phone, Bob Dugan says he needs—"

"Patti, Dugan can get whatever he needs from Martin. I filled him in on the Brewster merger before I left."

"I understand that, sir, but he said—"

"You just tell him what *I* said, okay?"

After he hung up, Jonathan was exhilarated. If he wanted to know everything there was to know about Andrianna DeArte, he'd do the legwork himself as he got to know her . . . as *they* got to know each other. And how much more exciting it was going to be, how much more of a challenge to unveil the mysteries of this exasperatingly intriguing woman on his own! It would be like those very first deals, when he'd done all the background research himself and the victories had been all the sweeter for it.

It would not only be a hell of a lot more fun, but it would spare him the embarrassment of her learning that he'd had her investigated. Expedient? Yes, but he had no doubt that a woman of her obvious breeding would see it as a tasteless, tawdry act.

And even at this stage—when they hadn't as much as spoken a word to one another—it was important to him that she think of him as worthy of great respect, even as a man of honor, old-fashioned as that sounded.

Andrianna let her silk robe fall to the floor before she slipped under the covers. She thought about the handsome young American whose name she didn't know. He was a luxury she couldn't afford, but she could dream, couldn't she? What avenging god or demon—the keeper of the fates—could be so cruel as to deny her one tiny dream? What had she done, after all, that was so terrible that she couldn't at least have that?

But she *was* being punished, and she still didn't know why—for what crime. For having been born to Elena Duarte, who had lived too foolishly and died too soon and entrusted her daughter's future to a man who had cared too little?

If only, just this once, she thought wistfully, she could do all the lovely things any woman might do with an attractive stranger when they found themselves at sea with nothing else to do for five days. Nothing else to do except fall in love. Five days, such a tiny slice of time to ask for out of all eternity . . .

No, it wasn't so much to ask, not for the ordinary woman. But then she, Andrianna DeArte, born Andrianna Duarte, returning to the land of her birth for the first time in thirty years after leaving it as a little girl, wasn't exactly your ordinary woman, had never even been an ordinary little girl. What ordinary little girl, flying from San Francisco to Baghdad of all places, discovered, in midair, that she was no longer who she'd been but a stranger named Ann Sommer who was going to live with other strangers?

Terrified, unable to understand what was happening to her, she turned her face to the window to look out unseeingly, and when Miss Hadley said, "You may call me Eva," at the same time insistently calling her Ann, she neither turned around nor responded.

"You're being very rude, Ann, and if you want to get along in your new home, you're really going to have to do better, or you'll find out that not everyone is as patient as I am. Do you understand me, Ann?"

"I'm not Ann! I'm not Ann! My name is Andrianna Duarte! And I'm never going to be Ann Sommer!"

Eva sighed and closed the magazine she was reading. It wasn't that she didn't feel for the little girl. Actually she admired the child's spunk. But she had her orders.

"Since I know you're such a smart little girl, Ann, and that you can understand what I'm telling you if you try very hard, I'm going to tell you a secret I learned a long time ago. Certain things are going to happen to you no matter how you feel about them, and there are two ways you can take

49

them. One way is easily, which means behaving yourself like a nice little girl. The other way is the hard way—fighting—which will only make things harder for you. And the truth is that, no matter what you do or say, from now on you *are* Ann Sommer, and you'd just better get used to it because there's nothing you can do about it. Do you understand me, Ann?"

Andrianna turned around to face her tormentor with tear-swollen eyes, darkened with hate and terror. "My name's not Ann! My name's not Ann! My name is Andrianna Duarte!"

When the stewardess brought their dinner trays, Andrianna took one look at the beef Burgundy and retched—all over the food, all over herself, and partially over Eva Hadley.

There was a car with a driver dressed in strange-looking clothes waiting for them when they finally landed in Baghdad after changing planes twice. And then, as they drove through streets full of odd-looking people dressed in funny clothes just like the little man driving the car was, Andrianna thought, this sure is a funny-looking place. All the buildings were really funny-looking too, so different from the house she and her mother and Rosa had lived in.

Then, after holding out for so long, the tears began to flow, and she rubbed at already reddened eyes with hard little fists and whispered piteously to Eva Hadley, "I don't like this place, and I don't want a new name. I want my old name back, please. And I want to go home! Please, can't I go home? Rosa's still there. I want to go home to Rosa. Can't I please go home and have my real name back? I promise I'll be good. I'm sorry I vomited on you. I didn't really mean to. And tell Mr. Wyatt I'm sorry if I was bad. Tell him I promise to be very good . . ."

The tears became sobs. "I won't ever be bad again."

Eva Hadley shook her head helplessly and took Andrianna in her lap. "I know you're not bad, honey, and Mr. Wyatt knows it too." She rocked the small child, her own tears falling on the little girl's face. "You'll be happy, you'll see," and she could only hope that it would be so.

Then she hoped that Helene Sommer and her husband were decent people. She also wished that her boss, Andrew Wyatt, had done his own dirty work. Or, at the least, had let the poor kid stay in her own country instead of sending her halfway around the world to a place so foreign she was bound to be scared half out of her wits.

Four

Thursday

When Jonathan took up his watch outside Andrianna's stateroom at the break of dawn on the off chance that she loved this time of day and would come out of her stateroom to experience it more fully, he didn't feel the cold at all.

As a matter of fact, he felt terrific even though the mist that hovered was so thick and laden with moisture that he couldn't even see his own warm breath hanging in the frigid air as he enthusiastically inhaled and exhaled. The sweats and big leather jacket he had bought at Harrods the previous day helped, though at that time he had had no idea he'd need them for this odd vigil at daybreak.

After a couple of hours passed without a sight of her, he began to feel the cold even with the sun beginning to show some signs of life, and he took to running in place every few minutes or so just to keep the blood flowing. Still, he was determined to continue with his surveillance even if it meant forgoing breakfast entirely, no matter that he felt in desperate need of — at the least — a steaming cup of coffee.

He didn't leave his post until he saw the steward wheeling a dining cart to her stateroom. Then he felt it was safe for him to go off to get his own breakfast, for at least as long as it took her to finish her meal. But then he was so eager to get back to his station that he took only enough time to wolf down a roll along with two cups of coffee, grabbing another roll for the road.

Sooner or later she had to leave her stateroom, he reassured himself. To get a breath of air, to go for a swim or a workout, maybe to visit the Elizabeth Arden Salon he'd noticed the day before when he'd gone shopping. Maybe she'd want to do some shopping of her own.

Still, even when it became apparent that *nothing* was going to entice her from her cabin that morning, he remained the stalwart sentinel, feeling somewhat noble in his endeavor. Surely she'd emerge for lunch, he told himself. But then a steward appeared, steering a dining cart up to her door once more.

When the steward came back out again, he inquired pleasantly, "Is Ms. DeArte feeling all right?"

"Why, yes . . . I believe so, sir. She appears to be fine. Seems to be in good appetite as well."

"That's good. That's very good. I'm glad to hear it," Jonathan stated emphatically. Then, reminded of his own extremely healthy appetite, he asked, "Do you think you might bring me some lunch too?"

"Of course, sir. Shall I fetch you a menu?"

"No, that won't be necessary. Anything will do. What's Ms. DeArte having?"

"The swordfish seviche. As a matter of fact, Ms. DeArte mentioned that it looked most appetizing. Would you care to try it?"

Jonathan considered for a moment before shaking his head. "No, thanks. Just a sandwich will do. Make that two sandwiches. A club and a roast beef. Rare."

"And what would you like to drink?" The steward permitted himself a tiny smile before adding, "Ms. DeArte is enjoying a pot of tea."

"Ah, but she's English," Jonathan laughed. "We Americans prefer our coffee."

"Very good, sir. Coffee it is. Shall I bring the lunch to your stateroom?"

"No, thank you. I'll eat right here. On deck."

"But isn't it a bit nippy up here, sir, to be dining *al fresco?*"

"Not at all. I like it this way. Bracing, you know. Besides, it looks like the sun is just about to come out."

"Of course. I'm sure you're right, sir."

But the sun never came out in full force. Rather, it appeared for a while and then disappeared to emerge again a half hour later, repeating this pattern all afternoon until the day had come and gone, and without a single sighting of his quarry.

Puzzled and frustrated, he finally went to his cabin to change for dinner. She couldn't stay cooped up indefinitely, he reassured himself. Surely she'd emerge to take advantage of all the amenities this finest of ships offered. Otherwise, why hadn't she simply flown the *Concorde,* as he himself had originally planned to do? Clearly she was in no hurry to reach the States. What awaited her there?

Jonathan found his head spinning with questions, and not a single answer among them. When she did come out, what would it be—dining, dancing, gambling? Roulette or blackjack? Or did she prefer the slots? Maybe instead of dancing or gambling she'd catch a movie at the ship's cinema? And after that, one of the cabaret shows?

Whatever her choice, he could picture the heads turning, the eyes ogling as she made her entrance. He could see her fending off one admirer and then the next, as smoothly as she had brushed off Dwight Rumson—not unkindly, but with a finality that would brook no protest.

At least he *hoped* she'd fend them off . . . all of them. Then he wondered exactly what kind of man she wouldn't want to turn away from . . . what it took to arouse first her interest and then her passion . . .

Then he thought of how it would be to make love to her. That her body would be lovely he took for granted, but would she be sweetly supplicant? Content to match her rhythm with his? Or would she be all over him, clinging like a second skin? Would she be hot and wild or cool and deliberate? Slow to arousal? Or would she cry out—ecstatically

54

eager or savagely demanding—for him and fulfillment? Whatever her style, whatever her preferences, he'd be willing to bet his last dollar that with the right man Andrianna DeArte was a woman of supreme passion.

Dressed for the evening and ready to step out on deck, Jonathan whistled softly, his mood definitely up. But even before he closed his stateroom door behind him, he saw a stewardess wheeling a dining cart up to Andrianna's door yet one more time!

He was so infuriated by the sight of that cart he wanted to grab it away from the young woman, to pick it up—dishes, food, and all—and heave it overboard, to watch it disappear into the black waters. But almost instantly the intense fury left him. Exhausted, bewildered, exasperated, and disgruntled all at once, Jonathan went back into his cabin, having lost his appetite for the evening as well as for dinner.

He sprawled on the sofa in the sitting room. *What the hell is she doing in there?*

He rose from the sofa to pace. *What does she find so fascinating about her suite that she can't leave it?*

He climbed the small flight of stairs to the bedroom.

Is she spending all her time on the transatlantic phone? And whose conversation does she find so damn interesting?

He threw himself down on the bed.

Is she writing love notes, or is she watching a video? Is she listening to music on the stereo?

He could almost imagine that he heard the muted sounds of the music. Sad songs of love gone wrong. And with a deep sense of melancholy he yearned only to sing along.

Andrianna had not been unaware of the stranger's vigil outside her cabin door all day long. Unable to sleep, she'd been staring out through her porthole at the black night well before dawn broke and had seen him when he first came out on deck to take up his station. And more than once during the day she'd peered through the porthole to see if he was still there, pacing the deck, to and fro, back and forth endlessly.

But whatever he was doing at any particular time, she knew exactly what he was after—waiting for her so that they could make contact. And she knew that she yearned for the same thing. Contact with her handsome stranger.

She rationalized, trying to find excuses for her preoccupation with his preoccupation with her. It was only a way to pass the time, she told herself. Nothing more.

But then, when the afternoon was about to become a memory and he was still there, she found herself—*admit it, Andrianna*—becoming even more intrigued. Gradually she became as fascinated by his presence outside her door as he was by hers behind it. Many men had wanted her, and some had succeeded—at least they'd thought they'd gotten her, for a while. More than a few had gone to extraordinary lengths to achieve their goal. But never before had she come upon a man who, after catching such a brief glimpse of her, had been willing to wait around in the cold for hours on end on the chance of seeing her again. A woman he had never met, about whom he knew nothing, without any assurance that once he did get to know her he would even like her . . .

Was it just a game?

Well, if it was a game they were playing, he would find her a formidable opponent. Now, even if she'd been thinking of coming out of seclusion to go to dinner, she wouldn't, eager to see what he would do next.

But then, realizing exactly how *much* she was intrigued and fascinated by this stranger, her mood changed and she became angry. How dare he impose his presence on her without knowing whether it was welcome or not? Because that was what he was doing. Just his silent vigil outside her door was a tease, conjuring up all kinds of impossible notions and visions to dance in her head and make her dream of what could never be, tempting her into deluding herself.

And years ago, when she was only seven going on eight, she had already promised herself never to be fooled again.

By the time they arrived at the Sommer house in the outskirts of Baghdad, Eva Hadley had persuaded Andrianna to give her new name and home and the Sommers themselves a chance.

"You can't be happy," Eva told her, "unless you're *willing* to be happy. And Mrs. Sommer won't be like a mother to you unless you make up your mind that you're going to love her and she's going to love you. She and Mr. Sommer don't have any children of their own, so that means that they're going to be very happy to have *you* as their adopted daughter. And adopted is very special. It means the parents *chose* a child, and choosing means really wanting."

But it wasn't like that at all. Not from the very second she and Eva walked into Helene Sommer's house. Very thin, very petite, with the palest of blue eyes and the lightest of blond hair, Helene Sommer didn't kiss her. She shook hands with Eva Hadley but only stared at her, the child who was supposed to be her chosen daughter.

Helene Sommer's tongue flicked over her lips gingerly as if she tasted something faintly sour. "Well, from the looks of her it's a good thing she's supposed to be my husband's niece and not mine," she told Miss Hadley. "I had no idea she'd be this tall or that her hair would be *that* dark or, for that matter, that she'd look this . . . well, *exotic*. You've explained the situation to Ann, I take it?"

"I'm not sure what you mean by the situation." Eva blinked.

"I'm referring to Ann's supposed background," Helene Sommer snapped. "The story that Andy — Mr. Wyatt — and I have worked out is that she's the daughter of my husband's poor deceased brother, Hugh Sommer, who was, of course, an Englishman, a businessman working and living in Spain who married a Spanish woman of aristocratic background. That will explain the girl's coloring. She speaks some Spanish, I presume?"

"I'm not sure . . ." Eva faltered. "I wasn't aware of—no one told me about this . . . this background, and we've spoken only in English—"

Helene Sommer made an impatient gesture. "Do you speak Spanish, Ann? Yes or no?"

Andrianna, sucking her thumb, a habit she had given up years before, did not answer.

"Well, no matter," Mrs. Sommer said impatiently. "We'll just say she's always had English governesses and attended American schools in Europe, and that will take care of the language business. She'll call us Aunt Helene and Uncle Alex, and there should be no problem with any part of the story.

"In any case, she'll be away at school most of the time. As a matter of fact, since we will be moving to Zurich in several weeks—did Mr. Wyatt tell you that Mr. Sommer has been assigned to a post there?—I've been thinking it would be best for all concerned if Ann was sent away to school as soon as it can be arranged. An English school, I should think, so that she can learn to speak her English with a British accent rather than a California one."

She gave a short laugh. "I lived in San Francisco for a time, you know, and frankly speaking, I didn't find the accent particularly attractive, no offense intended, of course. Yes, I think the English countryside is the right place for our Ann."

Eva Hadley took a quick, remorseful look at Andrianna's bewildered expression and rushed to say, "Well, I've been thinking—I was planning on staying on in Baghdad for a few days anyway—I have a friend here who works for an American oil company . . . Well, I could stay *here* for a couple of days with Andrianna until—"

"Ann," Helene Sommer corrected her, smiling icily. "Really, Miss Hadley, how can we expect a child to get the bloody thing straight if a grown woman can't? And no, it won't be necessary for you to stay on here with her. The quicker the child learns to stand on her own, the better off everyone will be. However, why don't you go upstairs with Ann now for a

58

bit? You can go over her story with her until she gets it down pat, and then you'll be free to go."

When it was time for Eva to leave, with Helene and Alexander Sommer watching, she hugged Andrianna to her, whispering in her ear with a conviction she hardly felt, "Things will get better, you'll see, little Ann Sommer."

But Andrianna pulled away from her, no longer trusting her, crying out, "My name is not Ann Sommer. My name is Andrianna Duarte . . . Andrianna Duarte . . . Andrianna Duarte!"

It was almost as if she were repeating it over and over again so that she would never forget it.

As soon as Eva was gone, Helene Sommer fixed a frigid eye on her charge. "I think it will be best if you go to your room right this minute, Ann, and I think you'll have to stay there until you know what your name is. Perhaps you should try saying over and over to yourself, 'My name is Ann Sommer, my name is Ann Sommer,' until you have it exactly right."

Going up the stairs, Ann heard Aunt Helene say to Uncle Alexander, "Did you hear her saying that her name is Andrianna Duarte over and over? The ungrateful, surly little wretch. That's what happens when one takes up with one's inferiors, I suppose. I wonder what that fool Andrew was thinking of when he—"

She heard Uncle Alexander laugh. A nasty kind of laugh. "I realize how it must pain you, my dear, to be stuck with the bastard child of your rich but former lover and the Mexican fluff for whom he threw you over."

"Pain me? I'll tell you what pains me. It pains me that I have to be stuck with the brat because of *your* inadequacies. If you weren't such a loser, I wouldn't have to take her just to get us out of this hellhole into civilization."

"And how did we get here in this hellhole in the first place but because of *you,* my sweet? Because your ex-lover, the prick, was so eager to be rid of you he used his influence to have me assigned here."

"Well, I didn't see you turning down the Zurich appointment because it was the prick who got it for you. And I don't see you turning down your share of the money either."

But their words meant nothing to Andrianna as she continued to trudge up the stairs. She was concentrating on not crying and saying over and over again to herself, "My name is Andrianna Duarte. . . ."

A week later Andrianna started school at Huxley, where the offspring of the European crème de la crème pursued their education while their parents ostensibly pursued power, prestige, and greater fortunes. When she saw the Sommers again, they were living in a lovely chalet in Zurich, where Alexander Sommer was installed at the British Consulate. But even then she didn't get to see much of Helene. It seemed that just as she was arriving for her holiday from school her aunt was just leaving for a fortnight's shopping trip to Paris, a pattern that would continue for the next several years. Which was fine with Andrianna. She had needed only that first meeting to know that Helene was never going to be even a friend, much less a mother to her.

Andrianna shook her head angrily to rid herself of the single tear that she had been unable to suppress. *Damn Helene . . . and Alex . . . and Andrew Wyatt—damn all of them for still being able to make me cry!* Then she gave a brief and bitter laugh because she knew it was *she* herself who had been truly damned.

Five

Friday morning

When his bedside phone rang, Jonathan came awake almost instantly. In a single automatic gesture he reached for the instrument and glanced at the watch that he rarely took off. *Seven o'clock. Damn, I overslept.*

"Jonathan West here," he said, clearing his throat.

"Good morning, Mr. West," came his secretary's cheerful voice. "I'm sorry about the hour, but I wanted to catch you before your morning workout . . . Did I wake you?" she added incredulously.

"No, no . . . But what is it, Patti?"

"It's just that *Time* magazine called. They want to do an interview with you, and they're on a tight schedule and need an answer right away. They want to angle the piece on you as one of the *Forbes* Four Hundred—you know, that annual list of the four hundred richest people in the country."

"Yes, I do know," he said dryly. "But why me? I'm not anywhere near the top of that list." This a touch ruefully.

"But you *were* on it. Anyhow, it's *you* they want to interview. They said you were one of the more *colorful* listees."

"Is that what they said? Colorful?" he drawled, making fun, but actually he was pleased since he never eschewed publicity.

"Yes, sir. Colorful. And they referred to you as the California *wunderkind.*"

61

"In that case you'd better call them back and tell them that the California *wunderkind* would be pleased to be interviewed. When do they want to schedule it?"

"That's the catch, Mr. W. They don't have much time. They want to do it next week."

"Okay, I'll be swamped when I get back, so schedule it for Thursday or Friday."

After he hung up, Jonathan realized he hadn't asked Patti whether the article was to be a cover story. Not likely on such short notice, he decided. Still, a feature in *Time* was nothing to scoff at. It was one more confirmation of his status as a major player, and as far as he was concerned, *any* publicity had always proved to be good news. There had been the *Los Angeles Times* piece on him after he'd made his first million, which had led to the resort deal in the mountains near Santa Cruz. That buy had drawn the interest of *Forbes*. Then as he'd acquired more West Coast hotels, *Business Week* had hailed him as the "California whiz kid," and then there had been the feature in *Fortune*. And the list went on. He was no longer sure which came first, success or publicity.

As he stepped into a steaming shower, Jonathan wondered whether a woman used to being in the company of the Dwight Rumsons of the world would be impressed by *less* than a cover story. And then, with a sharp twinge of pleasure, he realized why he'd slept beyond his usual six o'clock. He'd been dreaming of consummation with the beautiful Andrianna. Recalling little cameos from that imagined tryst, he felt wonderful . . . fulfilled, suffused with an incredible sense of well-being and infused with renewed determination.

Veni, vidi, vici. I came, I saw, I conquered. He smiled as the phrase flashed through his mind. Caesar's words and his own call to arms. The conquest of Andrianna DeArte would soon be a *fait accompli.* He was sure of it!

As he dressed for breakfast, he saw that the sun was streaming in through the portholes strong and bright. *A good sign.* He checked the time. Five after eight, and he was starved—almost as if he *had* spent the night in frenzied passion.

He carried out his morning routine as if he were at home—his body going through the motions necessary to eat breakfast, have a shave at the barbershop, work out in the gym, and swim in the sculptured pool, his mind focused on planning his strategy for the day. But instead of sorting through tactics he might employ in, say, a hostile takeover, he deliberated his next move in the battle to win Andrianna. Yesterday's plan—waiting outside her stateroom for her to appear—had been inappropriate. He chided himself for having approached her as if she were a Mom-and-Pop concern rather than a well-defended multinational conglomerate. Andrianna DeArte was a sophisticated woman, and therefore a more sophisticated strategy was in order.

Jonathan took one glance at the display of flowers in The Greenery—and ordered the entire contents of one refrigerated showcase sent to Ms. DeArte's suite. The manager of the shop didn't raise an eyebrow. On the *QE2* all things were possible, especially when a rich Yank was involved.

Asked if he wished to write a note to accompany his offering, Jonathan considered briefly and then decided on only his business card and the name of his suite. *You don't breach the defenses of a savvy corporation by stomping in and announcing your intentions.* Then he went back to his stateroom to observe the delivery of the flowers through his porthole.

An hour later he saw eight stewards struggling under their massive burden appear before Andrianna's door. Then he settled back on the sofa to watch a "Dallas" video, chuckling at J.R.'s machinations—*Would that the real business world were always that entertaining!*—while he waited for his phone to ring with her thank you.

63

A few minutes later there was a knock on his door, and he jumped up from the couch. *She'd come to thank him in person!* Combing his hair back in an unconscious gesture with one hand, he flung the door open with the other to see all eight stewards returning his flowers.

He was filled with crushing disappointment, and the disappointment made him angry as he watched them placing the flowers around the room, overpowering him with their fragrance. *Who the hell does she think she is?*

But then, digging into his pocket for some bills to give the stewards, his anger dissipated, and he smiled to himself. Returning the flowers was exactly the right touch—a challenge! Andrianna DeArte knew how to play the game with finesse.

He reconsidered. *Had* he overplayed it? Was a roomful of flowers too lavish, too showy? In that case he'd just have to alter his style—go with something less grandiose.

He picked up the phone and ordered a bottle of Cristal champagne, thinking that Cristal was the obvious, discerning choice for a woman of obvious discernment. Directing that the wine be sent to Ms. DeArte's suite along with his compliments and *two* glasses, he requested that a couple of ounces of Petrossian caviar be sent along too. Then he went back to the sofa and "Dallas" to await developments. But he paid scant attention to what was happening on the screen, his own unfolding drama being a thousand times more engrossing.

Would she again refuse his gift? Or would she appreciate his change of tactics, accept his gift, and call, thanking him for this thoughtfulness and inviting him to join her in a toast?

Or would she show up at his door herself to extend the invitation?

On the other hand, she might dash off that note of thanks but *without* an invitation to join her, leaving *him* to make the call suggesting that they share the champagne.

It took just twenty minutes for the champagne and caviar to reach her door—he checked out the porthole every few minutes. After another four minutes—he was watching the second hand on his watch—he had a response. He took a deep breath, went to the door, and again flung it open, only to see the cart and the steward with a note in hand.

He tore the note open. "I adore champagne but never eat caviar. So why don't *you* eat the caviar while I drink the wine?"

Jonathan was dumbfounded. There wasn't even a signature, much less a thank you. And she really hadn't given him any room to pick up the phone and invite himself over to help drink the champagne. He burst out laughing.

Ms. DeArte two, Mr. West zero.

He couldn't remember any contest he'd ever taken part in that had been this much fun.

Andrianna, watching through her porthole, saw Jonathan leave his suite, whistling, happy as a lark. *The damn fool! Where is he off to? What is he up to now?*

When the flowers had arrived at her door, a million of them seemingly, in a dazzling array of colors, she'd been astonished. She'd even forgotten for the moment that she had decided the night before that she couldn't afford . . . hadn't the time . . . to play the stranger's game.

But then she'd convinced herself how annoyed she was with such an ostentatious offering, and she'd ordered the stewards to return the flowers directly to—she consulted the business card he'd included—Mr. Jonathan West.

Once they'd left with all her beautiful flowers, she'd wanted to cry. *It isn't fair!*

And she'd curled up on the sofa, his card clutched in her hand. At least now she knew his name! Jonathan West! And it was kind of ironic that Mr. West lived in California, the place where she'd been born.

And then she did cry.

When the champagne and caviar arrived, and she realized that he still wasn't giving up, she was so overcome with feeling—and relief—that she weakened. Oh, it couldn't hurt if she played along for a day or two. Besides, she was sure that all he wanted was a shipboard romance to while away the crossing and that nothing serious was going to happen. Surely there was no harm in that.

As she scrawled her reply and handed it to the steward, she realized how much she was beginning to enjoy this game. *How clever are you, Mr. Jonathan West?*

Walking through the promenade of shops, Jonathan pondered his decision. He was dealing with a lady who returned flowers and caviar but kept champagne. The thing to do now was to send her a present that would further establish exactly what she would keep and what she wouldn't.

He knew that he wanted something fairly intimate. Still, a delicate balance was called for here. He wanted *intimate,* but then again, not *too* intimate. In the end he chose a silvery satin Christian Dior hostess gown that came with a matching coat. He thought the ensemble struck exactly the right note. The gown *could* be worn for intimate occasions . . . but then again, not necessarily.

But then, being a man given to excess when aroused, he selected a bottle of perfume to be included with the gift—a small flacon of something called Passion, a name that captured his imagination. Still he felt unsatisfied.

Then he knew what he wanted to do. *Jewelry!* But would she find a gift of jewelry insulting? Too presumptuous? Would she resent it? She might, but wouldn't she also be impressed? And it would be interesting to see what she would do about it.

He selected a slender bracelet fashioned of yellow gold set with small diamonds and sapphires—not *that* showy or blatantly expensive.

Then, with his triple-pronged attack set in motion, Jonathan went back to his stateroom to await developments.

Before settling down to toast herself with her champagne, Andrianna decided she would make an occasion of it, set the scene just as she might if Jonathan West himself were sitting across the room from her, or perhaps next to her on the pale blue silk damask sofa . . . sipping his wine as he gazed into her eyes.

First of all, she would have scented candles burning. She ran to a trunk to find some. She always traveled with a supply of them, enjoying the luxury of a bubble bath with the room illuminated by their seductive light, permeated with their heady fragrance. Long ago she had come to rely on these small solitary pleasures to sustain her, to soothe her spirit as much as her body.

And then she decided that was exactly where and how she would drink her champagne—in the whirlpool. In the pink marble bath with the perfumed water swirling all about her, with the Renaud candles lit and music filling the room.

Like a child playing at being a grown-up, she ran about setting everything in motion: placing the champagne close by the tub, spilling in the lavender bath salts with a lavish hand, lighting the candles and inhaling their fragrance—violets—and selecting a cassette from the suite's library of tapes for the stereo. Something smoky and sultry, she decided. Edith Piaf? No—too French, too sad, and possibly too apropos. Then she found it: Billie Holiday. Still sad, but the fact that Billie had been an American seemed suitable. Then, as she sank into the tub, the plaintive melody drifting through the room, she brought the flute of bubbling wine to her lips.

She could hardly wait to see what he would do next. He *would* make another move; she was certain of it. Would he extend an invitation for them to do something together?

What was his idea of the ideal romantic evening, here on the world's most luxurious ocean liner, where one's every whim could be fulfilled? Or would he send her another present?

She was not unused to receiving gifts from men. Hardly. It was a large part of the fabric of which her life was fashioned, but she had always prided herself that no one and no gift had ever bought her. Some presents she had kept, and others she had returned, strictly according to the way she felt about the donor and not the gift.

For all of that, even those expensive items she did keep meant little to her — even the most exquisite pieces — usually having no sentimental value. They were nothing more than a piece of her security blanket, something to be hoarded against that time when she would desperately need to exchange a piece for cold cash . . . when she was absolutely vulnerable.

It was a pattern that had evolved out of circumstance and need rather than out of any preconceived design. Although it had become a way of life for her, she had never dreamed in the beginning that it would evolve this way . . .

Sometimes she likened herself to Blanche DuBois in *A Streetcar Named Desire*, a role she had essayed in London a few seasons back — a woman dependent on the kindness of strangers. But the truth was that no matter how many gifts she accepted or how dependent she seemed to be on strangers or friends, she had managed to live her life independently, beholden to no one. No matter *what* she accepted, she gave no promises in return. And that was the way she intended to keep it. She would live and die . . . oh, yes, she would die . . . but owing nothing to anyone.

As for the gifts, some — like the men who offered them — had been lots more fun than others.

Her first real gift from a man had been a nightgown — a pristine one, cotton rather than satin or silk, but hand-embroidered. The present, surprisingly enough, had come from Uncle Alex, and the occasion had been her arrival from school for a week's holiday.

Uncle Alex brought the prettily gift-wrapped box up to her bedroom on the second floor of the chalet in Zurich and explained as he handed it to her that Aunt Helene hadn't been able to wait to greet her because she was off for a cruise on Ari Onassis's yacht in the Mediterranean.

Ann nodded. By this time she'd become inured to the fact that Helene Sommer wanted as little to do with her as possible. And certainly she had no feeling for Helene unless it was an aversion — as intense as Helene's apparent aversion to her. She didn't know why Uncle Alex even bothered to try to explain his wife's absence.

"It's okay," she reassured him, unwrapping the gift to find the pretty, innocent-looking nightie. "Oh, Uncle Alex, it's lovely. Thank you!"

She was really delighted with the gift, more for the idea of it than for the present itself. Although she was hardly the normal unsophisticated thirteen-year-old, she was still child enough to be excited about receiving a present. Especially when it came from her adopted uncle, who, while he was certainly more pleasant than his wife, had paid her scarcely more attention over the years. In truth she was hungry for the least sign of affection.

"Try it on! Hurry!" Alex cried, seemingly as elated to give the present as she was to receive it.

She disappeared into her bathroom to do as he requested, and a couple of minutes later she called through the bathroom door, "It's darling, Uncle Alex! It fits perfectly."

That wasn't quite the truth. She had shot up recently and filled out at the same time, and the gown was too small, not quite covering her maturing body. The newly burgeoning breasts with their delicate pink nipples strained against the sheer white cotton and spilled out the sides of the deep armholes, and the thin fabric pulled tightly across her newly rounded, womanly buttocks. But since Alex would never actually see her in the nightgown, she saw no reason to disappoint him or spoil his pleasure by revealing that it was at least a size too small. Maybe without his knowing it, she thought, she could exchange it for a larger size.

But then Alex called, "Well, come out here and show me how you look!"

She hastily demurred. Even if Alex wouldn't realize that the gown didn't fit properly, she was much too shy to display herself wearing nothing more than a nightdress that revealed so much of her.

But, suddenly, he was in the bathroom with her!

"You look so sweet," he murmured, "just as I imagined you would. So sweet . . ."

He reached out, and instinctively she stepped back, but he only laughed softly. "I just want to take your hair out of that ridiculous ponytail."

She stood very still while he did so, allowing her long, dark hair to flow free, well past her waist.

"There," he said, breathing hard. "That's much better." And he turned her around to face the mirror, positioning himself behind her. "Look, isn't that much better? Don't you look sweet, my dear? So sweet and young and virginal . . ."

At first she only thought it strange that while his eyes were moving up and down her body he didn't even notice that the nightgown didn't fit her. Or if he did, he didn't mention it. But then, seeing in the mirror that his eyes had taken on a kind of weird glazed look, she grew apprehensive.

When he asked her, his breath coming in gasps now, "Do you realize that you'll never look quite like this again?" she barely heard him, too conscious of his body pressing hard against hers from behind.

Now she was more than apprehensive. Now she was frightened, and she tried to wriggle away from him, reaching for her clothes on the vanity bench, blurting out, "I guess I'd better change now. I guess we'll be eating dinner soon."

"Not so fast, my little virginal princess . . ." And then his expression changed and he looked angry. "You *are* a virgin, aren't you?"

She blushed furiously. "Of course," she said, trying to sound normal, but now she felt herself panicking, wanting to escape.

She tried to get to the bathroom door, but he was too quick for her. Before she could grasp the doorknob, he caught her and pinned her against the door, whispering savagely, "Let's see exactly how virginal you are . . ."

"No!" she protested. "No, no, no!" she screamed as she tried to get away from him. But both her struggles and her shrieks were in vain; no one else was in the chalet. Alex ripped the new nightgown, leaving her breasts and loins completely exposed. One hand reached out for a breast, and then she felt a terrible pain as his other hand thrust between her legs.

Was he trying to test her virginity with his fingers? she agonized, terrified. Would he tear her apart as easily as he had the thin white nightgown?

He thrust again and again until his fingers finally went into her. She went into a half-faint and slid to the hard white-tiled floor. Semiconscious, eyes closed, she didn't move. Not even when she felt the wetness of his ejaculation on her exposed, supine body.

In the morning she was gone, knowing that she would never see the Sommers' chalet in Zurich again. But two weeks later a simple yellow gold bangle bracelet from Uncle Alex arrived in the mail, followed by several other small gifts of jewelry in the next few months. Was he trying to buy her silence? Andrianna wondered. But then Alex Sommer hardly knew her . . . couldn't know that it was hardly the few baubles that kept her silent but rather a deep sense of shame.

So all she did was store the pieces of jewelry away in a box—it not even occurring to her to wear these symbols of her shame. But then, when she couldn't bear her own silence any longer, she called Aunt Helene.

Helene merely *laughed*. Laughed and told Andrianna she'd do well to keep her lips buttoned since people would think she was either a disturbed child who imagined things or a wicked brat who told vicious lies. In either case she'd be sent away to a place she wouldn't much like.

After that Ann spent her holidays either at school or at other girls' homes, and she passed her summer vacations at camps and summer schools. Under the circumstances, that arrangement was fine with her. The one thing that did bother her, though, was that she didn't know if Helene really thought she was making the whole thing up or actually believed her.

But gradually she came to understand that even that didn't really matter . . . And then occasionally she would even wear one of Alex's gifts. Why not? They were only pieces of metal, with or without pieces of stone, and had neither conscience nor memory . . .

When Jonathan's presents were delivered to her suite, Andrianna could barely contain her excitement. Jonathan West's gifts were in a whole new category from those she usually received. These were just for *fun*, especially since there could never be, no matter how much she might want one, a relationship between them . . .

No, any presents he gave her were only pawns in a game of chess only the two of them could play. He would make a move and she would counter. It was a game that would, hopefully, amuse them both and one that, by the time they docked in New York, would end in a checkmate.

Accordingly and even though she adored the gown and coat and they fit her perfectly, she placed the ensemble carefully back in the box. Then she inhaled the perfume and found it to her liking too, but sighing, she put the bottle back into the box as well. And then, putting on the bracelet and admiring it on her wrist, she picked up the phone to ask for a steward so that the box could be returned to the sender and sat down to write an accompanying note: "Thanks all the same, but the gown and coat are not exactly me, and the perfume is not one for which I have a Passion."

She didn't mention the bracelet at all, but it was, most assuredly, *not* one of the items returned. Keeping it was what it was all about—a potent move in this game of chess.

The next move would be his . . . and she hoped for both their sakes that it would be a brilliant one . . .

Six

Jonathan read Andrianna's note over and over again, forced to admit that she was really spinning his wheels. Here was a woman who wasn't fond of caviar or Passion but loved champagne. And while she sent back flowers and negligees, she kept gold bracelets studded with diamonds and sapphires. Was there an obvious conclusion to be drawn here?

It was just possible that, for once, he was in way over his head.

He deliberated his next move. Should he send her another present? One just to test her? A diamond tennis bracelet accompanied by an innocuous box of chocolates, along with a silly note such as "Sweets for the sweet"? What would she keep and what would she return? He was no longer sure if he really wanted to find out.

When a stewardess brought Jonathan the bucket of ice and the bottle of Glenfiddich he'd ordered, he made the young woman a gift of the Dior ensemble and the perfume. When she tried to stammer her thanks, saying, "I don't know what to say," Jonathan smiled and told her, "A wise man once told me when in doubt about what to say the best thing is to say nothing. I've found it to be excellent advice."

By the time Jonathan had worked his bottle of scotch

down a quarter, he was telling himself that when a wise man didn't know what else to do he did nothing. And that's what he would do—absolutely nothing. Let *her* make the next move. If she chose to end the game in stalemate, she wasn't as worthy an opponent as he'd thought, and she could go to fucking hell!

Andrianna moved restlessly from the stereo to the video monitor finally shutting off both to try concentrating on one magazine after the other. Still, her thoughts constantly and consistently returned to the man installed in the next suite. *Would* he send her another present? When?

When the hours passed and nothing happened, Andrianna grew increasingly disconsolate. Her tiny, little, innocent, harmless flight of a flirtation hadn't even gotten off the ground, and there were only two full days and three nights, including this evening, before their crossing was over. *Fini!*

She checked the hour. There was still time for her to dress and go to dinner.

Should I or shouldn't I?

I shouldn't, and if I were really smart I wouldn't.

But in a couple of days they would dock in New York and she'd never see him again. Really, what difference could three nights and two days possibly make in the larger scheme of things?

Damn it, I shouldn't, but I will!

Since she had never intended to leave her cabin except to get a breath of fresh air, she hadn't bothered to unpack much—a couple of robes, a couple of pairs of jeans, a few sweaters. Now, almost in a frenzy, she tore into her luggage to find a gown for the evening. A gown that would knock Mr. West's eyes out, make a smashing impression. Then she blushed. She was being utterly ridiculous! She was throwing caution to the wind! But then again, it was just this once, a kind of last hurrah. And then it would be over . . .

Viewing herself in the floor-to-ceiling mirror, she held one dress after another against her. First a short dress with a strapless top of orange silk, its skirt a flip of pleated gold gauze. No, not the look she wanted. Too much bare skin and too little mystery.

A Scaasi—long and emerald green. But had emerald green ever really been her color? Only when it came to the real thing.

A dinner suit of red taffeta with black velvet soutache, a long narrow skirt, and a bolero jacket was discarded next. She couldn't image why she'd ever bought it.

A white Valentino with a draped elongated waist—Dwight had insisted she have it—was eliminated from the running, as was an Oscar de la Renta (circa George Phipps, whom she had met in Monte Carlo), which featured a sunburst beaded top with a very full satin skirt the color of café au lait.

She finally settled on a strapless tube of black velvet that showed off her long neck and sleek shoulders and made her appear even taller than she was. But if the gown was simple, the shoes she selected were not. They were black velvet too but almost entirely embroidered in pearls.

She did nothing more to her hair than blow it dry, allowing it to sweep back from her forehead in a cloudlike drift of apparent careless profusion.

The selection of jewelry to complete her look was not nearly as simple. Should she wear the long strand of Aegean pearls that would match her shoes? Was she in the mood for pearls? When she was a schoolgirl, she had thought them lovely until a classmate had told her that pearls reminded her of teardrops on a string, one sorrowful tear after the other, all in a row. The same girl, months later, had jumped to her death from a Swiss steeple, and after that Andrianna had never felt the same way about pearls again.

No, tonight was not the night for teardrops all in a row.

In fact, she wouldn't wear the velvet shoes embroidered with them either, and she fished out a pair of black suede pumps with four-inch gold kid stiletto heels. That was more like it.

She pawed through the trays of her jewelry case, fingering drop earrings of pink gold and rubies, considered a topaz pendant that hung from a double string of diamonds. *Very sumptuous . . . but no.*

She tried on a brooch fashioned of diamond and yellow gold flowers with leaves of emeralds, studied the effect, then unpinned it. She lingered over a gold cuff watch with a pavé diamond cover before deciding against it, too, then slipped a huge ring of clustered diamonds and onyx on her middle finger where it reached past the knuckle. But then she pulled it off quickly as if it seared her flesh. She had always liked that ring, enjoying the weight and feel of it, until she discovered its donor—a munitions maker with an ancient Prussian title—had a penchant for sadomasochistic fun and games, whereupon she had gotten rid of him but kept the ring. Still, she hadn't worn it ever again. And when she was in need of cash, it would probably be the first item to go.

She picked up Jonathan West's present, the diamond-and sapphire-studded bracelet, and weighed it in her hand, trying to make up her mind. While it was a simple piece of jewelry compared to the rest of her collection—such as her bird of paradise pin—executed in platinum, diamonds, sapphires, rubies, and citrines that had been designed by a famous Parisian artist in the twenties—it was exactly the right piece to wear tonight. Only the single bracelet and nothing more—no necklace, earrings, or rings. When Mr. West saw that she was wearing *only* his gift, it would give him something to think about.

Dressed, she drew a cape of white mink around her shoulders and consulted the list of scheduled events for the evening. The captain was hosting a cocktail party before dinner. Maybe she would find Jonathan West there . . .

As she passed his stateroom on her way to the party, she discreetly checked his portholes to see that the interior of his cabin was dark. Good, she thought. He had already started on his evening. He was already out there on the ship, waiting for her to find him.

When the captain came forward to welcome her, he had already as always, thoroughly briefed himself on his passenger list and knew exactly who this splendid-looking woman was—Andrianna DeArte of the English stage.

"I regret that I've never had the pleasure of seeing you on the stage, Miss DeArte . . ."

Andrianna, trying to be gracious, but at the same time searching the room for Jonathan, answered somewhat distractedly, but smiling, "Oh, don't feel bad. There are several million people who haven't experienced that dubious pleasure."

"Your modesty is refreshing," the captain said, "although, I'm sure, not merited."

"Oh, but—"

A woman of impressive size shouldered her way between them, interrupting their conversation without bothering to excuse herself to state aggressively, "I am Lady Spencer, and you're the entertainer Anna della Rosa, are you not? I believe I saw you in a Parisian revue some while ago, isn't that so?"

"Hardly," Andrianna retorted, laughing faintly. "My name is Andrianna DeArte, and I've never been in a revue." Then, taking advantage of the moment to excuse herself she smiled sympathetically at the captain and walked quickly away.

"She *is* Anna della Rosa! I'm never wrong about these things. Never!"

The captain, chagrined that his conversation with the lovely actress had been so abruptly aborted, barely managed to say soothingly, "When one travels extensively as you do, my dear lady, and meets so many people, I'm sure it's difficult not to confuse them occasionally."

"Don't be ridiculous, Captain. I am never confused!"

Andrianna wasn't too disturbed by being recognized as Anna della Rosa by the dreadful Lady Spencer. In the course of many years, various names, and several different occupations, such recognition was not an infrequent occurrence.

Sometimes she denied the name with cool detachment as she had tonight. And on those occasions when an identity could not possibly be denied—the playgrounds of Europe in the end being a small world with too many of the players popping up in the same place at the same time—she shrugged the whole thing away with a laugh and an "Oh . . . one of my professional names. I do get so bored with the same old name, don't you?"

That usually ended it. When it didn't, she often allowed her eyes to fill with sadness, implying that there were some things just too painful to be discussed.

Still, it was happening more and more frequently, and it was one of the reasons she had decided to give up on England and the Continent. Then too, she was increasingly weary of all the places she'd already been and the lives that she had lived in them.

Of course there were other places where one could bury oneself, places where the odds were no one would know her or recognize her for who she really was: the daughter whom no father would claim, the young woman who had no real talent for anything except attracting powerful, rich men to her side, and finally the woman with a secret that could strike a fatal blow when she least expected it . . . when she was so foolish as to dare to be happy.

But she was already weary of all the places she hadn't been as well as the places she had.

What she really wanted was only to go home again. To

be little Andrianna Duarte again . . . as she had been before everyone taught her that to be Andrianna Duarte wasn't very much . . . almost the next thing to being no one at all . . .

Andrianna hardly felt as high-spirited as she had when she'd first left her stateroom, but she was determined to see the evening through.

You will feel strong. You will enjoy yourself. You'll have fun. You are very much a someone . . .

Deftly evading those seeking to make her acquaintance, she finished checking out the room and, convinced that Jonathan West was not among the revelers, left the cocktail party to investigate other corners of the ship where people were mingling, talking, laughing. She hoped Jonathan would be one of them, but when she discovered that he wasn't, she reassured herself that he was bound to be at dinner.

"Oh, yes, Miss DeArte!" The maître d' was delighted to see her. "We have a seat reserved for you right next to Mr. Jonathan West. Is that agreeable?"

She nodded and smiled discreetly.

But as the table filled with other diners, she found herself barely able to make polite conversation.

Where is he? Isn't he coming to dinner? Has someone else caught his interest?

Some brazen little snip who knew a good thing when she saw it, who made no secret about being attracted to him, who wanted him desperately and told him so?

Were they sipping drinks in her stateroom, having dinner there—just the two of them—thinking about what would follow as inevitably as night the day?

Oh, she was a fool for ever having left her cabin this evening! . . .

Jonathan awoke to find himself lying on the sitting room sofa in the dark, instantly remembering that his intention had been to drink himself into a state of forgetfulness. But he had succeeded only in falling asleep and waking up in the dark with the day gone and a whopper of a headache.

He sat up, snapped on a lamp, then reached for his head with both hands. *Wow!*

He checked the time. It was going on ten. Then he checked the bottle of Glenfiddich. He had consumed half of it and had managed to sleep for over five hours. What he needed now was some air.

He had just opened his door to go out on deck when he saw an apparition. A hauntingly lovely vision dressed in black with a cloak of white fur floating behind her, the luminescent skin gleaming in the dark with a ghostly, pearly glow. The dreamlike woman was a dead ringer for Andrianna, and she was *staring* at him. Then she quickly disappeared into the real Andrianna's stateroom!

He shook his head as if to clear it. He must have really tied one on—now he was seeing apparitions.

By the time he realized that he wasn't *that* drunk and that the apparition he'd just seen was no phantom but the real thing, she had already closed her door. God, he was an ass! She had been wearing an evening gown. She had gone to dinner! She'd finally made an appearance, and he had missed her!

At first, closing her stateroom door and leaning against it for support, Andrianna was exultant. Here she had pictured him in some gorgeous young thing's cabin making love, but it was obvious from his clothes—a pair of jeans and a leather jacket—and from his tousled hair that Jonathan West had never left his own cabin that evening.

Then she was filled with remorse. Why hadn't she said something to him, even just a cool "Good evening"? Surely a man of his bold determination would have taken it from there . . . and then the magic would have begun.

Oh, she was a fool! She had spent hours getting dressed

for *him*, had searched the ship for a sight of him, and then had sat at that damn table in the dining room talking to all those people of no consequence, waiting for him to appear. And then, there he was, practically on top of her, and she had said nothing, had let the moment pass, had run inside her cabin—to do what? To hide from him again? To come back another day? But there wouldn't be another day . . .

Why hadn't *he* spoken? Made some move?

It could only mean one thing. She had waited too long to make *her* move . . .

Feeling as miserable as he had ever felt, Jonathan remained on deck, walking, sprinting, running, all the while haranguing himself for not following the rules he had set for himself early in life—to seize the moment, to grab at opportunity with both hands, believing that to him who grabbed belonged the spoils.

But then he stopped in his tracks. So he had let opportunity slip through his fingers. It had happened before, and what had he done then? He'd turned around to rectify the error, had gone back to reclaim the opportunity, to change the course of events. Usually it worked. Just maybe it would work again.

Andrianna tossed and turned. Was she ill? Her mouth was so dry that she got out of bed to get a glass of water. She turned on the tap, letting the water run a few seconds while she studied herself in the mirror. It was funny—she didn't look miserable, and she didn't look sick. If anything, her pallor was becoming.

Sipping from the tumbler of water, she stepped back to better view her nude figure. It was still the body of a young woman—firm, full, and desirable . . . and *desiring*. That was the rub. She wanted him, and he had tired of her before he had even had her. *Or had he?*

She had to find out, and not tomorrow. She had to do it this very night. She had spent a life of denial. Tonight she would not be denied! She rushed out of the bathroom, grabbed for her cape and, running down the little flight of stairs, wrapped it against her nakedness. If he wasn't in his cabin, she would comb the ship until she found him!

She flung her door open wide, prepared to rush out into the night, only to find him there, breathing as hard as she was, his eyes blazing with a fierce light. As his arms slid under her cape to pull her to him, she could almost feel the beating of his heart . . . beating as wildly as her own. And then, with her eyes closed and without an inch of space between them, she could actually *hear* the beat, and she thought surely it was the loveliest music she had ever heard . . .

Seven

Friday evening

It was almost completely dark in the bedroom of Jonathan's suite, its only illumination the brightness of the starlit night entering through the portholes. But it was more than enough light for Jonathan to see the beauty of the trophy lying next to him in the wide bed — the mysterious Andrianna.

No woman he had ever known could begin to compare with her in sheer magnificence; no satisfaction he had ever taken in any acquisition could equal what he was feeling now. She was everything he had ever dreamed a woman could be in bed — wildly passionate, responsive to his every touch, giving and yet demanding. And the wonder of it was that while she was so expert at the *craft* of sex, she made it all feel like *art* . . . the art of love.

And there was the superlative beauty of her body — the exquisite velvety quality of her skin, the superb elegance of her throat and neck, the matchless voluptuous breasts managing to be firm and pliant at the same time with their hard and pointed nipples that he found especially erotic, the long perfection of her legs as they coiled about him. And the face — the full lips, the aristocratic cheekbones, the eyes that glittered yellow in the semidarkness. He had the haunting feeling that once having looked into those eyes in the closest, most intimate proximity he would never be the same again, those eyes casting a spell on him that no amount of time would ever dispel . . . that he would be in her thrall forever.

He could see only her profile now as she looked straight ahead, seemingly lost in thought. His hand reached out to cup her chin, gently turning her face to his so that he could look into her eyes again, but now he found them completely enigmatic, and he was disturbed. Why weren't those eyes, if not her lips, smiling at him? Why wasn't she lost in the same grip of euphoria as he?

"What are you thinking?" he asked, realizing that, incredibly, these were the first real words he'd spoken to her outside of those uttered in the throes of passion.

She smiled at him now, but despite it, he saw that her expression was no more scrutable than before. "I'm thinking the same thing you're thinking—"

"Tell me," he whispered. "What am I thinking?" His lips grazed her throat before kissing her forehead, and she reached up to trace his lips with delicate fingertips, to smooth back his yellow hair with a tender hand.

The most wonderful hair . . .

"I was thinking, and I thought you were too, about why we were just lying here when we could still be making love."

Her voice was throaty, thrilling, and he moaned and covered her body with his once again.

He sat up, gave a Tarzanlike whoop, and announced, "I'm starved! What about you?"

She laughed aloud. Only seconds before he'd been the consummate, most sophisticated of lovers and now he was acting like a boy of eighteen, and she found this both amusing and endearing.

But then why do I feel so close to tears?

"I'm calling room service," he announced, snapping on the bedside light. "What do you feel like eating?"

"But what time is it? It must be the middle of the night—"

"Not quite. It's twenty past two. But who cares? I'm so hungry I could eat a horse, and since they promise the customers on this tub twenty-four-hour room service and just about anything they might want, maybe that's exactly what I'll order—a horse. Now, what would *you* like to eat?"

She laughed again. God, he was full of life! What was his secret? Great expectations? That life for him would offer nothing but the good?

"Hmm . . . What are you going to have just in case they're fresh out of horses?"

He grinned boyishly at her, large, even, very white teeth gleaming, and she thought, What a wonderful smile! What wonderful teeth! Was it true, as someone had once told her, that only Americans have wonderful teeth like that? But everything about him was wonderful!

Most of the men she had known had been rich, sophisticated, and powerful. Some had also been cultured, witty, and bright. More than a few had been quite handsome in a Continental fashion, and a couple had even been possessed of lean, muscular bodies like Jonathan's spectacular one. But none of them had had *everything* . . . so many dazzling attributes all rolled into one magnificent whole. None of them had been—she groped for the words—golden boys. Yes, that was the right term. Jonathan West was a golden boy . . . most golden.

"On second thought, I think what I'm really in the mood for is not horse but dessert, since I've already had the best in main courses," he confided, his lips inches from hers.

She stuck out a tongue at him, irresistibly drawn into his nonsense. "I hope it's not me you're referring to—as if I were a plate of meatballs and spaghetti."

"Hardly meatballs and spaghetti." His mouth reached for her tongue to taste it and savor it. "If I were to describe you in terms of food, I would have to resort to a menu

86

from the finest restaurant in the world, which I suppose would be French, but frankly, I prefer plain American cooking with a southwestern accent. And when I'm in the mood for exotic, I prefer Italian, if you can call Italian exotic, or sushi rather than escargots . . . no offense intended."

"Why would I be offended?"

"Well, you *are* French, aren't you? DeArte *is* a French name, *n'est-ce pas?*"

"No, actually it's Spanish."

She almost went into her usual routine, as if by rote. But the last thing she wanted to do now was to tell Jonathan West one of her fanciful stories:

DeArte is Spanish, my stage name. When I decided to go on the stage, I took my mother's maiden name. Mother was from an old Castilian family. She was very beautiful, and when Father, who was with the English Foreign Service in Madrid, saw her for the first time at an embassy ball—she was only seventeen—he fell madly in love with her. But of course her family wouldn't hear of her marrying an Englishman. Perhaps if he'd been the British ambassador himself, they might have overlooked his being English, but he was much too young for that. So they had to elope. It was a bit of a scandal, and Father was reassigned to Baghdad, where I was born . . .

But the last thing she wanted to do was lie to Jonathan West.

So instead she laughed, and when he asked her what the joke was, she said, "It's that *n'est-ce pas*. It's easy to see you're no more French than I am with that American schoolboy accent. You don't actually pronounce the *ce*—no offense intended."

"Offense definitely not taken," he said with a laugh. "To tell the truth, French was neither my favorite nor my best subject."

She sat up, pulled the sheet up to partially cover her nakedness, and settled back on the pillows, the better to indulge in the unaccustomed pleasure of this kind of sweet and simple getting-to-know-you talk. Their lovemaking had been incredibly good, but this kind of intercourse was incredibly satisfying.

"What *was* your favorite subject?" she asked, her amber eyes wide open and shining. "Was it the one you were best at? I was good at languages, but I always loved literature the best. Especially poetry. But I just bet you were the teacher's pet, and I'm sure your mother's pride and joy, weren't you? I want to hear all about it."

"You don't really want to hear all that, do you? I was just your ordinary American schoolboy who went to your ordinary neighborhood school in San Diego, California, which is a pretty nice place to grow up in, and it *was* fun, but I'm sure you had a childhood that was much more interesting . . . more exciting and probably more fun."

Oh, but wouldn't you be surprised to know the truth, Mr. West? It was interesting, I suppose, if you have a taste for freak shows. But only occasionally was it fun. As for you, I doubt that ordinary ever fit you.

"It was fine, but I really do want to know all about you and how it was growing up in San Diego. What did you like? What did you do?"

Now he leaned back against the pillows, totally relaxed. "Well, in San Diego people pretty much take life one day at a time, if you know what I mean. 'Laid back' is a state of mind that's supposed to apply to all Californians, but I think it's especially so in San Diego. Have you heard of the condition?"

"No, not really."

"Well, let me try to explain it to you. In southern California, and especially in San Diego, the sun shines practically every day of the year, and that tends to lull you into enjoying the day and not worrying too much about the next one, and that way you don't get too shaken by anything. The attitude is 'Why bother when life is really good and it's nice and warm and an earthquake or a tidal wave might come along tomorrow and put things out of commission for a couple of days? So let's relax and just let it happen.' So everybody wishes everybody else 'a good day' and thinks about taking the day off to head for the beaches, or the mountains, or maybe Disneyland. Especially when you're a little kid and all that's on your mind *is* going to the beach and riding your bike and wondering whether the manager of your Little League team will let you play in next Saturday's game."

"And did he?"

"Yeah. Usually."

"That's what I thought."

"Oh, you did? Why?"

"Because I'm sure you were the star hitter or whatever it is they call the boy who gets all the home runs."

"Well, I got my share," he admitted. "But then I practiced a lot, really worked on it."

"And I bet you were a Boy Scout and one of those newspaper delivery boys too."

"How'd you guess? Do they have newspaper delivery boys in Europe too?"

She shrugged. "I really wouldn't know. I never lived at home much. Mostly I was away at boarding schools. But were you a good newspaper boy? One of those boys who's named newspaper boy of the year . . . dependable, never late, making your deliveries through rain and snow?"

He threw his head back to laugh. "I think you're mixing up newspaper boys and mailmen. Besides, there is no snow in San Diego and hardly any rain to speak of. But yes, I must admit I was dependable and almost never late, and I *was* newspaper boy of the year, but I'll tell you a secret. The real reason I was boy of the year was because I couldn't miss. You see, I delivered more papers than any other kid in San Diego. I had three routes where the other boys had only one."

"You did? How did you manage that?"

"Simple. I was nine or ten at the time, and I parceled out the deliveries to a bunch of kids who were a year or two younger—kids who weren't old enough to have routes of their own but could throw a newspaper in the general direction of a front door. I was more of a sales manager than an actual delivery boy, and I gave the boys half the profit on every paper they delivered."

She was not surprised.

"That was when you were ten. Tell me what you did when you were twelve."

"At twelve I was selling used bicycles out of our backyard. All the kids in the neighborhood would bring in the bikes they'd outgrown and get a bigger or better one, for an additional fee of course. I had a slogan, 'If you'll trade, you'll make the grade, and if you come to West, you'll get the very best.' "

"Oh, I love it! That's wonderful. And I bet you made up the slogan all by yourself."

"But of course. I wasn't the fifth-grade rhyming champion for nothing. *Numero uno* every time." He inclined his head in a mock bow.

"Oh, my Lord, you must have been impossibly conceited."

And absolutely adorable . . .

"Confess. You had an ego as big as a house. I just bet you were the *numero uno* show-off in your class too."

And how I wish I'd been the little girl in fifth grade who sat at the desk next to yours . . .

"Tell me, wasn't there anything you weren't a champion at? Something you *didn't* do better than everyone else?"

"Well," he admitted, "I suppose there was French . . ."

She laughed and countered, "No, that doesn't count. I mean something you *chose*, that you really went after."

He made a great show of trying to recall *something*, but then he lifted his shoulders helplessly. "Sorry. I really can't think of a thing."

"Nothing? I can't believe it. I think you're just a big, fat liar," she accused, trying to keep a straight face.

He kissed the tip of her nose. "Me a liar? Well, listen

90

here, Miss DeArte, I don't know what they said where you went to school, but in my playground they used to say, 'It takes one to know one.' "

Andrianna felt her face flushing. *It takes one to know one.* Was he implying that he *knew* she was an accomplished liar? That practically her whole life had been a lie?

No. There's no way that he could possibly know.

"All right," she said. "I'm going to give you one more chance to tell me about life in sunny San Diego illustrating yet another of your superior accomplishments, withholding my decision as to whether or not you're a big, fat liar until I hear you out. Do you wish to proceed?"

"Very well, Madame Judge. Or are you the prosecutor?" He leaned down to brush his lips against hers.

"Please, sir, try to restrain yourself from attempting to unduly influence the court, keeping in mind that in the end it can only help your case."

She couldn't believe how silly she was acting, embarrassingly so. But then he was acting as silly as she.

"Would you mind clarifying that statement, your Honor? What will help my case? Restraining or attempting?" He kissed her again.

"I'm warning you, Mr. West. These diversionary tactics will only work in your behalf."

"Is that a promise?" One finger traced the curve of a silky-skinned breast.

Her senses reeled at even this slight touching, and she forced herself to pull away. "Enough of that kind of tampering with justice, Mr. West. Get on with your story."

"Okay . . . okay. Just give me a second to gather my wits. After all, a lot is riding on your decision, and I want to make sure I'm making the best possible presentation . . ."

"The truth is all it takes, Mr. West. The truth and nothing but the truth."

"All right, I'm ready. I'll tell you about the summer I turned ten. In September I'd be going into the fifth grade with the citywide annual spelling bee coming up in October, and naturally I had my heart set on winning although I was a lousy speller."

"So what *did* you do?"

"Nothing that revolutionary. I simply began to prepare for it that summer. I began my campaign by taking the dictionary to bed with me, staying up half the night every night studying and memorizing."

"But what made you think you could memorize a dictionary? Even a ten-year-old couldn't be that foolish."

"But I had a secret weapon."

Ah, yes, of course. A secret weapon. A true hero. They always had some secret weapon that rendered them invincible. And sometimes it was only that they were so pure of heart.

"I have this—well, call it a gift. The ability to remember almost everything I read if I concentrate hard enough. It's not a photographic memory, not total recall, but something close to it. Anyhow, I thought it was worth a try, and I stayed up half the night all through the summer, studying the dictionary, using a flashlight so my parents wouldn't catch on. I memorized the spellings of thousands and thousands of words I had never even heard of before. And it was the most marvelous feeling you can imagine . . ." His voice even now was full of awe.

"I felt like I was bursting with knowledge . . . that there was nothing I didn't know, couldn't do. I felt like I was king of the whole damn universe. I've never felt quite like that again. Oh, I've made a lot of big deals since. I've made millions of dollars, but that time—well, it was unique! Can you believe it?"

Yes, she could believe it. She could almost see him studying his trusty dictionary by the light of a flashlight after everyone else was asleep—a sturdy, special, handsome little boy who believed he was invincible.

But what she realized, even if he himself didn't, was that, win or lose, it really wouldn't have mattered. He could have lost the skirmishes; he had already won the battle. Still, she asked, "And you won? The citywide finals?"

"Yes, I won. How could I not? I even memorized words like *spirochaetales.*"

"Oh, no! I refuse to believe that you would even think that they would ever ask you to spell a word like . . . like *spirochaoticles* or whatever that ridiculous word is! You *are* a big, fat liar!" she laughed.

"Wait a minute! I never claimed they asked me to *spell* it; all I said was that I *memorized* it. If you must know, I still remember how to spell it." And he spelled out the word for her, letter by letter, affecting an injured tone. "You can write it down if you like, and check out the spelling, and—"

Then, suddenly he was very serious. "I didn't lie to you, Andrianna. Don't you know that I would never lie to you? Do you believe it?"

The thing of it was that she did believe it, totally. And she had never known a man before about whom she would swear . . . swear that he would never lie to her . . .

The truth was, she realized, that she was totally beguiled . . . lost in the wonder of him, in his golden glow, bedazzled by his sincerity, his shining virtuosity, and his utter belief in himself. She believed not only his words but *in him,* as she had never believed in herself.

And she was incredibly saddened.

Maybe if she had met Jonathan West a few years sooner, somewhere in California—someplace between the beautiful northern country and sunny San Diego—some of what he was might have rubbed off on her, a kind of by-product of love, and she would have come to better believe in herself. Maybe then she could have looked up at a sky aglitter with stars and thought, I'm Andrianna Duarte and I can catch any one of you. I'm Andrianna Duarte, and there's no one—nothing, be it man or time or illness—that I can't beat, fair and square . . .

But now it was too late.

He slipped his arms around her. "Well, I'm still waiting

for an answer. Do you believe me? You look so solemn. What are you thinking?"

She grinned at him. "I believe you. And if you must know, I was thinking, 'Oh, my God, this man is incredible! What a speller!' "

And they both broke up, laughing and hugging at the same time until suddenly he stopped laughing and buried his face in her dark hair. "Andrianna! Andrianna!" he murmured, and then, "I love you, Andrianna DeArte."

Then she stopped laughing. He had said the magic words. *I love you, Andrianna DeArte.* But the problem was there was no Andrianna DeArte. There was only the woman who was one part Andrianna Duarte, one part Ann Sommer, and so many tiny parts of so many women that she couldn't keep the percentages straight in her head.

The whole is sometimes greater than the sum of its parts. She'd read that somewhere, and it had sounded terrific, but she didn't believe it. If anybody were to ask her, she'd put it the other way around: the whole of the thing is often diminished by its different parts.

When had it all started—this diminishing of the whole? When she had kissed Rosa good-bye at the airport in San Francisco, still Andrianna Duarte? Or was it with that first lie told when she'd landed on Helene Sommer's doorstep as little Ann Sommer? Was it when she had first figured out that Andrew Wyatt was her father, or when she'd first begun to suspect that Helene truly despised *her* and not just her intrusion into the Sommer household?

Did it happen when she'd been raped by Alex when she was not yet fourteen? Or did it happen after the rape, when she'd told Helene about it? After Helene's cruel response she had thought that nothing else could possibly shock her . . . or move her to tears . . . or make her any more cynical than she already was . . .

But she was wrong. There had still been some way for her to go. And it hadn't been until she found out *why* Helene despised her so that she had determined to be as cold and as hard and as unfeeling as the "aunt" she'd been foisted on.

It was Patricia Smithers, otherwise known as Bitsy, Andrianna's schoolmate from San Francisco, who let the cat out of the bag when she returned to Huxley after her Christmas holiday in the States.

"Oh Ann!" Bitsy trilled. "Did you know that my mother actually *knows* your Aunt Helene from way back when?" Bitsy winked at the circle of girls around her, a coterie of her friends whom she'd rounded up so they could witness snooty Ann getting her royal comeuppance.

Catching the wink and sensing that whatever Bitsy was leading up to was going to be unpleasant—Bitsy had had it in for her ever since Andrianna had resisted Bitsy's attempts to draw her into her catty clique of friends—Andrianna decided she just wouldn't listen and turned to walk away so briskly the pleated plaid skirt of her school uniform fanned out above her knees.

But then Bitsy spoke again, riveting her to the spot. "As soon as I mentioned the Sommer name to Mummy and told her that your uncle was the British something or other in Zurich, she knew exactly whom I was talking about. Did she ever! It seems she remembers the Sommers really well from the time your uncle was the consulate in San Francisco *before* they were sent into exile or whatever it is they do to people in foreign service who disgrace themselves."

While Bitsy's friends tittered, Andrianna's mind raced. This was the first time she had heard that the Sommers had actually lived in San Francisco, so close to where she'd been born.

Not wanting Bitsy to know how well she had captured her attention, Andrianna smiled loftily. "I haven't the vaguest idea of what you're talking about, but I do know why they call you Bitsy. They must be referring to the size of your brain."

"Oh, really? Well, maybe *you* don't have any idea of what I'm talking about, but Mummy has more than a vague idea of what *she's* talking about. She remembers *everything* about your aunt . . . *all the juicy details*. Did you know that Auntie Helene was a public scandal when she was in San Fran, fooling around with a married man named Andrew Wyatt?"

Fooling around with Andrew Wyatt! Andrianna actually felt her heart skip a beat.

"Mummy says that right from the beginning your precious aunt was carrying on with all kinds of men until she got her hooks into Andrew Wyatt, who is first-class San Fran society and owns banks and stuff like that."

Andrianna unconsciously moved in closer.

"Mummy says Helene and Andrew Wyatt had a really hot affair going until he threw her over for some little Mexican girl from the boonies."

A little Mexican girl from the boonies? Elena! Bitsy was talking about her mother! Andrianna's chest tightened so she could scarcely breathe.

"Can you imagine?" Bitsy turned to her audience. "Ann's fancy-pants aunt being thrown over for some Mexican slut who probably didn't even speak a word of English? Isn't that a gas?" she demanded and was rewarded with the proper gasps and giggles.

Now Andrianna felt the blood rushing to her head, her face burning. At that moment the stunning news that her father, the man her sweet mother had adored, had believed in, had worshiped, had been Helene's lover too hardly mattered. All Andrianna could think of was that Bitsy had called her mother a Mexican slut! *A whore!* She thought at that moment that she might wrap her hands around Bitsy's skinny neck and choke the breath out of her, but she was as if immobilized.

"And then," Bitsy went on blithely, "the Sommers were laughed right out of town and were sent to Baghdad.

Probably no other country would take them. And Mummy says it took them years before they worked their way back to civilization, which I suppose is what you can call Switzerland.

"Of course Mummy's furious that Huxley, which is *supposed* to be an exclusive school, would even take you, Ann, which is an attitude, of course, that I don't share," Bitsy declared, her tone suddenly self-righteous. "It's just not right. I told Mummy that *anyone,* no matter how lowly, deserves the benefit of a good education, no matter who they are or what kind of people they come from, however trashy. That's the American way," she explained to her audience piously.

But Andrianna wasn't listening anymore. All she could think of now was that afternoon, that next-to-last afternoon of sweet Elena's too-short life when she, believing in the beauty of love that she and her Andy had shared, spoke to Rosa about that love . . . those golden moments stolen from eternity, not knowing that before her there'd been Helene Sommer, who had also enjoyed stolen moments with Andrew. Poor naive Elena, who didn't know that what glittered like gold was only brass — and tarnished brass at that.

No wonder Helene hated her! She had lost Andrew Wyatt to Elena. *Hate my mother . . . hate me!* And she had agreed to take her off Andrew Wyatt's hands for money and to get out of Baghdad. It all added up. No sooner had she arrived in Baghdad than the Sommers had made their move to Zurich. Her father, the prominent millionaire, obviously had bought the new appointment.

But then Bitsy's voice, still going strong, filtered through her consciousness: "I finally talked Mummy out of demanding that Ann be thrown out of school," she told the girls. "It really isn't her fault that she's the niece of a woman who is *très déclassé*—no less tarty really than that little Mexican grape picker if you think about it, only British, of course, and with a zillion pretensions. Anyhow, I *did* talk Mummy out of it, and I don't even expect any thanks—"

It was then that Andrianna lit into Bitsy—hitting, cracking, smashing, slamming, slapping, kicking, and gouging. She even bit her. She flayed and she raked and she scraped and she pulled at Bitsy's hair until her tightly clenched fist held a bunch of Bitsy's yellow curls and Bitsy was a bloody mess and she herself was drenched in sweat, exhausted . . .

Huxley held both girls accountable for what they referred to as the "disagreement." But when neither girl had anything to say for herself, it was agreed that the whole matter would be dropped with no letters sent home on the condition that the incident wasn't repeated.

After that Bitsy gave her a wide, wide berth. Still, in one way Andrianna was grateful to her. At least, if nothing else, she understood a lot of things much better than she had before.

Yes, the whole incident had been another link in the diminishing of the whole, but hindsight allowed her to see that it really hadn't added up to much in the scheme of things.

Right now, at this very moment, there were only Jonathan West and she, not Andrianna Duarte or Ann Sommer but Andrianna DeArte, and they had two days, just forty-eight more hours that, no matter what the future held, nothing or no one would be able to snatch back. Those few hours would be hers to hold and to hoard, a golden time to treasure like a precious jewel against an uncertain eternity . . .

Eight

Saturday

Andrianna never went back to her suite that night, and it was dawn before they finally surrendered to sleep. He drifted off first, while she held out a few minutes more, watching him as he slept, marveling at how young and innocent he appeared.

As she struggled to stay awake, she felt jealous of each passing minute, reluctant to give even one up and already greedy for more. Was that the price of experiencing real love? Never being truly sated, always wanting, demanding, craving, pleading for more?

Then, as her eyelids insisted on closing and she felt herself sinking into sleep, she instructed her inner clock to wake her before too long, hoping that that mechanism at least would obey.

When she came awake, slowly at first, she was drowsily aware of him leaning over her. Then, when she became sensuously aware of his lips moving across her shoulders and down her breasts, she moved against those lips, wanting only to luxuriate in the moment. But when she saw the sunshine streaming into the room through the portholes, she sat up abruptly. "What time is it?" she asked urgently.

"I don't know. I haven't looked. Nine . . . ten, maybe. Why? What difference does it make? We're not going anywhere." He laughed, bent his head again to tickle her throat with his tongue. "Or are we? You haven't made an appointment to play shuffleboard or anything, have you?"

"No," she admitted, feeling foolish.

She leaned back against the pillows, smiling up at him, trying to appear utterly relaxed even if she wasn't. "No appointments. But I *would* like to know the hour, please. It's a thing I have. I have to know what time it is or I feel disoriented."

"Okay. The last thing I want is to have you disoriented. I need your full attention." He checked the wristwatch he'd left lying on the nightstand. "It is exactly nine forty-two. Feel better? I had no idea that time was your master," he teased. "Not a lady like you."

Time is not my master — it's my enemy.

"And what kind of lady do you think I am?"

A question of no consequence, a trivial one, but not a waste. It was a lover's question and therefore most relevant. Especially when she knew what he would say. Lovely things, wonderful things . . . and he said them, every last one of them.

"Hungry?" he asked.

"Well, we never did have dinner last night."

"No, we didn't, but I didn't miss it, considering . . ." He grinned. "Did you?"

She laughed back at him. "Not a crumb. But we should eat to keep up our strength. Isn't that what people always say? Besides, I *need* coffee, pots of it."

"I guess it's settled then. We will go to breakfast."

No, please don't ask me to squander my precious hours so wastefully!

"Must we *go* to breakfast? I'm feeling much too comfortable and lazy for that. Why don't we have breakfast right here in this lovely bed? So much cozier. So much more . . . *intime*, shall we say?" Her voice caressed the word, and he, sensitive to her every nuance, her every intonation, became immediately aroused.

"Shall we indeed," he agreed solemnly.

It was he who objected when after breakfast she proposed that she go to her own stateroom to brush her teeth, shower, and get herself something to wear. At least a robe.

"No, I won't hear of it. You may not leave this room."

"My goodness, you're bossy," she said, as archly as a sixteen-year-old. "What will you do if I don't obey you?"

"Try me and find out."

"Will you punish me?"

"I will."

"Promise?"

"I promise."

"Oh, good! Punish me! Punish me with kisses . . ."

She brushed her teeth in the white-tiled bathroom using his toothbrush, wearing nothing at all, while he stood behind her, his arms encircling her waist, his eyes meeting hers in the mirror and smiling into them, and she thought, what a lovely way to brush one's teeth. And then, when she felt his erection hard up against her, pushing, seeking, she thought, Oh, yes, the loveliest, the very, very best.

They shared a shower after he insisted on pulling her into the stall with him. At first she had objected, saying there wasn't really room for two. But then, as she soaped him slowly and conscientiously, followed by his soaping her in the same manner, solemnly and as precisely, followed by their just standing together, arms wrapped about each other, just letting the water stream down on their uplifted faces and over their bodies for endless minutes, she understood the ritual of the shared shower as a lovers' experience.

It was as lovely an act as they had thus far performed . . . until they lowered themselves to the tiled floor in a sitting position and she felt him slipping into her, and then it became another thing altogether. Then it was both as exquisite and as erotic as anything she could possibly imagine.

When Jonathan had gone downstairs earlier to take the breakfast tray from the steward, he'd found a sheaf of phone messages slipped under his door—the consequence of his having taken the phone off the hook the afternoon before. Now he flipped through them quickly. Each message represented a frantic call from his office, his staff seemingly hysterical at not being able to reach him.

"Christ," he muttered.

"What is it? Something wrong?"

"Not really. It's just that all of a sudden people who earn better than a couple of hundred thou per don't know what they're supposed to do next just because I've been out of touch for—what, a day? You'd think I was the President of the U.S. and suddenly I up and disappeared."

"Have you ever been out of touch for a whole day before?"

"I guess not."

She smiled. "Then you've only yourself to blame."

"I guess you're right. Maybe I should hire you to work for me since you're so smart. Let you whip everyone into shape. My executive assistant? How about it? Good salary, terrific benefits."

She laughed. "Those benefits are very tempting, but I'm

afraid the job would be a little bit out of my line."

Of course they were only kidding around, but he was suddenly conscious that while they'd talked about a thousand things they hadn't talked about *her*—hadn't touched at all on her plans—and it was essential to his well-being that he know all about them.

He had made love to her over and over again in the past hours and was by now on intimate terms with her body. He had watched her every expression, studied her every feature at length so that, eyes shut, he could reproduce her facial image faithfully, down to every exquisite pore. Yet he still knew almost nothing about her, and what little he did know was what he'd learned before he called off his investigation, which added up to practically nothing.

He had talked endlessly about *his* childhood but hadn't learned anything about hers. He didn't even know *why* she was going to the States. Whether she was planning on staying in New York or whether, like him, she was planning on flying to the coast immediately. An actress, she might very well have business in Hollywood.

But he would have to start from the beginning. Ask her what it was she did. He couldn't very well confess at this point in their relationship that he had initiated an inquiry into her past even if he'd called it off almost immediately. While some women might even be flattered by this kind of reaction at the first sight of her, he didn't think Andrianna would be. More likely she would resent it fiercely, and he wouldn't blame her. It had been an incredibly nervy, even sneaky, thing to do.

But he'd own up to it later on in their relationship. When they'd be able to laugh about it together. It might even become one of those funny stories couples told on themselves—how they met and the ridiculous things they'd done.

He slouched down in the big, comfortable chair facing the bed. "So what *do* you do?"

"Do?" She licked her lips, stalling for time, not wanting to pursue this avenue of conversation.

Rich girl, poor girl, beggarman, thief . . .

"I'm an actress. Not an important one, not even a very good one. But it's what I do, more or less."

For a second he was distracted from what he really wanted to know—where she was headed once they docked. "What kind of attitude is that?" he reproved. "More or less?"

She shrugged, not wanting to discuss her lack of interest in the art of emoting or her lack of ambition in general.

"You don't approve?" she asked with a little smile.

"Hell no, I don't approve. If you're an actress, then you're the best or at least you *think* you're the best. If you don't at least think it, you never will be."

She made a joke of it. "I'll tell you a secret if you promise not to be shocked or hold it against me. I haven't the least desire to be the best even if I could be."

On the one hand he *was* shocked. He couldn't imagine not wanting to be the best. It was a concept completely alien to him. On the other hand he couldn't help being impressed by such indifference. But maybe that was what set her apart from everyone else.

He never did get around to asking her about her plans once they landed in New York. But he figured that they'd get to it before they docked. Besides, he wanted to think about it. Just in case she *wasn't* planning on flying to the coast, he wanted to be ready with an offer—a good one. An offer she couldn't refuse.

It was nine o'clock before they thought about dinner, and he asked her to order while he stood at the Queen Anne desk, glancing through the latest dispatches from his

104

office.

"All right." She picked up the phone that sat on the coffee table in front of the gray-blue sofa. "What do you think you'd like to eat?"

He strode across the room's plush carpeting to reach her. "You . . ." He grinned.

"I don't think I have any problem with that," she whispered and gently hung up the phone.

Before they thought about food again, it was very late, and he said, "You know what I'm really in the mood for? A party. A real celebration."

It was on the tip of her tongue to ask, "And what are we celebrating?" But then she thought better of it. She *knew* what he wanted to celebrate, and it was better that the words weren't spoken. Maybe it was even time for her to let him know that what he wanted to celebrate was at most worthy of only the tiniest of celebrations. But they still had one more day, and she wasn't ready . . .

"And what do you think a celebration calls for in the way of food? A fat, juicy hamburger with lots of grilled onions and a double order of fries? Certainly no *ris de veau aux morilles*. I know! A hot dog with lots of mustard and dripping with pickle relish!" she teased.

"You're making fun of me and my pedestrian American tastes, but I forgive you. I know what culinary snobs you Continentals are. It matters to me not at all, and furthermore, I'll tell you exactly what I'm in the mood for."

"Tell me," she begged, contrite.

"Fudge brownies and double chocolate layer cake and raspberry tarts and ice cream sundaes. Definitely ice cream, all flavors—chocolate chip and maple walnut and rocky road and vanilla rum all gooey with peanut butter brittle running through it, not to mention pistachio mint—"

105

He picked up the phone and asked for room service. "You got me so excited my mouth is watering. What flavor ice cream would you like? Name it and it's yours," he said grandly as if offering her her choice of diamonds, emeralds, or rubies or simply the moon and the stars.

She laughed and shook her head. "You're like a little boy at his own birthday party, thrilled with his presents and ready for the ice cream and cake. Is that what life is to you? A great big birthday party?"

He looked at her, amazed, and laid down the receiver. "Yeah. At least that's what I'd like it to be—a kid's birthday party with all the presents tied with satin ribbons."

"Balloons?"

"Balloons and party hats and streamers. Why the hell not? What do *you* think life should be like?"

Oh God, what do I think life should be like?

"I think I'd like life to be like . . . like . . . sex in the afternoon . . ."

He had had no idea what she would say in reply to his question, but her answer so startled him that without thinking his eyes darted to the time displayed on the video equipment facing the bed. Fifteen minutes to twelve. And then he looked to the portholes, where moonlight, not daylight, filtered in. He sat down on the bed to look into the shadowed amber eyes. "Like sex in the afternoon?" he repeated. "How do you mean?"

She smiled faintly. "You know—a wonderful surprise . . . unexpected and spontaneous. You make love and look out the windows, and the whole world is bathed in a warm, soft, golden glow, and . . . and it's so delicious, as if you've stolen golden moments from life . . . from eternity!"

Her eyes were glistening, and he sat motionless, captivated by her words. "Yes?" he prompted her to go on.

"And you *know* . . . deep down you know that it's more than just sex you're experiencing—it's love at its most glo-

106

rious . . . most extraordinary. It's as if you're making love on sheets of pale pink satin or on white fur. It's like walking on crimson velvet and drinking sparkling wine and feeling the bubbles exploding inside your head all the way down to your soul, and it's hearing wonderful music that only two people can hear. It's breathing in the scent of the most incredible perfume in the world in a roomful of flowers and laughing all the way . . ."

Now, as she leaned back against the mound of downy pillows, the dark hair cascading around naked satin shoulders, her eyes were half closed, her lips slightly parted, as if she were somewhere else apart from him, lost in her own vision.

"Yes . . ." Her voice was a husky whisper. "That's what life should be like. Like sex in the afternoon, a wonderful surprise before the sun goes down."

He was mesmerized. She had painted a picture for him, a vision that, even if he lived to be a hundred, he would never get out of his mind. His mouth was dry, and he felt like he had almost ceased breathing. He couldn't think. He only knew that he had to have her again, immediately, at that very moment, but he also knew that he wanted it to be as she'd described it—not ice cream and chocolate cake but champagne kisses, love on satin sheets in a room full of golden light . . . lovemaking stolen from eternity.

He retrieved her fur cape from the wardrobe and spread it on the floor and then went to the portholes and closed them against the moonlight, leaving the room in complete darkness until he went from lamp to lamp, turning on each one, bathing the room in a bright yellow light. "There . . ." He picked her up from the bed and laid her carefully down on the fur, kneeling beside her. "I've turned the night into day, changed the moonlight into sunlight . . ."

"So you have," she murmured, looking at his beautiful bronzed body glowing in the golden artificial sun he had just created and into the shining light of his eyes, and she knew that even while the sunlight was fake, everything else was real. As real . . . as perfect . . . as it would ever be.

She held out her arms to him, and he took her with a violence bred out of lust. But even as he submerged himself in his hot passion, he knew that it was conceived out of love—love for this beautiful, exotic woman. And he knew that he wanted this more than he had ever wanted anything . . .

She was laughing, thinking of how she had finally cheated eternity, stolen a lot more than a few of its golden moments, but when he asked her why she was laughing— suddenly jealous of anything about her that he wasn't a part of—she told him she was laughing only because she was happy. And that satisfied him because he felt as if he too were bursting with happiness.

"We're getting married in the morning."

"What?" She stopped smiling. "What did you say?"

"You heard me. We're getting married in the morning. There's a song that goes like that, you know," and he sang a few bars for her, oblivious to the fact that he was more than a little off key.

Marriage! She stared at him as if he had lost his mind.

Why is he doing this to us? Why doesn't he know that this is just a shipboard romance, not meant to go on forever?

Frantic, she gestured at the brightly lit stateroom. "All this sunshine must be going to your head. Don't you know that too much of it is bad for you?"

He laughed. "I'm a California boy, and we get along fine with the sun. We know how to cope with it."

"Ohhh!" She waved a hand at him in frustration.

He laughed again, thinking that all the talk about the sun and her apparent anger were just cover-up noise while she composed herself—that she was just a little overwhelmed by how fast things were moving.

Not that he blamed her. He was a little overwhelmed himself. He had never asked a woman to marry him before. And while he had been damned sure that they were going to get together right from the start, his thinking hadn't really gone much beyond that. He'd been thinking perhaps of a relationship. Living together. But now he knew that nothing less than marriage would do. Living together was for those who wanted to try on a relationship for size, or for fools, maybe, who didn't realize that when you saw what you wanted you grabbed for it with both hands and tied it up before someone else got there first.

"Look, forget that sunlight business. It was beautiful and it was exciting, and given a choice, I wouldn't have it any other way. And I hope that it will always be sex in the afternoon for us. I fully expect that it will. But the point is, I'm willing to take you for better or worse, in darkness or in sunlight. Don't you understand that?"

She understood only too well. But *he* didn't understand. "Oh, be serious!" she cried.

"But I am. Will it help if I start from square one and do it by the numbers? I love you, Andrianna DeArte, and I will do my best to make you always laugh with happiness just as you were laughing before. I will treasure you always. Given those facts, will you be mine? But you can't take too long to give me an answer. I want the captain to marry us first thing in the morning, and I think it's only the decent thing to give him a couple of hours' notice."

"And what about me?" she asked indignantly. "Don't I get a couple of hours' notice? No, never mind that. I don't need any notice. The whole idea is ridiculous, and my answer is no! Get it? N-O. No!"

He didn't really understand why she was acting this way—putting on this show—but he didn't think for a moment that she was serious. He was sure she had fallen in love just as he had. He felt it too strongly to be wrong.

"Is it more courting you want? I know we just met, and there's no time for spooning on the front porch for six months, but I can promise you a whole *life* of romance."

He tried to take her into his arms, but she evaded him while she tried to think of what to do next.

Obviously she was taking the wrong tack, acting like she was angry. What was anger going to do? No, the right thing to do was to make a joke of it—make him think that she had thought he was just fooling around all along . . . give him a chance to take back his words and save face.

"Not funny, West," she reproached him teasingly. "Just suppose I was the kind of woman who took your funning seriously? You could have broken my little heart. No, not funny and not very nice either. Kind of mean, really."

With a sinking heart she saw that he wasn't smiling. Instead his eyes narrowed as if he were coming to a slow boil, and he asked, "What *is* it with you? I'm in love with you, and my gut instinct tells me you're in love with me. So why are we playing this game?"

No, there would be no saving face here, no salvaging of anything. It was just a matter of her getting out of there with as little pain as possible to either one of them.

"Game?" she inquired coolly. "I wasn't aware that we were playing any games. I only thought we were having a good time. You know, enjoying ourselves? Enjoying each other. And we did, didn't we? So no harm done, right?"

Exit time, she thought, trying to swallow the lump in her throat.

Her fur cape was still spread on the floor, and she picked it up and wrapped herself in it.

"And that's it?" he asked flatly. "A fucking good time and you're out of here? Is that it?"

No, no painless way either.

The problem was that for all his money and success, Jonathan West was so damned naive. He thought that

110

wonderful sex and what smelled like love *was* love . . .
"until death do us part" love. Well, it wasn't, and somehow—any way that she could—she had to show him that it
wasn't.

"What did you think?" She smiled into his eyes with just
a touch of nastiness, hoping she wouldn't spoil everything
by crying. "A couple of really good fucks and I was
hooked?"

She headed for the small flight of stairs and went down
them slowly. She walked through the sitting room and
then, just before she opened the door, turned to look up at
him as he stood there stunned at the top of the stairway.
"But you *were* good. *Really* good. The best I've had in
years . . ."

At first Jonathan was angrier than he'd ever been in his
life. He called her every ugly name he could think of.
Then he told himself he was well rid of her. Suppose he
had talked her into marrying him? She was the kind who
first dragged you through the mud and then bled you dry.

Overcome with fresh anger, Jonathan ran to the wall adjoining her suite and kicked it as hard as he could and was
further enraged when he didn't even make a crack. All he
did was hurt his bare foot, and then he was furious with
her for that as well.

Then, sinking down on the couch, cradling his sore
foot, Jonathan knew that what he felt was sorrow rather
than rage, and all he really wanted to do was cry. And
then he tried to console himself. You win some, you lose
some, and big boys didn't cry. Even he, Jonathan West,
who had won so many battles, couldn't win them all.

At first Andrianna didn't know for whom she was crying
more—herself or her poor Jonathan. She'd wounded him

111

badly.

First she had lured him into falling in love with her . . . seduced him, and not with her body but with a lie—her deceitful golden vision of love.

Then after having lured him and lied to him and succeeded in making him love her, she had rejected him. And what did it matter that she was rejecting him for his own good? That it was hell for her too? That didn't lessen his pain. Wouldn't make him hate her less.

Why shouldn't he hate her? She was guilty. Guilty of thinking that she could be happy for even a few hours and drawing him into her delusion. If that hadn't been a crime, she didn't know what was. At the very least it had been a terrible mistake.

"Well, chalk up one more mistake for Andrianna in the great heavenly book of mistakes," she said aloud to the mirror, wiping away at the evidence of the tears she'd shed. She had to have her own page in that book, an extra-long page, so what was one more item? But she started to cry all over again, knowing that this mistake had been worse than all the others . . .

Nine

Jonathan spent his last day at sea working on contracts and talking to his office, trying to accomplish in one day what he had neglected in four. He tried not to think about Andrianna—she was a closed file in his life.

They had a special file cabinet at West Properties that was referred to as the cemetery, but painted bright yellow, the color of a perfect California lemon. Inside this gorgeously colored cabinet were the records of those deals that had come to a premature death, gone sour before consummation.

Occasionally Jonathan might ask to see one or the other files from its recesses just to refresh his memory, to recall what had gone wrong in a specific case or maybe to check out what had been a problem from the onset, but mainly to see that an error in judgment or execution wasn't repeated. Mostly the files remained untouched, one of Jonathan's rules for success being that you didn't waste time dwelling on the lemons but got on with it. And very rarely was a deal reopened once its file was consigned to the cemetery.

Still, as he tried to concentrate on a contract—the culmination of several months' work that would add the Wilshire West Hotel, a prestigious "small" hostelry on the Wilshire Corridor (that pricey stretch of high-rise edifices

113

between Beverly Hills and Westwood) to his ever-widening portfolio of holdings — Jonathan couldn't banish from his mind the image of Andrianna lying in his bed, as exquisite as any masterpiece, her eyes glowing brilliantly as she described her vision of sex in the afternoon. And he couldn't forget how exciting it had been to make love to her. Or how he had felt . . . Even if he lived to be a hundred and one, he doubted that he would ever recapture that feeling.

He attempted a mental exercise — picturing burying Andrianna in his "cemetery," squeezing the glorious length of her between the yellow hanging folders. But it didn't work — she kept emerging, popping up, refusing to be vanquished.

He kept asking himself, *Why?* Why couldn't he just chalk her off as a deal that went sour, one of those projects that had had a basic problem right from the start?

He kept coming up with the same answer. Because the whole thing didn't ring true! The Andrianna who had kissed him off so succinctly and with so much expertise at the finish was not the same woman with whom he had done such beautiful business in the beginning.

Nothing was going to convince him that he'd been so wrong about her. Andrianna DeArte *couldn't* be the cold bitch she purported to be when she had walked out of his stateroom and his life after he had said he wanted her to be his wife. He was never wrong about these things, not when he felt it so strongly. There had to be more to it than that but he was damned if he could figure out what it was, and he only hoped that he wouldn't go to his grave still wondering.

Andrianna tried to concentrate on getting through the hours, telling herself that if she could get through this last day at sea she'd be all right. Once in New York she'd have enough on her mind to keep the image of Jonathan West at bay.

She *could* get the works at Elizabeth Arden, she deliberated. Manicure, pedicure, hair, skin toning, massage. Maybe she'd even try an entire new makeup, or did they call it a makeover? Maybe that was what was called for — a complete makeover — a new Ann Sommer, a new Andrianna DeArte, take your pick.

That should at least get her through the morning, would perhaps even take her into the afternoon. It was worth a try.

With her long fur coat thrown over a sweatshirt and jeans, she slunk past Jonathan's stateroom, careful to avert her eyes. But as good as her intentions were — not to let her eyes stray in that direction — a quick use of peripheral vision confirmed that the window curtains were drawn against the light of morning, against all chance passersby.

Despite all the ministrations, the new makeup, the new hairdo, all the magazines glanced through, and lunch taken in the salon, she was back in her suite by two.

What would she do with herself now? she wondered as she looked at herself in the mirror, this way, that way, front face and then in profile. She didn't think she liked the dark lipstick they had painted on her mouth so painstakingly, nor the very pale foundation they'd applied, complemented with a brightly colored blush. It seemed to her that they had given her the look of an old-time movie star when filming in black and white had called for intense contrasts. And she didn't like her new hairstyle — the big but shorter curly look with wispy bangs — any better. It might be the latest in contemporary hairdos, but it wasn't Andrianna DeArte, any more than it was Ann Sommer or, for that matter, Anna della Rosa.

She applied a vigorous hairbrush to the curls until the

115

mass of hair once again swept back smoothly from her forehead to fall past her shoulders with a will of its own. Then she cleaned her face free of the makeup, deciding to leave it bare for the remainder of the day. Her friend Nicole, who had been taught numerous beauty secrets while still at her mother's French knee, always insisted that the skin had to be given an opportunity "to breathe, breathe, breathe. . . ."

Nicole had so instructed her when they'd still been schoolmates, a long time ago. But Andrianna still followed her friend's cautionary advice, Nicole and her long list of rules being one of the fondly recalled memories of the past.

With that, Andrianna turned away from the mirror, wondering what she'd do next. Sleeping pills to make it through the day just so she wouldn't be able to think?

No, she would go through her things, find some clothes she could discard. Less was more when it came to rolling stones, a lot of moss impeding motion and fast getaways.

But she gave up less than halfway through, having already gone through everything before she left England, the chaff already separated from the wheat—the good stuff, wickedly expensive monuments to the great gods of style and fashion, with the artist-designer label discreetly sewn into the seams. These masterpieces weren't meant to be discarded easily. Each creation, vested with hundreds of man-hours of work, was made to last, through depressions and bull markets, the good times and the bad, through wars and other catastrophic events. Good clothes were timeless in more ways than one, and at this moment Andrianna found the thought depressing. Her wardrobe was going to outlast her.

Then she thought of making an inventory of the contents of her jewelry case even though there was already an existing inventory—each piece listed with a full de-

116

scription along with the date of acquisition and place of origin. The insurance company had a copy, and there was a duplicate in the jewelry box itself to facilitate going through customs, which she so often did. There was another copy with her "important papers" and one more in her purse . . . just in case.

But the inventory-taking she had in mind was something entirely different. It was deciding which pieces she would sell first when she needed money. And she began to lay the jewelry out on the bed, intending to sort the pieces into different piles, starting with a "keep" pile since that would be the easiest . . . the smallest pile of all.

First there was the hospital bracelet fashioned of pink and white beads that spelled out her name—the name she'd been born with. Rosa had given it to her with the few other simple pieces of jewelry that had been her mother's—presents from Andrew Wyatt, Andrianna assumed—just before she had left for the airport that day her whole life had changed. She placed these in the "keep" pile, along with the bracelet Jonathan had so recently given her. But then she snatched it back and put it on her wrist, not quite ready to relegate it to Pandora's Box, which was what she called the jewelry case.

Next came the child's charm bracelet that Andrew Wyatt had given her on her seventh birthday. She started a new pile with that one—the victim's pile, she thought.

Then came the additional pieces of relatively small value from Uncle Alex. Should she start another pile with these? The extortion pile, she could call it, since they'd been given to her in the hopes of buying her silence. No, they were not really the spoils of extortion. More they were the price of her being victimized one more time.

She threw Alex's presents on top of Andrew Wyatt's charm bracelet and then threw herself down on the bed, burying her face in the pillow . . .

Yes, she had been a victim. Fate's victim as well as people's. But, uneasily, she realized that somewhere along the line she had become her own victim too, gradually, subtly, with no distinct edges to mark the when and the where. With the passing of time those lines had grown smudged and indistinct.

When had it really begun? When had she passed over that invisible boundary line and become her own victim? Was it when Alexander Sommer died and the rules by which she lived were altered?

She was fifteen and at Le Rosey in Switzerland when they called her into the school's office to inform her that her uncle Alex had suffered a massive heart attack and subsequently an untimely demise. She was offered the school's sympathies and told that arrangements for her immediate return to London had been made.

"What for?" she asked.

Return to London? That was a hot one. She had never lived in London, much less even seen the Sommers' house there.

"What for? Oh, my dear. So that you may be a comfort to your aunt, of course, and so that you may attend your uncle's funeral," the headmistress told her, smiling sadly.

Her roommate, Penny Lee Hopkins from Dallas, was working on her French accent when Ann went to her room to pack the required necessities. Penny's mother had told her daughter that if she didn't acquire a really good French accent—or at the very least a proper English accent—out of her ridiculously expensive schooling abroad, she might as well pack it in, the cost of a foreign education being what it was and the bottom falling out of oil.

"But you have to understand," Penny Lee enjoyed explaining, "that's what people in the oil business are always saying—that the bottom's falling out. Still, I don't know a single person who's selling his jet."

"What's up, honey chile?" Penny asked now, grateful for a reprieve from her odious task and forgetting for the moment that she was no longer supposed to sound like a little old gal from Texas.

"My uncle died and I have to go to London for the funeral."

"What I wouldn't do to be in your shoes! To get out of here and get a few days in London! Get to a few clubs and hear a little decent music for a change. Maybe even the Beatles. Get in some shopping on Carnaby. Believe me, sugar, what I wouldn't do would turn even a colored nun's cheeks the color of an overripe tomato."

"Well, it's too bad we can't change places, Penny. I wish it *were* you instead of me going to London."

"Oh, I do beg your pardon, honey. I guess that all did sound a little insensitive, your uncle dying and all."

"You don't have to be sorry about that. Actually I haven't seen Uncle Alex since the day he raped me . . . that is, if you count using a hand instead of you know what—"

Penny gasped. "Oh, Annie! He *didn't*, really, did he?"

"Oh, yes, really. And I haven't the slightest idea why my dear aunt even wants me at the funeral. She hates the sight of me, and I assure you, the feeling is mutual."

Actually there'd been very little communication between her and Helene even *before* the telephone conversation when Andrianna had informed her aunt of what had transpired between her and Alexander. The infrequent holidays in Zurich when Helene was mostly absent. The boxes that arrived in the mail—a present for her birthday or Christmas, occasionally something *très luxueux* like a silk blouse from Paris or an enormously extravagant bottle of perfume or, more usually, something practical, such as a durable leather purse from Italy or Spain. And then there were the boxes of necessities.

Every fall there were two new school uniforms, consisting of a blazer and skirt and a gray Shetland sweater (to be interchanged with white blouses), and twice a year—according to the season—there were a coat, rainwear, and a jacket of some kind. Then there were handkerchiefs and underwear, bathrobes and nightgowns, assorted white blouses to go with the uniform, a Sunday dress for chapel, and two party dresses.

Once a month there was a small check—her spending money—and twice a year there was a check for other expenses, for necessary travel and the purchase of shoes and boots and bras (when she was old enough to need them), since those articles were best personally fitted on the wearer.

But then, ever since the telephone call when Helene had called her a vicious little liar, only the box of necessities, minus its more frivolous articles, and an expense check cut by half arrived in the mail, the gifts and allowance having been eliminated.

Having so little money to spend was a considerable sore spot but otherwise the arrangement suited Andrianna fine. By this time she had come to take a perverse pleasure in being despised by her aunt, having long since passed the point when she cried herself to sleep.

Andrianna took one look at the dress she was to wear for the funeral—a black velvet with a big white lace collar and a full skirt that would reach almost to the ankles—and her mouth dropped open. "This is for *me?* Aunt Helene, I'm not a child"—she looked straight into her guardian's eyes and saw that Helene knew exactly what she was talking about—"and I'll look ridiculous in this."

"Then stop acting like a child," Helene hissed. "What were you expecting? The latest from Mary Quant or a bizarre little something from Petticoat Lane? Did you think I was going to allow you to make an exhibition of yourself in a dress that barely covered your crotch?

"Oh, don't think I missed that photo of you in *Elle* in a mini so short I could actually count the hairs. Where was it taken? Oh yes, Saint-Tropez, one of your seemingly endless holidays with one of your school chums. Who was it this time? The girl in the picture with you and those two toughs? That little Swedish tart with the father who's made a fortune manufacturing toilet bowls?"

"Jean Paul Polignac and Teddy Roberts, the toughs you refer to, are schoolmates who just happened to be in Saint-Tropez at the same time I was. And Pia Stromburg and her father, who is a famous industrial designer, were kind enough to invite me to Saint-Tropez only because they knew I had nowhere else to go on holiday. And that skirt was one that Pia and her father bought me, among other things like jeans and sandals and bikinis, because I didn't own anything that even resembled what the other girls were wearing in Saint-Tropez, and the only money I had wouldn't have covered the cost of a pair of tights."

"Oh? In that case I have a suggestion for you to follow in the future. *Don't* go to Saint-Tropez, and then there shouldn't be any problem. After all, where is it written that a fifteen-year-old *has* to go to the Riviera, much less with a wardrobe more suitable for a trollop than a schoolgirl?"

"Where, then, would you have me go, when everyone else goes home or on holiday with their families?" Andrianna asked evenly in a low voice.

For a second Helene was taken aback, but she recovered quickly. "Don't be such a bore, Ann. Even *you* should be able to find an appropriate friend or two to associate with. That's why you're being given this opportunity to attend one of the most exclusive schools in the world. Do I have to pick the right friends for you too? Haven't I done enough for you already?"

Oh, yes, dear Auntie Helene, you've done more *than enough.*

Andrianna stared at the black velvet funeral dress draped over Helene's Chinese Chippendale sofa in Helene's gold and white drawing room in Helene's great Georgian mansion in fashionable Grosvenor Square. Then she looked all around the room, at the gilded sconces and the Meissen jardinieres on the marble mantel, at the ancient hanging tapestries and the paintings on the walls.

When she had first entered the room, she had gone from one painting to the other, amazed at the signatures, all of which she'd recognized from her art appreciation class. Two portraits by George Romney, a Gainsborough, two Constables, and a Turner. Helene had a fortune in art alone . . . for which she had given so little in return. Even at that, she had shortchanged the buyer, the millionaire who hadn't even bothered to check whether he was getting what he paid for. If nothing else, Andrew Wyatt was a bloody terrible businessman.

And *she* was supposed to be grateful!

She picked up the velvet dress and threw it on the marble floor. "I'm not wearing that dumb dress. I'd look like a freak in it—which I suppose is what you really want."

"Don't make me angry, Ann. That is a very expensive dress, and I specifically chose it because when you go back to school you'll be able to wear it to dances and things, the *proper* sort of things, hopefully."

"Dances? What kind of dances do you think we do? Actually, I wouldn't be caught dead in that dress at a cricket match! If you think it's so great, why don't *you* wear it?" She made a point of staring at Helene's black silk suit, its hemline a discreet but stylish one inch above the knee.

"I'm warning you, Ann. Pick that dress up, go upstairs, and put it on. Because if you don't, there won't be another new dress for you for years, not to mention shoes or boots or skis or riding clothes or anything of that sort. And there won't be any expense money for you *at all,* so you won't be traipsing about to Saint-Tropez or the Greek isles or the Costa Emeralda with all those friends you think are so fond of you. Believe me, you'll find out that they won't be nearly as fond of you if they have to keep shelling out all those lire and francs to pay your way. And then where will you be when everyone else is having fun? In the cold and empty dormitory at school, all by yourself."

Andrianna snatched up the velvet dress from the floor. She knew when she was hopelessly outclassed.

"Just tell me one thing. Why did you bother to drag me to London for this funeral? You know I despised Alex, and you can't stand the sight of me, and believe me, the feeling is mutual. Why did you want me here?"

"Honestly, Ann. You are here for the sake of appearances. You *are*—were, anyway—Alexander's niece, and he was your legal guardian."

"Appearances," Andrianna repeated dully.

"Yes, of course, appearances. And although you're right about one thing—I really can't stand the sight of you—I will give you some very good advice. Sometimes that's all that really counts—appearances. Otherwise, why would I go through with this charade of an elegant funeral, considering the expense? Especially since Alexander's death is, if anything, an embarrassment to me, considering how and where he had his heart attack."

"An *embarrassment:* What do you mean? Where did he

123

have his heart attack?"

Helene laughed nastily. "Never mind, my dear. Let's just say I've been used to the task of keeping up appearances for a *long* time.

"Now, you'd better get upstairs and change into your dress. We don't have all that much time."

Just then she noticed that the draperies at the bank of windows at one end of the drawing room were hanging a trifle askew. She sighed heavily as she went over to straighten them, as if all the burdens of the world rested on her own frail shoulders.

When she finished and turned to see Andrianna still standing there, just staring at her, she snapped, "Are you still here? I thought I told you to get upstairs and put that bloody dress on!"

When Andrianna came down the stairs two hours later, she was wearing the black velvet dress, cut to six inches above the knee. There had been no need to hem where she had cut; she had simply fringed the edges by pulling threads. For once, she thought, she'd gotten the better of Helene.

But Helene proved as good as her word. There were no new dresses for Andrianna in the months that followed, no shoes or even panties. There wasn't so much as a tuppence by way of spending money either, much less travel expenses, and Andrianna was forced to learn to adapt.

Friends, she quickly discovered, were the key to getting along, and some she chose not necessarily only because she liked them, as she had chosen Penny Lee Hopkins, Nicole Partierre, and Pia Stromburg. With the right kind of friends a girl could have the best of times in the best of places and never be lonely again.

Le Rosey was the perfect place to start life all over again. The school was a kind of crossroads for the children of the international set—those of more-or-less noble lineage, those who were merely very rich, and those who were only famous, as well as those who combined all three to the best advantage. Some of the students were real royalty with thrones in their futures, others—near misses, only pretenders to the throne—a special breed of European aristocracy who ruled only in a never-never land, having title but no domain.

They were *all* fascinating to Andrianna—to a one they seemed to live fabled lives—but it was the pretenders to the throne who held a special attraction for her. She too was a pretender, and all the pretender had to do, really, was *just be,* radiating a glamour that was infinitely romantic and alluringly mysterious, unburdened by the responsibilities a real princess, for instance, might face. Like duty and obligation . . . or even the need for truth.

Andrianna placed all the jewelry back in her Pandora's Box. Was it then, at that time of her life and at Le Rosey, when she had begun to be one of her own exploiters, caught up thereafter in a maelstrom she was unable to control?

Well, she was landing in the New World tomorrow and, theoretically, at least, embarking on a new life again. Maybe there was still time to turn things around.

But did she really believe that? Or did she know, as she had always known, that it was already too late . . . too late before it had ever really begun?

Part Two

New York
November 14-16, 1988

Ten

Jonathan was already inside the limousine that had been dispatched to meet him at the docks, with the engine running and the chauffeur ready to move out, when he looked at the long lineup of limousines still waiting for their passengers.

One of them is waiting for her. A woman who's occupied the Queen Anne suite and is of a generally reclusive nature, as Andrianna appears to be, isn't about to stand around scrambling for an available cab.

"Hold it!" he told the driver.

"Sir?"

"Turn off the engine. We'll just sit here awhile."

"Yes, sir . . . But we don't have all that much time for you to make your flight—"

Jonathan nodded, well aware of the time situation.

He had been one of the first to line up for customs that morning, anticipating the typically hellish Monday morning traffic from the city to Kennedy. Despite having a couple of hours before his plane was due to depart, he'd still be cutting it close.

Then, as he'd moved quickly through the crowd getting in line for customs, he'd found his eyes involuntarily searching the crush of disembarking passengers for a glimpse of Andrianna. And when, in spite of everything,

129

he'd still found himself wondering where she was headed once she left the ship, he'd told himself it was all to the good he hadn't spotted her. He might have run up to her, grabbed her, and shaken her like a rag doll, demanding to know why she had lied to him . . . why she had denied loving him when he knew she did!

No, it was better this way, he had told himself. *I've already relegated her to the dead file, and only an ass wouldn't be grateful when the dead didn't rise up to haunt him.*

Still, here he was now, acting on impulse, changing his plans, all because of his lovely nemesis. He really was a damn fool.

Yet when the driver prodded him with a "You never know how the traffic's going to run. You might miss your plane," Jonathan smiled pleasantly. "Well, I guess if I miss one plane, I'll just have to catch another. That's what's so great about commercial aviation today—the planes take off all day."

The driver shrugged. He got paid by the hour, and it was all the same to him. "Yes, sir. You're right about that. But would you have any idea of how long we'll be sitting here? I should call in—let them know . . ."

Eventually, Jonathan reminded himself, he'd have to call his own office and let them know he'd be delayed . . . an hour, a couple of hours, a day. *Oh, hell, what's the use of being a millionaire if you can't call the shots, if you can't decide how you're going to spend your own time?*

He leaned forward. "What's your name, pal?"

"Rennie, Mr. West."

"Okay, Rennie, call in. Tell them I'll be keeping you for the day."

"Yes, sir!" Great. He'd just as soon sit here as spend his time fighting traffic. Besides, he could always smell a good tip from a mile away, and his nose was twitching.

"Would you care to see the morning news, Mr. West? The remote is right there on top of the TV, and the *Times* and the *Wall Street Journal* are in the pocket there. And if it isn't too early in the day for you, sir, you'll find that that little bar there is stocked pretty good. Or, if you'd like, I could mix you a drink and fix you a tray of cheese and crackers and pâté. It's all ready to go in the trunk. It would just take a minute . . ."

The time dragged almost intolerably as Jonathan's eyes scoured the crowd of disembarking passengers. He should have known that Andrianna would be one of the very last to leave, avoiding the inevitable early mob scene. That would be her pattern.

Then, suddenly, he spotted a familiar face, a friend and Malibu neighbor—Hal Cramer—heading for one of the waiting limousines. Hal was one of the few people Jonathan really respected in L.A., even though he wasn't what one might call a major player . . . an attorney whose private law practice took a backseat to what Hal earnestly considered his civic and humane responsibilities.

Quickly he flicked the switch that lowered his window. "Hal!" he called out. Breaking into a grin, Hal trotted over to Jonathan's car.

"Yo, Jonny! Fancy meeting you here!"

"I can't believe you've been on the *Queen* these last five days and I didn't catch hide or hair of you, Hal. Where've you been hiding?" Jonathan demanded, forgetting that he himself had hardly ventured out into the public arena.

"Jesus, Jonny! I caught this goddamned cold in London, and I haven't been able to shake it. Would you believe that for the last five years I've been promising myself this trip and then when I finally manage to squeeze it in I had to confine myself to quarters nursing the son-of-a-bitchin' thing?" He sneezed and then blew his nose heartily as if to confirm his plaint. "But tell me, how was it enjoying the pleasures of the *Queen?*" he asked somewhat pathetically.

131

Jonathan laughed. "To tell you the truth, I was more or less confined to quarters myself. You know how it is . . . I had a briefcase full of papers . . ."

Hal sniffled, blew his nose again, and chuckled. "Same old Jonny. Business first and everything else second."

"What can I say?" Jonathan grinned. "We can't all be my pal Hal with all his do-good causes. But look at it this way, pal. Where would all your philanthropies and high-minded causes be if there weren't some of my kind with their noses to the old grindstone, making money to donate to same? We need each other—we balance each other out."

"Point well taken, old buddy. And I'm glad you brought it up, because God knows when we'll have the time to talk about this once we get back to L.A. As a matter of fact, I was planning on giving you a call first thing. I need your help. But we've got to make this fast. I've got a plane to catch! Hey, maybe we're booked on the same flight and we can take one limo to Kennedy and talk about it on the way and then on the plane—" He turned away to cough.

"No, I'm not leaving until later in the day, and I'm not exactly sure when. And if you must know, I'm not all that eager to spend that much time in your company"—he grimaced and laughed—"considering all those germs you're spreading. But spit it out. I don't need a long spiel. What's the worthy cause, and how much is it going to cost me?"

"No, Jonny. Not money this time. This time I need a little of your *time* and the benefit of your thinking. It's this project the council's been bogged down on for three years already—the Hill Street Performing Arts Center. It's been one problem after the other. Zoning. Building codes. A really lousy budget. One builder after another quitting on us. We don't seem to be able to get the damn thing moving."

Jonathan nodded. "So I've heard."

"Well then, you've already got a handle on the situation. And it occurred to me that maybe the master builder him-

132

self, my friend Jonny West, might lend us his expertise. How about it, Jonny? Can I send over the files for you to take a look at—the figures and the specs? You might have some ideas on how to get this thing rolling."

He moved closer to the window, pressing. "Hell, Jonny, I might as well level with you. I want *more* than your ideas. What I'd really like . . . what I really want is for you to think about heading up the committee on this thing.

"It's a very worthy venture," he urged, his voice husky with his cold and with his intensity. "It would not only give theater in Los Angeles a healthy boost—it would also go a long way in revitalizing that whole downtown area. What do you say? Will you at least think about it?"

Jonathan looked hard at his friend. Hal was a man who always had a dream in the offing, as he did, only Hal's dreams always transcended the personal, so on a certain level he was never really disappointed—his efforts on behalf of his dreams were always sufficiently gratifying no matter the ultimate results.

Jonathan made a decision on the spot. He'd go for a different kind of dream this time, one that—like Hal's—transcended the personal.

He smiled at Hal. "Tell you what I'm gonna do—"

Hal leaned forward eagerly. "Yes?"

"I'm going to build that center for you . . ."

"What do you mean? Literally build it, or what?"

"I mean I'm going to take it completely off your and the city council's shoulders . . . build it for you at no expense to the city or its citizens, get it done in less than a year's time, and present it to the city as West Properties' gift to the people of Los Angeles . . ."

"You're kidding."

Jonathan laughed. "No kidding."

"Come on, Jonny, what's the catch?"

"No catch."

"You don't want special considerations for something

else you're building? No tax abatements, no—?"

"Nothing. I'm just making your dream *my* dream. You don't mind, do you?"

"Mind? Hell, *no!* If you must know, I think you're one sweet son of a bitch!" Hal offered affectionately.

"Well, there *is* one thing I might want out of this . . ."

"Yes?"

"I might expect that you'll want to call it West's Center for the Performing Arts. What do you think?" Jonathan grinned.

Hal grinned back. "Like I just said, Jonny, you're one sweet son of a bitch!"

It was at least another hour later when Jonathan finally saw her. She was wrapped in the same fur coat as when she'd boarded ship and carrying the same square jewelry case, and she was claiming one of the two remaining limousines.

His pulse pounding, Jonathan leaned forward and did something he had longed to do since he was a kid. "Follow that car!" he shouted at Rennie.

The chauffeur sat up, clicked off the radio, laid down his copy of *Sports Illustrated,* shook off his lethargy, and cried, "Yes, sir!"

This is more like it, thought Rennie. Every driver dreamed of having someone get into his car and say exactly that, but in all his years of driving for a living the situation had never come up. Rennie glanced in the rearview mirror to get another look at his passenger. *What's this guy's story?* He looked too classy to be a private dick trying to get the goods on a cheating wife, and he didn't fit the profile of the nondescript FBI or CIA agent. Besides, a stretch limo wasn't exactly your ideal undercover vehicle.

What the hell, Rennie thought as he maneuvered the car smoothly into traffic. If I run into trouble, I can always say that the son of a bitch told me he *was* with the CIA and it was a matter of national security. *Let's go for it!*

Much to Rennie's disappointment, the ensuing chase turned out to be a bumper-to-bumper crawl taking three-quarters of an hour to get from the West Side to East Fifty-ninth Street. And they didn't lose sight of the woman's white stretch for a second. When it pulled up in front of the Plaza Hotel's entrance on Fifth, they were right there, three cars behind.

Wouldn't you know it? Jonathan thought wryly. Where else would she land but at *Trump's* Plaza Hotel? Fate's little twist of irony. While Donald Trump might very well have never heard of Jonathan West, the master of the deal played a prominent dual role in his life—the business tycoon he most wanted to emulate and, at the same time, the billionaire he most envied, the fancied adversary he dreamed of besting in a deal of the century.

But that had nothing to do with the action at hand, and when Rennie, now his cohort, asked with dramatic urgency, "What do we do now?" Jonathan, after a moment's hesitation, said, "We sit tight."

He watched as Andrianna's extensive luggage was removed from the car and she disappeared into the lobby. He ached to jump out and follow her right up to the registration desk, but then what?

He forced himself to sit for a couple of minutes before he jumped out, telling Rennie to "stay" as if he were an attack dog, and walked quickly into the lobby to position himself where he could watch Andrianna check in but still remain unobserved. Just in case she did spot him he had a line ready. He'd grin and say, "We really must stop meeting like this . . ."

Then, when he saw her following the bellman to the bank of elevators, he was tempted to run over to learn which floor they were headed for, to follow them to discover exactly which room was hers. But he could hardly do

135

that without revealing himself.

Damn, how did a private eye handle a situation like this? In the movies and in books they usually talked to the room clerk. They slipped the guy a bill, ten bucks for a flea bag or a cheap motel, at least a twenty in a better-class hotel. At these rates the Plaza should go for at least a fifty, and he would have gladly turned over a hundred-dollar bill or even two, but he suspected that at Mr. Trump's Plaza the ploy wouldn't work. He would have to be more subtle than that.

"But you must have a reservation for Jonathan West!" He was properly indignant. "My secretary made the reservation from Los Angeles at least two weeks ago, and she's the soul of efficiency. If there's a mistake, believe me, it's the Plaza's, not hers. In all the years I've been coming here this has never happened before."

Actually he had never stayed at the Plaza before, but he doubted that they'd check. The gentleman *did* consult his computer to announce, as Jonathan thought he might, that there'd been a cancellation and they could, after all, accommodate him. For how many days would Mr. West require the suite?

Jonathan shrugged. "Two . . . three days. It depends . . ."

"Of course."

The bellman had the key, and just before Jonathan turned to follow him he said casually, "Oh, by the way, I thought I saw a friend of mine checking in a few minutes ago. Andrianna DeArte? A tall, beautiful woman with dark hair?"

The clerk blinked. "Well, I did just check in a young woman who fits that description. But her name wasn't Andrianna DeArte. It was della Rosa. Anna della Rosa." He checked his computer again. "Yes, that's correct. Anna della Rosa."

Della Rosa? What the hell is that all about?

"A striking woman. Dark hair, and her eyes were an unusual color. I couldn't help noticing."

"That's Andrianna, all right. I was pretty sure it was she. She's the actress, you know, and I guess she's trying to keep a low profile. Doesn't want the press to know she's in town." He laughed. "But I'd like to surprise her. What's her room number?"

The young man smiled tightly. "It's not our practice to give out room numbers. Security, you know. But if you'll go to the house phone and ask for the guest by name, you'll be connected to the proper room, and then the guest can give you the number if she so chooses." A smile.

Since his bag and briefcase were still in the car, Jonathan had no reason to go to his room. He went instead to the hotel florist shop, where he ordered thirteen white roses to be sent to Miss Anna della Rosa. Declining to write out a card, he asked when the flowers would be delivered, planning to wait outside the shop and follow the bellman right to Andrianna's door.

"Within the hour."

"Why can't they be delivered immediately? She's going out, and I want her to have them before she leaves."

"Very well, sir. Immediately it is."

The thirteen roses were selected and approved, and Jonathan watched the clerk pick up the phone and ask for a bellman, then hit another key and ask for Ms. della Rosa's room number. The clerk listened for a few seconds before telling Jonathan, "There seems to be some kind of a problem — it appears that they can't find a listing for Ms. della Rosa."

"That's ridiculous. I saw her check in myself just a little while ago, and I saw her go up to her suite!"

137

"She has just checked in," the young man said into the phone, and then, "I see . . ." He replaced the receiver, telling Jonathan, "Just a bit of confusion. Ms. della Rosa checked in under her own name, but she's occupying Mr. Gaetano Forenzi's suite. He keeps it on a yearly basis."

Gaetano Forenzi! Jonathan knew the name. Italy's Forenzi Motors.

"Suite 924," the florist confirmed, writing it down. "We're all set now, I believe, and Ms. della Rosa will have her flowers in a few minutes."

"Great," Jonathan said, but he left the shop in a state of confused dissatisfaction. Now that he had all this new information—that Andrianna was staying in Forenzi's suite as Anna della Rosa—what was he going to do with it?

When the roses arrived with no accompanying card, Andrianna immediately assumed Gaetano had sent them. Who else, besides Penny, knew she was here, and who else but Gae would choose thirteen roses with total disregard for superstition? Other people *occasionally* dared to cross Lady Luck, defiantly walking under ladders and crossing in front of black cats. But Gae only laughed in the lady's face. No matter what, Gae shrugged and laughed. Or at least with rare exception.

And the memories washed over her like a spring shower, persistent but not threatening, with a hint of a rainbow in the offing, its promise never quite realized, but warm and gentle and sweetly familiar all the same . . .

She'd been not quite sixteen when she and Gae had first become acquainted, and he was a couple of years or so older, devastatingly handsome, and Le Rosey's most charming but naughtiest boy. Maybe that's why she'd been drawn to him from the start, even though she'd never

138

dreamed that the two of them could be friends. So sweet and so bad at the same time, Gae Forenzi had been a Le Rosey legend in his own time.

Gae broke all the rules but remained unscathed. He smoked constantly no matter where he was—classroom or playing field; stayed out all night whenever he pleased; left for holiday early and returned days late; showed up for class inebriated more than once; and was frequently discovered (so frequently it boggled the imagination, since only a limited number of ladies were available within Le Rosey's boundaries) in bed with a lady who was no lady but someone's wife—a member of the faculty or an athletic coach or someone like that—after which the disgraced lady, alone or in the company of her humiliated husband, left the school and the area, while Gaetano remained, still laughing.

There was even a rumor that he'd been discovered in a state of fellatio-cunnilingus with a girl from South Africa in the girls' locker room, but this story had never been either confirmed or elaborated on. Even so, Gaetano's exploits and the fact that he never suffered any retribution, as far as anyone could tell, left Andrianna breathless with admiration. But then, when she was not quite sixteen, anyone who broke the rules without paying a forfeit was, to her, a hero of gigantic proportions.

Sometimes it was Gaetano's indulgent father who, using his money and his influence, bailed his son out of numerous scrapes, and sometimes it was just the fact that no one, including Le Rosey's headmistress, could hold out against that Latin charm, that dazzling smile, the soft voice like kisses dipped in honey, those warm, velvety brown eyes.

Andrianna always thought of Gaetano's eyes as the color of brown pansies, if pansies came in brown, which as far as she knew they didn't. But *if* they had, they could have named the variety after Gae the way they named roses

139

after people, like *floribunda Winston Churchill*. She didn't know the Latin name for pansy, but she did know that the gay, perky little flower was sometimes called heartsease, and for a while Gaetano had been exactly that—her heart's ease.

Every year Le Rosey moved from Rolle to Gstaad for the winter season, when skiing replaced all the other activities on the school's sports program. This emphasis on sports was an integral part of the curriculum for a student body hailing from forty different countries, all of whom were equally keen on athletics and competitive games, no matter in which of Le Rosey's two sections they were enrolled—the English-speaking, which prepared a student for the American Advanced Placement Examinations and the British G.C.E., or the French-speaking, preparing for the French Baccalaureate and Swiss Maturity exams.

It was on the skiing trails of Gstaad that Gaetano actually spoke to her for the first time, although they'd been conducting a flirtation of the eyes since the term had started in the fall. This quaint but romantic phrase—*a flirtation of the eyes*—came from Andrianna's friend, Nicole Partierre, but it did not originate with her; it was her sophisticated Parisian mother who had advised Nicole that a flirtation of the eyes was so much more romantic than the real thing.

"But then again, you can't really trust *Maman's* advice," the usually serious Nicole said with a laugh. "I think she just wants to keep me pure while she herself is very *ooh ooh, la la,* if you get my meaning."

Andrianna and her roommate Penny definitely did get her meaning, and all of them, including Nicole, wondered what it would feel like to be very *ooh ooh, la la* . . .

At first Andrianna was inclined to agree with Madame Partierre's assessment. But then, by the time school had adjourned to Gstaad, she was getting a bit bored with the lack of action, her eyes growing increasingly fatigued, and she wondered whether Gaetano Forenzi's eyes were also tiring of the game. Why it was like . . . like *practicing sex without penetration!*

Andrianna was so delighted with her own phrase, thinking she had coined a totally original one, that she directed Nicole: "Ask *Maman* what she thinks of *that!*"

But Nicole only sighed dramatically. *"Pour moi, Maman* would think sex without penetration was very *ooh ooh, la la,* but for herself — how do you say it? — not a chance in hell!"

But Nicole made that observation when she was feeling frivolous, not serious and practical, so Andrianna couldn't really go by what she said.

The day when Gaetano finally spoke to Andrianna she had just taken a bad spill and was lying on the slope with her eyes closed and her left arm collapsed and folded under her in a peculiar way, enveloped in excruciating pain. Then she opened her eyes, and there were Gaetano's velvety ones gazing commiseratingly into hers.

"Hurts like the bloody devil, doesn't it?"

His words were a shock. He sounded almost like one of her English friends, but knowing that he was Italian and that he looked like a medieval Italian painter or even a poet, she had dreamily imagined that he would sound like a poet. That, under the circumstances, he would have murmured something like "Think not of pain, oh lady fair. Think rather of a beauteous day, all too rare."

And then, lying there in the snow and hurting like the devil, she laughed . . . at herself. Of course he spoke al-

141

most like everyone else at Le Rosey—those enrolled in the school's English-speaking section, anyway. And if he had talked like a medieval poet, what would she have done? She would have run like mad, thinking he was the epitome of what Penny branded the worst kind of turkey. Besides, what was important was not what he said but how he said it, and how he said it was music to her ears—the Italian accent a soft, furry accompaniment to his speech, like a cloak of velvet.

Velvety eyes, velvety voice, she thought, not feeling the pain half as much.

"It's not unbearable," she breathed, trying to appear the brave heroine, blithe though under attack. Being a brave heroine was romantic too, easily as romantic as a flirtation of the eyes.

Evidently Gae thought so too. He took her mittened hand, the one that didn't belong to the arm folded under her, and brought it to his lips, whispering, "You don't have to be brave, *cara mia!* You may cry as long as you don't move. Not moving is the most important thing until they see what sweet part of you is broken."

Cara mia! Sweet part of you! He *did* speak like a poet after all!

They kept her in the clinic for two days and two nights, and although the personnel and atmosphere at the clinic were as cold, as sterile, and as generally prohibitive as Andrianna imagined they might be at a women's prison, she cheered up when Penny and Nicole came to visit bearing gifts.

Penny brought her a bottle of My Sin, with which she sprayed Andrianna from head to toe, as well as the entire room, to kill what she called the "spermicidal smellums."

"Ugh! That sounds horrible. What are the spermicidal smellums?"

"You know, it's how the guck you put in a diaphragm smells, *if* you have a diaphragm, which you don't presently have but which you're going to need now that you're on speaking terms with Gaetano Forenzi. Isn't that right, Nicole?"

"Oh, mais oui!" Nicole stated so earnestly that the three of them dissolved into a fit of giggles.

Nicole brought her a see-through nightie from her own cache of hidden treasures—a black chiffon number with a little red satin bow on each narrow shoulder strap that she insisted Andrianna put on at once.

"Mon Dieu! Suppose Gaetano comes rushing in, dying for a sight of you, and he sees you in *that!"* She gestured with disgust at the clinic's starched short hospital gown. "He would be—how do they say?—turned off. He might even retch."

"Oh, you're from Nutsy Country!" Andrianna protested, borrowing one of Penny's pet phrases. "First of all, he won't come to visit. Why would he?" Then, *"Will he?* Why do you think he will?" She looked hopefully from Nicole to Penny.

"He will because he is mad with love for you," Nicole said quickly with conviction while Penny put her head to one side and deliberated for maddening seconds, during which time Andrianna thought she could happily throttle her.

"He'll come," Penny finally announced and then pounced on Andrianna to help Nicole tear off the clinic's gown, which accommodated for Andrianna's left arm being in the cast, and trying to pull the black lace nightie over her head, which *didn't.* While they were struggling with it, with the cell-like room wafting with My Sin and with almost all of Andrianna bare, the nurse who most reminded Andrianna of what she thought a nurse in a women's prison might be like—Nurse Stromm—trounced in and, sniffing with a vengeance, threw both girls out, along with

143

the lace nightgown.

"There will be no more visitors for you tonight," she snapped, clicking off the light.

It was only twenty minutes or so later that Gaetano appeared as if by magic. She couldn't see him at first in the darkened room, but she heard *someone,* and it occurred to her that it might be he. Then, when he leaned over, no more than a faceless form in the night, she was almost sure it was he, and when he kissed first her eyelids and then her throat, she knew. Oh, she knew! And she opened her eyes and there he was! Now she could make out his face in the dimness, could see his eyes shining darkly liquid. And she buried the fingers of her free hand into the coal black of his curls and drew his face down again until their lips met and opened . . .

When they stopped kissing only to breathe, Andrianna murmured, "But how did you get in? The witch of a nurse said I couldn't have any more visitors tonight."

"I talked her into it."

"Really? Nurse Stromm?" She was open-mouthed in admiration. "But how did you do it?"

He laughed in answer, then bent over her again and whispered in her ear.

"Oh, no! Nurse Stromm? I can't believe it! But how?"

He climbed into bed with her and snuggled under the covers. "This is how . . ." he whispered.

And she believed him.

"You're crazy," Andrianna whispered as Gaetano pushed her against a wall in a lavatory at a concert hall in Lausanne. "Someone will be coming in at any minute, and—"

But by then Gae had already pulled down her tights and thrust himself into her, and then by the time a woman had entered the tiled room it was over and Gae was tenderly pulling her tights back up into place. He turned to the woman and explained as they made an unhurried exit, "She has so much difficulty keeping the impossible things in place. They're forever falling down about her knees. We have to watch them all the time . . . like a hawk."

Andrianna was constantly amazed at how many places—given the parameters of their small world—Gaetano could find to make forbidden love. He was endlessly inventive and innovative. In his room, in hers, in water closets and in broom closets. In his red Forenzi, of course. Even on the slopes. When she protested that they would freeze certain parts of their anatomy off, he reassured her that the heat of their passion would not only keep them warm; it would melt the snow for kilometers around. She believed him, believing in their passion for each other.

And despite her mother's example of loving foolishly with blinders on, Andrianna now believed in endless love, that Gae would love only her until the end of time. Andrew Wyatt may have been a cold, uncaring man, but Gaetano was her darling true love, another species altogether. But then she was only sixteen and in love with the first person she had found to love in almost ten years.

Andrianna was more irritated than anything when just before spring holiday Penny, who was flying home to Dallas for the break, asked her to ask Gae to get her some really good weed before she left.

At first Andrianna thought she hadn't heard Penny right. "I beg your pardon. *What* did you say?"

"I said, would you ask Gae to get me a couple of grams of that terrific pot he had the last time? I'm not sure I'll be able to get any stuff in Dallas, or good stuff anyway. Everyone thinks just because we're practically over the border from old May-he-co we can get all we want, but you'd be surprised. They're awfully tough on drugs in Texas, and I've been away from the scene so long, I hardly have the right connections. Besides, my Dallas friends will want to die once they sample Gae's pot! It makes the Mexican shit taste exactly like that . . . shit. Still, all I want is a couple of grams."

"Only a couple? Are you sure that's *all* you want?" Andrianna asked, the hollows of her cheeks sucked in as far as she could manage. "Why are we being so modest in our demands? Why not a couple of kilos while you're at it?"

Penny looked at Andrianna strangely, mystified as to what was bugging her. "No, I don't want a couple of kilos or even *one* kilo. I just want a couple of grams. Just in case I get caught going through customs, I don't want to have enough stuff to be charged with intent to sell. Would you please just tell Gae I want a little grass without this big stink? From the look on your face you'd think I'd insulted you or Gae or something. What's your problem? Why are you so pissed?"

"Why? I'll tell you why. Just because Gae is so sweet and generous, always willing to share a joint with everyone under the sun when we could just as soon keep it to ourselves like everyone else does, you have the nerve to ask him for a couple of grams. I don't *believe* how greedy you are!"

Now it was Penny's turn to be miffed. "Well, I wasn't asking for a present. It would be different if I expected him to *give* it to me as a gift or if I were asking him for a break on the price. But I'm prepared to pay the going rate, whatever it is, and if you must know, I think your attitude sucks. We are best friends, after all, and I don't think—"

"What do you mean you're prepared to pay the going rate? What do you think Gae is anyway? A supplier?" Her voice was full of contempt.

"For God's sake, Annie, don't you know? Gae *is* a

146

dealer. Maybe he's small-time as far as dealers go, but here at Le Rosey he's as big as they get. I mean, Jamie Pritchard deals, but he's so chicken all you can get out of him is a couple of joints at a time. But honestly, Annie, I can't believe you didn't know. How couldn't you?"

At first Andrianna thought Penny had somehow been misinformed. She and Gae were so close . . . soul mates as well as lovers as well as constant companions. How could Gae be *anything* she didn't know about? How could any part of him be someone with whom she wasn't acquainted?

But when she told Gae what Penny had said, he didn't deny it. He just laughed, as he usually did. But this time she was neither admiring nor amused. It didn't bother her so much that he was Le Rosey's chief drug lord as that she, like a wronged wife, was the last to know.

"But why didn't you tell me? I thought we were as close as two people could be. How could you keep this from me?"

He wrapped his arms around her. "But I didn't keep anything from you, *cara mia.*" He kissed her mouth persuasively. "Everyone else knew, so why didn't you? You're not less clever than they. I thought you didn't know because you didn't want to know, and that was good with me. I'm for everyone knowing only what they want to know and not knowing what they don't want to . . ."

But he was wrong, Andrianna thought; she hadn't known. Or had she? Had she fallen, like her mother, into the trap of closing her eyes to any faults her beloved might possess? She didn't have the answer to that either, so she asked Gae what she thought was a reasonable question.

"But why do you do it? Your father sends you more money than you can spend around here, and you already have everything you need. Think of the danger. Suppose you were caught?"

That *was* a terrifying thought. Gae in jail. Taken away from her. "I don't know how you can take that risk."

This time Gae didn't laugh; he merely shrugged. But she knew the answer. He did it *only* for the risk. When you weren't quite nineteen, not yet a man in the eyes of the world, and you already had everything else—the good looks, the breeding, the Forenzi money and the Forenzi cachet, and a father and a girlfriend who adored you—what else *was* there but the danger and the risk—the excitement of living life on the edge?

She insisted that he give up dealing drugs. Even if he was willing to risk discovery, she was unwilling to risk it for him . . . for them both. "Please," she begged. "I don't think I could bear it if you were caught and had to go to jail. Don't you know I love you? That you're the only one I have in the whole world outside of Penny and Nicole . . . the only one I can depend on?"

It was one of the few times she ever saw Gaetano serious. "Which is it—that I'm the only person you love or the only one you can depend on?"

She refused to see the difference. "Same thing."

"They're not. And I think it's wonderful that you should love me, but not so wonderful if you depend on me too much."

Andrianna was instantly suspicious. "If I love you and you love me, why isn't it wonderful if I depend on you?"

Now he was either growing uncomfortable with the conversation or bored by it. He was doing what he always did when he didn't want to talk about something—tickling her ear with his tongue. But she persisted: "Why isn't it wonderful if I depend on you?"

He smiled at her tenderly, playing with a tendril of her hair. "All right. It's wonderful if you depend on me, but just not *too* much, if you please."

She knew she shouldn't say any more. But she was powerless to stop. "Why not too much?"

"Because if you depend too much on a person, then you are sure to be disappointed, and I would despise for you to be disappointed in me."

She was relieved to hear him say only *that*. She'd been afraid he might say that he didn't love her enough to take so much responsibility for her or that he no longer loved her, *period,* because she was such a pain and a bore.

She threw her arms around his neck. "I could *never* be disappointed in you."

Still, she kept at him until he agreed to have nothing more to do with drugs except for smoking the infrequent joint. "Now, promise. Say these words after me: 'I promise that I will never—' "

"Enough! I promise! And you are a terrible *pulédra*," he said affectionately.

"Oh? And what is this *pulédra?* What does it mean?"

He thought for a second or so. "I think the word for it in English is a nag. You know, like a woman who sells the *pesce* in the marketplace."

"Oh!" she screamed in outrage. "You're calling me a fishwife? That's a terrible insult in English. For that I will *never* forgive you!"

He tried not to laugh. "Oh, that's too bad. And I had such wonderful plans for holiday. My father has asked us to join him at our villa in Port'Ercole. He'll be so disappointed to hear that you aren't able to come . . ."

"Oh? Well, in that case, I will *have* to forgive you, won't I?" She pretended to pout. "I wouldn't want your father to be disappointed. Poor man, he has enough trouble with you for a son. Besides, I've never been to Port'Ercole, and it will just kill my Auntie Helene to hear that I'm going to holiday where she's never been. She's been dying to go there ever since she heard that the Radziwills had rented a place there and Jackie Kennedy was their guest . . ."

But once she mentioned her aunt's name her mood changed and she grew despondent, and then Gae had to remind her that Helene Sommer wasn't really part of her life. "You haven't even seen the bloody bitch since your uncle's funeral. What do you care about her so long as she keeps paying the tuition?" he offered with a Latin practicality.

He rubbed his cheek against hers, caressed her breast to make her forget all about her aunt, who wasn't worth discussing. And once he did that, one thing led to another and Andrianna forgot about everything else—Gae's promise not to deal in drugs or that he had been concerned about how much and how hard she depended on him.

But she hadn't really heard what he was telling her . . . didn't realize exactly how much love he was expressing for her by warning her against loving him too much.

Utilizing the elegant resources of the hotel's Palm Court, Jonathan personally carried lunch out to Rennie. "I don't want you to leave the car," he explained. "I want you to be ready to take off. I don't know when or what. But I want to know you're here. If you don't hear from me before then, I'll see to it that you get your dinner. And you can call in that I'll be needing you tomorrow too."

Rennie considered asking when he'd be going off duty that evening but thought better of it. Jonathan West, who had remembered he had to eat just like anybody else, would do the right thing. He guessed that at this point they were both playing it by ear.

Jonathan stationed himself in a comfortable armchair not too far from the elevators, where he wasn't likely to be spotted but where he could keep an eye on who came and went. He buried himself behind a copy of *USA Today*, a publication he usually didn't read, but it didn't matter since he was barely able to read more than a sentence at a time, the elevator traffic being what it was.

Besides, the print was but a blur before his eyes. The

only image he could make out was one that was purely in his mind's eye—a photo he'd seen in some popular magazine or other in the past couple of months. A picture of the darling of the world's playboy set (if there still was such a thing), the dashing, mustachioed Gae Forenzi, astride his polo pony, movie-star handsome, his name linked to one international beauty after the other—Monaco's Princess Stephanie, America's own post-debutante, Cornelia Guest, some actress whose name he couldn't remember. The caption under the picture had posed a question: *Will Italy's king of cars play or reign?*

The text had gone on to reveal that rumor had it that the heir to the Forenzi car fortune had been given an ultimatum by his aging father: give up either the fast lane or future control of the family-owned company.

So that was it, Jonathan thought. Andrianna had registered under an assumed name to keep her and Gaetano's tryst a secret from the gossip-hungry press and/or his father, who objected to her as one of his "fast" companions.

Then he tried another plot line on for size. She and Gaetano were meeting here at the Plaza to discuss the possibility of formalizing their long-standing affair. They had made love in dozens of countries, skied the slopes of Switzerland hand in hand, shaken and undulated while gazing into each other's eyes in the clubs of Rome and London, blown kisses across baccarat tables in casinos up the Italian Riviera and down the French. But now their playtime was over. It was time for them to marry in order to meet the demands of his father, who would accept a stable marriage as a sign that Gaetano was ready to settle down and accept his responsibilities.

"You can do it, Andrianna," he would urge. *Or does he call her Anna?* "You can convince my father you are exactly the right wife for me and that with you by my side I will shape up and become a father as well."

Oh, yes, she could do it! Jonathan thought with savage

jealousy. Who could play that role more convincingly than she? Besides all her physical virtues, she was a superb actress! Who knew that better than he?

Jonathan's arms ached with the urge to smash both of their beautiful people faces!

He could barely sit still in his chair now, convinced that Forenzi was definitely going to show up to claim Andrianna DeArte, or Anna della Rosa, or whatever the hell her name was. And crazy as he knew it might be, he wanted to stand guard by the elevators to keep the son of a bitch from going up to the suite where his girlfriend was waiting for him, panting and impatient and hot to get him crazy with her own tantalizing version of sex—her sex in the afternoon!

He didn't even know why he was continuing to sit there like some besotted, calf-eyed asshole, yet he was powerless to move, consumed by the feeling that wouldn't go away—the knowledge that when they had been together, she had loved him as much as any woman could love any man . . . with as strong a hunger as his own.

He didn't leave his post for the rest of the day. It would take only a minute or two for her to come out of the elevator and leave the hotel or for Forenzi to ascend to the suite on the ninth floor, and he would miss them—not know for sure what was happening.

When evening fell, he summoned a bellman to fetch a fresh supply of newspapers and magazines and a waiter so that he could order dinner for Rennie and a drink for himself.

When it was already past midnight, he went outside to retrieve his briefcase and one piece of luggage from the car and to send Rennie home, telling him to be back at eight

152

sharp, when something was bound to happen. Andrianna DeArte wasn't holed up in Gaetano Forenzi's suite at the Plaza for nothing. And then he went to his own suite on the eleventh floor to try to get some sleep even though now he had a feeling it was already a lost cause.

Eleven

Jonathan was up at six, had breakfast in the Palm Court at seven. As instructed, Rennie arrived at eight on the dot and, after a conference with Jonathan, took his position in front of the Plaza on Fifth. At eight-ten Jonathan took up his own position near the elevators after stocking up on the *Times,* both New York's and Los Angeles's, and the *Wall Street Journal.* All he was really certain of at this point was that if Andrianna emerged from Gaetano Forenzi's plush cocoon of a suite he and Rennie were ready to follow her into the great unknown.

Or maybe today was the day Gaetano Forenzi would show up, he thought morosely, turning the pages of the *Journal.*

Then, attempting to concentrate on a report about a possible takeover of Radson International Products by Allied Global, it occurred to him that it was entirely possible that Forenzi had shown up in the middle of the night and he had missed his arrival.

He berated himself for not having sat there through the night. Or, if not that, why hadn't he at least put a team of private investigators on the case? To hell with his scruples about doing it all himself—at least then he would have known for sure if Forenzi was up there.

Andrianna placed the vase of thirteen white roses squarely in the middle of her room service breakfast table, wanting to inhale their fragrance while she ate. But then she saw that the flowers had already begun to lose their first flush of freshness—an almost imperceptible wilting, a certain loss of dewiness.

Oh, yes, the bloom was definitely off the rose, she thought, saddened. Gaetano's exquisite roses . . . But it was inevitable. That was the way with roses, she mused, suddenly overcome with the vague ache of melancholy. Perhaps the more spectacular the bloom, the quicker decay set in. Still it happened little by little, so gradually one could barely detect the deterioration. Just like that first sweet burst of young love. In the beginning you think it will go on forever . . .

When they first arrived at Gae's father's villa in Port'Ercole, only an hour-and-a-half drive from Rome on the old Aurelia Roman Road, Andrianna was overwhelmed by the splendor of it all. The Forenzi villa had been built on a rocky shoreline jutting out into the sea—land bought from the Borgheses, the great Italian family who had been Port'Ercole's first aristocratic settlers. Facetiously called Bedlam, the villa was much grander than any home where she'd been a houseguest. Its marble floor tiles were laid out to resemble a chessboard, and it employed a cunning system of mirrors through which the shoreline was actually visible from every room.

She was even more impressed by Gae's father, Gino Forenzi, who was practically a mirror image of his son, only older, of course, with a head of black curls and the same velvety eyes. And then she couldn't help being impressed by Gino's roster of international guests.

Everyone seemed to have a title—the duke of this, the

count of that, the princess of someplace Andrianna had never heard of—and if they didn't have a title, they had a famous name, a fabulous career of some kind, or a fabled position in one of the arts. Like Beatriz de Ayala, the Italian film actress, who was known more for her tantrums and endless repertoire of vicious gossip and tasteless stories than her talent and was Gino Forenzi's current *inamorata*.

Andrianna thought the actress incredibly ugly, with a too-thick nose, coarse skin, and heavy, hairy legs. Why did Gino Forenzi—along with everyone else at the villa, man and woman alike—appear to be so enchanted by her?

It was the fourth night of their holiday, and as on the three preceding evenings, Beatriz sat in the hostess's chair at dinner and dominated the conversation. Also as on the three preceding evenings, Gino Forenzi ate heartily, drank many glasses of wine, and laughed harder than anyone else at the actress's acid comments about different people they all seemed to know, her gibes at one or the other guest's expense, and at all her jokes, one more repulsive than the other. For her part, Andrianna found it all so revolting she not only didn't laugh, she barely ate a forkful. Was this what amused supposedly worldly, sophisticated people?

She tried to tune out the actress's voice, concentrating on the pattern of the flowered Limoges dinner plate in front of her, until the Baroness Theresa von Lichenhaus, no shy little violet herself, begged the actress to recite a few of the ribald limericks for which she was notorious, and then Andrianna couldn't help listening.

"There was a young man from Capri
Who raped an ape up a tree.
The result was so horrid,
Nine balls and no forehead,
Six cunts and a purple goatee."

156

Everyone at the table, including Gae and his father, was convulsed with laughter, except for Andrianna, who thought she had never heard anything as disgusting. Instead of laughing, she stared down at the blush pink napkin in her lap, her cheeks flaming the same color.

When Beatriz saw Andrianna's eyes cast downward, she snickered and said, "What is the matter, little one? Don't you know what a cunt is? Can it be that you don't have one?"

Then, when everyone laughed again, she called out loudly to Gaetano down at the far end of the table from her, "And what's wrong with you, lover boy, that your little *putana* doesn't even know she owns a cunt?"

This time when the actress's audience again roared with malicious merriment Gino raised a hand for all to desist. But Andrianna, thoroughly humiliated, had already run from the room.

Gae found her outside, looking out to sea from one of the villa's many terraces. He tried to comfort her, putting his arms about her and rocking her back and forth. "You mustn't let her upset you. It was only a joke."

"A joke? Well, then it was a particularly repulsive one. And she's a thoroughly repulsive woman. What *is* her attraction? Can you explain that to me?"

Gae gave one of his characteristic shrugs. "It's true she's the complete opposite of beautiful; still she acts like she's a great beauty. And while I doubt she's ever had any schooling, *she* thinks she is clever and a great actress. So that is how everyone else thinks of her. The answer is that no matter how she looks or talks, she has a huge style, a large presence. Her presence is bigger than life."

A huge style. A presence bigger than life.

Moodily Andrianna reflected on that. Her mother had been beautiful for sure, her spirit easily as lovely as her face. But a huge style, a large presence? Hardly. Was that why her mother had been so shortchanged by life and the beastly Beatriz seemed to have it all?

Andrianna struggled to understand. "Is this big, showy act Beatriz puts on—all the carrying on and the sweeping around in costumey clothes and that loud, raucous voice and the dirty stories—is that what you mean by style and presence? Is that what's important, above anything else?"

Gae traced the curve of Andrianna's cheek with a tender finger. "More important than what, *cara mia?*"

"Well, being *nice*, for one thing? Or being really beautiful?"

She knew for sure that her own mother had been beautiful, and she supposed that she herself was since a lot of people said so, especially Gae, who told her so almost daily.

She watched Gae's face carefully while she waited for a response, waited for him to reassure her, to tell her that she was right, even as she was apprehensive, seeing that for once there wasn't a hint of a smile on his full, sensuous lips and none at all shining from the liquid eyes. If anything, Gae appeared to be more serious than she had ever seen him and even, suddenly and mysteriously, melancholy.

"Being nice is a very nice thing to be but of little *importanza* in the long run, I'm afraid. And being beautiful, which, of course, you are, *is* of great importance. But—" he shook his head morosely—"I think being beautiful must be like being born rich and getting a little poorer every year . . ."

Andrianna was stunned, not quite sure what Gae was telling her. Was it that inner beauty didn't count for much and that outer beauty didn't last? That it was only this great style and stupid presence thing that really mattered? That seemed pretty shallow to her and awfully cynical too.

"You sound almost like my Aunt Helene," Andrianna accused. "She doesn't give any points for purity of the heart either, and she would be sure to agree with you that putting on a big show is what really counts."

"Come with me," Gae said brusquely and seized Andrianna's hand to pull her into the house toward the sweeping, centered marbled staircase and up the steps to the second story of the villa. Then he pulled her down the hall until they reached the far end and entered a huge room with a twenty-foot-high ceiling painted in cathedral fashion, with lots of blue sky, white clouds, and gilded angels.

Andrianna looked around, stunned. Nearly every inch of wall was covered with paintings hung in bewildering confusion, an eclectic mix of sixteenth- and seventeenth-century Italian artists, Flemish paintings of flowers, early Picassos, and seemingly all the French Impressionists.

"But I had no idea this gallery was here. Why didn't you show it to me before?"

Gae didn't answer but led her to the far end of the gallery to a niche where two large pictures hung. One was by John Singer Sargent, and it was of a tall, imperious woman in a long red dress and a picture hat, her hand resting on a long black umbrella. The subject was more "interesting" looking than a beauty, but the painting made a very dramatic statement, especially when compared to the picture hanging beside it. This one was of a young woman with subdued good looks, her blond hair neatly coiffed, her pale blue eyes matching the blue of her dress. She was sitting in an armchair, wearing a long string of pearls, and holding a small dog.

It was a wonderful painting, Andrianna thought, but something about it disturbed her. And then she realized what it was. While the picture was obviously a portrait and the woman in the blue dress its subject, it was as if *she* were the background for everything else included in the painting—the long, glistening rope of pearls, the George III gilded armchair, the appealing, furry little dog in her lap, the bright silk taffeta curtains hanging behind her, the pilasters and ornamental moldings on a wall to one side, and even within the picture, another picture—a small Dutch interior—reflected in a Louis XVI mirror. It was as if the portrait painter, one Carlos Brunetti, had feared that the woman herself wasn't enough of a vivid subject, that possibly she might fade away and then there would be nothing at all . . .

Andrianna looked again from the dramatic Sargent portrait to the Brunetti and saw that they were as different as night and day. The subject of Sargent's portrait was obviously a woman of great style and presence who needed nothing but the counterpoint of a plain black umbrella, while the blonde with her quiet elegance had no presence at all and all but disappeared into her painting's props.

It was obvious to Andrianna why Gae had taken her here to view these two paintings. At first she was unable to speak, the words caught in her throat. Finally, she said, "Who is she?"

He didn't ask which woman she meant. "The woman in the red dress was some duchess or other—it doesn't matter. And the woman in blue is . . . was . . . my mother."

"Was?"

"Was." He looked deeply into her eyes, and Andrianna saw that his were suspiciously wet. Then he turned away. "She killed herself when she was twenty-nine."

"Oh! How awful! But how? Why?"

"She cut her throat."

"Oh, no! . . . But why?"

He turned to face her again, and now the tears were gone from his eyes and his voice was toneless. "She was in a sanitarium in Switzerland. They say she was disturbed"—he tapped his head—"which was why she was in the *clinique* in the first place. But I suspect that she was disturbed here . . ." He placed his hand upon his heart. "A disturbance of the spirit. The French have an expression—

160

chagrin d'amour . . ."

Andrianna said nothing. And Gaetano smiled a sad little smile. "You see, I think my mother did not have a great sense of her own presence and had no true understanding of style at all."

"Oh, my poor Gaetano." Andrianna put her arms around his waist and hugged him tight to her. "How old were you when she—?"

"Almost nine. My father told me I had to accept her death like a man and that when I was *really* a man it would all be *chiarire* . . . clear. But I think even then it was already *chiarire,* you know?"

Andrianna didn't know exactly what was clear. All she knew really was that both she and Gaetano had lost their mothers when they were children and both their mothers had been ladies of great beauty but of too frail spirit.

"I understand," she whispered. "My mother died when I was only seven, and she too was—"

"What? What did she die of?"

"I really don't know." But then she thought that perhaps she did. Maybe it was as Gae had said. Maybe her mother had died, as his had, of too little style and presence, which led to a terminal case of *chagrin d'amour.*

They stood in front of the two paintings, locked in each other's arms, more connected in sorrow than they'd ever been in joy.

Later, when she was alone in her room preparing for bed, Andrianna studied her nude reflection in the length of mirror that covered one complete wall to see if she was really as beautiful as Gae claimed. Her eyes were large and luminous and the amber color that everyone thought so unusual and interesting. Her cheekbones were high and distinct, leaving hollows to form below—the kind of cheekbones all the girls at Le Rosey both envied and admired.

Her chin was not thrust forward too much, nor was it receding. Her skin was fine and poreless. And everyone agreed that her dark cloud of hair was her best feature. So much for the face.

She ran her fingers over her soft-skinned firm breasts, their nipples pointing slightly upward. They were the kind of breasts that her friend Penny called "good soldiers," standing upright and at attention. Her hands moved down to her waist, properly small and flowing into rounded hips, a proper ten inches wider than her waist.

But what did it matter even if she were really beautiful? She was sure that she had neither style nor presence, and without them, apparently, one ended up dead, too young and too sad.

She thought of how she'd run from the table when Beatriz, the Wicked Witch of Style and Presence, had taunted her, and she was filled with self-contempt. Why hadn't she stood her ground, drawn herself up to her full height, and tossed her hair, taking full advantage of her youth and beauty to show up the dumpy and ugly and much older Beatriz, and then delivered some terrific *bon mot* to completely demolish the vulgar actress?

She could have quoted one of the great poets, which would have shown everyone that while Beatriz had to rely on nasty, disgusting limericks, she herself was a great wit. And probably with that crew she could have gotten away with the quote as her own creation and even twisted the words around to suit the needs of the moment. There probably wasn't one person there who would have known the difference. She could have recited only the first verse of Cary's "When Lovely Woman":

When lovely woman wants a favor,
And finds, too late, that man won't bend,
What earthly circumstances can save her
From disappointment in the end?

162

But then instead of giving the second verse, which in answer advised the woman to cry, she could have mockingly asked: "Is it the cunt?"

Well, next time she would try to do better, she resolved, getting into bed to wait for Gae to slip into her room as he had every night since they'd been at the villa.

But Gae never came, and she anguished over why he hadn't. Had she said or done something wrong?

Finally she fell asleep, after promising herself that she was going to be, first and foremost, a woman of tremendous style . . . a woman with an overwhelming presence.

The next day she rose before anyone else in the villa, put on her bikini, and went down to La Scalera, the farther away of Port'Ercole's two beaches. It would take Gae that much more time to find her when he came to look for her, and he did deserve to be punished just a little for deserting her last night.

There were no cabanas at the beach, so after taking her swim Andrianna simply lay down on the sand to bathe in the warm, loving sun, turning her face upward to meet its sympathetic rays. She had had so little sleep during the night that she drifted off almost immediately, drowsily wondering how long it would be before Gae awoke and came to hunt her down.

Actually Andrianna was the third thing Gae thought of when he awoke that morning. The first thing was how starved he was and the second was the shower he decided to take before he went down to breakfast. Then on his way down to eat, he knocked on Andrianna's door. When she didn't answer his first knock, he rapped three more times and then decided that if she were sleeping like the dead he would let her be.

He joined some of the others at the glassed-in terrace where breakfast was usually served—his father, Beatriz, Lady Patricia, the industrialist Silvio Pucci and his friend, a small Oriental man incongruously called Marco Polo, and the Princess Marita Cortina, who was actually an American heiress from Oklahoma City—to find everyone in a discussion as to what they'd do that day.

The matter was settled when one of the Cerruti sisters, who had a Moorish-style house near the quay, sent her chauffeur with an invitation for whoever was available to join them for a pre-lunch swim to be followed by lunch, to be followed by dancing, to be followed by drinks. Princess Grace, their honored guest, was expected to arrive at any moment, so it was necessary not only that there be an immediate response to the invitation but that everyone who was coming come immediately and come "as you are."

Gino decided they'd go the short distance by yacht and that they would leave shortly, warning everyone that they'd better hurry to ready themselves or they'd be left behind. He himself went to rouse his other guests.

Gae knocked again on Andrianna's door to tell her they were leaving shortly. But receiving no response, and hurrying to meet his father's deadline, he decided again to let her be. If she wasn't beguiled by Beatriz, the Italian actress, she probably wouldn't be intrigued by the American actress turned Princess of Monaco.

When Andrianna awoke, she was dizzy, covered with a blazing red rash, and so weak she didn't think she could even make it to her feet. As she tried to accomplish this seemingly impossible task, and found her limbs had absolutely no strength, she attracted the attention of other sunbathers, who came to her aid, aghast at her terrible case of sunburn.

"*Mon Dieu,* how long have you been lying here?" a

woman asked. Andrianna tried in vain to answer, but it was as if she had lost her power of speech.

When she managed to reveal that she was staying at the Forenzi villa, two men undertook to take her there. The houseguests who had been left behind marveled over the extent of her rash and instructed a couple of the servants to put her to bed since she was consumed with fever and unable to stand on her own.

When the Forenzis returned hours later, Gino put in an emergency call to the doctor, and a remorseful Gae sat by her bed, holding her hand, whispering reassurances, and kissing her fingertips.

Dr. Roncello pronounced Andrianna a victim of the worst case of sun poisoning he had ever encountered and prescribed various ointments and salves.

"But it wasn't only this rash," Andrianna protested feebly through blistered lips. "I could barely speak, and my arms and legs felt so heavy it was like they had turned to stone."

"Sun poisoning is not something to sneeze at, young lady. You were a very foolish girl to allow yourself to fall asleep under the sun," he reproached her. "The sun is not everyone's friend. For some people it is a deadly enemy."

Still the doctor was puzzled by the extent of the burn and the severe reaction. Despite being English, the girl was not particularly fair, and usually dark-haired people had a far higher tolerance for the sun's rays.

"Well, it should all clear up within a few days. Just use the ointments and stay in bed, and the next time you go out into the sun be sure to wear a large hat. If you intend to sleep at the beach, do so under the large umbrella. *Si?*"

For the next few days, even with her strength back, Andrianna remained in bed, embarrassed to be seen by the other guests—particularly Beatriz—with her skin reddened and blistered.

Gae, feeling at least partially responsible for her condition, was lovingly attentive. He sat by her bed for hours, often eating breakfast and lunch with her, playing board games (he loved Monopoly in particular), and even teasing her gently by constantly telling her that she really didn't look *all* that terrible. But Andrianna sensed he was growing restive.

At ten that night, bored and not having seen Gae since early that afternoon, Andrianna got out of bed, put on the exquisitely embroidered kimono Gino Forenzi had gifted her with to raise her spirits, and went in search of her sweetheart. She found him in the villa's card room, a medley of pinks and oranges, kneeling at Beatriz de Ayala's pudgy feet, vigorously performing the act of cunnilingus.

Andrianna's mouth fell open, and she froze. She and Penny and Nicole had read a description of the act in one of those books dedicated to the art of making love.

Cunnilingus: The tongue is applied to the clitoris, at which point the man will feel the delicate trembling of that organ in response to the touch of his tongue. His taste buds will enjoy a slightly salty flavor, which is not unpleasant and will add to his own excitement. Also, due to the special sudoriferous glands located about the labia and vagina, this area has a most distinctive smell, which most males will find sexually arousing.

As in the case of fellatio, where the woman takes the man's penis into her mouth and feels the excitement of his organ throbbing against her lips, the most desirable use of cunnilingus is to make the final stage, which may be penis-vagina interaction, as exciting as possible.

Andrianna, horrified, with the actress smiling across the room at her in malicious triumph as Gae catered to her, didn't wait around to see if the act of cunnilingus would be followed by the act of fellatio, or by the act of simultaneous cunnilingus and fellatio, or, for that matter, by penis-vagina interaction. Soundlessly she fled the card room.

But later, when Gae came to her room, Andrianna

wasn't able to hold back the torrent of hurt and angry words. "How *could* you? That beastly woman!"

Gae was visibly upset, but Andrianna could tell that what embarrassed him was not so much the act he had performed on Beatriz but the fact that he had been caught at it.

Still, he was only a *little* contrite, explaining that what he'd done had not been for reasons of giving himself pleasure, and certainly not to give pleasure to the actress either, but only to please his father.

"Please your father? I . . . I don't understand . . ."

"Then I will explain it to you. It seems that quite suddenly my father has developed a taste for the fair Lady Patricia . . ."

Andrianna raised her eyebrows in disbelief.

Gae shrugged. "It's true. As you well know, Beatriz is quite a handful to deal with, and if she thought she was being thrown over for another, well . . . So I was merely helping out at my father's request by keeping Beatriz entertained while he was occupied with Patricia. But it was no big deal. It's not even worth talking about."

"Oh, but I think it's definitely worth talking about! Your father asked you to entertain her, so you got down on your knees and buried your face in her . . . in her . . ."

Gae shook his head at her reproachfully. "It only makes things worse to talk about it. I was only doing my father a favor. Now, can we forget about it and not waste our last couple of days here fighting?"

But Andrianna was unable to forget about it. She felt that she had to confront Gino Forenzi, even though she was still in awe of him, and she waited for an opportunity to find him alone.

When Andrianna, embarrassed, nervous, and blushing furiously, asked Gino how he could ask his own son to *en-*

167

tertain a woman like Beatriz, Gino was at first angry, then cold, then—what? Saddened? Disturbed?

"You'll have to forgive my son," he finally said softly, apologetically. "He's young and has a lot to learn, like any young animal."

Was he saying that he *hadn't* asked Gae to entertain Beatriz for him and that she had to forgive his son for lying? Or was he saying that she should forgive Gae his act of infidelity? Did Gino even take fidelity seriously? Nicole claimed that French and Italian men barely knew the meaning of the word *faithfulness*.

Her confusion must have shown on Andrianna's face, because then Gino smiled at her kindly. "If you were my daughter, little Anna"—he had insisted on calling her that ever since Gae had introduced her as Ann—"I would caution you not to take the words of my son or any other wild young animal too seriously . . . at least not until the boy comes into his maturity, and maybe not even then."

But apparently Gino's advice to her didn't mean that he wasn't angry with Gae, and she heard them arguing all afternoon through the library doors, catching a phrase here, a sentence there.

"How dare you? In my house?"

"What difference does it make? She's a pig, not your wife."

"That is not the point. A boy does not make love to another man's woman, especially if the man is his father."

"Then the man should act like a father."

"Perhaps he would act more like a father if the son acted more like a man and not a spoiled punk."

"Maybe the father should set a better example for the son, and then he would act like a man."

"You've been nothing but trouble ever since—"

"Say it! Ever since my mother died. And whose fault was it that she died with the blood running out of her like she was a stuck pig? Only she wasn't, was she? The pig.

No, the sows were all your other women . . ."

"I'm warning you, Gaetano. Unless you learn to have a civil tongue in your mouth, unless you begin to shape up, you're not going to see another lira from me."

"I'll get by. See if I don't. And then you'll never see me again."

"What are you going to do? Sell your body to rich American women vacationing on the Riviera like you did last year in Nice?"

"They were amusing. More so than your *prostituta*."

"Ah! Is that so? Then why did you dip your beak in the *prostituta's* hole? Do you hate me so much?"

But eventually their words softened until Andrianna could picture them hugging each other with the tears coursing down their cheeks.

"Ah, Gaetano, you must learn what is right and what is not appropriate. And you have to learn when it is time to play and when it is time to be serious. How are you ever going to take control of our company?"

"I will, Papa. Give me time."

"I will, Gaetano. But how much time is necessary?"

Gae's answer was mumbled, and Andrianna couldn't make it out, but then she could hear them both laughing, and then it was quiet inside the library and she imagined that they were silently toasting each other with Napoléon brandy.

Of course she was pleased that they had made up, but she was also disappointed, because not once had she heard her own name mentioned—as if Gae's betrayal of *her* was of no importance.

But then she remembered the conversation she and Gae had had just before they had left for their holiday, and it suddenly occurred to her that he had *known* that in the end, inevitably he would disappoint her.

By the time they returned to school Andrianna, like his father, had forgiven Gae his transgression. Gae, in return, had forgiven her for reporting him to his father, which he regarded as a less than honorable act.

But Andrianna arrived back at Le Rosey a much smarter woman than she had been before her sojourn at Bedlam, convinced now of the wisdom in not depending on Gaetano *that* much, even as she knew that it would never be quite the same between them again . . .

She had also learned two other things. One, that great style and presence were more important than true virtues in a woman. Second, that it was vital for her to stay out of the sun.

Andrianna plucked one of her roses from the vase to bring it to her nose. Its scent was, if anything, more pungent than the day before. How strange it was that flowers, on their descent into death, always smelled stronger, *sweeter* . . . even as their beauty slowly faded away.

Twelve

It was almost noon when Jonathan finally saw Andrianna, again wrapped in her fur coat, step out of an elevator into the lobby. After the long wait her sudden appearance caught him off guard, and it took him a few seconds to recover, to remember to bury his head in his newspaper. But once she was past him, headed leisurely toward the hotel's Fifth Avenue entrance, he sprinted out a door on the Fifty-ninth Street side to run around the corner, to beat her out.

He jumped into the limousine, slamming the door closed as he yelled to Rennie: "She'll be out in a moment! Get this baby running and be ready to move!"

"You got it!" Rennie grunted.

When Andrianna came out, they saw her look up and down Fifth as if to get her bearings, then speak to the doorman briefly, after which she started walking.

"No car or cab," Jonathan shouted excitedly. "She's walking!"

How did they put it in the movies when the cop on stakeout was transmitting via walkie-talkie? *Subject is proceeding on foot, headed south on*— "She's headed south on Fifth!"

"You want me to stay with her?"

"Yeah. Cruise. Just stay a bit behind her, okay?"

"No problem," Rennie said, "if the guys behind me don't blow me out of the street."

But he had no difficulty keeping pace with their subject since the traffic was moving only the occasional couple of feet.

When they saw Andrianna cross to the south side of Fifty-seventh and then turn right, Jonathan burst out, "She's heading west! Where's she going?"

Rennie shrugged, taking a right at the corner. "Maybe she just wants to take a walk? Do some window-shopping? A lot of people who visit the city like to do that. Take a look around."

"Maybe . . . Look, I'm going to follow her on foot." Jonathan already had one foot out the door before Rennie could pull the car to a full stop. "You just follow. Look for me or I'll catch you . . ."

Ignoring the traffic, he zigzagged across to the south side of the street, conscious that he was acting out of character, was even a little out of control. He would never dream of jaywalking in L.A.—it just wasn't done.

Halfway down the street, still headed west, he saw Andrianna turn into the Russian Tea Room. In L.A. the restaurant was referred to as the Polo Lounge of the East, which meant that it was a power restaurant where the leading lights of show business in from the Coast congregated to eat blini and caviar when they came to town to meet with other leading lights from either coast.

Obviously she had an appointment for lunch, but with whom? He couldn't follow her inside—she'd be sure to spot him.

Catching sight of Rennie slowly cruising by on the opposite side of the street, Jonathan waved him down and darted out into the middle of traffic, oblivious to the standard New York cabbie salute he received when a taxi jolted to a stop to avoid hitting him. "Hey, asshole, where d'ya think you are—Saskatchewan?"

Refusing to get into the car and out of collision range,

172

as Rennie wryly suggested, Jonathan said impatiently, "You see that restaurant across the street?"

"You mean the Tea Room? Sure."

"She went in there. So I want *you* to go in there, have some lunch, and see who she's lunching with."

"How am I going to identify who the person is? I'm not exactly familiar with every face in the social register, ya know?"

"Well, you could at least tell me what he looks like."

"Yeah? And what about the stretch? I can't leave it here double-parked in the middle of Fifty-seventh Street!"

"I'll take the wheel."

"You?"

"Yeah, me."

"This is a big baby," Rennie said doubtfully. "And you hear those guys behind us leaning on their horns?"

"Let them lean. Come on. Out." He opened the driver's door. "You don't have to worry about me. I'm a California boy, and we drive before we're out of diapers."

"Mr. West, would you please close that door before a car hits you and takes my door with you? This is a commercial vehicle, and I'm sure you don't have a license to drive a commercial vehicle. Besides, I walk in there in this uniform and one of them snooty maître d's is gonna have me out the door before I even get a fix on your lady."

My lady? No, she's not mine yet, Rennie. I'm not even sure she's a lady.

"Look, Rennie," he countered, "how would you like to come to Los Angeles to work for me at double your present salary?"

Rennie perked up. "As what? Your chauffeur or your private dick?"

Jonathan laughed. "How about a combination of both?"

Rennie had always dreamed of going to California, where they guaranteed you only twenty days of rain a year and there was always one or another racetrack in operation. "You got a deal, Mr. West. Only you haven't asked me what my present salary is."

"Right, I haven't. So you get the picture. Now that that's settled, this is what you do. You go in and tell them you've been dispatched to pick up a client — give them any old name. And while they check it out, only to find that there is no one in the restaurant by that name, you'll have time to check out the tables and at least see who she's with.

"And maybe, once you spot her and the guy, you can play it dumb and say something like 'That gentleman over there with the dark-haired lady? What's *his* name? I have a feeling that he might be my man.' Who knows? Maybe they'll tell you the fellow's name just to show you you're mistaken."

"Yeah. I *could* do that." Rennie got out of the car, and Jonathan took his place in the driver's seat. "What name should I use? How about Rudolph Pinkney?"

Jonathan smiled. "Rudolph Pinkney?" He had been right about Rennie. He was a man with imagination. "That's a fine name," he said.

Ten minutes later Rennie found Jonathan parked in a bus stop down the street. "She's not having lunch with a *guy*," he reported. "It's a lady. A big, gorgeous redheaded broad . . ."

"Penny darling, I've never seen you looking so well," Andrianna raved, and she meant it. Penny was now a stunning, statuesque woman who had clearly come into her own, whereas at sixteen she'd been a skinny gawk in search of a style to call her own and breasts she could call voluptuous. The breasts had already been augmented the last time Andrianna had seen her, when Penny had flown into London to see her open in *Lady Georgina,* but the burst of fiery red tresses was new and flattering. There was a certain something else, though, and Andrianna struggled to put her finger on it.

She studied Penny as her friend sat in her beige cashmere knit cinched with a trio of gold chains hanging low on the waist, her sable coat slung carelessly around her shoulders, her wrists clattering and clanking with gold bracelets, a fashion statement Penny had been addicted to even at Le Rosey. Finally Andrianna decided that the big difference was in her friend's expression. She had the look of a pussycat who had just discovered a bowl of thick, rich cream.

"Oh, Penny, I just can't tell you how good it is to see you! It's like the sun bursting out after days of rain."

"You only say that because you're English," Penny said with a giggle, managing to pick up an entire blini oozing caviar, sour cream, chopped egg, and onion with her fingers and taking a healthy bite without losing one bit of fastidiousness or one pearly fish egg. "The English always use the sun as a point of reference. Boobie said that was because as a race the English suffer from sun deprivation."

She followed the bite of overflowing blini with a healthy swig of straight iced vodka.

"Boobie?"

"Harold Poole, my first," Penny said dryly. "Remember?"

"Yes, of course I remember Harold. Didn't I celebrate with the two of you at the Ritz after you and he eloped? I just didn't know he was also called Boobie."

Peggy giggled again. "Oh, that was Mama. She gave him the nickname, and it kind of stuck. It was just after I brought him home to Texas, and Mama said, 'Penny! I know that I thought it would be nice if you married a member of the European aristocracy, but I must say, lord or no lord, you're a little old asshole to have married *that* boob!'"

Now it was Andrianna's turn to giggle. "She didn't!"

"Yes, she did! Of course, Daddy turned it around. He said I was the boob to have married the little old asshole who didn't have a buck to his name. But Boobie *did* have his sweet points." She tossed off the rest of her vodka, signaled the waiter for another, and sighed wistfully. "I wonder who's calling him Boobie now . . ."

Andrianna thought she sounded sad. "Oh, Penny! Are you sorry you divorced him? Do you still miss him?"

Penny's eyes opened wide. "*Miss* him? Are you bonkers? Of course I don't miss him! Whatever gave you that idea. In fact I haven't even thought about the old boob in years." She shook her head. "I see you're still hopeless, just as sentimental as ever, the same old Annie."

Andrianna laughed and took a small forkful of her shashlik. The truth was she had never been sentimental about anything or anyone outside of Penny, Nicole, and Gae.

"But say what you will, Boobie was a gentleman compared to Rick. Rick Townsend was the biggest bastard Texas ever spawned, and you know how it is in Texas — they have the biggest in everything, including bastards. *Really* big."

"But you loved him when you married him. At least you said you did."

"Well, I *thought* I loved him, which isn't quite the same thing, is it? Actually I kind of suspected from the beginning that Rick 'Bus' Townsend — the nickname *Bus* was actually in quotes on his business card — was strictly ten-carat gold-filled, but . . . well, after Boobie, Mama and Daddy had had their fill of fancy European titles and they were hot for me to marry a good old Texas boy and —"

The waiter set down a fresh glass of vodka, and Penny immediately brought it to her lips, telling him to bring the bottle, while she adjusted the sable coat, which kept slipping from her shoulders, and continued talking without taking an extra breath. "Let's face it. Rick *was* big and handsome, and he had just miles and miles of good old Texas ranch land, not to mention a standing army of oil derricks. And I figured that since I'd already bought foreign goods — Boobie — and it hadn't worked out, I'd do the patriotic bit — you know, like the slogan, 'Buy American.'

"And what did I get for my patriotism? Well, you already know the answer to that one. A broken jaw, that's what."

Andrianna had heard the story several times before, but she wasn't about to stop Penny. She usually didn't get to see her more than once a year, and wasn't that what true friends were for, to listen without interrupting, to let the friend get it all out?

"Then to top it—when I was lying in the hospital with my jaw wired, taking only liquid nourishment, and all I could do was shake my head from side to side for no and up and down for yes, in waltzes my daddy, defending the *mother,* saying that while Rick had been wrong to bust my jaw, a woman *could* drive a man to it with her incessant yapping and there'd been plenty of times he himself would have given a million dollars to plant one on Mama's jaw.

"What Daddy wanted, believe it or not, was for me to forgive Rick—Rick was prepared to say he was sorry and wanted to kiss and make up. And there I was with my jaw wired shut, not even able to scream my head off. All I could do was shake my head from side to side till my teeth rattled. There was no way in hell I was going to make up with that jaw-busting maniac, even if he stood bare-assed naked in Neiman Marcus's window.

"At least Mama got the message. She asked, 'Penny, do you wish to see the son of a bitch?' and I shook my head no. Then she asked, 'Penny, under any circumstances, would you care to make up with this son of a bitch?' and when I shook my head no again she asked if she should make immediate contact with the biggest son-of-a-bitch divorce lawyer in Dallas on my behalf. Well, you better believe I moved my head up and down so hard I almost unwired my poor little jaw . . .

"Then the day I got my decree and my twelve-million-dollar settlement Mama said, 'You're an independently wealthy woman now, Penny Lee, and you don't have to listen to us anymore, not that you ever really did. Still, I want to give you a piece of advice. When you pick out your next husband, just you make sure he has more money than you, so at least you'll know he loves you for yourself and not for your money.'

"And Daddy almost broke my heart. He was actually crying when he gave me his advice, even though I wasn't sure if he was crying for my pain or his own. The poor demented man had actually loved Rick like a son. But I'm glad to say—even though I have sometimes viewed it as an act of disloyalty on Daddy's part—that he and Rick have sustained a relationship. They still play golf together a couple of times a month.

"As for Daddy's advice, he said that when I picked out my next husband to make damn sure he was possessed of a peaceable nature that wasn't affected by a few hits of Wild Turkey, since he had no doubt I would continue with my ways, which could send any man into a wife-beating frenzy. Which all leads up to *where* I am today—" Penny concluded, reaching for her honey-brown crocodile envelope handbag.

Andrianna sat back in her chair. "Where you are today," she repeated. "And *where*, specifically, is that?"

Instead of answering, Penny clutched her purse to her breast and pointed to Andrianna's black crocodile one lying on the table, crying out, "Oh, look, we have the same handbag, only in different colors!"

It wasn't surprising to Andrianna that she and Penny should have the same handbag. The bag was expensive enough to be regarded as one of a collection of purses by an owner who collected expensive handbags like some women collected antique jewelry or even paintings and other objets d'art—the kind of woman who wouldn't be caught dead clutching anything but a purse costing upward of three or four hundred pounds.

That's the kind of women we are, Penny and I, Andrianna reflected wryly. We know the value of all the really relevant things in life. Like expensive accessories, more relevant even than the suit or dress from the most bally-

178

hooed designer in Milan or Paris or New York. Oh, yes, we know what's truly important . . . that the irreproachable bag and really fine shoes are the primary barometer of the impeccably turned out woman, as important even as Gaetano's huge style and large presence.

"You bought yours on the Via Veneto too?"

Andrianna shook her head. "No. Actually it was the duty-free shop at the airport in Athens. But let's forget about the purses. What I want to know is where you're *at* today . . . specifically. That *is* what we were talking about . . ."

"Yes, we were, weren't we?"

Penny reached into the crocodile handbag for a crushed pack of Marlboros, fished out a cigarette, and lit it with a hot pink Bic lighter.

"What?" Andrianna teased. "My friend Penny Lee Hopkins Poole Townsend using a plain Bic lighter and not a Dunhill or Cartier? I don't believe it."

Taking a deep drag on the Marlboro and letting out a long curl of smoke, Penny said, "Gae made me give my gold Cartier away to the maid at the Hôtel de Paris in Monaco . . ."

"*Gae* made you? Gae Forenzi?" She'd caught herself just in time. After all this time she'd almost said "*my* Gae."

"Yes, of course, Gae Forenzi," Penny said nervously. "How many Gaes do we both know? Well, anyhow, Gae and I . . . *together*—" she stressed the word—"made a vow to swear off everything—cigarettes, coke, grass, pills, even liquor, except for the occasional glass of wine. You might say we're going straight *together*. That's why you can't tell him that you saw me smoking or drinking vodka. You won't, will you? Do I have your word on it?"

"Of course," Andrianna said automatically, trying not to show exactly how much this conversation was rattling her.

She smiled brightly. "So! Is that it? You and Gae . . . *together*? So *that's* where you're at. Is that what you were going to tell me?"

"Yes. When Gae told me you were coming to New York and were going to use his suite at the Plaza, we decided that I should fly in to talk to you—to tell you about *us* before you heard it from someone else. That's why I'm in New York. I came here straight from the airport to meet you . . . to tell you myself. And then I'm flying to Dallas tonight."

Andrianna drained her glass of champagne and signaled the waiter for another while she chose her words carefully. "While I'm pleased as anything to see you, Penny darling, as always, there really was no need to—"

"But *I* felt there was a need. Gae felt there was a need. That it was the least we should do . . ."

Andrianna forced herself to laugh. *"Need?* But why? Whatever there was between me and Gae was over years ago . . . twenty years ago. A lifetime ago. My God, I was only sixteen . . . seventeen. A lifetime ago . . ."

She grabbed for the fresh glass of champagne the waiter set before her. "But I must admit that . . . that I'm speechless. You and Gae! When did all this happen?"

Penny squashed out her cigarette and lit another. "Last year at the Prix de Paris. Gae was racing his Forenzi, and I was there with the Alperts. You know, George and Elaine. George was in the race too, and the night before we all met at Regine's, and . . . well, you know how it is. Actually, we're a natural, Gae and I. We understand each other; each knows exactly what the other one needs. And Gae's father is adamant that Gae settle down if he wants to take over at Forenzi Motors. Actually, he's pretty scary, isn't he? Gino?"

"No, I can't say that I ever found Gino *scary* exactly." She chose her words carefully. "Overwhelming at times, true. But I always thought he was a wonderful man. Very strong. Warm, caring, very kind."

"Let's not go overboard here, please. Anyway, Gino's after Gae to settle down, and he fits my parents' requirements too. Can you think of anyone better-natured than

Gae? Once in a while he might get maudlin, but surly? Never. As for Mama, Gae probably has a hundred or a thousand times more money than I do. Oh, Annie, we make such a good couple, Gae and I, with all the qualifications for a good, solid marriage . . ."

"*Marriage?* You and Gae are actually getting married?"

"Yes, of course, marriage! What did you think I was talking about? Just another affair? The truth is, Annie, that I'm really, at last, in love! Head over heels in love. And I'm pretty sure Gae feels the same way about me. Besides which, I'm inordinately attracted to him, sexually speaking. Who wouldn't be in love with Gae or terribly sexually attracted to him? Those eyes. You could drown in Gae's eyes—and how that man is hung! Me oh my, it is to die! But I don't have to tell you about that, even if it all happened between you two twenty years ago, do I?" she asked coyly.

Then she took a hard look at Andrianna. "You know, you do look a bit pale, Annie. Are you sure all this is *really* okay with you?"

"Of course. Gae and I have remained dear friends over the years, and whenever I needed anything Gae's been there for me, and I will always have a special place in my heart for him. He will always be as dear to me as you are, Penny darling."

She reached for her friend's hand and squeezed it. "But for us . . . as lovers? Well, that was finished by the time we left the Costa del Sol . . ."

"Ah, the Costa del Sol! What a time that was. Of course I was only there for a third of the time you were. Remember? I came to visit for a week and stayed for at least two months! I'll never forget that time. We barely ever went to bed. To sleep, that is. It was one of the best times of my life. God, but it was fun!

"You know, I think that's when I was first attracted to Gae . . . that time in Marbella. He was like a young god, wasn't he? The tousle of black curls, that bronzed muscled body. And so naughty, in his sweet way. Oh, God, what young girl wouldn't have been attracted to Gae Forenzi?" Then she flushed, was embarrassed. "Hey, you don't mind that I was attracted to Gae back then . . . when you two were still an item?"

"Oh, Penny, don't be foolish. You and I and Gae were only children then, playacting at being adults. Staying up all night and sleeping our days away at the beach. Drinking, dancing, partying while the *real* world was going crazy with Vietnam and other issues we were oblivious to . . ." her voice trailed off. "Oh it was *such* a long time ago and we were only children . . . No, Penny, I don't mind a bit. I'm very happy that my two favorite people in the whole world are going to be married and live happily ever after. Oh, Penny, I wish you and Gae the best of everything!"

And with a rush of feeling, she knew that she would never say any truer words. She wished them well . . . she wished them love!

"It really was the best of times, wasn't it?" Penny demanded. "Marbella. The Costa del Sol. The three of us together."

"Yes, of course. It was the best of times."

And while it had been twenty years ago and she no longer loved Gae the way she had then, with the kind of passion only a teenager desperately in love with love could feel for a boy, the Costa del Sol was one of those places she couldn't bear to return to. And when anyone even mentioned Marbella, she always quipped, "Oh, the Costa del Sol? It's not what it used to be. I wouldn't dream of going there anymore . . ."

And she found herself thinking of the opening line from *A Tale of Two Cities*. "It was the best of times, it was the worst of times. . . ."

Thirteen

London and Switzerland
Spring 1968

That best and worst of times began not long after Andrianna and Gae returned to school following their holiday in Port'Ercole, when Helene again summoned her ward to London. Again the reason for the visit was death, but this time it was the demise of Andrew Wyatt.

They sat in the drawing room, Helene's favorite room, where she could simultaneously talk, survey her treasures—the paintings and the signed tapestries—and look out on Grosvenor Square, which was a constant reminder of how far she'd come, despite her late husband's many deficiencies.

"We've never actually discussed this, Ann, but you're a big girl now, and I assume you're cognizant that Andrew Wyatt was your benefactor. And I suppose you've figured out by this time he was your father as well? Or, at the very least, he thought it was *possible* that he was your father since he assumed financial responsibility for you."

For a moment Andrianna thought of Elena, remembering how she'd adored Andrew Wyatt—how there'd never been another man who had so much as visited at their home. "Oh, he's my father, all right," she snapped. "Don't you doubt it for a minute!"

"Was, Ann, was. He is no more."

Andrianna had been slouching on the gold Chinese Chippendale sofa. Now she sat up straight. "What do you mean—is no more?"

"I mean exactly that. He's dead, Ann. Your benefactor is dead."

"Oh, no," Andrianna moaned involuntarily.

Helene laughed. "Don't tell me you actually *feel* something? That's a bit much."

Andrianna glanced down at her overly long fingernails, which Nicole had insisted on painting with silver frost polish, claiming that it was all the rage in Paris.

Yes, she *felt* something. She felt . . . *grief*. And a strange kind of utter desolation.

The truth was that somewhere in the back of her head, in spite of never having heard from Andrew Wyatt personally, she had nursed a dream. One in which she and her father were reunited, loving each other, their love reinforced by their mutual love for Elena. And now he was gone, her father and her mother's true love, and it was never going to happen. The dream was dead forever . . .

But then Helene's cool voice brought her back to the real world. "Do I imagine that you're actually feeling grief over Andrew's passing? Well, perhaps you *will* mourn dear Andy more than you think. The fact is with the death of your benefactor an era has come to an end for you, Ann dear. The good times are over. There won't be any more funds to keep you in the style to which you've become so comfortably accustomed. No more school, no more clothing allowance, no more expense money. In other words, you're totally on your own."

She was overwhelmed. On her own? She wasn't even seventeen yet!

"But didn't he make any—?"

"Provisions for you in the event of his death? No, he didn't. Naturally, since I was affected too, I checked into it. There's no trust fund, no bequest. Nothing. It's pretty simple, I should think."

Simple, Andrianna thought, but hardly pretty.

The millionaire father who had never formally acknowledged her in life—not even privately between the two of them—had simply forgotten about her in death. As if she had never truly existed for him at all.

She sat in silence for a couple of moments, numb with the pain of that. Then she managed to stammer, "But what about money?"

"My, you *are* being dense. *There is no more money.* Still, I'm prepared to be generous with you. There were always two checks from Andrew, one for me and one for you, and I'm going to give you the balance of your latest check. Mind you, I don't have to do this, but"—she waved an airy hand— "let us just call it an act of *noblesse oblige* . . .

"In fact, I'm going to write you out a check right now and be done with it. That way we'll be out of each other's lives for good and there will be no need for us to be in touch ever again. That sounds good to me. How does it strike you?"

"But what will I do?"

"Well, you're paid up at Le Rosey until June, so I suppose you could stay there and finish out the term."

"But . . . but I won't even be graduating from Le Rosey then. And I always thought—"

"What? What did you always think?"

"That after Le Rosey I'd be going on with my education. That I'd—"

Helene laughed nastily. "What you thought was that you were going to get a free ride for life, is that it? Well, we'd all *like* that, but I'm afraid it's not in the cards for all of us. Would you believe that some of us must actually work for a living?" she drawled.

Frightened now, Andrianna forgot that she was appealing to the wrong person. "But where will I live? What will I do? What *can* I do? The education I do have hasn't taught me how to *do* anything! And I'm only sixteen . . ."

Helene chuckled. "So you are, but cheer up. Soon you'll be seventeen, and a year later you'll be eighteen. As for what you can do, I'm sure you'll think of *something*. At least you'll have until June to figure out just what you're best fitted for—and you know? I already have a pretty good idea just what that occupation will be."

She looked Andrianna over deliberately and winked.

In a state of soundless shock Andrianna watched as Helene went to the Queen Anne secretary, sat down, removed a checkbook from the top drawer, and started to write.

"Now, there's some four hundred pounds or so left in your account, and just to show you that my heart is in the right place I'm going to round that out to five hundred pounds. Now that's a tidy sum, and if I were you I'd put it in the bank against a rainy day. But perhaps what you should do is spend your money for air passage back to California. You should be able to manage that with what you have. Yes, that's *exactly* what you should do," Helene urged.

"You really don't belong here. And there, well . . . there must be people who knew your mother and would feel some obligation to you."

Rosa . . . She's talking about Rosa, Andrianna thought.

But she had never heard from Rosa. In the beginning she had written Rosa letters, desperate letters, begging Rosa to help her, to try to get her back, but she had never received an answer. No! In California she would be only a stranger . . . a stranger in a foreign land. At least here — in England and on the Continent — she was familiar with how things worked, knew the terrain. And here she had friends, in addition to her three special friends — Penny, Nicole, and Gae.

But Helene would like it if I went back, Andrianna realized.

She wants me gone. Out of her vicinity. But why? What's it to her since she doesn't plan on having anything to do with me? Obviously my father wanted me out of his country years ago because he was afraid I'd be an embarrassment to him. Is Helene afraid that I'll be an embarrassment to her now?

But she's hardly the type to be embarrassed by much. It has to be more than that. Something legal? Like the fact that officially I'm her ward and that legally she just can't abandon me? I am only sixteen. Doesn't a legal guardian have certain responsibilities until a child turns eighteen? ·

And, then, of course, there was the business about her falsified English passport and birth certificate. Officially, with an English birth certificate and an English passport, she *was* Ann Sommer. But if that was a lie, which it *was,* then wasn't Helene guilty of some kind of fraud?

Andrianna, ignoring the check held out to her, tried the shoe on for size. "But Auntie Helene, I'm only sixteen, and don't you, as my legal guardian, have to see to it that I'm at least fed and clothed and have a roof over my head until I'm eighteen?"

Helene flushed. "Perhaps. But no one says what *kind* of food or clothing or shelter. Would you like to find out exactly what the law requires? You bloody well might not enjoy it."

"Maybe not. But at the same time maybe we could find out what the law thinks of an abandoned child who has an assumed name, a fake birth certificate, *and* a fake passport. What do you think they'd think about the woman who was responsible for that?"

Helene laughed. "I hardly think they'd hold that poor deluded woman responsible. After all, it's Alexander's name you bear, and it was *his* brother's child you were supposed to be, and I, the poor deluded wife, was as much a dupe as anybody. You see, all the arrangements were instituted by Andrew and made in Alexander's name. It was he, not I, who obtained the birth certificate that made you a citizen of the United Kingdom, and the passport, of course. And whom would anybody question? One can't question corpses. And if you doubt any of this, I suggest you hire yourself a solicitor and good luck to you. But I don't think you'll *have* much luck. Solicitors, like anyone else, like to see the color of your money before they make a move."

Andrianna bit her lips in disappointment. She was sure that, in the end, it would be as Helene said—no one would pay any attention to anything she said. She had no power. That was the way things worked. No money, no power.

But then she saw Helene's eyelids fluttering as if she were thinking rapidly. *What is she thinking?* That she, Ann, the pesky little fly on her papered wall—no matter how ultimately insignificant her bite—was still capable of provoking tiny but annoying eruptions on the smooth surface of things?

Yes, that must be it! And how much *was* an insignificant but irritating baby fly worth? Another five hundred pounds? A thousand? More? She might as well go for it!

"I suppose that, as usual, you're right, Aunt Helene." She sighed as if in capitulation. "There's not very much I can do about anything. And I think you're right about my going back to California. I guess that's where I really belong, and then, at least, I wouldn't be an embarrassment to you — which isn't much, but it is *something.* The only problem with that is, how can I really go back to the States without so much as a pound to my name? You did say that five hundred quid will *just* about buy me an airplane ticket home, didn't — ?"

Helene cut her off. "How much?"

"Five thousand pounds."

Helene laughed. "You flatter yourself. Even as an embarrassment you're not worth half that. But all right. Three thousand pounds altogether, including what I was going to give you anyway. Take it or leave it."

"I'll take it."

"Good."

Helene ripped up the old check and wrote another.

"But a piece of advice for you, Ann. When you're ahead of the game, don't push your luck by getting greedy. Just keep in mind that this is the last pound you're getting out of me."

Helene held out the check, and Andrianna snatched it. "Well, I'm off to the bank," she said cheerily. "Would you please be so kind as to call them to expect me so that they'll have my money ready?"

Helene was amused. "Afraid I'll change my mind? Don't you trust me?"

"Why, Auntie Helene, it was you who taught me to trust and depend on no one except myself."

Then she thought of the question that had remained unanswered in the back of her mind for a long time. "There is one thing I'd like to know—"

"You might as well spit it out so we can get this thing over with once and for all."

"When I was at Huxley, there was a girl there from San Francisco who said her mother knew you when you were living there, and she said that you had an affair with my father . . . *before* my mother. Is it true?"

"Yes, it's true. Now, is that all you wanted to know?"

"Did you love him?" Andrianna blurted out. "Really, truly love him?" *Like my mother did . . .*

Helene laughed. "Oh, it *was* fun, but only a fool gets what's fun mixed up with the things that really count."

"Like money?"

"Like money."

Helene was many things but no fool, Andrianna thought. Only Elena had been a fool . . . a lovely, trusting fool . . .

She was almost out the door when Helene said, "By the way, how *was* your holiday in Port'Ercole, Ann dear? So clever of you to get yourself invited by that Forenzi boy. But what *did* you do when you got there? I've heard that the father, Gino, is a most attractive man, extremely virile, and just between us girls, I must confess, when it comes to this sort of thing, I tend to go for the older man myself. True, the boys do have the energy and the drive—the old willie ever at the ready—but then the sophisticated and more experienced older man has the *savoir faire,* don't you think?"

Helene's meaning was clear, and Andrianna could feel her cheeks flame at the nasty implication. No, Helene was no fool, she thought again, and probably Helene knew everything about money that there was to know. About how to get it and how to spend it. But there were things she knew nothing about. Like love . . .

So all she did in response to Helene's taunt was smile at her most pityingly.

As soon as she was back at school, Andrianna went in search of Gae, bursting with her news, only to find that Gae

189

had news of his own, equally devastating. Several kilos of hashish had been found in his room, and the school was kicking him out even though he was supposed to graduate in June. They were even threatening to turn him over to the Swiss authorities.

"Gae, you promised me you wouldn't . . . But your father? Can't he do anything about it?"

"He could if he wanted, but he doesn't want to. He said that this time I will have to get myself out of my own hot water. He's washing his hands of me."

"But he probably doesn't mean it! He would never let you go to jail."

Gae smiled knowingly. "I don't think so either. But I'm not sticking around to find out."

"But what about your graduation?"

Gae just laughed.

"But what are you going to do? Where will you go?"

Gae laughed again. "Do not concern yourself, *cara mia*. I will go where the sun shines and where the living is — how do they say? — easy. The south of Spain. The Costa del Sol. Marbella, to be more *preciso*. It will be a lot more fun than here, I assure you. I have friends there. One is a special friend. An Englishman. You see, Marbella is a favorite spot for Englishmen on the run. It's beautiful and the weather is superb. You know what they say? That the English invented the rain and the Spanish the sun. And I want you to come with me, Anna."

It was a mandate from heaven, Andrianna thought. Without even giving her a chance to tell him her troubles, Gae had provided her with a solution. A place to go, something to do, someone to love her. Her tuition at Le Rosey was paid up until the end of the term, but she wouldn't be able to return the next year, so why wait until June?

"When are we leaving?" was her answer.

Gae hugged her. "You are my sweetest love. But we'll have to wait a couple of days before we can go. I need a little bit of time to raise some money. It's of *importanza* that we go first class. It is a matter of impressions."

190

She didn't ask questions. If Gae said it was important, it was. He knew more about these things than she.

"I have some money," she offered. "It's in pounds . . . three thousand pounds."

"Pounds, lires, francs—it makes no difference. But three thousand pounds? Where did you get it?" he asked, astonished.

She was proud. "I squeezed it out of my Aunt Helene."

He was proud of her too. *"Bravissima!* We will leave tomorrow then. You must pack. You can leave your school uniforms and whatever is not of the best. But your *bagaglio?"* He remembered that the couple of bags she'd taken to Port'Ercole had been Louis Vuitton. "Is it all Vuitton?"

"Yes," she answered, puzzled. What difference did it make what kind of luggage she had?

"Then be sure to take it all."

She nodded. Whatever Gae told her to do, she would do.

Penny cried when she kissed Andrianna good-bye, even though she thought not finishing out the school year was excruciatingly fun to begin with and to go to live in Marbella of all places was excruciatingly exciting.

Nicole was equally tearful when she bade Andrianna adieu but not as sure as Penny that Andrianna was doing the right thing. When Andrianna had first told her her plans, Nicole had immediately run to call her mother and then reported that *Maman* had thought the whole thing unwise.

"Maman says that while an alliance with the only son of the house of Forenzi would be a marvelous thing ordinarily, but since Gae is only an irresponsible boy whom you can't count on, and it is highly unlikely that Gino Forenzi would ever approve of his son marrying a penniless girl with no family connections to speak of, it is not such an idea hot.

"Most likely, *Maman* says, you will end up in a bad way because Gae will end up going back to his father as soon as he crooks his finger in Gae's direction, leaving you without a wedding ring on your finger."

"Oh, my Lord!" Penny had exclaimed. "Who's talking about *marriage?* Annie's got years to go yet before she thinks about anything as boring as marriage. She's not even seventeen, and we're only talking about a real good time here . . . fun!"

"Besides, Gae would never leave me in a bad way. I'm sure your mother means well, Nicole, but she doesn't know Gae. Or understand that he really does love me. I *can* count on him. Besides, what choice do I have?"

Then her friend proposed an alternative. *"Maman* is a practical woman, and she likes to present practical solutions. She says that if you would like to come to Paris, she would be willing to take you under her wing. You would live with her . . . with us . . . and she would undertake to train you as her social secretary. That way, she says, you would have a profession to fall back on no matter what happens."

"Oh, shitty-poo!" Penny said in disgust. "That sounds like as much fun as going into a nunnery. Is that what poor Annie is supposed to be doing while the rest of us are finishing school, having good times, and then marrying rich so that we can go on having good times? Really, Nicole, how can you suggest such a dreary thing to our Annie?"

"Maybe because I don't know what else to suggest?"

"Then maybe you should keep your big mouth shut?"

"Please, girls, don't fight, and thank your mother for me, Nicole. It's so kind of her to offer to help me. But I'm going to Marbella with Gae, and it's going to be wonderful!"

She was positive that she was right. And when a little voice that sounded a lot like Gae's told her not to depend on him too much, that he might disappoint her again, she ignored it. Gae was not only her knight protector and her friend; he was her sweet, funny, darling love.

Fourteen

Tuesday, one o'clock

"You know, you really are impossible today," Penny said petulantly. "You're not paying attention to a word I say."

Andrianna reached across the table to take Penny's hand. "I *am* sorry. I was just daydreaming or something. But seeing you and hearing about you and Gae takes me back, and I was just remembering . . . you know. Now, what were you saying?"

"I was just asking you if you thought Gae and I were going to be happy."

"*Happy?* I think you and Gae are going to make happy sound like the understatement of a lifetime!"

"Good! Now tell me what you think about my wearing virginal white at the wedding. I know you're not supposed to if you've been married before, but—"

"Wear it! Today anything goes, and besides, do you really care what anyone says? That's not the Penny I know. I say, if that's what makes you happy, do it!"

Penny beamed. "That was what I was hoping you'd say, because I saw sketches of this gown at Valentino's that I really had my little old heart set on and . . ."

And Penny was off, launched into a soliloquy that fortunately needed no responses, because Andrianna's thoughts had already turned back to a time when the good life had been a near guarantee on the Costa del Sol for all kinds of people . . .

* * *

There were the patricians who seemed to favor Marbella. And then there were the hippies of various nationalities who mostly congregated, along with their ubiquitous backpacks, in Torremolinos and Málaga, who seemed to get by with almost no money at all—sleeping on the beaches, hanging about the cafes, and constantly riding the ferry back and forth across the Strait of Gibraltar to Tangier in Morocco, the exotic appealing almost as much as the readily available hashish. The Costa del Sol also offered a haven for those with limited assets but great pretensions, provided they were attractive and entertaining enough, even for those with a dark and shadowy past if they were sufficiently charming and knew how to live by their wits.

For her too it had been the good life at first, even though at the time she hadn't been quite sure into which category she and Gae fitted. But then, had it really been necessary to know? She knew all the really *important* things—that Gae loved her madly (he told her so several times a day); that it was imperative to have huge presence and style (as he had told her in Port'Ercole) as well as a great wardrobe and fine luggage (which he had told her just before they had left Le Rosey). She also knew that it was important always to go first class, which Gae had explained to her even before they reached the Costa del Sol . . .

They flew first class to Madrid, where they had a connecting flight to Málaga, which worried Andrianna. While Helene's three thousand pounds *seemed* like a lot of money, she knew it was hardly a fortune and certainly no bottomless well that could afford first-class tickets.

Sipping the champagne the flight attendant had provided, diplomatically not inquiring whether the imbiber was old enough to be served alcohol, Andrianna asked Gae, "Shouldn't we have traveled coach and saved the money?"

Gae, drinking Napoléon brandy, shrugged her question

194

away. "It's important always to go first class since one can never be sure whom one will meet on a plane. Just suppose, for instance, Cary Grant, who's seated two rows behind you at this very moment, saw you proceeding into coach. What would he make of you? That you were simply another tourist, however beautiful, and not a woman of high style and importance."

"Cary Grant? You're fooling."

But when she turned to see for herself, there was Cary, looking every bit as devastating as he did in his films. "It *is* Cary Grant! Penny and Nicole would die! And goodness, do you know who he's talking to at this very moment?"

"Who?"

"Audrey Hepburn!"

"I'm not at all surprised," Gae said smugly, as if he were personally responsible for Grant's and Hepburn's presence on the plane. "Audrey and her husband, Mel Ferrer, have a house in the area."

"And Cary?"

"Oh, he's probably going to be a houseguest of the Windsors, or maybe Generalissimo Franco's daughter, who is married to the Marques of Villaverde."

"Do you know them?" Andrianna asked breathlessly.

"The Windsors? Of course. As for Franco's daughter—"

"Not *them*. I mean Cary Grant and Audrey Hepburn!"

"No, not really," Gae said a bit hesitantly as if reluctant to admit this shortcoming, but then he winked at her and got to his feet. "But it's not a problem if you would like to meet them."

"It isn't?" She was incredulous.

Andrianna had no idea what Gae said to Cary and Audrey, but it wasn't too long before the three of them were laughing together and Gae was calling her over to be introduced.

Later, back in their own seats, when Andrianna demanded to know how he'd managed to get so friendly so quickly, Gae dismissed the whole thing breezily. "No big deal. It's a matter of having mutual friends and acquaint-

195

ances. By the way, Cary invited us to a party on the fifth."

And so Andrianna learned another rule for the good life. It was called "having mutual friends and acquaintances."

But it was a rule that worried Andrianna. While Gae was used to living it up with friends and *their* friends and acquaintances, he'd always been on an equal footing with them, spending freely, dispensing largesse. Now that would no longer be the case. Now he would be cast in the same role she had always played, and having played it, she knew what it meant—dependence on friends, on their goodwill and even their charity. It meant ceaselessly hopping on one foot to be agreeable and amusing.

Now, with only her three thousand pounds in their pockets, less the money for their airplane tickets, Gae was going to experience a side of life he had never even considered before. He was going to have to learn a whole new set of rules as far as friends and mutual acquaintances went—how to exist in their world without a vast reservoir of money to fuel the high cost of driving in the international fast lane, especially once the word got out that he had been disinherited by his formerly overindulgent father.

Was Gae up to it? she agonized. Would he be able to adjust to a new lifestyle? What would he do when their money ran out? And she found herself wishing that they weren't going to Marbella at all. It was too rich for their blood and, therefore, too dangerous. They should have gone to Paris, where they could have lived on the Left Bank among other kids in the same financial situation—students, poor would-be writers and artists, whoever. That would have been fun without requiring lots of money. Or they could have gone to Greece, where the living was easier, or even Rome.

Now it was too late for that. But at least she could try to convince Gae to stop spending money so freely.

"It's been lovely to fly first class," she murmured, proceeding cautiously so as not to offend him. "And simply terrific to meet Cary and Audrey. But we'll have to be careful about money until we figure out how we're going to earn some more. Don't you think that's a good idea? We should try to

196

get some inexpensive place to stay in Marbella and then look for work. I've heard that there are lots of jobs available in resorts if you're not too choosy."

"What kind of work?" Gae laughed at her. "Waiting on tables? Washing dishes? Do you know what I think? I think you worry too much," he told her, placing his hand under her skirt on her inner thigh, trailing his fingers up and down the soft skin, getting recklessly closer and closer to her area of excitement, his head bent to her neck, where his lips left a trail of tiny kisses.

"Sweet Anna. Leave the worrying to me."

His free hand rang for the attendant, who came immediately, and Gae requested a throw. "The lady feels a chill." And then, just as the young woman turned to get the blanket, Gae said, "Get two, *por favor*. I too feel a chill."

Once the blankets arrived, Gae placed one tenderly about her up to her neck and the other about himself, adjusting it to cover him from the waist down. And then, as the fingers of his left hand found her clitoris, his right hand undid the zipper of his trousers and he took her right hand and placed it on his penis. And then as her pulse rate increased and all her muscles tightened and the centrifugal forces of sexual excitement took over her physical being and her mental process concentrated on giving ultimate pleasure to *his* physical being, Andrianna found herself too occupied to give another thought to how they were going to fare in Marbella on a limited budget.

When they landed in Málaga, Gae immediately went off to make a phone call, leaving Andrianna to wait for him in the terminal. "Now sit there like a good little girl while I call for our ride and don't talk to any strangers while I'm gone. Especially not gypsies. I don't want to come back and find you missing. The gypsies have an eye for proper, beautiful English girls with rosy cheeks, you know. They'll steal you if you're not careful and sell you to the highest bidder."

She laughed uneasily, but it wasn't because she paid any

mind to Gae's silliness. It was the reference to her being a "proper English girl." Once she told Gae the real story of her origin she'd feel less dishonest, relieved, and much more relaxed.

"Oh, you big liar! You can't fool me. I read in a book about Spain that it's Granada where the gypsies hang out, not Málaga. Besides, I don't have rosy cheeks."

"Oh, you read it in a book, did you? Well, that just shows that you shouldn't believe everything you read. How long will it take you to learn that it is only I you should believe?" He pinched her cheek. "There. Now the cheek is definitely rosy.

She watched him walk away—shoulders broad, waist narrow, and what Penny called "his cute little buns" molded by the tight white pants. No matter what Gae wore—formal dress, skiing togs, or blue jeans and a tee—he was always just a little more elegant than anyone else, a natural elegance. There was never any doubt that Gae was a rich man's son and used to the best of everything.

"A limousine will be by in a few minutes," Gae told her when he returned, not in nearly as high a mood as when he'd gone off to call. Had the person he'd called not been as receptive as Gae would have liked? Andrianna wondered. But instead of probing that issue, she asked, "A limousine? Can we afford it?"

"We can't afford *not* to afford it."

That had to mean that they were going someplace where they had to make an impression, Andrianna reasoned. "You still haven't told me where we're going to stay."

"At the Marbella Club. That's where my father always stays when he's here. It's run by the Hohenlohes. And in Marbella if you don't know the Hohenlohes you might as well kill yourself. The Princess Hohenlohe is a most charming woman . . . knows everyone," he told her, lighting a cigarette and taking quick, short puffs. "Her father was an Iturbe, one of Mexico's finest and oldest families."

"And that's good?" Andrianna asked hopefully.

"Of course it's good." Gae spun the butt of his cigarette through the air in an arc of dismissal. "How can it not be good to be descended from a fine old family? It's only in America, my father says, that they don't pay attention to these things. There only the almighty dollar counts."

Andrianna felt a twinge of resentment at hearing her native land slandered, even though she hardly thought of herself as an American. What arrogance! What hypocrisy! Was she supposed to believe that Gino Forenzi and other people like him, the rest of Europe's superrich, were too fine and cultured to care about their millions?

But she said nothing to Gae, not wanting to have even the smallest of disagreements with him since he was already uncharacteristically tense, pacing back and forth as they waited for their car, lighting one cigarette after another and discarding each one after only a couple of puffs. Yet she continued wondering and worrying. Whom had Gae spoken to when he went to make his calls and what had been said to make him lose his usual impeccable cool?

By the time the liveried chauffeur presented himself, Gae was so worked up about the long wait that he acknowledged the driver's presence with only a curt nod and directed him to their pile of luggage with a silent gesture. He himself picked up one small bag and offered his other hand to Andrianna, who picked up one of her larger pieces. Then Gae, removing that bag from her hand firmly and setting it down, picked up her cosmetic case and handed it to her.

"When a lady travels, she carries only her purse and her jewelry box. When she does not have a jewelry box, she may, if she wishes, carry her own cosmetic case."

Andrianna clicked her heels. *"Ja wohl, mein führer!"* she teased. Still she was aware that she'd just learned another rule for living life in the luxurious lane, and it was one she would never forget. If Gae was nothing else, he was a most proficient tutor in the rules of living grandly.

And so grandly did they live . . . for a while.

They stayed for a week at the Marbella Club, sleeping in after exciting late nights, waking to a Continental breakfast of wonderful Valencia oranges, hard rolls, and countless cups of the marvelous Spanish coffee before playing some tennis, followed by swimming or a sail, not having lunch until three or four. And they toured the countryside in their leased white Forenzi convertible. "No matter what," Gae said morosely, "the Forenzi is still the car close to my heart."

Forgetting for the moment that she had resolved not to ask too many questions, Andrianna wanted to know what had happened to Gae's own red Forenzi.

"I drove it to Gstaad and left it in the streets."

"You just left it there? But why?"

"Because it was registered in my father's name. Oh, they'll find the car eventually and it will be brought back. But I just wanted to make it a little more difficult."

Although she fretted in silence about the cost of leasing the white convertible, she enjoyed the rides they took through the countryside, past olive orchards and orange groves, visiting the ancient towns. Wherever they went was the presence of mountains nearby or in the distance, semi-tropical plants and incredibly lush greenery dappled by sunlight, with the incredibly blue sea never too far away.

"It is much like southern California here, the climate and the topography," Gae told Andrianna.

"Have you been?"

"To California? But of course. My father and I always went at least once a year. Father has many friends in Los Angeles. And you?"

Andrianna knew that if she was ever going to tell Gae the truth, this was the time. But she hesitated too long, and soon her moment of truth had come and gone.

"No, I've never been to California. But I'd love to see it. California and New York too. All of it."

"You will. We'll go there together," he said, recklessly taking his hands off the wheel to give her a quick squeeze.

"Gae!" she screamed. "Watch the road!"

"You're right! I must pay more attention to the driving. But it is all your fault!"

"My fault?"

"Yes. You distract me. But we can remedy that." He unzipped his jeans to take out his penis, hard in erection. "There. Now I can keep my eyes on the road and my hands on the wheel and still enjoy the pleasure of your company."

She giggled. He was irrepressible. With Gae all conversations invariably led up to one thing, much like all roads supposedly led to Rome. Maybe it was because Rome and he were both Italian, she reasoned, as she began to stroke him first languidly and then faster and with more energy, inspired by his moans and groans and ecstatic praise of her beauty, which, he swore breathlessly, he would worship forever . . .

After a week they moved from the Marbella Club over to the Casa de las Palmas, the home of the Swedish actress Inga Strolman and her husband, the Duke of Molino.

They had run into the actress at the casino late one night, where, to Andrianna's delight, Gae had won several hundred pesetas . . . before losing it all back in one turn of the roulette wheel, at which point she was plunged into gloom.

The very tall, very blond actress tried to cheer Andrianna up. "You mustn't take it so to heart, little one. It's not a vast sum of money, after all. And here on La Costa, you must adopt an attitude of easy come, easy go."

Andrianna was more annoyed than consoled. She found Inga Strolman's words patronizing, and being tall herself, she didn't like being called "little one."

But then the actress turned to Gae and said, "You must bring your little friend and come stay at our house for a while. Why don't you move in tomorrow?"

Even though behind Inga's back Andrianna vigorously shook her head no, Gae accepted with alacrity, almost as if he had been anticipating or at least hoping for the invitation.

"Inga has the best guests, the best food, and gives the best parties in the region," he told Andrianna later when she complained that she didn't want to be Inga's houseguest. "Everyone dies to come to her parties. Do you have any good reason you don't want to stay there?"

"I don't know. I just don't like her. It's a feeling. Besides, I think what she's really after is *you!*"

Gae laughed. "Don't be silly. And don't act like a baby. We'll have a marvelous time."

The Casa de las Palmas, built into the hills overlooking Marbella, was surrounded by great palms, naturally enough, and olive trees and layered terraces. Andrianna could not help being impressed by its magnificence even though the international crowd—the beautiful people—snidely referred to it as the California Palace, claiming it resembled a Hollywood movie star's grand illusion more than a whitewashed Mediterranean villa, replete as it was with such lavish accoutrements—fountained courtyards, sunken bathtubs with solid gold fixtures, huge expanses of marble floors and mirrored walls, clothes closets as big as huge rooms, plus a spectacular sound system and a very large staff.

But no matter these snide remarks, Andrianna saw that what Gae had said about everyone dying to go to Inga's parties was nothing less than the truth. Almost every night Casa de las Palmas filled with the same beautiful people who made the sneering references, all eager to see and to be seen, to dine at Inga's spectacular table (she'd brought her own French cook along with her), and to dance the night away. Flamenco dancing, which Inga adored, was always featured, with musicians to play the lively music and professional dancers brought in both to perform and to instruct the uninitiated, since Inga was adamant that everyone participate.

In general, life at the villa was exhausting. On those nights that Inga didn't entertain at home they went out—to dinner at restaurants or other people's homes, followed by bar hopping and dancing at clubs, both private and public, or perhaps to the casinos. It was the rare evening that anyone went to bed before six in the morning, not to rise before two in the afternoon to begin a full complement of daytime activities. Even when the soiree was at the Casa, dinner wasn't served before midnight, with the flamencos beginning at 2:00 A.M.

Andrianna took to the flamenco as if born to it, the professional instructors insisting they had never seen an Englishwoman perform the dance as well as she did and in so short a time, much to Gae's pleasure and pride. So much so that he made a special trip to Seville just to buy her an authentic flamenco dress, a lavishly beautiful lace mantilla, and high-heeled slippers to match. Andrianna was so thrilled with this unexpected present—easily as thrilled as she would have been if the gift had been a huge diamond or a star sapphire—that she burst into tears of excitement.

That night she took an especially long time to dress and fix her hair. And as she made her preparations, all she could think of was how tonight she wanted to make Gae really proud of her, prouder than he had ever been. It was the least she could do in return for all his goodness to her.

When Andrianna descended the marble staircase long after the party had started, wearing the yellow dancing dress that swirled into a burst of ruffles low on the hips flowing from a tight-waisted revealing bodice, with her black hair drawn tightly back from her face and topped with the long, flowing mantilla attached to a big silver comb, and with silver earrings dangling from her ears, there was stunned silence. It was as if an incredibly lovely Spanish princess had stepped down from an Old Master painting.

Then, when she danced for the jaded crowd—a solo exhibition—accompanying herself with silver castanets, there was a solemn hush more eloquent than any show of clapping hands or stamping feet. And there wasn't a sound until she

203

kicked off the yellow satin high heels to dance barefoot, and then a wave of enchanted murmurs of approval swept through the room. And then it was a long, full minute after the final *olé* before the audience broke into thunderous applause. But no one applauded harder or louder than Gae, who ran up to Andrianna to embrace her, to whisper fierce Italian endearments in her ear.

But it was Inga who seemed the most entranced. "Brava, little Anna! An extraordinary performance considering that you are so new to the flamenco!" She turned to Gae. "Are you sure your Ann Sommer doesn't have a little hot Spanish blood under that proper English schoolgirl demeanor?"

"Nothing about Anna would surprise me any more than her dancing did tonight. There is nothing she cannot do or be!"

"That's good." Inga smiled obliquely. "When you two run out of money, perhaps Ann will be able to support you with her dancing. Not in Spain of course. We have more professional flamenco dancers here than anyone needs. Anna, as you so charmingly call her, would have to do her flamenco in countries like Sweden and England, where they couldn't compare her to the real thing. There they'd be more likely convinced that she was truly a Spanish princess or whoever it was she pretended to be. But I'm sure wherever Anna appeared, all would be beguiled."

Andrianna wasn't sure what Inga was driving at or whether she was making fun of her and her dancing. That was the thing she found most disturbing about Inga—she was never sure what the actress was about.

On the other hand, there was no mistaking what Gae wanted. When they finally went to bed that morning, Gae, enflamed by her dancing, made love to her as he had to Beatriz, and she didn't object. Then, when he reversed their positions and their roles, she didn't object to that either. It didn't matter, she thought, *how* one made love. Love itself was the thing—and the person with whom one made it.

* * *

The next morning all the other houseguests, Gae included, went down to the beach earlier than usual, but Andrianna remained in bed, exhausted. Never in her life had she felt so tired, every bit of her aching—each arm, each leg, even her fingers. And she felt so weak that all she wanted to do was sleep.

When she came awake slowly, her eyes still closed, Andrianna felt a delicious sensation in her loins . . . the delicate touch of a clever tongue flicking and licking. Mmmm . . . she moaned, not wanting to come fully awake, wanting only to enjoy the sensations coursing through her body. *Gae!* He was insatiable! Oh, she did love him!

She reached out a hand to caress his head, his hair, but instead of the familiar curls she touched smooth, silky hair. Her eyes popped open to see that it was Inga bent over her, her tongue inflicting the sweet thrusts of pleasure, Inga in black net stockings and a lacy black garter belt!

"And I thought it was *you* she was after! God, what a bloody ass I am! I should be arrested for stupidity!" Andrianna told Gae when he finally came back from the beach to find her furiously packing their clothes.

She'd thought he'd be as mad as she was, but he just sat on the bed, ran his fingers through his curls, and laughed.

She was so outraged by this reaction that she began to whip him about the head with the denim jacket she was about to throw into a suitcase. "So, you think it's funny, do you?"

"Well, if it's not exactly funny, it's not *not* funny either." He tried to stifle his laughter. "Don't you think you're—what is the word?—overreacting?"

"Overreacting? After that . . . that woman, that—"

"Prostituta?" he suggested amiably. "Isn't that what you wanted to call her?" He moved to put his arms around her.

205

"You think this is a big joke, don't you?" She pulled away from him.

"Well, it's not so terrible either. What did she do, after all? She didn't rape you or beat you. All she did was kiss your little pussy. That's not so bad. Some girls might even like it."

"Oh, would they? You're just as bad as she is. You're just as . . . as . . . perverted!"

Again he laughed, and again she lashed out at him, this time with her hands, and he tried to protect himself. They wrestled, but as the wrangling went on and on, the first flush of her anger began to dissipate until she too finally began to laugh, too exhausted to go on fighting.

He started to unpack the suitcase.

She sobered immediately. "What are you doing?"

"Putting the clothes back."

She sat up straight. "No, Gae. I'm not staying here another night." This time she didn't shout or sound angry, only determined. "I mean it."

This time he didn't laugh. "But we're not ready to leave. I still have to make some arrangements."

"What kind of arrangements?"

"A place for us to stay. A way for us to make money. Your three thousand pounds are gone, you know."

"We can get work. In one of the English bars. And we can get a room cheap, I bet, in Torremolinos."

"No, I hardly came to the Costa del Sol for that."

"What did you come for?"

He smiled a little sadly. "The good life."

She looked at him soberly. "I thought we *had* it . . . the good life. But only because we were together. I can't stay here another night under any circumstances. I won't."

"What will you do if I don't leave with you?"

"I'll go to Torremolinos by myself, find a place to stay, and look for work. I'm sure I'll get something."

"You would go without me?"

"If you won't come with me, yes."

He thought about that for a second, shaking his head in wonderment. "In that case you'd better finish with the packing . . ." He walked toward the door.

"What packing?" she asked, frightened. "Just mine? Or yours *and* mine?"

"Yours and mine. When you are through packing, just put on your chastity belt and wait for me." He managed a smile. "Like some general or other once said, 'I shall return.' "

"But where are you going?"

"Where else but to make the necessary arrangements?"

"Wait a moment . . ." She ran to him to throw her arms around him, to shower him with kisses. "My hero!"

He was pleased. She could tell. Still he shook his head. "That one . . . Inga. She really is a *putrefatta prostituta*."

"But didn't you know? Didn't you suspect?"

"Suspect what? That she was a whore?"

"That she likes women . . . girls. That she would try to—"

"But she doesn't like girls. I mean not any more than she likes boys. She is a woman who likes her pleasure wherever she finds it, and that is not so rotten."

"No? Even when she forgets that little formality of asking first? Is that something you forgot to tell me about the good life, Gae? That you just help yourself to what you want, and everyone else be damned?"

Gae looked baffled for an instant; then the beguiling smile returned. "But you are irresistible, *cara mia* . . ."

No, thought Andrianna. There are a million beautiful girls on the Costa del Sol. Why did Inga choose me?

"Besides," Gae continued, "she's a rotten whore only because she messed up my plans. Made me make my move before I was ready . . ."

Late that afternoon they moved into Harry Mansfield's stunning all-white triplex located in a luxurious complex between Málaga and Marbella right on the sea.

The first thing Andrianna noticed about pink-cheeked, flaxen-haired, green-eyed Harry, who was as opposite in coloring from Gae as one could possibly get, was that he was easily Gae's counterpart when it came to charm, assuming one liked Harry's particular brand of the commodity. She didn't think she did, any more than she had liked Inga's.

She finally figured out what it was about Harry that turned her off. It was something that happened between his lips and his eyes when he smiled. The smile was warm and radiated an "Aren't we having fun?" kind of camaraderie, but when it reached his eyes it changed into laughter—the eyes laughing at you rather than with you.

It was not that different from how it had been with Inga, only with her it had been the contrast between her words and her voice. The words came out fine; the voice mocked you.

But maybe it wasn't a question of Harry's eyes opposed to Inga's voice, she thought. Maybe it was more a matter of whom Gae found more entertaining, with whom he'd rather be, and that certainly seemed to be Harry. And then she remembered that even before they had come to Spain Gae had told her that he had friends in Marbella and had mentioned an Englishman in particular, a fabulous chap who owned a fabulous fun club. When, the very same night, Harry took them to his Rogue, she knew, without asking, that Harry and the fabulous chap were one and the same.

Then she told herself that she must be wrong about Harry. If Gae liked him so much, he had to be fabulous, *didn't he?* But what were all those arrangements that had to be made before they moved in with Harry, and why had Gae been reluctant to make the move, saying he hadn't been ready?

It was only a couple of weeks later that everything fell into place . . .

"We're going to Tangier today," Gae announced. Andrianna was excited. Although the exotic continent of Africa lay only two hours or so away by ferry across the strait, they hadn't been there yet, and she was dying to see it.

"What shall I wear?"

208

"Not your safari outfit," Gae kidded. "This isn't Africa at its darkest, you know."

She gave him a look. Of course she knew that Tangier was a metropolis where the merchants in the "real" shops spoke fluent English and peddled expensive Oriental carpets and leather goods, and the impoverished inhabitants in fezzes and caftans peddled whatever they could, chasing down the narrow and dark alleys of the sokko after the foreigners, bargaining as they ran, going from five dollars (or whatever currency they suspected the foreigner was familiar with) down to a dollar in the space of twenty seconds. Tangier was the crossroads where the mysteries of Africa intertwined with the sophisticated inroads of European civilization and where the kids—English, American, German, or wherever—went to see the sights and smoke the best dope they'd ever smoked.

But to Andrianna Tangier was the overwhelmingly romantic Casbah, featuring a darkly handsome Charles Boyer longing to break out into the bright daylight of the sophisticated world from the shadowed alleys of the quarter, and a beautiful Hedy Lamarr, the gorgeous, glamorous foreigner, as featured in the movie *Algiers*. Very romantic, heady stuff!

"How long will we be staying?"

"Just overnight." And then, seeing the disappointment on her face, Gae said, "Don't feel bad. We'll be going back . . . again and again."

She presented herself in an hour, ready to go in a cool white silk shirtdress, little rhinestone and pearl buttons running down the front, her Vuitton overnight bag packed, her cosmetic case in hand.

"I'm sorry," Gae apologized. "I should have told you before when I told you no safari costume. The order of dress is jeans and an old jacket . . . it will probably be windy on the ferry. Well, I suppose you *could* take a little sexy something for the evening, but take your backpack, not your Vuitton."

When they got into the white convertible for the ride to

the Algeciras, where they'd park the car before boarding the ferry, Harry surprised her by jumping into the backseat. She had had no idea he was planning to accompany them.

"Thought I'd help show you the sights, love," he said.

But Harry wasn't wearing jeans like she and Gae were. Rather he looked like a rich tourist in well-pressed white slacks and a navy blazer decorated with gold brass buttons, and he was carrying a burnished leather suitcase from Mark Cross. He also carried two large straw hats. One he placed rakishly on his own head and the other on Andrianna, carefully adjusting the tilt of it to his satisfaction. "If we sit outside on deck, the sun can be murder what with the reflection on the water, and I burn in about three seconds. And you should wear a hat just in case you're ultrasensitive to the sun too."

Thoughtful Harry . . .

Once they parked the car and went to purchase their tickets for the ferry ride a tall, gorgeous German girl with white-blond hair rushed up to shower Harry with kisses. She was dressed in raw silk and beige linen — Andrianna suspected the House of Dior — with a Rollei hanging from a gold chain around her neck and carrying two expensive-looking black and tan leather bags.

"Darling Harry, I thought you were never going to show up," she breathed.

Harry returned her kisses, protesting that for *her* he would show up crawling on his hands and knees if necessary.

Charming Harry . . .

As far as Andrianna could see, the passengers on the ferry were divided into distinct groups. One were the native Moroccans with many packages and bundles and cheap suitcases held together with rope and tape who huddled together, away from the others. The second group were the hippies and students in their jeans and jean jackets, sneakers or sandals, the more affluent among them wearing down vests, and fancy cowboy boots. They extended the hand of

210

friendship to one another, regardless of their country of origin, singing Beatles favorites, strumming guitars, retelling stories. "You wanna hear what happened to me in Amsterdam? . . ."

Next were the middle-class tourists who sat outside on deck, taking the sun, oblivious to the heat, or inside at the tables eating the food they'd brought with them, not sure that they would find food or acceptable drinking water on board. And then there was a relatively smaller group wearing conservative dark-colored suits. These were the Spanish businessmen, carrying briefcases and attaché cases or the salesman's sample case, going to Morocco just for the day.

The last group was no more than a handful of American, English, German, and French tourists, but obviously "rich." The men were dressed much like Harry in his natty blazer and perfectly creased trousers, Rolexes or Cartier tank watches on the wrist, their luggage discreetly shouting "first class." And the women, young and old, were dressed much like Heidi, Harry's friend, in silk and cashmere and linen. And if they carried a camera, it was no less than Heidi's Rollei. They passed the time by playing the slots in the little gaming room that opened as soon as the ferry's engines roared, shoveling in twenty-five-peseta pieces with a compulsion.

Andrianna, Gae, Harry, and Heidi sat inside, out of the sun, and drank gin straight up, washing the gin down with swigs from a bottle of mineral water *con gas,* while Heidi giggled a lot and Harry regaled them with amusing tales of various misadventures riding the same ferry back and forth.

When the ferry docked, all the passengers surged forward to line up in a reception area with their passports and luggage ready for inspection. As soon as their foursome entered this arena, Andrianna and Gae were curtly directed to the line of students and hippies by an expressionless official whose face lit up with a huge smile when he looked at Harry and Heidi. And then Andrianna was amazed to see a distin-

211

guished man in a fez and flowing caftan approaching Harry and Heidi and pick up their luggage himself to escort them to the front of a line where the official behind the desk broke into a smile, shaking hands with Harry, stamping their passports, and bowing them on.

In a matter of minutes they were free and clear and Harry was waving to them, cheerily calling out across the reception room, "See you later, chums. We'll have the drinks ready," while Heidi threw them a pitying but brilliant smile.

Andrianna was outraged. "What's going on?"

"Don't be so upset." Gae laughed. "What's going on is that you are witnessing the benefits of traveling rich from Spain to Morocco and back again. One can avoid entirely the rigors of customs inspection. As it happens it doesn't really matter going from Spain to Morocco except for avoiding the long lines of the less privileged traveler, but back again? From Morocco to Spain? There's a fortune to be made . . ."

A fortune to be made? But of course! God, but she was incredibly stupid!

Why else would Gae, who loved his comforts and his pleasures probably above all else, even more than he loved risk and the exquisite high of danger, go through all this pretense of playing the penniless hippie if he didn't have something more solid in mind than teaching her how one was treated by virtue of outward appearances?

It also explained why, in so short a time, there'd been so many rich young women in Harry's bed. After all, how many girls, out of all the girls who landed in Harry's bed, were willing — daring enough — to make this trip just for the thrill of it? Harry needed many to weed out the few.

And then, once willing, how often could the same rich girl, with the same expensive luggage, make the same trip in a certain time period carrying precious dope, without raising suspicion when reentering Spain? Not too frequently without risking apprehension. Not to mention that rich girls were notorious for tiring quickly of things. Before too long they were gone . . . on to new thrills, new places, new men.

But she, Ann Sommer, the poor girl who had lived as a

212

rich girl and knew how to act like one, who was madly in love, was a *constant* both Harry and Gae could count on.

As their line moved another few inches forward, Andrianna grabbed at Gae's arm. "So that's what you have in mind for me? Smuggling dope. You want *me* to smuggle dope for Harry."

"For Harry?" Gae put his arms around her. "Of course not. For *us*. We're in this together, Anna. You and me."

"No, Gae! I don't want to! For you it's exciting, but not for me. I hate the whole idea! Don't you understand? I'll be a nervous wreck. I'll break out in hives. And besides, you promised me!"

Gae kissed her cheeks, her chin, her hair, and murmured soothingly into her ear. "What did I promise you?"

"That you wouldn't deal drugs. And suppose we got caught? What would your father say?"

"My father? Forget my father!" Gae told her harshly. "It's only you and me now." Then his tone softened again. "Besides, hashish isn't *hard* drugs. And we won't get caught. It is foolproof, this scheme. And it is Harry who does the selling, not us. *Cara mia,* would I let you do something that was dangerous? Never. But you can't let me down."

Andrianna shuddered, knowing that inevitably she would do what Gae wanted. She couldn't . . . wouldn't . . . let him down.

Besides, as Gae had said, he wasn't doing this just for himself but for her as well. After all, it had taken them a while before they got to Harry's. She remembered the day they'd first arrived in Spain . . . how upset he'd been at the airport after making his telephone calls. Maybe before he had called for their limousine he had called Harry and had learned the true price of a haven with him, and had then . . . at first . . . decided that the price was too high.

Then later, maybe if she hadn't given him an ultimatum about moving out of Inga's, he wouldn't have been forced to throw their lot in with Harry's. He *had* been reluctant.

No, she had to bear at least some of the responsibility for the situation they were in.

Still, she was relieved that for this trip anyway it was Heidi who wasn't letting anyone down and not she. And she consoled herself that most likely she'd be required to do it only a couple of times. Once or twice, maybe, and then, like the rich girls who tired of things quickly and moved on, Gae would tire of the whole thing and of the Costa del Sol, and they too would be moving on to new places and new experiences.

She desperately hoped so.

Fifteen

When Jonathan returned to the car with their lunch from the Carnegie Deli — a combo of tongue and pastrami on rye with extra pickles and two cartons of chocolate milk — Rennie had nothing new to report on the activities of the two ladies dining at the Tea Room. But he did have something to say about Jonathan's choice of beverage: "A cold beer would have gone nice."

"I *like* chocolate milk," Jonathan retorted defensively and proceeded to chew his piled-high sandwich silently while he pondered the significance of his having wasted another couple of hours in fruitless pursuit of his mystery woman. Obviously it was some kind of commitment, but a commitment that was completely alien to him since it was the first time he had placed anything or anyone before the business of doing business . . .

"You're not listening to a word I'm saying, Annie," Penny complained again.

"Of course I am . . ."

"Then what did I just say?"

Andrianna looked at Penny blankly.

"You see!" Penny trilled triumphantly. "You *weren't* listening. What I said was that Nicole was coming up from

215

Palm Beach to see us—you and me—since we're both in New York. She's probably already here. She and Edward have a place at Trump Tower, you know, and she's expecting us for dinner tonight, and I'm accepting no excuses. I don't care if you've a date with the mayor himself. You don't, do you?"

Andrianna laughed. "Would it matter? You've already told me that you're not accepting any excuses."

Why not? It would be fun to be with her two oldest friends, to gossip and giggle like the schoolgirls they used to be, to let go and forget that she had so recently fallen in love with the one man she could have lived happily ever after with, provided all other things were equal and constant, which of course they weren't . . . and never would be. And it would be good to forget for a little while about her appointment tomorrow morning . . . the appointment that should give her a pretty good idea of where she stood in relation to the rest of her life.

"No, I don't have any plans for this evening, and yes, I'd love to have dinner with you and Nicole. But what are your plans, Penny? How long are you staying in New York and *will* you be staying at the Plaza tonight?"

She hoped not. She didn't want Penny asking her a million questions when she set out to keep her appointment in the morning.

"No, I'm not staying over. I told you—I'm catching the old red-eye back to Dallas tonight. I have much to do there. And you? Are you going to be staying on in New York? Oh, I know! If you have no immediate plans, how about coming back to Dallas with me? I need lots of help with the wedding arrangements and with keeping Mama off my back. And you've always had such great taste, unlike Mama, whose taste is in her butt, I swear!"

"No, Penny darling, I'm afraid I can't go back with you."

"Why not?"

Andrianna shook her head. It was the same old Penny. She thought that everyone could do just what she did, which was any old thing she wanted.

216

"Because I have things to do . . ."

"What kind of things?" Penny persisted.

"Things."

"I know!" Penny squealed. "It's a man, isn't it?" She leaned over the table, her eyes shining with excitement. "You came to the States because of a man."

Andrianna laughed. Penny really hadn't changed. She always thought there was a man behind . . . or above, or below . . . every move a woman made.

"Times, they are a-changing, love. Women don't do things anymore just because of men. Not *all* the time, anyway."

Penny snorted. "The hell they don't! If it's not love, or what passes for love, it's something close to it. Like sex or romance. And don't give me any of that liberation bull, either. I mean having your very own guy to screw is very liberating too. It means you're liberated from walking around so horny you're forced to fuck the gardener or the UPS man or someone you'd really rather not. The other kind of liberation, doing it all on your own without a man, might have its compensations—I'm sure it does—but it can lead to all kinds of complications. Like being lonely at three o'clock in the morning or having no one to sit up with you when you're sick or just not having anyone to nag."

"Hear! Hear! The prophet of Dallas, Texas, speaks! Is that why you're marrying Gae? So you'll have someone to nag at three o'clock in the morning?"

"Believe me, I can think of *worse* reasons to marry a man. Take Nicole. It was amazing that with her background she married an American in the first place, and an old fogy from Boston at that. And I don't give a fat fuck about the fancy house in Paris, the estate in Palm Beach, or the apartment at Trump Tower. He's thirty years older than she, and he's been retired for years. He must be as much fun as screwing a statue. It wasn't like she had to marry for the money, and God knows she wasn't marrying him for the sex. Why do you think she *did* marry him?"

"I haven't the faintest idea. I never asked her, and she never said. But maybe it's that she really loved him, even if he isn't as sexy as you would like. In any case, I'm sure she's very fond of him. Respects him totally."

Suddenly Penny's eyes narrowed. "Why didn't *you* ever marry, Annie?"

Oh, God!

"I guess it's because I never met the right man. Or maybe it was because I put my career, such as it is, first . . ."

Penny looked at her sidelong, disbelieving. "Somehow I don't believe you. I still think there's something you're not telling me." Then, abruptly, she leaned forward. "It's not because of Gae, is it? That you never married, I mean?"

"Really, Penny, if you mean what I think you mean — that I'm still in love with Gae and he's the reason I never married, the answer is no!"

"Well, what I really mean is that now that Gae and I are getting married, I'm selfish enough to be thrilled that you two never did tie the knot, but I wouldn't want to think that — well, that time in Spain, I was sure you two were a forever item. And I was *so* jealous!"

"Oh, Penny, how could Gae and I have been *forever?* We were both so young, and . . ."

"And what?"

"I guess we wanted different things. I guess in the end we were really worlds apart."

"No one would have ever thought that seeing the two of you together. The two of you were *so* close . . . Oh, that was a summer to remember. The glorious days at the beach just lying in the sun wearing only bikini bottoms. The bullfights and the casinos. Standing at the top of the Rock of Gibraltar. Going from club to club all night long. Drinking gin and tonics at the Rogue. Do you know that one of Harry's dishes at the Rogue has remained in my memory as one of the very best to this day?"

"Oh?" Andrianna drawled. "What dish was that?"

"The steak and kidney pie. I know the Rogue was

hardly gourmet, but that pie! It was definitely one of Harry's specialties."

Andrianna struggled to keep from sneering visibly. She didn't remember *any* of Harry's dishes as being special. And if anyone had asked her then what Harry's specialties were, she would have said hashish, the charm of an asp, and pale green eyes that sent shivers up her spine . . .

"You know, Annie, sometimes I lie awake at night just trying to remember what specific dance we were doing that summer and who I did it with, what boy and what place and whose bed I ended up in in the wee hours of the morning. But most of all, I think, the best fun was being with you and Gae. It's great, you know, being someplace wonderful, but it's best if you're there with friends . . . best friends, sharing the fun with the people you really love."

Andrianna was so moved by this declaration that she reached out to squeeze her friend's hand, and then Penny touched a finger to her own lips and leaned across the table to place it on Andrianna's. "As Humphrey said to Ingrid in *Casablanca,* 'I love you, kid.' "

"That's not what he said at all," Andrianna protested with tears in her eyes. "What he said was 'Here's *looking* at you, kid.' "

"Well, here's looking at *you,* kid." Penny raised her glass of vodka to find that it was empty and set it down again. "Are you *sure* you can't come back to Dallas with me?"

"Positive."

"Well, all right. But I still expect you to be my maid of honor," Penny said, lifting the now half-depleted bottle of vodka to fill her glass again.

"We'll see," Andrianna said as she gently removed the bottle from Penny's unsteady hand and signaled for the waiter to remove it.

"What do you think you're doing, may I be so bold as to inquire?" Penny asked stiffly. "You know, now that I think of it, you were *always* something of a killjoy."

"What? When did I ever kill any of your *joie de vivre?*"

219

"Well, as I'm starting to recall the actual details of that time in Spain, you weren't exactly a bellyful of laughs."

"Oh? Just a while ago you were saying what a wonderful time that was and that it was so wonderful because you were with me and Gae, because you loved us so much. Has all the vodka you've been swilling changed your mind?"

"I can handle the vodka. I'm fine. If you must know, what vodka does for me is give me a clarity of vision. That's why I'm beginning to remember exactly how *crabby* you were at the time. I mean, you really had an itch to bitch."

"Oh, come off it, Penny." Andrianna laughed.

"No, I'm serious. At first I thought that maybe you were just cranky because, while you and Gae were really tight, the two of you weren't actually getting along *that* well."

That was true enough, Andrianna thought, remembering the long line of rich, pretty girls practically begging to do the Tangier-Spain run with Gae since she herself wasn't doing it more than once or twice a month and how she had wondered what else those girls were begging to do for Gae. Not that she had actually voiced her anxieties. She'd learned early on that even if she did confront Gae directly he'd only laugh at her—kiss, caress, and embrace all her questions away. Still, all the unanswered questions had festered like an untreated wound . . .

"And then, when I did the hashish caper with Gae—you know, the ferryboat bit—I thought that maybe you resented that," Penny said thoughtfully. "Like I was cutting into your exclusive territory."

Andrianna gave an abrupt, mirthless laugh. "My exclusive territory! Oh, Penny, I never hated anything more than that Tangier business. I was so nervous, and I always felt so sordid. It's true that I didn't want you to do it, but only because I was worried about you. Worried you'd get caught. When it was one of those other girls, I was always just grateful that I didn't have to do it, regardless of what a thrill it was supposed to be."

"It *was* thrilling. But then Gae and I always had that in common—wanting to experience the more exciting highs life has to offer. Willing to expose more of ourselves to the risk and the challenge. Now you, Annie darling, are not one for exposing yourself to anything."

Andrianna cringed inwardly, reminded of the risk she'd allowed herself to take on the *QE2*. *Falling in love!* She should have known better.

It's not true, Penny, that the bigger you are, the harder you fall, that the more you have, the more you have to risk. You and Gae had everything, and the risks you took were never really risks at all since you always had it all to fall back on—money, family, a name.

"Even back then I thought about that—how Gae and I had that in common," Penny went on. "Maybe that's why I had a case on him even then. But you didn't know that, did you? So that couldn't have been the reason you were kind of crabby.

"And you know, at first I thought that maybe you were crabby because you were pregnant. And under the circumstances, who could blame you? You were only seventeen and to be strapped with a kid? Besides, Gae was hardly ready to be a father, was he? But then, as it turned out, you weren't pregnant after all."

No, she hadn't been pregnant when Penny arrived in Marbella, but she had been only a month or so before . . .

She didn't blame Gae for being upset when she told him that he was going to be a father. He was barely twenty, and it was hard to think of how a baby would fit into their lifestyle. She'd been ambivalent herself, *wanting* the baby, but scared, doubting herself, not sure of the future, unsure of *them*—her and Gae—as parents . . . as a couple.

The first thing Gae said was "This is not so good. What will my father say?" which said something about how Gae still felt about Gino Forenzi. And she thought then that *if* she did have the baby and it was a boy, they would name

221

it after Gino, and that would please both Gae and his father. But, of course, if it were a girl, she'd call it Elena . . .

But in the end it wasn't her decision, nor was it Gae's. In the end it was Harry's. He said, "Christ, man! What the bloody hell are you going to do with a snotty-nosed kid with a shit-filled nappy?" His graphic turn of phrase did the trick.

Still, there'd never been a question of anything but the best for her, even in Catholic Spain. She had to grant Gae that. She didn't know how he managed it—the proper connections, she supposed—but there was no dark room and dirty sheets, no old woman with a bloody apron and a rusty hanger like in the stories she had heard. Rather, it was first class all the way, the only way that Gae believed in. A white-walled, meticulously clean clinic and a doctor performing the procedure, one with proper credentials, Gae assured her, he standing by, wiping her brow himself. "It won't hurt, *cara mia*," Gae promised her. "I would never let anything or anyone hurt you."

And it didn't *really* hurt . . . hardly at all.

"But pregnant or not, you were definitely out of sorts for sure! Was it because I was making it with Harry? There was one time there when I thought you might have been resentful or jealous that I was sleeping with Harry."

Andrianna was outraged. "Jealous that you were sleeping with Harry? Why in God's name would you have ever thought that? I *despised* Harry!"

"You did? I never knew that! But *why* did you hate Harry? He was the epitome of charm! Sweet as bee's honey."

"*Sweet?* Harry?"

"Well, he *was* kind. Remember how he used to let you sing at the Rogue? You accompanied yourself on that old upright and sang 'Golden Earrings' and that oldie that goes 'We're drinking, my friend, to the end of a—'" Penny hummed a couple of bars. "Remember?"

"Yes, of course I remember. That was all Gae's doing." Andrianna smiled slightly, recalling. "He insisted that I sing. He *loved* it whenever I sang or danced. But why do you say that that was *kind* of Harry?"

Penny giggled. "Well, it was kind because it was *his* place, after all, and no offense intended, but you were pretty awful in those days."

Andrianna laughed. "I have to agree with you there. I *was* pretty awful, and the truth is I never did get much better. All I did was develop a better style. I learned how to *sell* a song. But I would hardly call Harry kind for letting me sing at the Rogue. It was hardly a class spot."

"Well, I don't think you're giving Harry enough credit. He was very generous actually. As soon as anyone hit town—especially the kids from England or Australia or the States—they ended up at Harry's, and it never mattered if they didn't have any bread. If they were hungry, thirsty, tired, and broke, they got fed, watered, and given a place to sleep, and he was *always* good for a reefer or two. Don't you remember?"

Yes, she remembered, but unlike Penny, she *knew* why Harry was always generous with the giveaways. It was to make people grateful, so grateful that they'd die to return his favors, become his slaves forever. And wherever, whenever, in whomever he spotted a weakness, he went in for the kill.

She was having one of her bad days and didn't feel strong enough to make the run with Gae, so he and Harry decided Gae would take Polly, who waited tables at the Rogue, to Tangier with him, no rich girl being available on short notice.

Gae and Harry had a lot of fun dressing Polly up in one of Andrianna's elegant "traveling" outfits, Polly having nothing suitable of her own. Then they arranged Polly's hair while she watched from her bed, too listless even to offer suggestions. Then, as Gae and Polly left, Harry went off too, telling Gae that he was not to worry. "I'll keep an eye on our poor little sick Anna while you're gone . . ."

She didn't see Harry again until that evening, when he came home earlier than usual, specifically to check up on her, he said, and to bring her a bit of supper from the Rogue—a mess of fish and chips. But just looking at the cold and greasy food that, from the smell of it, had been too liberally doused with vinegar, made Andrianna queasy. As did being alone with Harry.

She thanked him and told him that he didn't have to feel obligated to stay with her. "I was just about to go to sleep anyway, and I know that it's still early for you and you probably have someplace to go . . . a party or something. So don't let me keep you."

"You're not keeping me from anyplace I'd rather be, love. And it *is* late." He sat down on the edge of her bed and looked at her with those pale green eyes. "I'd be willing to wager Gae and Polly have already hit the sack in their room at the hotel."

"Room?"

"Of course, *room*. Did you think it was *rooms?*" He laughed while the pale green eyes mocked her and his hand stroked her arm ever so gently.

But by now she knew Harry and his bag of tricks too well to react. "Get out of here, Harry," she said quietly.

"Don't be a little fool, Anna. What do you think Gae and Polly are doing right this moment?"

"I haven't any idea because I haven't given it a moment's thought, and I don't intend to."

Harry just smiled in response and got into the bed beside her, blithely ignoring her protestations and easily resisting her attempts to push him out.

Leaning his head back against the pillow, he drawled, "I'll tell you exactly what they're doing. Probably, at this very moment, Polly has Gae's willie in her mouth . . ."

"You're vile! Repulsive!"

"Maybe so, but I'm also right. I *know* pretty Polly. She's

The Publishers of Zebra Books Make This Special Offer to Zebra Romance Readers...

AFTER YOU HAVE READ THIS BOOK WE'D LIKE TO SEND YOU 4 MORE FOR *FREE* AN $18.00 VALUE

NO OBLIGATION!

MORE PASSION AND ADVENTURE AWAIT... YOUR TRIP TO A BIG ADVENTUROUS WORLD BEGINS WHEN YOU ACCEPT YOUR FIRST 4 NOVELS ABSOLUTELY *FREE*
(AN $18.00 VALUE)

Accept your Free gift and start to experience more of the passion and adventure you like in a historical romance novel. Each Zebra novel is filled with proud men, spirited women and tempestuous love that you'll remember long after you turn the last page.

Zebra Historical Romances are the finest novels of their kind. They are written by authors who really know how to weave tales of romance and adventure in the historical settings you love. You'll feel like you've actually gone back in time with the thrilling stories that each Zebra novel offers.

GET YOUR FREE GIFT WITH THE START OF YOUR HOME SUBSCRIPTION

Our readers tell us that these books sell out very fast in book stores and often they miss the newest titles. So Zebra has made arrangements for you to receive the four newest novels published each month.

You'll be guaranteed that you'll never miss a title, and home delivery is so convenient. And to show you just how easy it is to get Zebra Historical Romances, we'll send you your first 4 books absolutely FREE! Our gift to you just for trying our home subscription service.

BIG SAVINGS AND FREE HOME DELIVERY

Each month, you'll receive the four newest titles as soon as they are published. You'll probably receive them even before the bookstores do. What's more, you may preview these exciting novels free for 10 days. If you like them as much as we think you will, just pay the low preferred subscriber's price of just $3.75 each. *You'll save $3.00 each month off the publisher's price.* AND, your savings are even greater because there are never any shipping, handling or other hidden charges—FREE Home Delivery. Of course you can return any shipment within 10 days for full credit, no questions asked. There is no minimum number of books you must buy.

crazy for eating cock. And she's the best. When it comes to giving head, no one can touch her. Did you know that? That she gives the best head on the Costa del Sol? Well, that *is* her reputation, and I can personally vouch for it. In fact, I can tell you exactly what they're doing this very second—a blow-by-blow description, if you will."

Andrianna knew that no matter what, Harry wasn't going to stop talking, and there was no way she could force him to. All she could do was not listen. She put her hands over her ears.

But Harry straddled her then, pulling her hands away from her ears and leaning over her, his face only inches from hers. Then he pinned her hands up and back, each hand held fast by one of his. In that position, and under the weight of his body, she couldn't move and was too weak even to struggle. But she was determined not to make a sound, not to give Harry one gram of satisfaction.

"Gae's stretched out in the bed, his legs spread apart, and he's hard already, just looking at pretty Polly kneeling between his legs. Now, she's stroking his John Thomas and singing to it—telling it how sweet it is. Now it's got a life of its own and growing bigger by the second. Now she's leaning forward over him and rubbing it between her titties. But she doesn't do that too long, else he'll be spurting between them instead of down her throat, and that won't do at all. You see, Polly likes swallowing the stuff . . ."

Andrianna groaned involuntarily, and Harry laughed and went on. "Now she's ready to really get down. First she licks the balls, gets them all juicy and wet, and by now Gae's dickey bird is so hot for her mouth he's got his hand entangled in her hair and he's pulling her away from the balls toward the cock. But first she licks it wet all over, and then her tongue reaches for the tiny hole at the end, and Gae's shaking all over and screaming at her to take it in her mouth, every last bit of it, and finally she does . . . takes it all in, down to her tonsils. Up, down, and all around. And now he's groaning and moaning, and he's ready to climb the hill, and there he goes, shaking and spurting, and she's swallowing it . . . every fucking last drop!"

Using a last-ditch desperate surge of strength and taking him by surprise, Andrianna wrenched her hands free to push Harry off her and laughed with as much contempt as she could muster: "Did you think you were going to turn me so green with jealousy with that little recitation that I would fuck you to get even with Gae? Or did you think you were going to get me so hot I was going to beg you to let me do a Polly on you? Well, sorry, Harry, old love, but I find you as enticing as a slimy toad!"

Now Harry's lips were no longer curved into a smile and his eyes were hardly laughing. He reached for the zipper of his jeans, and his intent was as clear as a cloudless blue sky.

"Try it, and I swear I'll bite it off!"

Harry looked at her hard with the green eyes turned mean, and she knew he must have believed her—believed the angry tone in her voice—because he got to his feet and walked from the room. In a few seconds she heard the front door slam.

But she never told Gae about the encounter. She wasn't sure why she didn't, but it was hardly because she was afraid he would make too much of the incident. Perhaps it was the very opposite that she feared. Or maybe it was that she somehow sensed that telling Gae wouldn't have helped . . . that it was already too late for that . . . that Gae was already in too deep . . .

"Harry was a slime," Andrianna told Penny, stony-voiced. "A maggot . . ."

Of course twenty years later it was easy to see that Harry had been another factor in the diminishing of the whole. Back then she'd thought mainly of Gae's reaction, but some part of her, deep within, had seen the whole incident as a reflection of who she was . . . or wasn't. Somehow, no matter the elegance with which she carried herself, the insouciance with which she played the game, the tough worldliness she could call up when the situation demanded it, the Harrys and Ingas of the world saw her as a girl who had no say in her own fate. They tried to take what they wanted from her not because she was young, beautiful, innocent, and thus vulnerable, but because they sensed that she was a girl who could not, as Penny could, say "Fuck off" and go her own way.

It had been a particularly hot day, and she and Penny had been shopping for hours. Andrianna was so exhausted she thought she might drop in her tracks if she didn't lie down for a while. She decided that, instead of going on to the Rogue with Penny as planned, she'd go back to the apartment. "Tell Gae I'll catch up with him later . . ."

The apartment with the white draperies drawn against the sun was deliciously cool, and before Andrianna headed for her bedroom she went to the kitchen for a cold drink from the fridge. And then she heard the muted sounds from the living room. What was it? Had someone left the telly on?

Taking her Coke with her, she went to see, and what she saw were two naked men — one sitting on the extra-deep, overstuffed white sofa, with his arms folded behind his flung-back head, eyes closed, and the other kneeling at his feet . . .

Her glass of Coke made a loud crash as it hit the white-tiled floor, causing both men to turn in startled shock — Gae on the sofa, Harry, kneeling on the floor . . .

Hours later, when she finally unlocked the bedroom door, Gae said exactly what she knew he would say. "Why do you always make such a fuss over every little thing?

You take everything so seriously. I swear, it was nothing."

Her tear-stained face was covered with bright red blotches. "Nothing? I hardly call it nothing when my lover is having his cock sucked by another man!"

"What is so terrible? I could understand that you would be upset if it were a beautiful girl blowing me. But a man? I was doing nothing more than obliging a friend. It's Harry. He says he's had so many women that they make him — how do you say it? — nauseous. If you had gone to as many schools as I have where there are nothing but boys, you wouldn't be making such a big thing of this. It doesn't mean that the boys are homos. It just means that when it comes to sucking, what does it matter who sucks you? You just lean back and enjoy it . . ."

Eventually she forgave (or said she did) Gae his dereliction, allowing herself to be persuaded that the whole incident did mean very little to Gae, if not to her. Gae was at least not evil. Gae was . . . well, *Gae,* and there was so much about him that was sweet and wonderful. Besides, she had a feeling that their time on the Costa del Sol was drawing to a close. Even in the south of Spain, where the days were full of sunshine, the sun still had to set . . .

Penny frowned. "Well, no matter what the problem was, *something* was bothering you the whole time I was there. Every little thing seemed to upset you."

"That's not true," Andrianna objected. "That's unfair. It was just that everyone expected me to go around grinning like a little fool no matter what."

No matter how ill I felt or what was happening between me and Gae . . .

"Well, remember that day we went to the beach and you got sunburned and swelled up like a balloon and had that peculiar rash on your face? When we all laughed, you got mad."

"Of course I got mad! What was so funny? That I was suffering? Was I supposed to laugh along with all of you?"

"But we weren't laughing at *you*. We were laughing at how funny you looked and at that really weird rash on your face. None of us had ever seen anything like it before . . ."

In all fairness, after Gae finished laughing he insisted on calling a doctor for her, as his father had done when she'd suffered the terrible attack of sun poisoning at Port'Ercole, even though she protested, feeling foolish to be in need of a doctor again after that last warning about exposing herself to the sun. After all, she knew what it could lead to—the rash, the swelling of her legs and arms, the weakness. As for her constant fatigue and loss of weight, all that was natural enough, she thought, considering she had so recently been pregnant, aborted, and plunged into depression resulting from so many things . . . too many things.

The doctor, much like the doctor in Port'Ercole, clucked like a mother hen and scolded, "What is wrong with you English girls? Don't you know enough to stay out of the sun or at least protect yourself with a hat and skin lotion?"

He examined her swollen joints and clucked some more, prescribing aspirin, ointments, and bed rest until all her symptoms were gone. "And you should eat more. You are much too skinny. Don't you know European men like women with some flesh on the bones?" he joked. "So you will eat more, no?"

Then, before he left, he studied the peculiar butterfly-shaped rash on her face again. He shook his head. "I have never seen that before. Very curious. It resembles nothing so much as the bite of the wolf."

Andrianna's eyes filled with tears.

"Oh, shit, Annie! Now I've gone and made you feel bad. Just because I said you were out of sorts years and years ago? That's so silly. Please, Annie, don't! I'm sorry . . ."

"No, no. I was just thinking back. Thinking actually

229

about the *good* times. And it made me feel—I don't know—nostalgic."

Penny, relieved that she was absolved from guilt, rolled her eyes. "Do I ever know what you mean! And it's not nostalgia. What it is is crying for one's lost youth . . ."

Andrianna nodded, allowing Penny to think that she had hit the nail squarely on the head. What she was really thinking about was a *what if . . . What if* she had told that doctor the rest of her symptoms? What if she'd told him about her being tired all the time, about the recurring terrible pain in her arms and legs, about the bouts of fever, or how sometimes every part of her felt heavier than lead?

What if, when he remarked on how thin she was, she hadn't let him think she was consciously trying to be thin but had told him instead about her loss of appetite, the difficulties she sometimes experienced in swallowing? *What if . . . ?*

Would he have figured out that the supersensitivity to light was not the problem in itself but only one more symptom of her real illness?

But it had never occurred to her at the time to reveal her other complaints. The truth was that at that point in her life she'd already been far too enmeshed in the habit of secrecy to reveal anything about herself that she wasn't forced to. She had already grown accustomed to not revealing her innermost feelings to anyone, of not lying but *withholding.*

Withholding . . . it was a pattern that would come to mold all the days of her life . . .

Sixteen

La Costa del Sol
Fall 1968

Recovered from her second bout with sun poisoning, Andrianna resumed her routine, but remembering this time to take much more care to protect herself from the sun. And she took to wearing really dark sunglasses nearly all the time since the shades not only blocked out the rays of the sun but prevented those on the outside from looking in too closely . . . the eyes being the mirrors of the soul. She didn't want anyone looking into the recesses of her soul . . .

When Penny left, she felt a deep void in her life, a void she was unable to fill. Oh, how she missed Penny's exuberance, her ability to "keep on truckin' and fuckin' no matter what," to quote her friend. But there *was* an up side. With Penny gone they'd no longer be a foursome—she and Gae, Penny and Harry. So she'd see less of Harry.

But then Harry had a new girl—a snowbird from Scandinavia—and a few days later a pretty bird from London, and then bird after bird, one distinguished from the other only by how quickly they came and went. And each time Harry expected . . . demanded . . . that she and Gae, he and his new girl, make up a foursome.

When she begged off, which she most often did since she could barely endure looking into Harry's green eyes, Gae would simply go on without her.

But then, when she thought her well of despair was bottomless, there was a ray of hope—Gae seemed to be tiring of Harry and his attractions. He was beginning to pick up on his old friendships—the jet-setters with whom, Andrianna guessed, he really felt more comfortable. Then there was a new question: did *she* feel at home with this crowd?

She wondered what was in Gae's mind as he went back and forth between the two worlds. Was it only that he was growing restless, that what he really wanted was to go home again, to his father and his old way of life? Or was he running away subconsciously, from Harry—even from her—torn, caught somewhere in the middle, between being a man and a boy?

Then, beginning to feel a little bit worse each passing day, she thought, What difference did it really make which crowd Gae was partying with when he was still running to Harry for solutions, still dependent on him for their living? And it didn't help when she insisted that they leave Harry's condo and get their own place, hoping that that was the key to their salvation. Gae would only shrug, smile, and say, "We will . . . in time. You're still my sweet, innocent little Anna. You don't understand that there is a time and place for everything . . ."

As her physical condition worsened, she tried to keep it from Gae. The pain was the hardest thing to conceal, but she couldn't have Gae running with *her* pain to Harry, who would most certainly prescribe dope. She was sure that, if Harry had his way, she'd get hooked on drugs, because everyone knew what happened to a junkie. Whether the addiction was to drugs, money, or the wrong kind of love, first you became a whore one way or another, and then one morning you woke up dead.

Then one morning she awoke feeling sicker than she ever had before, listless with fever, every part of her body aching. There was no way she could get out of bed, bathe, paint her face, arrange her hair, put on the white Chanel suit with the little gold buttons, and make the run to Tangier, even though all the arrangements had been made and the drugs were waiting to be picked up.

At the last minute Gae was able to persuade Cissy St. Cloud, the new girl in town, to make the run with him.

Sick as she was, Andrianna managed to kiss him good-bye, thinking how beautiful he looked in his all-white suit with his black hair curling down on his forehead. There was a distinctive Gatsby quality about him, she thought, although if she remembered the story correctly, Gatsby had been rough around the edges, while Gae was as smooth as silk all over.

It wasn't until after he was gone that she remembered Fitzgerald's Gatsby had been doomed from the beginning—a marked man—and she moaned in pain that transcended the physical.

But it was only Cissy who was caught when, inexplicably, the routine broke down and her luggage was inspected. And it was Cissy who was taken into custody while Gae was home clean, his bag having revealed nothing but the usual accoutrements of a man on a two-day excursion.

When Gae returned to the apartment free but more upset than Andrianna had ever seen him, it struck her that even though she had envisioned him, like Gatsby, as a marked man, it had never been he who'd been marked—it had been the girl, marked as both culprit and victim before she ever stepped foot on the ferry. This had been Harry's game plan: only one member of the team actually carried. Only Cissy hadn't been the intended victim—it had been Andrianna, and only her illness had intervened. Harry had wanted to get her!

Of course Gae would never believe this—not of fabulous, happy-go-lucky, easy-come-easy-go, generous Harry!

As she lay in bed completely miserable, Gae, his pretty white suit crumpled and stained, sat on the edge, running his fingers through his curls, nervously pulling on a cigarette. Harry sat on the white lounge facing them, languidly puffing on his cigar. "Cissy will be all right. Her rich dada and mum are most likely on their way this very minute to spring her."

Andrianna plucked at Gae's sleeve to get his attention: "What if they're not?" And Gae repeated to Harry, "What if they're not? Maybe they're washing their hands of her."

"Then that's her lookout, isn't it?"

"No, Harry," Gae shook his head in despair. "It's our lookout too. We can't just throw her to the dogs."

"What do you propose? That we turn ourselves in and say 'Look, old chaps, this girl is innocent. She had no idea she was carrying dope. *We're* guilty. Free her and lock us up'?" Harry laughed. "Believe me, Gaetano, my friend, a Spanish prison is no joke. Besides, they'll go easier on a rich foreign girl, and this is the way the plan's supposed to work—if one gets caught, the other goes free. If it was you who got nabbed, she'd be out of the country so fast it would make your knob spin. She knew the score, didn't she?"

"She knew, but she didn't know. I told her there wasn't a chance in hell of our getting caught."

234

Harry laughed again. "She deserves to be in the clinker for a few months for believing that bit of tripe. That's like believing the line: 'I swear I won't come in your mouth.'"

Involuntarily Andrianna groaned.

Harry was amused. "You must see to our Anna, Gae, while I toddle along and see what I can do about our disappointed clients who were waiting for our confiscated merchandise."

"But what about Cissy?"

Harry sighed wearily. "Look, Gaetano, this isn't my gig, and I don't propose to make it so. If *you* want to play the fucking asshole, that's your business. But do me a favor and vacate these premises first. I hate to be sticky about it, but these are my digs, and there's no room for excess baggage. I'll be back tomorrow, and I'll expect to find you two gone."

Once they heard the front door slam, Gae picked up Andrianna's hand and pressed it to his cheek. "I think I have to call my father. He will know what to do about Cissy."

Andrianna agreed.

Gae went into the next room to make his call. Then she could hear him talking softly, his words muffled by his weeping. When he came back into the bedroom, he said, "He's coming," and lay down in the bed beside her.

After a while he turned and put his arms around her, and then they lay there, not speaking, just holding each other tightly, knowing that a chapter of their lives was drawing to a close and nothing was ever going to be the same again.

It wasn't until Cissy St. Cloud was free to go merrily on her way that Gae brought his father back to the apartment to see Andrianna. A pale Gae stood behind a stern Gino Forenzi, whose countenance grew more forbidding as he looked at her. She was frightened, assuming he was going to yell at her, blame her for Gae's most recent fall from grace, for having helped to corrupt him.

But Gino only demanded angrily, "How long have you been ill like this?"

"I'm not sure," Andrianna whispered. "It's been on and off—"

Gino wheeled to demand of Gae, "And you? You were too busy being the big drug dealer to see to her, is that it? To notice how thin she was? How pale? How weak? How swollen? Too occupied being the important drug lord? Or was it that you were too busy being the playboy to call in a doctor?"

"No, no." Gae held up his arms as if to defend himself. "We *had* a doctor. It was only a couple of months ago. Isn't that right, Anna? When she had another case of sun poisoning like the time in Port'Ercole. At least the doctor *said* it was sun poisoning, just like the time . . ." Gae's voice died away before he took a deep breath and resumed. "And then after a while she seemed much better . . . until this time." He hung his head.

"It's not Gae's fault, Mr. Forenzi," Andrianna whispered hoarsely. "Most of the time when I didn't feel well I didn't even tell him, so you see he really didn't know . . ."

Gino shook his head morosely. "No, you're right; it is not Gae's fault—it is mine. I raised him poorly. I have been a bad father, so, as a result, my son is not a man."

She heard Gae sob, but she didn't look at him, not wanting to see him crying like a chastened, miserable little boy. "Oh, no, Mr. Forenzi, you mustn't blame yourself and not Gae either. He's been very good to me. And the drug business—of course that was wrong, but he did that only to make enough money for us to live on. He didn't know what else to do."

Gino wiped his face with a dazzling-white linen handkerchief. "Ah, that is the problem, isn't it? He didn't know what else to do. But I have a feeling that *you* did. That if it had been left up to you, little Anna, you would have thought of other ways to earn a living."

That was true enough, Andrianna thought. She had wanted them to wash dishes for a living, wait on tables, get work as clerks in stores—anything but work for Harry Mansfield. But she had never really insisted. That had been *her* weakness.

It was funny. She barely knew Gino Forenzi, but at that moment, when he called her by the affectionate "little Anna" and attributed more virtue to her than she possessed, she had never felt more like an impostor.

And she felt a tremendous urge to confess to Gino Forenzi, to tell him that little Anna didn't really exist. That there was only Andrianna Duarte, the bastard daughter of a beautiful but foolish woman without any social significance and a man who thought her too worthless to claim as his own.

But Gino Forenzi wasn't here because of her. This wasn't her scene, only Gae's and his father's. And as a sudden pain streaked through her, she tried not to reveal how much it hurt by forcing a smile to her lips. "Gae is really a good person, Mr. Forenzi. He has so many wonderful qualities. He's very sweet, and he always makes me laugh . . ."

But Gino Forenzi saw right through her. "You're in much pain, aren't you?"

"It's not so bad. Please, Mr. Forenzi, forgive Gae . . ."

As Gae wept in the background, his father leaned down and kissed her on the forehead.

"It is not a matter of forgiving. Loving someone is not a matter of forgiving. If it were, I would ask *you* to forgive Gae. And maybe I would ask both of you to forgive me . . ."

He turned to Gae and held open his arms, and Gae rushed into them, crying, "Papa! Papa!"

Yes, Andrianna thought, it *was* Gae's and his father's scene, and she herself was only part of the background.

It was dark by the time Gino Forenzi left, telling them that he would be back the next day, after he had made some arrangements. And after his father was gone, Gae went about the apartment putting on all the lights.

It was with sad affection that Andrianna watched him. Was he going to make love to her? she wondered. So frequently that had been his solution to problems. And once, in a moment of extreme feeling, she had told him what her mother had said about sex in the afternoon being golden. Just once.

Was that why he was putting on all the lights, to cast everything in a golden light? Or was he just a little boy afraid of the dark?

"Everything is going to be all right," she told him. "We don't need all the lights."

"Yes, I know. Papa will take care of everything. But it will be more cheerful with the lights on, no?"

"Yes," she agreed.

She had always gone along with what Gae wanted, and old habits died hard.

After all the lights were on, Gae got into the bed with her, to kiss her, every inch of her, as if trying to commit all of her to memory—her hair, her eyelids, her cheeks and throat, her arms and fingers, her breasts and belly, her thighs and legs, and each of her toes.

Then, very gently, he made love to her, more tenderly, more golden than she could remember, and she knew that this was but a farewell, a tribute to a time that had already passed.

For them that special, golden time was over. They

would never be lovers again, but they *would* be friends, and maybe that was even better. Maybe friends were even more golden than lovers . . .

Seventeen

"We've been here for hours," Andrianna said, motioning to their waiter for the check. "They're probably ready to throw us out."

Penny checked her wristwatch, an ostensibly plain creation of stainless steel highlighted with touches of gold but with a diamond bezel. "But it's only ten of four. What will we do with ourselves until seven, and I'm willing to bet my last dollar that Nicole won't serve us a speck of food until at least ten. Since all over the world anyone who is *anyone* is not dining before nine, Nicole will be sure to be an hour later. She always has to be a little bit *more* than anyone else. Like those little pots of home-grown herbs she brings over from her chateau in France, packing them herself in baby bunting for their voyage to the States. Did you know that she has complete sets of them for each of her kitchens all over the world? I think it all started when her *maman* commissioned the nuns at some otherwise obscure nunnery to crossbreed chives with chervil or something . . ."

"Really, Penny, you are too much!" Andrianna laughed.

"No, seriously. I think it was a much more worthwhile project for the nuns than embroidering silk panties for Princess Di or Princess Caroline. No? Well, still, it would be nice if Nicole gave me a set of herbs as a wedding

240

present, but potted in sterling silver, of course, instead of plain little clay pots. Now, *there's* an original idea. Just what every bride should have, *n'est-ce pas?* God knows, what I don't need are any more silver candlesticks from Tiffany's or crystal punch bowls from Cartier's or place settings from Neiman's. Mama still has all the loot from my ill-fated marriage to Mr. Richard 'Bus' Townsend wrapped up in tissue paper and sealed in plastic, awaiting better days."

"Good, I'll keep that in mind when I go shopping for the bride who has everything. At least I know now what *not* to give you. But I'll be hard-pressed to think of something as original as a set of French-grown herbs in silver pots."

"Why don't you just send us a bottle of champagne for our wedding night? Mumm's or Cristal, nestled in a great big bouquet of flowers.

"Anyway, you can be sure Nicole will make sure everything's *more* than perfect tonight, even for little old us. I assure you before she left P.B. this morning she had already alerted a florist to fill the apartment with giant tulips presented in charming Saint-Porchaire faience."

"How can you be sure the flowers will be tulips?"

"Oh, you silly girl. Because tulips are now the *très chic* flower, and cymbidiums are yesterday's news. Don't you know anything?"

Andrianna attempted a hangdog expression. "Much as I hate to admit it, I didn't know that cymbidiums were out."

"Well, goodness, how are you ever going to be a great hostess if you don't keep up?" Penny asked in mock horror.

"I guess the answer is I'll never be one. But *you* can be. You're *almost* as well qualified as Nicole. You know tulips are in and cymbidiums are out, and you're going to have a husband with homes all over the world too."

"No, I don't think playing the great hostess is my bag. I mean, really, does it matter if the apartment in New York is kept up to the highest standards while Nicole is in Palm Beach or if the Palm Beach estate is manicured to a T with rotating seasonal plantings when she's in Paris? See my point? With Nicole's talents she could be running countries or international companies instead of just keeping up appearances for some old nothing."

"Really, Penny! Edward is hardly nothing. When Nicole married him, he was the United States Ambassador to France!"

"Big noogies! She still didn't need him or his money."

"Need? Who knows what anyone really *needs?* Did you *need* Boobie? Or Rick Townsend? Well, maybe you *did,* for reasons you weren't even aware of."

"This is getting to be pretty heavy stuff. So tell me, why do you think I *need* to marry Gae? While he has oodles of money, I don't really *need* his money. Do you think it's the terrific sex I *need?* A really great fuck? Well, it *is* true that I put a high premium on *really good* sex, but while that commodity is not exactly growing on trees, it's still available without signing on for life. Do you think, then, that it's friendship that I need—a good old pal? Or do you think?—can it be?—that I *need* love? Because I do truly love Gae, you know."

"Oh, Penny, I would think *everyone* needs love."

Penny cocked her head to one side. "And you, Annie? What do *you* need? Are you really so different from everyone else? Don't *you* need love?"

Oh yes, I need love. Maybe more than most . . .

She had certainly needed Gae's love, but he had been incapable then of giving her the kind of love she needed. A man's love.

She thought of all the men she had known. Never the

242

right man, never the right kind of love . . .

Oh, yes, Penny, I've had my share of Boobies and Ricks. But I never could bring myself to take the risk, like you did. Maybe in the beginning it was Gae—they all seemed to pale next to that first sweet passion. At first there were some I ran away from—I couldn't bear to tell them the truth. Then, as the years passed, I got so good at the game, at staving off their questions, that they stopped asking. And then I would see it in their eyes—here was the woman of their dreams, the woman they'd always wanted, and the she that didn't exist was there for the taking. That's when I'd make my exit—but always gracefully, with "great style and presence."

As for Jonathan West, he was possibly the very rightest kind of man full of the right kind of love . . . but not for her.

Oh, the problem lay definitely with her. Love meant giving as well as receiving, and what did she have to give?

Oh, Jonny, Jonny, you're the boy who came too late to the fair.

Penny was still waiting for an answer to her question: did she need love like everyone else? Andrianna smiled mysteriously. Mystery was her thing, after all—it was the thing she did best. "And what makes you think I *haven't* had love . . . as much love as any one person needs in a lifetime?"

Penny looked at her for a long time before answering. "If you tell me that you have it . . . *had* it . . . as much love as anyone can need, I don't really believe you, but I sure as hell hope it's true."

The check came, and they tussled a bit over who would take it. "Let me," Andrianna said. "I *need* to take a check every once in a while."

Penny picked up her crocodile cosmetic case at the coat check—"My only piece of luggage," she explained—and they went out onto Fifty-seventh Street, where the day

243

had turned bitter and it was already growing dark.

"I *hate* this time of day in New York in the winter, don't you?" Penny said, huddling into her sable coat.

Andrianna pulled her mink tighter against her body. "I really don't know. I've never been in New York before, not even in the spring."

"That's right, you haven't. Well, this time of day at this time of the year, when it's cold and it's raw, and somewhere between day and night, makes me nervous. As if I have to run home to be safe, you know?"

Andrianna knew. What she didn't know was where her home was or if she would ever be safe anywhere.

"Hey, there they are!" Rennie blurted, elbowing Jonathan, who was sitting beside him in the front seat of the limousine parked directly across the street from the restaurant. "Your friend and the redheaded broad! They've just left the restaurant, and they're proceeding on foot, headed east!"

Jonathan took a quick look and then ducked down out of sight, chuckling at how quickly Rennie had picked up the vernacular of the surveillance business. "Well, what are we waiting for? Turn us around and let's see where they're headed."

While they'd been waiting for Andrianna to reappear, Jonathan had been using the time to take nips from a bottle of scotch from the limousine's bar and to catch up on his reading. He had learned, courtesy of the *Wall Street Journal,* that he had taken a licking to the tune of a quarter of a million dollars on the stock market since, busy as he'd been with his pursuit of the elusive Andrianna, he had not been minding his store.

He had had an educated hunch just before leaving London that it was time to get out of Jax International

Properties and quick, but then he had forgotten all about it. Now it was too late. The stock had plummeted, leaving him with considerable egg on his face. But such was his state of mind—actually he felt numb—that the loss didn't bother him too much. What did anything mean if he couldn't have the beautiful, mysterious Andrianna?

"What is it, Annie? You look as if you've seen a ghost."

Andrianna thought it extremely possible that she had. For a second she had thought she had seen Jonathan West in the limousine parked across the street. But when she looked again, there was only a chauffeur sitting in the front seat. Thinking of him so hard and longing for him, her mind and her eyes had combined to play tricks on her. As if she didn't have enough problems . . .

"So what shall we do? Go back to the Plaza?"

"We could walk around. Window-shop?"

"I don't know about you, but I'm freezing my ass off." Penny shivered in her fur. "Wait a minute! I know what we should do!

"The Sherry has a Harry's Bar now. You know, just like in Venice and on the Via Veneto. They call it Cipriani's here. Let's go there for old time's sake. Remember when we were there together? You and me and Gae's father, Gino. That time when I came to visit you in Rome? The funny thing is he sort of scared me even then, *before* he was my prospective father-in-law. He's such a *big* man, and the image he presents—powerful! Overwhelming, really!"

Andrianna remembered that time in Rome very well. But she hadn't thought of Gino as forbidding then. To the contrary. She had found him exceedingly kind, exquisitely considerate, and above all else, loving . . . in every way.

Soon after Gino took them back to Rome, he had Gae back at Le Rosey to complete his credit requirements so that he could get started on his higher education and had Andrianna launched on her first round of doctors in search of an answer to her medical problems.

Then, before too many months had passed and with a few strings pulled here and there, Gae was off to Harvard in America. That was where at least half the fathers who sent their sons to Le Rosey intended for them to finish their educations—where the boys, most often heirs to great fortunes, could go on to get their graduate degrees in business administration and be better equipped to run financial empires and administer the family fortunes.

Before he left, a subdued Gae came to say good-bye to her at the clinic in Milan where she'd been directed after the doctors in Rome had failed to diagnose her ailment.

"I'm going to try to make a success of myself at Harvard," he said, sitting at her bedside, holding her hand. "I'm going to try to make Father proud of me. Who knows, maybe I will even graduate magna cum laude."

"Oh, you will! I know you can. You can do just about anything, Gae, if you try! But your father is already proud of you. He told me so."

"Perhaps . . ."

He gave her that Latin shrug she knew so well. "Anyway, I'm prepared to give it the old college try. That's what they say in America, you know. Give it the old college try! And I will be on the crew and the soccer team

246

and do whatever else I'm supposed to do. And I will never drive any faster than twenty-five miles an hour," he smiled, "no matter what. I promise. You are not to worry about me."

"I won't. You're going to have the time of your life with all those girls at Radcliffe." And then her eyes filled with the tears she'd been fighting back. "Oh, Gae . . ."

His eyes immediately filled with tears too. That was one of the most wonderful things about Gae, she thought. There was always that immediate *simpàtico* reaction.

"And I don't intend to worry about you either, sweet Anna. I know you are in the very best of hands. Gino Forenzi's hands. I am sure Papa will take much better care of you than I ever did."

And then he gave her a farewell gift, a gold bracelet with charms all in a row.

"See, here is a little schoolhouse. That represents Le Rosey, where we met. And here is a little gold ski. That is for the time you broke your arm and—"

"And we became lovers."

"Yes, lovers. And here is a heart, because no matter what happens, you will always be part of mine."

"Oh, Gae. You will always be part of mine too. Forever."

There were other charms on the bracelet, but Gae had to leave, and she was showing signs of fatigue. So all he did then was to fasten the bracelet on her wrist and kiss her, first on both cheeks and then once on the lips . . .

"You have nothing to fear from Gino Forenzi, Penny. He's probably the most wonderful man I've ever known— the wisest, the strongest, and probably the most caring."

247

Penny looked at her curiously, then her eyes widened. "You were lovers, weren't you?"

Andrianna just shook her head enigmatically. *Lovers?* So many men had been her lovers. Gino Forenzi had been so much more . . .

Eighteen

Rome 1971-1973

SYSTEMIC LUPUS ERYTHEMATOSUS! Finally her illness had a name. Systemic lupus erythematosus, more commonly called by the single word *lupus,* the Latin term for wolf—the only link between the disease and the wolf being the pattern of the butterfly the facial rash sometimes assumed, the same pattern the bite of the wolf left.

She had had the butterfly rash only once—that time in Marbella when everyone had thought it so funny. Still, Andrianna knew that it would be a long time before she stopped seeing a reflection of a wolf's face rather than her own every time she looked in a mirror.

The doctors, explaining the nature of the disease, addressed their remarks more to Gino than to her, sensing that like a father, he was in charge.

There were two types of lupus, which was essentially an inflammatory connective tissue disorder. There was the discoid form, which was largely confined to the skin, and the systemic form—Andrianna's—which was a great deal more serious, since in addition to the skin problems the condition usually affected the joints, producing arthritislike pain and swelling, and as the illness progressed, it could lead to extreme anemia and complications involving the heart, lungs, kidneys, and muscles, sometimes leading to coma—even death.

At the word *death* Andrianna gasped, but Gino shook his head, rejecting this possibility, and took her hand to comfort her. "We will never let that happen. Trust in me, Anna!"

And she did, more so than in the doctors. Gino, more savior than any doctor, more avenging knight on a white steed than any mere man, more father than she had ever known, would never let anything bad happen to her.

The doctors explained that the illness was something of a mystery. While they knew it occurred most frequently in women in their twenties, they didn't know much more—what caused it or how to cure it. It was more a matter of trying to *control* it medically, allowing the patient to live a normal life, slowing the progression of the disease with drugs, some of which worked for one patient while not for another . . . a matter of experimentation.

"We will control it; be assured, Anna," Gino said confidently. Again she believed him.

While they searched for the drugs that would prove most beneficial—a slow process of trial and elimination— she was to faithfully take her vitamins and painkillers and large doses of bed rest. In addition, the doctors recommended two other things—protection from the sun and lots of prayer.

"Prayer for what?" Andrianna asked, tearing her eyes away from Gino to look at the team of doctors. "Recovery? Or just not to die?"

"Since there is no complete recovery as far as we know now, what you must pray for, Miss Sommer, is remission. There are patients on record who have gone into remission for decades."

Remission. The magic word. But it seemed these to-be-prayed-for remissions were as baffling as the illness itself. Like lupus, they appeared mysteriously, and then, like welcome but capricious guests, they came and went as they pleased, staying for as long as they desired, moving on when the spirit took them, leaving a mournful host in their wake.

But Gino, surrogate father, was also the all-powerful magnate who hadn't gotten where he was by settling or believing in mysterious happentance. Barring the possibility of a cure, he refused to accept anything but a complete remission as an alternative.

"We *will* achieve this remission, Anna—one that will last forever. You will see."

Again Andrianna believed him. But she never stopped praying.

Finding the right medications took less time than the long search for the diagnosis but proved even more arduous. But now that Andrianna knew what she was up against, the enemy out in the open, she was better able to cope. And whenever she grew depressed or dispirited, Gino was there to buoy her up with his unflagging enthusiasm and tremendous gusto. He was determined that she fill her days with things other than just going to doctors while they experimented with the different drugs that would control her condition.

First he insisted that she continue her education, if not formally at a school, then with private instructors, and he hired them, all kinds. She perfected her French and learned Italian. There was a tutor to drill her in art history, an artist to teach her how to paint, and a sculptor to show her how to carve and mold. There was even a tutor to instruct her in the principles of architecture and one for science and advanced mathematics. There was a voice teacher, a dance instructor, and a dramatics coach, because she had always enjoyed dramatics. She learned to play the piano, not brilliantly but adequately, and the guitar simply for fun.

This was the period when Gino became her teacher as

well as her best friend and personal rooting section. In fact the best parts of her days were the evenings, when Gino talked to her about the world and its people, about the car business and the world of finance in general, about wine and fine food and the art of good living.

Then, when the regimen of drugs was finally worked out and she felt *almost* like any healthy person, the doctors pronounced her condition under control and told her that she could live the normal life of any young woman as long as she didn't overtire herself or expose herself to the rays of the sun and remembered to take her various medications and vitamins.

That evening Gino took her out to celebrate. They went to the Hostaria dell'Orso, a restaurant Andrianna thought more romantic than any other throughout Europe. There, in a sixteenth-century palace, the restaurant's patrons ate under a ceiling of gold and by the light of candles flickering in ancient silver candlesticks, their ears filled with the music of strolling violinists.

Wearing a long, body-clinging dress of white crepe, its portrait neckline revealing the swell of her breasts, Andrianna felt like a fairy-tale princess, excited but, even more, intoxicated . . . like something else wonderful was going to happen to her that day. She felt it was even conceivable that her Prince Charming, growing weary of waiting in the wings, would pick this evening to reveal himself.

And then, after several glasses of wine and a rather wonderful entrée of veal baked with foie gras, followed by an equally wonderful cheesecake bathed in rum and cups of espresso and snifters of Frangelico, something did happen. From his inside coat pocket Gino withdrew a little velvet box and presented it to her. With trembling fingers she opened it, and what she saw took her breath away.

Through the bad times there had been many presents from Gino — a pearl ring, a gold bangle bracelet, a tiny heart on a chain, a pin in the shape of a turtle with sapphires for eyes, a string of pink pearls. Presents intended to cheer up a young girl. But this ring was a *serious* piece of jewelry, a huge emerald surrounded by diamonds, the kind of ring a lover gave the object of his love, a fiancé his fiancée . . .

Shyly she looked up at Gino. What did the ring mean? Was he going to ask her to marry him, incredible as the idea was, or was it a present that signified the end of one relationship and the beginning of a new one? *Was* Gino her Prince Charming, suddenly transformed as he might be in a fairy tale?

"Oh, Gino, it's beautiful! I don't know what to say."

"There is nothing to say except that you like it and that you will wear it in good health."

"But it's too much! And it's not even my birthday."

"Today is more than your birthday. It is the day you have become a 'medically controlled young woman.'" And that sounded so funny that they both laughed. "It is a day to be marked by a special gift."

"Still the gift is much too elaborate . . . too big and too expensive. And you have already been so generous . . . far too generous. No, Gino I can't accept it."

Then he took her hand and kissed her fingertips. "Now, listen to me carefully, Anna, and listen well. Since I am Gae's father, I am certainly old enough to be *your* father, and I am going to give you some fatherly advice, which you are old enough to understand. When someone offers you something valuable, be it wise advice or something of material value, take it! Seize it with both hands and enjoy it or save it up against a rainy day. Life is capricious. One day it goes with you, and the next it can as easily go against you, and the more you have stored

253

up for the future, the better off you are. Now, here, let me put it on your finger."

She stood up and extended her right hand, and he slipped the ring onto her third finger, where it fit perfectly. Then he stood and kissed her on both cheeks and they went home.

As she prepared for bed that night, she thought of how something wonderful *had* happened tonight. One way or another, she and Gino had stepped over some invisible line. From tonight on she and he were going to be less father and daughter and more *real* friends, as only two adults could be.

But then, after she turned off the light and got into bed and under the covers and was lying in the dark, she wondered why, in spite of everything, something nagged at her heart—a vague discontent . . . a sense of disappointment . . .

In the following months she and Gino became not only friends, on a nearly equal level, but good companions in every sense of the word, even as they continued their old relationship of teacher and pupil.

One of the most exciting activities they shared was when he began taking her to the great couture houses of Paris and Milan, instructing her in the art of fashion as he made the choices. It was he who decided what her look should be and which colors best suited her black hair and ivory complexion. And as they visited the fashionable showrooms and attended the showings, it never occurred to her to question either his selections or his definition of her style.

"While at a bare twenty-one years of age you are still a very young woman, Anna, you must always keep in mind that you are nevertheless a great lady, and you must dress like one, which means clothes of elegance and timeless style, not the fad of the moment. It means fine fabrics and fine cut, a look of refinement. But it doesn't mean you should be the subdued brown mouse either. Each and every piece of clothing you wear, even the play clothes, must make a definite statement."

Accordingly, he chose every last article with an eye to the dramatic, from the Dior jumpsuits and the little Halston skimps and the Chanel suits to the magnificent gold lamé ball gown by Saint-Laurent. No facet of her wardrobe was neglected. There were furs from Fendi and shoes from Balley and Ferrigamo, and riding boots, soft as butter, hand-fitted and handmade by the best bootmaker in Rome.

There were handbags from Gucci and scarves from Hermés, and always there was the jewelry, each piece a dramatic statement by itself. And there was a new set of matched luggage. The luggage she had first crossed the ocean with and then the Strait of Gibraltar was not only battered and shabby by now, but bore the wrong initials—L.V. for Louis Vuitton. Gino insisted that a great lady's luggage bore *her* initials . . . a discreetly stamped-in-gold A.S. for Ann Sommer.

They became a team. Gino put her to work, and just in case anyone should ask, he gave her an official title. She was Gino Forenzi's special assistant, a kind of executive secretary who took care of all the little details. When Gino was in Rome, she was in Rome. When he went to the car plant in Milan, she went along, as she did when he went to London or Paris on business.

And when he took a holiday, whether it was to Port'Ercole or Biarritz or a hiatus on his yacht, the *Gaetano*, she was always present. But by her choice, the one place where she never accompanied Gino was to America, whether it was New York or California or Cambridge, Massachusetts, when Gino went to visit Gae.

And thus a lady exquisitely well dressed, beautifully well mannered, and superbly well informed, Andrianna played out her role as the right hand to the president of Forenzi Motors. She kept the appointment book, made the decisions as to how Gino's time was allotted, advised him when he had to be where and meeting with whom, monitored the production schedules of the car plants, and often was Forenzi's official spokeswoman.

She also played the hostess, whether it was the villa in Rome—old-world magnificence with gilt chairs and gilded ceilings—the chalet in Saint Moritz, more simply furnished, or the *Gaetano*, with red velvet and marble and solid gold appointments in the bathrooms, easily as opulent as any yacht moored in the harbor in Monaco opposite the Hôtel de Paris.

And she did it all magnificently, schooled as she had been by the master teacher himself.

It was the day the doctors told her that she was in remission—did it really matter whether the remission was the result of her prayers, Gino's will, or the enigmatic caprice of the disease itself?—and she was wild with excitement! It was the day they'd been waiting for—she and Gino—and she could barely restrain herself from calling him on the phone, from running through the streets to him, from shouting it over the rooftops of the city. But restrain herself she did. She wanted it to be a special occasion, a special party, for just the two of them, when she told him her wonderful news.

She arranged for a candlelit dinner in the villa that night with all the dishes that Gino enjoyed most—*insalata di peperoni all'acciugata, lumache alla Borgognona,* followed by *misto di pesce fritto* and then an extraordinary chocolate mousse. Then, when they were enjoying their coffee and brandy, she would tell him . . .

There were a few moments of silence while she waited breathlessly for Gino to speak, to exclaim, to shout exuberantly, to roar with pleasure, but he seemed speechless. Then he very deliberately set his demitasse cup back in its saucer and stood, holding his brandy glass high, to toast, most solemnly, her everlasting remission.

Then he said, "Come to me, Anna," and she did as she was told, rising from her chair and walking the length of the long dining table until she was there, in front of him, and he took her in his arms.

Then they went upstairs, where slowly he undressed her, his fingers dexterous as he undid the fastenings of her dress, his hands displaying much expertise as he touched her here and then there, with a sure knowledge of a woman's right places. When she was completely naked, he stood back to regard all of her and said reverently as if he were standing before a great work of art, "You are very beautiful, my Anna."

He allowed her to undress him — the coat, the shirt, the tie, then the belt, the trousers, the undershorts. When he too was nude, he picked her up to lay her on the bed, still covered with its heavy satin spread, and proceeded to brush every inch of her body with his full, sensuous lips, stopping to linger now and then at her most receptive places.

And then, without speaking a word, he indicated that they should reverse roles and positions, she leaning over him now and caressing all of him with her mouth, which she did gladly, eager to please, and continued to do so until he indicated, again mutely, her next move.

Accordingly she took him in her mouth as he lightly held her head and she sucked him gently. When she felt the increased pressure of his hands on her head, she took

257

him deeper into her mouth, increasing her pace and the pressure of her tongue and contracting the muscles of her cheeks until he moaned softly but then withdrew himself.

Again he assumed the upper position, inserting his hardness into her, and with deliberate, knowing thrusts brought them both to climax, after which he again kissed and caressed her, but this time murmuring sweet, warm words, creating a perfect after-glow.

And Andrianna was pleased that they were at last lovers, happy that she was able to give so much pleasure to her lover.

The next evening they made love again. But this time it was all passion and violence and a torrid eruption of sex rather than tender and unhurried love, and when they were finished there were tears, sweat, and even blood from the biting and tearing and scratching.

The next time they made love was different again, when she dressed for her role rather than undressed, wearing a lacy black corselette with garters attached to black net stockings and red high-heeled pumps in which she danced for her audience of one.

It wasn't until they'd been lovers for several weeks, indulging in the varied rites of sex, that it dawned on Andrianna that they weren't really performing as lovers, the common denominator being love and passion, different in their needs perhaps but still equals. They were lovers but still teacher and student—Gino teaching her, the eager pupil, how to be the perfect mistress, knowledgeable in all the ways there were to please a man.

But she didn't object. After all Gino had done for her, pleasing him was uppermost in her desire, superseding all other needs and desires. She loved him! How could she not? And certainly he loved her. He showered her with love in a million different ways.

The day Gae came home from Cambridge with his master's degree in hand, ready to take his place in the family business alongside Gino, they threw a great party at the villa, Andrianna planning it all and choosing a theme. It was to be a white-on-white party from the food and table linens and flowers down to the canopied terrace and the umbrellas that shaded all the little round tables, and the invitations instructed all the guests to dress in white only.

Andrianna, in white chiffon, her ebony hair a cloud of contrast under a big, white garden-party hat, thought she had never seen Gae look so stunning. The white suit he wore complemented his dark good looks perfectly, and she thought of how in Marbella he had often worn all white yet had never been as beautiful then as he seemed to her now. Maybe it was because he had been but a boy then, and now he was a man, mature and brimming with self-confidence.

He hugged her continuously as if the best part of the party was that she was there. "You are especially beautiful today, Anna."

"That's funny." She laughed. "That was exactly what I was thinking about you."

He shook a finger at her. "A man is not beautiful and I *must* be a man. I am no longer a schoolboy, after all. You must call me handsome now, not beautiful."

"I'm sorry," she said, "but the father is handsome and his son is beautiful."

"Ah, my papa. I am still the pretty boy, and he is still the handsome one, still the only man in the family."

Gae said it in humor, but she detected an edge.

"Oh, Gae, it's not like that at all. It's just that—well, I think you will always be beautiful to me." She took his arm. "You don't really mind, do you?"

He shook his head. "I could never mind anything you

259

say, Anna, or anything you do. You will always be too special to me for me to mind anything about you."

She hoped that this was true and that he would feel the same when he found out that she and his papa were lovers. She wondered when Gino would tell him. That night? Or maybe Gino would think that the next day would be best, when everyone was rested and everything was quiet.

"Your father is so proud of you . . . so happy that you're going to be working with him at Forenzi Motors."

"Can I tell you something?" He bent down and whispered in her ear. "I'd still much rather race cars than make them."

She laughed, shaking her head at him. "Oh, Gae, you *are* still the same, aren't you? You haven't changed at all. You're still the naughty boy."

"You wouldn't want me to change all that much, would you?"

No, she thought, not all that much.

"*You* have changed, you know," he said thoughtfully. "Quite a lot."

"Maybe it's because I'm well now. Reasonably well, anyway." *Or maybe it's just that I've grown up.*

"Yes, it's a year already that you've been in remission. That's so good, Anna. So good!" And he hugged her again and kissed her.

And then Gino was there, all smiles and hugging them both, pleased to see that they were still friends.

Then, when Gae drifted off to talk to other old friends, Gino said, "You didn't say anything to him . . . about us?"

"No. I thought you would want to do that."

"Yes, of course. But I don't think we should be in any hurry. I think we should give Gae a chance to settle into things. To reorient himself."

They hadn't discussed this before, although they should have, Andrianna reflected. "Why? Do you think he will resent . . . mind us being lovers?"

Gino shrugged, a gesture much like Gae's own. "Who can tell? Perhaps . . . And I don't want to get off on the wrong foot with him now that he is finally back for good."

Then, never having taken his eyes off Gae, he frowned. "Look who he's talking to now! That shark, Lucianna Capriatto! And look how she's rubbing up against him! She has her teeth out for every good-looking man with a few lire to his name! Why did you invite her?"

Andrianna laughed. "Because Gae and Lucianna were friends when they were young. You told me to invite all of Gae's old friends. Besides, Lucianna is hardly a shark. She's an exceptionally pretty girl who has plenty of money of her own."

"I don't like her. She runs with a very fast crowd. And you know I am always right about these things, Anna. Would you do me a favor and go over there and break it up? Take Gae around yourself to meet all the people he doesn't know."

When the party was about over and Andrianna, exhausted, was looking forward to a quiet evening relaxing with Gae and Gino, Gino suddenly invited everyone still left at the villa to join him and Gae and Anna for a late dinner at Galeassi's in the Piazza Santa Maria di Trastevere, a particularly lovely spot. She was amazed. After being with so many people for so many hours, didn't Gino want to be alone with her and Gae?

But even then, after dinner and well past midnight, Gino invited everyone to go on to the 84 Club, where they sat in the back, these being the "good" tables reserved for the elite of Roman society and whatever jet-setters were in town. The Emilio Puccis were there as well as the Infant Beatriz of Spain, and Gino asked them to join their party, telling them the 84 was a favorite of his because of its excellent band. But no sooner had he said that than he refused to dance with Andrianna, claiming he was too tired and, probably, too old as well. He insisted that she and Gae dance together since they were both superb dancers, a treat for everyone else to watch.

By the time they came home again it was past four, and there was no question of Andrianna joining Gino in his bedroom. Then, when she awoke in the morning, Gino was gone and there was a note saying he had an emergency in Milan to deal with and probably wouldn't be back for several days. But in the meantime, before he knew that he would be called away, he had served notice on the captain of the *Gaetano* to get everything ready for a few days' cruise, and since everything was in readiness, why didn't she and Gae go ahead without him? He would see them when they got back.

But when she and Gae did get back after a wonderful four days spent mostly reminiscing about the good old days at Le Rosey, they found Gino at home immersed in business, and he barely greeted them before telling them that he was dispatching the two of them to Japan to investigate the possibilities of opening a Forenzi plant there. By now Anna was knowledgeable enough to handle such an assignment, and it was a good way for Gae to get his feet wet. Gino had already made arrangements for them to leave the following day.

That night Gino went out, having made private plans for the evening, and when he returned Andrianna, desperate to speak with him alone, found his bedroom door locked and no response when she knocked.

But it wasn't until she was alone in her hotel room in

Tokyo, suspecting that she'd been sent off on a wild-goose chase with nothing really happening, with Gae off somewhere in a geisha teahouse or taking one of those baths (the leopard not truly changing his spots), that it all sank in.

She had had sex with Gino Forenzi, but they had never really been lovers. They had only been master and disciple, with her in training to be the best kind of knowledgeable and cultured wife, one who knew how to please a husband in *every* way, from bedroom to boardroom, from restaurant to dining room to salon, and looking great all the way.

There was no anger, just regret. Gino *had* cared for her, cared enough to choose her out of all the others for Gaetano's wife. But in doing so he had sold the three of them short.

"I can't stay here with you and Gae any longer. You must realize that the situation has become impossible."

"Don't be too hasty, Anna," Gino warned. "You need us, and we—Gae and I—need you. There is no one else who—"

"But don't you see?" she interrupted him. "Your whole premise has been wrong from the beginning. Gae and I . . . our time has come and gone. All the affection I had for him and he for me—it's still there but in a different form. There's only loving friendship left between us, and it's not enough for—for what you want . . ."

"And us? You and me?"

She knew he was just playing for time now, trying to think of something to say that would keep her there.

"Oh, Gino. You probably saved my life, and for that I will always be grateful. And you've been wonderfully good to me, only I'm afraid that as far as you and I are concerned, we existed as a couple for the wrong reasons.

263

And it's hard to make something that started out wrong come out right."

"I do love you, Anna. Very much. I loved you so much that I wanted you for—You must stay here with us and work in the business until you're ready to go out on your own."

"I'm ready."

"You are not!" he said sternly.

"I must be."

"But where will you go? What will you do?"

In answer she gave him one of his and Gae's Latin shrugs. "I will go somewhere. I will do something."

Finally Gino accepted that it was over and he wouldn't be able to change her mind. "I will make a settlement on you. At least enough to keep you until—"

"No. I know you mean only the best, Gino, but I have to strike out on my own. It is time. And I'm returning all the jewelry you've given me."

"No, that I will not accept. Whatever else my intentions—and I cannot really be faulted for wanting a wonderful, courageous woman for my son—the jewelry were gifts given in love . . . more love, perhaps, than you will ever realize." His eyes implored her to understand.

And then she did understand. In his way Gino Forenzi was making a supreme sacrifice in the name of love. Love for his son. Oh, he loved her too. She would never doubt that. He loved her very much, but not *quite* enough. He loved her both as a lover and as a father. But the problem was as a father he loved *more,* and as a father he would always put Gae first, and he could not, would not, take the chance that Gae would not understand, would not accept them—Andrianna and Gino—as lovers or as man and wife.

"I understand," she said.

"Do you? Then you must keep the jewelry. It is bad

luck to return gifts of love and bad luck for the giver to take them back. And one more thing, Anna, that I beg you to remember — you are only in remission, and in the future you may need whatever you can turn into cash. Keep the jewelry and hoard it against the future. But don't turn it into cash until you must. There is one thing about precious stones and metals that you must remember. People will let you down, your own body can turn against you as you have already experienced, great companies can collapse, and countries will tumble and with them their paper currency, but one thing lasts and retains its value — the hard, cold currency of precious gems and gold. And the men and women who are in possession of this hard international currency will always survive.

"If I have taught you nothing else, let that be my supreme contribution to your education. Always keep what can be turned into cash no matter where you are and whatever your circumstances. And always remember that I am your friend, that I love you, and know that you can count on me . . . always."

"Oh, Gino . . . Gino!" She could not hold back the tears. "Do you think that of all the things you have taught me I haven't learned *that?*"

Yes, she knew that all of it was true. That he was her friend, even that he loved her, and that she could count on him always . . . until the end of time. But why, then, did she feel so cheated?

Nineteen

Tuesday, twilight

"Since we're here at Cipriani's, you must have a Bellini," Penny declared enthusiastically, shrugging off her coat.

"I'll bite. Why must I?"

"Because you always drink champagne, and a Bellini *is* champagne with peach juice or a whole peach, and it all started at Harry's in Venice. It was Hemingway's favorite summer drink. He drank them for hours on end—long, lovely, Venetian summer afternoons."

"That's fascinating, but I think I'll just have an Evian since I've already had quite a bit of champagne. And since you have had quite a lot of vodka, I suggest that you do the same."

"I agree, I've had enough vodka. So I'm going to have a Marty, which is a return to the martini as it was in its heyday, before it was corrupted by using vodka instead of gin."

"Oh, my, corrupted is it?"

Penny tossed her red mane. "Make fun if you will. You never did take the important things seriously, Annie."

"Oh? And what *are* the important things, Penny love?"

"Oh, you know, even if you pretend not to—marriage to a wonderful man, a home, babies, and a solid bank account."

"And drinking the perfect Marty, of course," Andrianna added dryly while she reflected that if Penny was right about what was truly important, then she herself had *nothing* of importance.

But that was beside the point, and she was determined not to let any more sad introspection spoil their afternoon. After the waiter went off to fetch their order, she said brightly, "So, you and Gae, I take it, are counting on having babies. How many are on the schedule?"

"Well, considering my age, which is, well . . ." Penny's voice drifted off vaguely.

"Honestly, Penny, we *are* the same age, so there's no use in beating about the bush with me. So why—? Oh, Penny, you *didn't* lie about your age to Gae, did you? Because he knows *my* age, and he knows that you and I are about the same age, so—"

"He's not the one I lied to," Penny said guiltily, lighting a cigarette with nervous, carmine-tipped fingers.

"Whom did you lie to?"

"Gae's father, Gino. But you won't tell him the truth, will you?"

"Of course not. Anyway, I haven't been in touch with Gino for years, and I'm not likely to be in the near future."

"But you will be—"

"Why do you say that?"

"Because my wedding is in January. And it's going to be in Los Angeles . . . in Bel-Air to be precise, at the Hotel Bel-Air, and he's coming and you're coming. As a matter of fact, Gino's going to be Gae's best man, and you are going to be my maid of honor, along with Nicole. Well, actually, Nicole's going to be the matron of honor."

Andrianna was taken aback. How could she possibly attend a wedding with Gae as groom, Gino as best man, in Los Angeles, which was Jonathan West's hometown? Even if all her reasons for *not* going were completely irrational, it was out of the question.

"Hold on, Penny. I never said for sure I'd be your maid of honor—"

"I'm not taking no for an answer, so you might as well make your mind up that you are."

"But I don't even know if I'll be able to *make* it . . ."

"Why not? Where will you be that you won't be able to make it? On the moon? May I point out that Bel-Air in Los Angeles, California, is completely accessible these days from any place in the world or—"

Andrianna saw that there was no reasoning with Penny. "All right. I give up. I'll come to your old wedding. So tell me. How old did you tell Gino you are?"

"Thirty-five."

"My, *that* old?" Andrianna drawled. "But why did you clip off only a couple of years? While you were at it, why didn't you take off a few more?"

"Well, if I'd said I was thirty or so, he might have thought I looked old for my age, and that would have been even worse than the truth. Besides, I didn't want to tell such a really *big* lie."

"But why lie at all?"

"Because of the babies. Look, I want Gino Forenzi to like me and *want* me for a daughter-in-law so there won't be any problems. And Gino wants babies, dozens of them. To him the bambinos mean that Gae means business and is really ready to settle down. And if I had said I was thirty-seven, all Gino would have had to do was a quick bit of arithmetic to figure out that all I had time for was a couple of kiddies, whereas thirty-five sounds like there's a little room there for some latitude."

The waiter set their drinks down, and Penny made a quick grab for hers. "Oh, Annie, I really want him to

268

like me."

"If you really want Gino to like you, Penny, all you have to do is convince him that you love Gae very much and that you're a terrific lady, which you are. And whatever you do, don't you dare even *think* of playing kneesies with him under the table just to ensure your popularity."

Penny gave a loud whoop. "Really, Annie, what makes you think it would ever even occur to me to do such a thing?"

Andrianna just gave her a look.

"Oh, all right, I might have *thought* of it, but I wouldn't actually *do* it! But I must admit, sixtyish or whatever, Gino Forenzi is still one hell of an attractive man, and as Lily Mae Turner back home would say, 'I wouldn't mind having his little old slippers parked under my bed any old time.'"

They giggled, almost like in the old days, and Penny took another sip of her martini.

"So how is it? Does it taste like the martini in its heyday?"

"How would I know? I wasn't even born then. Actually the only time I drank gin was in *my* heyday, when I was sweet sixteen. Well, not all that sweet. But it was in Marbella at the Rogue. Remember how we loved those gin and tonics?"

Remember? Oh yes! The trouble with old friends like Penny was that you never really got to quite forget the past.

"There's one thing I don't understand. Why *are* you being married in Los Angeles? I've always been under the impression that if there's to be a big wedding it's usually in the bride's hometown or, at the very least, the groom's."

"Well, Daddy's got this bee in his bonnet about the Hotel Bel-Air. It seems the hotel is a kind of Hollywood

269

landmark or something and very beautiful. Besides which, it's considered so chic that the Reagans' daughter Patti was married there. And Daddy says if the hotel's good enough for old Nancy's daughter then it's good enough for his. Anyway, the hotel is owned by one of our hometown gals, Caroline Shoellkopf, who's one of the Dallas Hunts, which probably doesn't mean anything to you, but the Hunts make the Ewings of 'Dallas' look like paupers.

"Well, anyhow, the story goes that Caroline and her daddy were staying at the hotel when Caroline said to Daddy that she'd just love to have the hotel for her own, and so Daddy just upped and bought it for her. So now *my* daddy's got it into his head that he wants to buy it for *his* daughter as a wedding present. You have to understand that everyone in oil in Dallas is very competitive, and Daddy figures what H. L. Hunt can do he can do. So we're going to have the wedding there and check the place out, and if we like it Daddy's going to make an offer."

"But is the hotel on the market? Is it for sale?" Andrianna asked, her brain whirling from Penny's long monologue.

"That's beside the point. Daddy says *everything's* for sale. All you have to do is make an offer they can't refuse. Understand?"

"I think so," Andrianna said, but she wasn't really sure she did. She'd always known that the really rich were different from everyone else, but now she was beginning to see that Americans—especially those from Texas, and maybe California—were even *more* different. Then she wondered if Jonathan West fell into this category. All she really knew about him was that he was different from any other man she had ever known . . .

When she'd made her exit from his suite on the *QE2,*

270

he had not reacted the way all the other men had. Certainly he'd been angry, but it hadn't been the anger of a man who'd lost a prize he'd thought he'd bought . . . or stolen. It had been the wounded rage of a man betrayed.

"You know, a terrible thought has just occurred to me," Penny said as she touched up her eyelashes at the table with a mascara wand.

"Oh, God! I hope it's not too terribly terrible."

"Well, it's all in how you look at it. We're due at Nicole's at seven, right?"

"I believe that's what you said."

"Well, if she doesn't serve her sure-to-be-extraordinary dinner until ten, and my flight back to Dallas leaves at one, that doesn't leave me much time to eat. Do you know what I think we should do?"

"What?"

"Without so much as a telephone call, I think we should pop in on Nicole right now."

"But it's only a little past five. I don't think she'd appreciate being popped in on almost two hours before she's expecting us."

"Exactly. You know Nicole. She always has everything so tightly under control that it makes my head ache. Before she stepped on the plane today, you can be sure her butler here had already received his instructions as to precisely which pieces of silver should be polished for our little dinner tonight, and the cook probably had the complete menu handwritten in French by Nicole herself. She probably faxed it in, and the cook received it on her own little fax machine, which stands next to all those little pots of homegrown herbs. Anyway, this is our one chance to catch Nicole unprepared, in an old bathrobe without her makeup on and with the canapés yet to be made! She'll probably faint at being caught with her panties down."

"No, Penny. It's too mean."

"Oh, come on! It will be like the good old days, when we used to do things that were naughty but fun, before we grew up and had to learn to do all these proper things adults do.

"Please, Annie, do it for me, do it for Nicole! Honestly, it will be so good for her to get a bit of a shaking up. It will teach her not to be so rigid and to give a little. Otherwise, if she's not careful, she'll turn into a stone. You know, like a pillar of salt, and then it will be all over for her. And it will be *your* fault, because you could have saved her but didn't, and then later, when she's on exhibit in a museum or a sideshow maybe, billed as the stone woman, you'll say sadly, 'Poor Nicole! She's a stone now. If only I had gone to see her that day at five o'clock instead of at seven, this wouldn't have happened. She'd still be *très chic* Nicole instead of this big, cold, hard rock.'"

Andrianna laughed so hard she couldn't catch her breath. "All right, we'll go pop in on Nicole. Anything to keep her from this terrible fate."

Actually Andrianna felt sorry for Nicole but was grateful to Penny. She hadn't laughed like that in years. Hoping that Penny would make another one of her funny observations, she asked: "So how do you think Harry Cipriani's in New York stacks up against Harry's in Italy?"

But now Penny sounded a bit sad. "How can you really compare the two? They're worlds apart, and there's the time span. The time in Rome was *then* and it was wonderful to be young and drinking wine on the Via Veneto, and you know what they say about Rome—see Rome and die. But this is today in New York and this is our life now and we have to get on with it. Right?"

Andrianna nodded. "Right. But the expression goes—see *Naples* and die—not Rome."

"Oh. Well, maybe there's a Harry's Bar in Naples too, so what the hell? Right, Annie old girl?"

"Right, Penny old love."

They walked out onto Fifth Avenue. "Trump Tower is a couple of blocks down yonder," Penny said.

Then Andrianna thought she spotted the same limousine again, the one in which she'd thought she'd seen the ghost of Jonathan West. She shook her head as if to clear it. All limousines looked alike really, and the real Jonathan West was back in Los Angeles, taking the sun and making his money grow.

"You look funny, Annie. You're so pale. Is something wrong? Are we walking the wrong way, you think?"

"I don't think so, but I'm not sure. This is foreign territory for me."

"Ah, Annie my love, isn't it *all* foreign territory?"

"They're going into the Trump Tower, boss."

"Do me a favor, Rennie, and don't call me boss," Jonathan said irritably.

Some boss he was! Wasting his precious hours waiting around for some woman he barely knew to emerge from elevators, restaurants, and bars while his financial affairs went down the drain. What the hell was he doing? The tremendous sum of knowledge he'd amassed for his trouble amounted to this: the woman he'd known as Andrianna DeArte was occupying the Plaza suite of billionaire Gaetano Forenzi under the name of Anna della Rosa and had a red-haired girlfriend who liked restaurants with a Russian flavor and the drinks at Cipriani's. *Terrific!*

"Call me Jonathan, Rennie, or call me Mr. West. You

273

can even call me dickhead, if you must. Just don't call me boss! Okay?"

"Sure, Mr. West. Whatever you say. But do you want for us to sit here until they come back out of the Don's Tower?"

"The Don's Tower?"

"Yeah. Didn't you know that's what Ivana—Trump's old lady—calls her husband?"

"Is that so?" Well, what the hell? It was cuter than calling him "boss" and safer. The feminists would really have chewed her ass out for calling him "boss."

"No, as a matter of fact, Rennie, I don't want for *us* to sit here. What I want is for *me* to sit here and for *you* to go into the lobby and find out where they went."

"Boy oh boy, Mr. West, you sure haven't learned much about tailing someone. Do you really think the security guys are gonna tell me who *lives* in what apartment, much less who's going where? You see, the Don himself and his Ivana have the penthouse apartment, a triplex. I read where it covers the whole top of the building and they're putting in a park and playground up there too for their kids, with statues and waterfalls and gazebos—the works. Now, if you lived in that penthouse with your wife and kids, would you dream of not having the best security in the world? The security's probably tighter in there than if they had the Secret Service on the job!"

Of course Rennie was right about the security. Donald Trump was no fool! Only he, himself *was* . . . the biggest fool and asshole in either New York or L.A.

Was it any wonder Trump had a fortune that ran into the billions while he himself hadn't even reached the half-way mark of the first big one? Would the Don waste his time sitting in cars and lobbies chasing a woman who had probably forgotten his name the minute she walked out of his door? No, he fucking well wouldn't, and he, the Don, owned the fucking hotel where he, West the asshole, had already wasted too many fucking hours sitting around.

Well, tonight would be the last of it. Tomorrow he would head on home. At least, if you took good care of it, nurtured it, and thought of nothing else, a billion dollars could give a man a hell of a lot more happy nights, or golden afternoons for that matter, than any woman could. Unless, of course, you were the Don, who had his cake and his Ivana too.

Twenty

Tuesday evening

"Oh, thank God, you're both here safe and in one piece. I can't tell you how worried I was about you two!" Nicole cried, greeting them with effusive kisses European style, while Penny stood open-mouthed with shock. Nicole had come to the door herself, clothed not in an old bathrobe but in a short black silk dinner dress, perfectly made up, every silvery blond hair immaculately in place.

Nicole quickly helped them off with their coats, which she handed to the waiting butler, Charles, and ushered them into the salon, where a friendly fire was going and a drinks table, complete with a Cartier crystal ice bucket, was set up.

Seeing everything in such perfect readiness, a chagrined Penny sharply demanded, "And why were you so worried about us, Nicole? Why, for God's sake, would you assume that we *weren't* safe and in one piece?"

"I was worried because I couldn't find you. When I tried to reach you at the Plaza, they said they had no guests with either of your names."

"That's not so hard to understand. I haven't even been to the Plaza this trip, and Annie's staying in Gae's suite, registered as Anna della Rosa for some reason or other. But why were you trying to find us? Did you think we were lost?" She grinned, enjoying her own little joke.

276

"No, you imbecile. I didn't think you were lost. It's just that I realized that since you are going back to Dallas late tonight it was foolish for you two not to come earlier than we planned. So it was my intention, if I reached you, to tell you to come over immediately. But apparently you arrived at the same conclusion since you are here and all is well. Now sit down, both of you, and I will get you something to drink."

As she turned away toward the liquor table, Andrianna took the opportunity to murmur to Penny, "See? Not so rigid after all."

In answer Penny tossed her head of bright red waves and gestured to the several flower arrangements standing on various tabletops around the room. Tulips only, in every possible color, set in faience cachepots just as she had predicted, as well as in crystal vases and Limoges bowls. "Do I know my business or do I not?"

She sat down next to Andrianna on the sofa upholstered in pale blue silk as Nicole said, "Now, what will you have to drink? An aperitif? White wine? Or would you prefer champagne?"

Andrianna said she would have the champagne, but Penny asked for a martini.

"A martini? *Hard* liquor? I refuse to make it for you," Nicole said severely. "If you insist on having one, you'll have to go to hell all by yourself. Perhaps Charles will be willing to prepare it for you when he brings in *les hors d'oeuvres froids*. But I can't guarantee that he will be any more willing than I am since he's French too, and I'm sure he thinks women should drink only wine, out of deference to their physical appearance, if nothing else."

"Oh, screw you, Nicole Austin, and your *hors d'oeuvres froids* and your French butler! I'll make my own goddamned martini."

Penny got up and went to the drinks table as Nicole stood over her nagging, warning her that she was going to be sorry when all that alcohol-inspired puffiness under her eyes ceased to respond to a water pill, and Penny retorted that a little alcohol was just what the doctor would recommend for Nicole—"to keep your already cold blood from freezing over."

"Come on, girls," Andrianna urged. "Let's get off it. We don't get together but once a year or so. Must you two spend the whole time going at one another?"

She knew, of course, that, yes, they must. That's the way it had been between them ever since the early days at Le Rosey. They were so different that, had it not been for their shared friendship with Andrianna, they probably never would have become friends themselves. And each had always resented certain qualities the other had. Like Nicole's just being *too* French for Penny's taste, with her redoubtable Parisian style never showing the slightest crack. There was no denying that everything Nicole did and everything she owned was perfection. Maybe what it boiled down to was that Nicole always made everyone else feel slightly déclassé. As for Nicole, what probably bothered her most about Penny was her "I totally don't give a shit" attitude, her warmth, openness, and total insouciance.

And perhaps, Andrianna admitted sadly to herself, she envied them both. Nicole knew exactly where she belonged in the world, and Penny was sure she owned it. But most of all she envied their tumultuous, yet undeniably close, friendship. In truth Nicole and Penny had seen more of each other over the years than either had seen of her, and despite the schoolgirl ties among all three, the ruse that had more firmly supplanted the real Andrianna with every passing year had left her on the outskirts of the trio, listening to *their* life stories while parrying requests for hers. More and more she had felt like a fading photograph of herself, propped up between her friends like any other memento of the good old days. Anyway, nothing she could say was going to stop the two of them from their squabbling, so she might as well lean back and enjoy it.

When Charles appeared with a huge silver tray, Nicole told him he could just set the tray down on the coffee table and return to the kitchen since he had enough to do there.

"What's going on here, Nicole?" Penny demanded, sucking on the olive from her martini. "Charles took the coats, Charles brought in *les hors d'oeuvres,* and now Charles has to go back to the kitchen to see about dinner. What's happened to the big staff?"

Nicole smiled. "You're behind the times, *cherie.* It is no longer the style to be so excessive and, shall we say, wasteful? In the world we live in today, with so many going hungry and homeless, it is inappropriate to maintain a staff in a *pied-à-terre* one occupies only infrequently."

Chalk one up for Nicole.

"Oh, I couldn't agree with you more, Nicole honey chile, but what about the standards? There's nothing more revolting, I always say, than *luxe* which is neglected. Inches of dust on the Louis XVI étagère and that sort of thing, with cockroaches running wild in the kitchen."

"You are so droll, Penny sweet. But there isn't a cockroach within miles of my kitchen or a fleck of dust anywhere. Charles maintains the apartment very well with the aid of cleaning women who come in by the day as needed."

Another half a point for Nicole.

But then Penny's eyes focused in on the tray of hors d'oeuvres—rounds of toast with caviar topped with a dab of sour cream, bright pink shrimp accompanied by a dip the color of dark red wine, delicate pale curls of *saumon fumé* resting on squares of dark bread, and *coeur d'artichaut au crabe*—and she screamed with the delight of discovery. "Now what do you call that if not excessive and wasteful? There are only three of us and enough *hors d'oeuvres froids* to choke a horse."

That's one for Penny.

279

But this time Nicole didn't have a tart rejoinder. It was more of a wounded reproach. Tossing pale blond hair that fell forward on one cheek and was tucked back on the other—the latest in French styling, Andrianna noted—she pouted, "You are such an ingrate, Penny. I was just trying to please you. Suppose I served only the artichoke hearts and you didn't like artichoke hearts. What then?"

"What then?" A chastened Penny, touched by Nicole's "I just wanted to please you," talked through a mouthful of smoked salmon and black bread. "Well, if there were only artichoke hearts, which it is true I despise, I wouldn't have a nervous breakdown. I would just do without and suffer along 'til dinner was served. And if, for once, you weren't the perfect hostess, the world wouldn't come to an end either. But speaking of dinner, you *are* serving it, I take it, even though there is no cook in residence?" Penny selected a shrimp and dipped it in the accompanying sauce.

Now Nicole laughed, showing her pretty white teeth, and poured herself some more champagne. "Of course I am serving dinner. Knowing what a greedy little pig my good friend is, how could I not serve you dinner, Penny my darling?"

"Up yours, Nicole. Better a greedy little pig than a fucking tightass." But there was no rancor in the remark.

"So, Nicole, who *did* cook dinner? Is it catered, or is that marvel of a French hausfrau, Charles, the guilty party?"

"Oh, Charles is looking after things in the kitchen now, but it is I who cooked the dinner." She laughed at the incredulous look on Penny's face.

"You? I don't believe it!"

"Oh, it is nothing very grand," Nicole said modestly. "And I am French, you know."

"Oh, Lordy, could we ever forget it?"

* * *

Dinner was, as Nicole had claimed, a simple affair consisting of only three courses. But Nicole named each of the courses in French—*la salade cresson et champignons, la côte de veau aux artichauts et tomates,* followed by *charlotte aux pommes*—with an accompanying commentary on each of the wines served with each course, which Andrianna knew was certain to drive Penny up the wall.

"You know, Nicole," Penny exploded on cue, "you really piss me off with all this French shit. If you're so in love with everything French, why the hell did you marry an American? Were you so crazy in love with him?"

And then suddenly, in a matter of seconds, Nicole, who had been discoursing animatedly and complacently, looked as if she might be cracking at the seams. But then she caught herself and straightened up, her back a ramrod in her chair. "I married Edward because he was eminently eligible and appropriate, and I have never regretted it."

"Haven't you?" Penny asked. "Are you sure about that?"

Now Penny was no longer kidding, but Andrianna, at least, could tell she wasn't trying to torment their friend. She just wanted to *know.* Still, by the look on Nicole's face, she could tell Nicole wasn't taking kindly to the inquiry.

"Excuse me for breaking in," Andrianna said hastily, "but before I forget, Penny, I meant to ask you if you wanted Nicole and me to wear matching dresses for the wedding. If you do, Nicole and I have to make plans to coordinate."

Both Penny and Nicole ignored her.

"I'm sure I made the right choice," Nicole said stiffly. "Edward has lived up to all expectations and has kept his part of the bargain. That is what a marriage is, after all—a bargain, a contract. And I have kept mine. Oh, I know what you think! That he's old and unexciting. And that I've been shortchanged, that I've missed out on something. What? Multiple orgasms? But I didn't get married for sex. A woman who marries for sex is a bigger fool than a

281

woman who marries for love. *Maman* said if the marriage was appropriate, love would follow, and she was right."

"So you *are* in love with Edward?" Penny was relentless.

Nicole was cold. "If you mean by love that there is caring and respect, yes. Edward is kind and considerate and has always been faithful. That is one of the reasons I was agreeable to marrying him . . . an American . . . an *older* American. Frenchmen have this tendency for love affairs on the side—it is part of the accepted pattern, which of course leaves the woman free to have her own love affairs on the side, and that is fine for some. But not for me. I refuse to dirty up my life with that sort of thing." She wrinkled her nose as if she smelled something bad. "And I didn't wish to tolerate it in a husband. Don't you understand? I knew exactly what I was getting, and I was not disappointed."

She looked down into her wineglass. "I have never been disappointed in Edward."

Penny narrowed her eyes. "What you mean, then, was that you married Edward simply because you were *afraid* . . . afraid of being disappointed, afraid of—"

"Penny, you're going too far," Andrianna protested.

"No, Ann, let her. Does it matter what she says? Look at her record. Two miserable marriages and two messy divorces. And now she's ready to rush headlong into her third, and whom does she pick? Gaetano Forenzi, who is not exactly poor—the money counts with her too—but who is, unlike Edward, fairly young, handsome, romantic, and sexy. Oh yes, very, very sexy. But steady, respectable, sincere, and trustworthy?"

Her mouth formed a thin, bitter smile. "At first there will be this thing called passion, and marvelous sex. At first he will be tearing the clothes off her body, but then in a matter of months he'll be tearing the clothes off someone else—an eighteen-year-old maybe, with a fresher skin and a firmer body—which she will then use as an excuse to

take her own lovers. Young, old, handsome, not handsome
. . . no matter. She will take whomever she can get. And
then what? Then there will be just another disgustingly
sordid marriage and probably another messy divorce."

"You cunt! You tightassed, smug little prig of a bitch!
What you can't stand to face is that Gae and I are in love!
Romantic, sexy love! Something you've never had. Or if
you had it, you were afraid to take a chance on it. That's
what's bugging you, isn't it?"

Andrianna couldn't bear to listen to their harsh, ugly
words. If she knew what to say to stop them, she would,
but she didn't know the words. But then who was she after
all, to interject herself into this conversation? What did she
know? Had she ever lived a *real life?* Barely. Rather, she
had lived on the fringes and in the shadows, a pretender at
the game.

Who was right? Penny, who had always rushed helter-
skelter into life, tasting, sampling, fingering everything like
a greedy child? Bound to get burned some of the time and
then doused with the cold water that was needed to put
out the fire, but in the process enjoying the laughs, experiencing the highs, reveling in the exquisite moments . . .

Or was it Nicole, who always played it safe, afraid to
take a chance, whether it was skiing, or even drinking
what she called "hard liquor," or disobeying her mother's
prescription for the "correct" marriage? Even now, correctly married and terribly chic as she was, Nicole always
wore black. Black was safe — one could never make a mistake wearing black. Even this apartment in New York,
where she could have experimented with bold strokes of
new images, resembled her apartment in France, down to
the same color scheme and the same Louis XVI appointments. As if she'd thought that if it worked once with successful perfection, why take a chance on something new?

When the turbulence in the room seemed to have died
down and the atmosphere appeared calm, Andrianna

turned her attention back to her friends only to hear Penny ask in a soft but intense voice, "If your marriage is so wonderful and your life so complete, what about children? Even men Edward's age — and you married him fifteen years ago — can still father children, and most men like him want an heir, so where are the children?"

There was dead silence for a moment, until Nicole answered with restrained dignity. "You are a good friend and a dear one, Penny, but there are some things that are to be discussed only between husband and wife."

Andrianna saw Penny flush with color, for once embarrassed at having possibly crossed some delicate line of suitable behavior, even decency. At the same time, Andrianna realized, Nicole had managed *not* to answer the question.

Where were the children? Having children was like buying a blind item at an auction, a risky business. You never knew for sure what you were going to get, and you had to be willing to take a chance.

Again Andrianna asked herself who was right. Penny, recklessly embracing life's pleasures, risking havoc and pain, or Nicole, with her built-in safety factors holding her tightly in their grip?

Somewhere in the back of her head, there was an echo. *No pain, no gain.*

They went back and forth at it, and sometimes it seemed as if there were no holds barred. But then, when Andrianna reminded Penny that if she didn't leave at once she was going to miss her plane, she was amazed to hear Penny answer blithely, "Screw the plane! They'll be flying in the morning, won't they? Can't you see I'm having a *très important* conversation here with my friend Nicole?"

And then she was equally amazed to see Nicole smiling, green eyes sparkling with pleasure, to hear her archly replying, "Since my friend Penny has been so irresponsible

284

as to have missed her flight, and since she has been so gauche as to have monopolized the conversation all evening, hardly giving me a chance to talk with you, Ann *cherie*, I insist you both sleep over instead of going back to the hotel. That way we'll be able to have a wonderful time talking all night, just like the old days."

Andrianna, delighted, shrugged and laughed and kicked off her pumps the better to settle in.

"We still have so much to talk about," Nicole said happily, kicking off her pumps too and tucking her off-black-hosed legs under her. "We have to discuss your wedding, Penny Lee Hopkins Poole Townsend, and decide what Ann Sommer—also known as Andrianna DeArte and Anna della Rosa, and God knows what else—and I are going to wear as your attendants that is compatible with our personal images and with each other, and of course we must talk about the menu and the wine list, because I insist on giving you the benefit of my superior knowledge on these matters. You agree?"

"Oh *certainement!*" Penny agreed. "But you will keep in mind that we can't have only French cuisine or French wines. I must consider the tastes of my prospective father-in-law—Italian . . . my daddy—down-home Texan . . . and the hotel—Continental with a California flavor. I don't know how they're going to feel about having a so heavily eclectic menu imposed on them."

"Worry not, Penny Lee. You forget my vast experience as an ambassador's wife meant pleasing all kinds of people and their individual, if odd, tastes. As for dealing with the hotel, that is also within my area of expertise. I'm quite willing to fly out there and, shall we say, 'handle' them?"

"That would be wonderful," Penny murmured, unwilling now to make any unsettling waves.

"And after we settle on a menu, or before, I have to find out from Ann why she's here suddenly, on this side of the world. Is it a part in a play, *cherie*, or is it a man?"

"Good!" Penny said, kicking off her shoes too. "Maybe you can get the truth out of her. I've been asking her that question all afternoon, and I haven't gotten anywhere. I say it's a man . . ."

Andrianna settled back into the sofa, already taunting her friends with her enigmatic and provocative smile in anticipation of their attack, ready for the game of fending off questions with silly, hopefully funny, wise-guy answers—their usual nonsense—which would inevitably end with her revealing nothing of consequence, with all three of them reduced to helpless laughter, putting aside for the moment all sad thoughts and all the troubling doubts . . .

If only she could forget completely for just a little while that her life was grounded in shifting sand, bound by the past and an uncertain future . . . tormented now by the image of a man to whom, if she dared, she could devote her future to . . . *if* she had a future. Oh, how tired she was of her empty life! And how tired she was of living it without hope or love . . .

"I just *know* it's a man," Penny said. "Why won't you just 'fess up, Annie? I know! We'll play twenty questions. And you have to answer yes or no and swear to tell the truth. Do you swear?"

"I swear."

"Okay, I'll go first. Is he bigger than a bread box—and if he is, aren't you the lucky girl?"

Twenty-one

Wednesday

Wearily Jonathan checked his watch. It was twenty after seven, and the new day hung dark and gray, but Fifth Avenue was already alive. He looked at Rennie, still asleep in the front seat, and decided to let him go on sleeping — there was no good reason to wake him. Nothing was happening, and Rennie hadn't fallen asleep until at least one in the morning. He knew because he himself hadn't drifted off for a second all through the whole dreary night as he sat futilely waiting for Andrianna to emerge. And for no good reason except that maybe it was a kind of fitting finale, a pointless ending to a pointless exercise.

Must have been one hell of a party, he thought. Not that it mattered anymore. Today, after he caught a few hours' sleep, he was going home, and Andrianna DeArte could go to fucking hell or wherever else she was headed.

But first he'd let Rennie sleep for a while longer. The poor guy had been through an exhausting two days with him, even though it seemed more like forever.

At nine-ten the redhead came out onto the sidewalk looking, Jonathan thought bitterly, as fresh as the proverbial daisy after what he presumed had been a hard day's night. Then a limo pulled up and, whoosh, the redhead was gone.

At a quarter to ten, just as a cool sun made a sudden incursion into the gray of the day, *she* emerged, and despite himself and his resolution that she was about to be a memory best forgotten, Jonathan sat up straight. He could feel his body reacting like crazy to the sight of her. And then he saw her looking straight at him, and he sucked in his breath until he realized that while she was looking at the limo—into it actually—all she could see was Rennie coming awake now in the front seat, stretching his arms, and nothing in the rear of the car, the darkened glass preventing it.

He grimaced in disappointment. While most of him knew that there was nothing to be gained from an eye-to-eye confrontation except maybe humiliation, part of him still yearned for it . . . that meeting of the eyes . . .

He watched her walk to the corner. Like her friend the redhead, she looked as fastidiously groomed as the day before, as regal as ever, and he was filled with the bitter taste of regret.

"Hey, there she is!" Rennie yelled, fully awake now, spotting Andrianna crossing the street. "Why didn't you say something? I'll start Baby up and we'll get going . . ."

"Forget it."

"Are you sure?"

"Yeah, I'm sure."

Still, they both kept their eyes on her fine, straight back as she headed for the Plaza, able to see her walking through the lobby doors. Jonathan sighed and said, "You might as well pull up in front of the hotel."

"Don't you want for me to stay with the car, ready to go, just in case?"

"No. Just leave it and come inside with me. We'll catch some breakfast."

"You sure about that?"

"Sure."

"I never ate here before," Rennie said, looking around the Palm Court. "It's real pretty. I bet these turkeys are wondering what you're doing breakfasting with a guy dressed in a driver's monkey suit."

Jonathan chuckled. "They're probably wondering what that clean-cut, clear-eyed, respectable chauffeur is doing with a red-eyed bum in rumpled clothes who obviously spent the night sleeping it off in some alley."

Rennie laughed. "Sorry about that, chief. You should have woke me."

"Look, Rennie, if you want to come and work for me in L.A., you have to stop calling me boss or chief or anything like that. Okay?"

"Sorry about that, Mr. West. Anyhow, I've been thinking about your offer, and while I appreciate it, I don't think I can take you up on it."

"Is it the money? If the money is wrong, we can do something about that. And if—"

"No, it ain't the money. Nothing like that. It's this woman friend I have . . ."

"Yes?" Jonathan put his menu down in order to give Rennie his full attention. "You two have something serious going?"

"Well, I don't know how serious it is as far as she's concerned, but I am. Her name's Judy Bryant and she's a schoolteacher. She teaches in the South Bronx, but you being from Cal, you probably don't know what the South Bronx's like."

"I've heard."

"Well, then you know it's a rough place. And Judy lives down on Twenty-third Street on the West Side and has to travel back and forth every day to the South Bronx, and I worry about her, you know? So whenever I'm not working early in the morning or late afternoon I take her to work and pick her up. It might sound foolish to you, but if I was in L.A. enjoying the weather, I think I'd be worrying about Judy riding the subway and walking those mean streets, and I'd feel . . . well, *bad,* you know?"

Jonathan nodded. "I'm sorry you won't be coming with me, but I understand. I really do. And I think this Judy Bryant must be very special."

Actually, he envied Rennie his Judy.

"Well, she's not the looker Miss DeArte is, but I think she's special. What she is is a tough Irish broad, feisty as hell, with a mind like a whip."

Jonathan picked up the menu. "Yeah, there's nothing like a woman who knows her own mind"—this a trifle ironically—"and I hope for your sake that she makes up her mind that she wants *you.*" He laid the menu down again. "But I've an idea. Why don't you pick Miss Bryant up and take her to California too? Then you wouldn't have to worry about her riding the subway, and you can both enjoy the good life, going to the track and the beach and—"

Rennie smiled, shook his head. "You don't know Judy. She's not the kind who'd just let you pick her up and take her anyplace. She *does* have a mind of her own, and she likes New York. She likes the opera and the plays and the museums. Every Sunday when I'm not working we go to a different museum . . ."

Jonathan chuckled. "Los Angeles isn't exactly a cultural wasteland, even if New Yorkers like to think so. We have museums too. But you talk it over with your Judy, and anytime you decide you'd like to give it a try, give me a call. I'll keep a place open for you."

"You're a sport, chief—I mean Mr. West. You're a real winner in my book."

"Sometimes, but not this time. Not in Miss DeArte's book anyway. I'm throwing in the towel on this one. After breakfast I'm going upstairs to sack out, then I'm catching a flight back to L.A. And you're free for the day. You can even go pick up your Judy this afternoon. All you have to do is pick me up later on and take me to the airport. Okay?"

"Okay, if you're sure that's what you really want. But without really knowing what's going on between you and this Miss DeArte, I feel kind of bad that you're . . ." He faltered.

"Giving up?" Jonathan smiled at Rennie's delicacy. "I think it's the only sensible thing to do. I'll try to explain it to you. A little while ago a hotel in Beverly Hills came up for sale, a very famous hotel where all the Hollywood greats stayed at one time or another and still do. And I wanted to own it for reasons that didn't have anything to do with money. It had only to do with owning the hotel for the prestige. The hotel was like an alluring woman, and the guy who owned her could enjoy all her seductive pleasures—her beauty and sitting at the number one table in her world-famous lounge, playing host to some of the most celebrated people in the world, feeling like a king.

"But there was a catch, a big one. Financially she was a loser. Still, there were a lot of people interested in buying her for the same reasons I wanted to. Men with more money than I had or really could afford to put on the line.

"Anyway, I was in on the early bidding, and for weeks while the negotiating went on I was in a sweat trying to figure out how to make the numbers come out right. But I couldn't come up with an answer, and in the meantime I was letting good, solid propositions pass me by because I was concentrating on the hotel and wanted to keep my credit free for her. And then I realized that I had to give her up. She was just this crazy fantasy, one that would never work because it was wrong for me right from the beginning, a dream I couldn't afford. And that's what Andrianna DeArte is, an ill-founded dream.

"I could follow her around for weeks . . . months . . .

291

and let everything else go hang, but it's not going to work out. She doesn't want me, which makes the situation a nonviable one from the word go. For a few days there I just lost my head. But it's reality time, and I have to face facts — she's one property on the Monopoly board that I just can't have, and chasing my tail around the block isn't going to help."

"Jesus, Mr. West, I'm sorry."

"Hey, no one ever said that anybody's entitled to everything they're crazy enough to get obsessed with —"

"Yeah, but I still think she's nuts. I think you're one hell of a guy, and if I was a broad, well, I wouldn't let you get by me." And then he realized how that sounded and looked down, embarrassed as hell. Jonathan threw back his head and roared as the waiter came to take their order.

"So as soon as I have my reservation, I'll let you know what time to pick me up, and you can give me my bill for the limo tonight and we'll put it on my credit card. But I think I'll give you your tip now." He pulled a checkbook and pen from his inner breast pocket and began to write.

"You don't have to do this now, Mr. West. You can put the tip on the credit card too."

"I'd rather do it now." He finished writing, tore the check from the book, and handed it to Rennie.

Rennie looked at it in disbelief. "Shit, Mr. West! This is for a thousand dollars. I can't take this kind of bread. There's no way I earned it."

"Don't be a sucker, Rennie. When someone gives you money for services rendered, take it and don't think about it twice. Just be glad that you're that much ahead."

"That ain't the point."

"Look, Rennie, you did a job as best you could, and you didn't whine about how many hours you were working or the meals you were missing. You acted like a friend, and I appreciate it. It's as simple as that."

"But you don't pay a friend for acting like a friend . . ."

"No, not usually. But I can easily afford it, and that makes a difference. Look, don't take the money for yourself. Buy Judy Bryant a present. A fancy watch or maybe even an engagement ring. Even feisty broads with minds of their own will soften up given the right present." *Sometimes anyway, at least for a while* . . . "Do it for me, okay?"

"Okay, boss." He grinned. "Now that I'm not working for you anymore, I can call you any damn thing I want."

"Oh yeah? Well, you're still working for me until *after* you drop me at the airport."

"Yes, sir, Mr. West. You're the boss."

"Just let me out at the curb, Rennie, so you don't have to bother parking the car. I'm fine."

"Hey, can't I go with my friend to the gate and kiss him good-bye? Besides, I'll just leave Baby at the curb. Don't you know by this time, chief, that nobody trifles with a stretch? They got too much respect."

Jonathan laughed. "Whatever you say. You're the boss."

"Now you're talking."

They had a few minutes before Jonathan's flight.

"So, Rennie, you never told me if you went shopping. Did you buy your Judy a pretty?"

"I didn't have time. That's what I wanted to tell you."

"Okay, tell me. For the next five minutes or so you have my complete attention."

"After we had breakfast this morning and you went up the elevator, I'm walking through the lobby, and who do I see? Miss DeArte, and she's checking out. So naturally I followed her outside, and she got into a limo with all her baggage . . ."

Jonathan's mouth compressed into a thin line. "I told you. That's a closed chapter—"

"Yeah, but it bothered me, you giving up like that."

"But I explained it to you. I wasn't giving up; I was getting out of a no-win situation."

"Yeah, I know, but still—Hell, Jonny. What I wanted to do was give *you* a present, like you gave me that thousand."

"It wasn't necessary," Jonathan muttered. Yet he couldn't help himself. "So, what next? You followed her?"

"Yeah. The limo took her uptown to the medical center there."

"She went to visit someone there or what?"

"I'm not sure what she's doing there, but the limo's waiting for her with all her luggage, so I know for sure she's coming out again—she ain't just checking in. So I mosey over to talk to her driver, and it's a guy I kind of know—we've talked before while we were waiting around like when there's an affair and there's a bunch of us drivers. We kill the time chewing the fat, you know?"

"I know," Jonathan said, impatient now for Rennie to get to the point. "And what did he tell you?"

"That the broad . . . excuse me, Miss DeArte . . . had told him she'd be inside for at least four hours or so, and after that she was catching a plane to California. Pan Am . . . She was booked on a five-ten flight. And that's it."

Jonathan automatically checked his watch even though he *knew* it was already twenty of six and he was at TWA's gate and not Pan Am's, and a sickening wave of regret passed through him. They could have been on the same plane . . .

So what if we were? We were on the same ship for five days, we were in New York at the same time for almost three days, staying at the same hotel, and at times we were within yards of each other. Still it hadn't mattered.

Then he remembered that Rennie was waiting for his reaction, probably waiting to be congratulated for ferreting

294

out this final and up-to-the-minute revelation, and waiting for him to be pleased to hear that Andrianna was up in the air, winging her way to the same place he was. That had to mean something, didn't it?

He didn't want to disappoint Rennie. He beamed at him. "Thanks, pal."

Rennie, his face creased in a big smile, gripped Jonathan's hand. "No thanks necessary, Jonny. Hey, what are friends for? I just couldn't see a stand-up guy like you giving up. And I figure with her being in L.A., on your own territory so to speak, and you being a big-time operator, you won't have much trouble finding her. And this time, don't just follow her. This time, really go for it! You know?"

"I think so."

It was time for Jonathan to board.

"Will you let me know if anything happens there? How things turn out? Here, take my card, chief. It's the limo service, but they always know where to reach me."

"And you know where to find me if you do decide to come out to L.A. My building's on the Avenue of the Stars in Century City, and there's a big sign that says West Properties. Got it? Wait a minute. Let me give you *my* card, the one with my private number where I can always be reached. But don't give it out. It's the line I keep free for friends only."

"Got you, friend." Rennie gave a quick salute.

It wasn't until he had been in the air for an hour, working on a scotch and moodily looking out the window into the dark, that he realized that all Rennie had really said was that Andrianna was on a Pan Am flight to California. *But where in California?*

They'd both assumed that California meant L.A., but there were hundreds of towns in California and at least five, six major cities that could be her destination.

He tortured himself thinking of all the places in California Andrianna could be headed for even though Los Angeles did seem like a natural for an actress and it was more than likely she had friends there. There was no shortage of Europeans in the Hollywood community, and she probably knew that whole English contingent who hung out together like members of a private club. Only a few weeks ago he had seen a bunch of them seated together at one table at Dudley Moore's 72 Market Street—Jackie Collins and Caine and Connery . . .

But if Andrianna *was* on her way to L.A., sooner or later maybe he *would* run into her. Somewhere . . . someplace . . . at some restaurant or party . . . across a crowded room, just like the song went.

Then again, she *could* be on her way to northern California.

Abruptly Jonathan snapped on the overhead signal, and within seconds a steward was at his side.

"I need to know where Pan Am's flight departing Kennedy at five-ten this afternoon is going. All I know is the plane's headed for California."

"I'll see if I can find out for you, sir. Be right with you."

Then Jonathan wondered about the other thing Rennie had told him . . . about the medical center. Had she been visiting a sick friend there for *so* long a time—four or five hours? But who knew anything? She was as much a mystery to him now as she'd been that first day he saw her.

Oh, God, but he was sick and tired of thinking about her! And he had made up his mind to forget her. So what the hell was he doing? What did he care *where* she was flying?

The steward was back. "I have that information for you, sir. Pan Am flight 623, departing at five-ten, arrives—"

296

"Forget it!"

"Yes, sir." The steward rolled his eyes and retreated down the aisle.

Still, Jonathan peered into the darkness as if, if he only tried hard enough, he would spot her plane out there, flying in tandem with his . . .

By the time Andrianna checked into the Stanford Court in San Francisco that night, she was completely spent. It felt like it had been the longest day of her life, even though she was on the winning end of the three-hour time difference between the East Coast and the West.

She, Penny, and Nicole hadn't gone to bed until nearly four in the morning, reluctant to put an end to the fun. They had talked about the good old days at Le Rosey, laughed (everything seemed funnier in retrospect), and gossiped about old acquaintances—who had married whom, who had had what parts of their anatomy plastic-surgerized even before they were forty, how many kids this one had and how many divorces that one, with Penny having something hilarious to say about every last one of them . . . even those poor souls who had been in and out of rehab centers.

But then Nicole had suddenly and abruptly remembered that she was supposed to be the responsible member of their trio and that it was *very* late, and she had practically ordered them to bed. After issuing heavy satin embroidered nightgowns with robes to match with a "you'll find all the necessities in the bathrooms," she had almost pushed Andrianna and Penny into the guest room, the one with the twin beds, telling them, "Since there is so little left of the night and you both are leaving first thing in the morning, it does not make sense to upset two guest rooms, *oui?*"

Then she had quickly disappeared into her own bedroom without another word, leaving Andrianna and Penny looking at one another, wondering what the sudden rush act was all about.

"What do you think got into her?" Penny had demanded of Andrianna. "There we were having a great old time, and all of a sudden it was like she got a bug up her ass. All I was doing was telling how Gae and I ran into Ursula Van Huber in Venice and how dippy old Ursula was on her honeymoon with this hunk who was so crazy about her he couldn't keep his hands off her and how Ursula was moaning about the joys of real love like a cow who just got kicked in her udder and how they couldn't wait to get rid of us so they could get back to their hotel to screw. Do you think it was that I offended Nicole's oh-so-delicate sensibilities?

After a couple of minutes of reflection, Andrianna had come to the conclusion that, no, it wasn't Nicole's sensibilities that had been offended but only that she didn't want . . . couldn't bear . . . to hear about other people's passion. And she could understand that.

But all she'd said was "It *is* four o'clock in the morning. Maybe Nicole just couldn't stay awake a minute longer."

Then, in spite of the hour, she and Penny had carried on where they'd left off, giggling and whispering so that Nicole wouldn't hear them, and it was at least another hour before they'd finally succumbed to sleep.

It seemed that she had been asleep for only minutes before Nicole was rapping on the door, demanding that she and Penny rise and shine—it was seven o'clock, and they all had to get moving if they were to meet their schedules. She also announced that a continental breakfast was being served in the secondary dining room at precisely twenty to eight.

"Oh, go screw yourself and your secondary dining room!" Penny had muttered and slept another fifteen minutes before groggily making her way to one of the three baths that were part of the guest room suite, not emerging, picture-perfect and exuberant, until it was too late for her to have more than a couple of gulps of coffee.

Penny had covered Andrianna's and Nicole's faces with a bunch of fast kisses as they sat in the rosy-hued room before she dashed out the door carrying her trusty cosmetic case, trailing her sable coat, and leaving them enveloped in a fog of Opium.

The second Penny was gone, Nicole, taking tiny sips of her inky black coffee, had complained that Penny was a *sotte*. "She talks of great love, but what she really thinks is that this marriage to Gae will somehow save her. But the truth is, he is as much a *sot* as she and cannot save anybody."

When Andrianna made vague sounds of protest, Nicole shrugged and went on to explain that she had specifically chosen various shades of rose as a color scheme for the junior dining room so that it would reflect favorably on the diner in the harsh, cool light of morning.

"A terrible time of day for the woman over thirty-five," she said despairingly.

But the rosiness wasn't working for Nicole this morning, Andrianna reflected. Perhaps Nicole hadn't been able to sleep after all. There were dark circles under the green eyes and tiny lines around her mouth that hadn't been there the night before.

She wondered what thoughts in particular had kept Nicole awake and agitated. Was it Penny and Gae's upcoming wedding—a marriage that promised love and passion? Was it Penny's questions about the inadequacies of Nicole's marriage? Or was it only the picture Penny had painted of dippy Ursula Van Huber and her hunk of a husband rushing off to screw? Was it the sour aftertaste of second thoughts that had kept Nicole tossing and turning?

Poor Nicole . . . Her strength had always been that she

believed in herself and the course she had chosen in life, in its suitability and its practicality. Had she tossed in her bed last night, plagued with doubts, asking herself whether playing it safe—not taking a chance on life . . . on love— had been worth it?

And then, suddenly, Andrianna saw that she and Nicole really weren't as different as she'd always thought. She had lived in many places, following various occupations, had had many men, and yet she too had never taken any chances, either on life or on love.

In her own way she too had been afraid and had played it safe, relying on the security of her jewelry case instead of people and, in the case of men, in the safety of their numbers. People, even people who loved you, could love you not enough, could love you for the wrong reasons, could falter when you needed them most. Jewels, cold and hard and impersonal, retained their beauty forever as well as their value. And men who were but temporary lovers could exact no promises, could demand neither commitment nor truth, and brought with them no risk of rejection.

And she knew at that moment, sitting across from Nicole, already perfectly groomed for her day in a black Adolfo suit with pretend gold buttons that matched chunky real gold jewelry, that she didn't want to live out her days the way Nicole had, secure but still afraid—and lonely.

Like Penny, she wanted to take a gamble on life, on love—even if it meant taking a chance on having her heart broken, even if it meant going for broke! Most of all she knew that she wanted Jonathan West!

After hours of testing, the doctors confirmed what she'd been told in London. She was still in remission, and for the present her physical condition was similar to that of any "normal" woman her age in reasonably stable good health . . . except that for her there really was no predicting if and when she might come out of remission.

And although she had asked the same thing many times before of many other doctors, she asked once again about her life expectancy, given that her symptoms recurred, just to be sure they would give her the same answer. After all, if you were going to love a man and ask that he love you, you had to give him at least an opportunity to get fairly decent odds.

But the reply was the same one she had received before—no conclusive answer. There were only statistics, and statistics were only averages, and no one person was really the average. But they did have an optimistic message for her: the survival rate was encouraging and constantly rising, with most cases "under control."

As for her life expectancy if she *never* came out of remission, that was a roll of the dice as it was for everyone.

And there was great hope—with each passing day they were learning more about SLE. Who knew what they would know if and when her period of remission came to an end? And there she was back again . . . to *ifs* and *whens* . . .

Children! She had to know about children, even if she was approaching that age when she was running out of time. *Could* she have a child? What were the chances of her giving birth to a healthy baby? And what were the baby's chances of having the disease too?

They told her that she could give birth to a healthy baby, barring the usual *ifs* involved in any pregnancy and birth, *if* she carried to term. That was the big *if*, the risk of miscarriage being higher for the SLE patient. And while they believed there was some genetic propensity for SLE, they knew that it wasn't transmitted in the DNA. The risks involved centered about the mother, not the child. Chances were that it would be a difficult pregnancy since there was stress on the kidneys, a highly vulnerable

301

area for the SLE patient, and there could be flare-ups with prolonged hospital stays. On the other hand, she could spend the months of her pregnancy in remission with a crippling flare-up *after* she gave birth.

"But it *is* possible to get through the pregnancy and give birth to a healthy baby?" she asked again, just to be sure. And they told her it was possible but that it was up to the woman—"what she is willing to endure and what she is willing to risk for herself."

Risk. The one thing she'd avoided for the last twenty years. *But all life is a risk. And the worst risk is in not living and the worst thing to be endured is to live without love.*

The doctors noted that Andrianna had written down that she didn't know what her mother or father had died of and asked her if there was any way more information could be obtained, particularly in the case of her mother since SLE was more frequently found in women.

"Aside from your own case, it would help us help others if we had more genetic history. If we had the name of your mother's attending physician, perhaps we could learn a great deal more than we know now."

Her mother's attending physician . . . *Dr. Hernandez.* She remembered that much, and she *was* going to northern California . . .

She was leaving that very afternoon for San Francisco and that little town in the Napa Valley where it had all begun. Before there could be new beginnings, there had to be proper endings, and she had already put it off for far too long . . .

Part Three

Northern California and Los Angeles
November 17-21, 1988

Twenty-two

Thursday

The Napa valley was as beautiful as Andrianna remembered it. Green and lush, even in the month of November. That was one of California's miracles, she thought, among others, not the least being that Jonathan West resided here.

Her chauffeur had no difficulty in finding La Paz, but it took them over an hour to locate the house she'd lived in. All Andrianna recalled was that somewhere near the sweet little house with a garden full of roses had been a white church, a cemetery, and a small schoolhouse. And some distance away had been a cluster of small, poor houses.

The house where Andrianna had lived with her mother and Rosa was almost as she remembered it, time having wrought very little change except for the garden, which apparently was now dedicated to growing vegetables instead of flowers. That seemed suitable. Vegetables were hardy and a staple of life, and flowers, while lovely and soul-satisfying, weren't strictly necessary. Like Elena, flowers were both delicate and expendable.

Andrianna got out of the car slowly, walked up the path hesitantly, approached the front steps with a heart beating rapidly, and rang the doorbell with trembling fingers.

If you believe in ghosts, stand up and clap your hands. . . .

She wasn't clapping, but it was possible—could it be, dear God—that Rosa *still* lived in the pretty house and would come to the door? *Oh, please God, let it be Rosa!*

But the woman who answered her ring and was looking at her curiously was more or less her own age, with a trim figure and a headful of dark, carefully tousled curls. She wore black stretch pants topped by an oversized soft black wool sweater and around her neck a gold chain from which hung both a gold cross and a little heart outlined in tiny diamonds.

She eyed Andrianna's full-length mink and snakeskin pumps; then her glance went to the limousine parked in the driveway. She laughed. "You're not the Avon lady, are you? The only Avon ladies I've seen are the ones in the TV commercials, and they don't look like you one bit—and I bet they don't ride in cars like that one either."

"No, I guess not." Andrianna smiled. "And I'm *not* the Avon lady. It's just that . . . I used to live here in this house with my mother and an old friend named Rosa. My name is . . ." She paused. It had been years since she'd said the name aloud. "I'm Andrianna Duarte."

The light of recognition filled the woman's eyes. "I remember you! I was three years ahead of you in school, but I remember you. You were the one with the dresses that were always nicer than everybody else's and the collection of fancy dolls. My mother said that was because your mother had a millionaire boyfriend. And my mother wasn't one of those women around here who gossiped about your mother. All she said, if I recall right, was that any woman as beautiful as Elena Duarte shouldn't have settled for anything less than a wedding ring."

She looked at Andrianna's fur coat again and put out a hand to touch the fur longingly. "But you look like you've done okay. I'm Gladys Garcia. Would you like to come in?"

Andrianna looked around the living room, trying to recall something about it that would be familiar, but there was nothing. When she'd lived there, the house had been furnished in a warm, comfortable but undistinctive fashion, and now the room was completely color-coordinated, everything fastidiously perfect and gleaming with polish, as if it had come out of the pages of a magazine, picture-pretty.

The wallpaper was brightly colored poppies—yellow and red and orange and hyacinth blue—against a background of white, and the overstuffed white plumpy furniture sat on a hyacinth blue carpet and was strewn with sofa pillows in yellow and red and orange. The focus of the room was the biggest TV Andrianna had ever seen, and perched on top of it was a VCR with a dizzying array of buttons.

The woman watched Andrianna's face for a reaction, obviously proud of what she had wrought.

"It's lovely," Andrianna said. "I think it's the most cheerful room I've ever seen."

"We just got the VCR. I didn't know anything about them. Tony . . . my husband Antonio . . . just told me to pick out the best one in the store. But my son, Tony Jr.— he's nineteen—he went with me to buy it, and you know how kids are today. If it's electronic, they know it like the back of their hands. So I let him pick it out."

"You have a son nineteen?" Andrianna was incredulous.

"Sure." Gladys smiled, showing perfect white teeth, enjoying her guest's surprise. "And Tony's not my oldest. There's Al. He's twenty-one. And Richie's eighteen, and Veronica is sixteen. Four in all. I got married when I was seventeen. But then, when Veronica was born, I said to myself, 'That's the last one.' I wasn't going to wear myself out having babies every year, you know? So I had my tubes tied without asking anyone's advice. I figured it wasn't anyone's business except mine, not even Antonio's or Father Gilberto's. Would you like a cup of coffee?"

"Thank you, I would." Andrianna followed Gladys into the kitchen, which, like the living room, was exceedingly

307

cheerful. It was also a marvel of equipment — a dishwasher of black glass matched the built-in double ovens, which matched the huge refrigerator-freezer with twin dispensers built into the door. The tiled counters held an impressive battery of every conceivable small appliance, plus an undersized TV, the kind that increased in price as the set got smaller.

As Gladys poured coffee into daisy-decorated coffee mugs that echoed the daisy-strewn tiles covering the walls, she said, "The fridge has an icemaker. I just got it last year. I always wanted one of those icemakers."

"It's a beautiful kitchen," Andrianna said. "You must love cooking in it. How long have you been living here?"

That was the question she'd been waiting to ask . . . the all-important question that translated into: when had Rosa stopped?

"Since I'm married. That's almost twenty-three years. Almost as many years as my husband Tony is older than me. He's almost sixty-five, about ready to retire. Surprised? Everyone who doesn't know him always is. But I'll tell you how it was. When I was seventeen, all I was interested in was boys and clothes and boys and dancing and boys. All kinds, but mostly the wild ones — the ones with the wicked eyes and the wicked hands and the hot bodies, the ones who talked real sweet and rode the fastest motorcycles and could give a girl a real good time." Gladys laughed.

"But my mother, may God be with her, was born here, not in Mexico, and she always warned me that the girls who went with those kind of boys or with the illegals who could barely talk English would end up with a houseful of babies and spend their lives never getting ahead and never having anything but grief. Marry for the right reasons, Mama said, and love would come later. And you know what? Mama was right. She herself fixed me up with Tony, who was no grape picker but a foreman at the Monticello Winery, and just like she predicted I moved into this house right away, and I never worked one day breaking my back. I certainly never picked grapes or anything else.

"And I've always had just about everything I wanted, and my kids have had it good too. My oldest, Al, is in insurance, and Tony Jr. is at the junior college, studying computers. And Richie's the real smart one, so we're counting on him becoming a lawyer after he finishes high school and college. And that's what I tell my Veronica. Marry a man who will take care of you and give you security instead of a broken heart."

She looked straight into Andrianna's eyes as if expecting a comment, one of agreement or even a challenge, but Andrianna didn't know what she could possibly say. So she merely made what she hoped were appropriate sympathetic sounds.

Apparently these sounds satisfied Gladys. "What about you, Andrianna? Are you married? Do you have any kids?"

"No. No marriage, no kids."

Gladys grinned, stroked the mink coat again. "Like your mother, huh? You don't believe in marrying them?"

Andrianna decided Gladys hadn't meant anything by her remark and just let it go.

She asked Gladys if she knew what had become of Rosa. "When I left California, she was living in this house, and I don't know what happened to her. Of course that was thirty years ago, and you moved into this house twenty-three years ago. That leaves seven years unaccounted for. Whom did your husband buy this house from?"

"Not anybody named Rosa. It was a bank. I wish I could help you out since I can see finding this Rosa is important to you, but frankly I remember you and I remember my mother mentioning your mother a few times, but I don't remember anything about this Rosa. But I'm sure someone around here would remember her and be able to tell you what happened to her. All you got to do is ask around . . ."

"Yes, of course." Andrianna stood up. "I'll do that. And thank you for everything."

"For what? I didn't do anything."

Andrianna smiled. "Oh, but you did. You were . . . kind. I'm a stranger, and you invited me into your house and gave me coffee and friendly conversation."

"Look. Sit down and have another cup of coffee while I call my sister Lily. She's seven years older than I am, and she'll probably remember this Rosa and what happened to her. Okay? Lily lives in San Francisco. She really did well for herself. She married this Italian, and he has his own business—an auto body shop, and you know how those guys clean up. Sometimes I wish I had married somebody who lived in San Fran. I don't really mean it, of course, but it's just that sometimes it gets awful boring around here, and it must be fun to live in the city."

Lily remembered Rosa. She also remembered that Rosa had died only six months after Elena Duarte. Andrianna was almost sorry she had asked.

Oh, Rosa! Rosa! I needed to see you so much!

"She wasn't buried in La Paz. Lily says a man—a brother, she thinks—came up from Mexico and arranged for her body to be sent back there for burial. Lily says it was a stroke that killed Rosa."

But Andrianna thought she knew better. Rosa had died of *chagrin d'amour,* her own version of love gone wrong.

"There's someone else I would like to talk to. A Dr. Hernandez. I think his first name was Geraldo, but I'm not sure. He was my mother's doctor," Andrianna explained. "There are a couple of questions I must ask him. You know him? Of him? Where I can find him?"

"Of course I know him. I mean *of* him. I know his son. He's *my* doctor. Dr. Jerry Hern. Dr. Hernandez, the

310

father, died about ten years ago, and Jerry took over his practice. Jerry was in my class at Central High before I dropped out to marry Tony. His office is on Vista Way, in a new complex they built over there. I guess La Paz is growing up, getting bigger anyway. And you should see the house Jerry and his wife built on the outskirts of town—a great big white house right on the La Paz Country Club golf course! Jerry's a real doll, but his wife, Melissa—she's a real cool pale blonde—she doesn't bother much with anyone around here. Considering, I guess it's not likely that she would. I don't really know her, but it's my guess she's a class A stuck-up gringa bitch." Gladys laughed, but it had a bitter edge.

"People around here say she's the one who made him change his name from Geraldo Hernandez to Jerry Hern. I don't know if that's true, but I wouldn't be surprised if she was one of those girls who found Geraldo's Latino eyes sexy but didn't want the rest of what went along with them, if you know what I mean. But who knows? Maybe it was her family who didn't like his name, and she just wanted to make them feel more comfortable about her marrying him."

She laughed again, but now Andrianna thought the laugh sounded wistful rather than amused.

"But, anyway, Jerry's as sweet as sugar and a wonderful doctor, and maybe he can help you out. I'm sure he'll try."

Yes, she'd go to see Jerry Hern. Even if his father was dead and he himself knew nothing about Elena Duarte's case, he had inherited his father's practice, and very possibly the records that could reveal how strong "the propensity" for her sickness raged in her genes.

As she stepped back inside her waiting limousine, she waved to Gladys. She had entered her home a stranger but was leaving it, somehow, a friend. And she felt she knew Gladys Garcia very well. She was Nicole Partierre Austin in another skin, a Nicole in black stretch pants instead of an expensive little black dress but a Nicole just the same—

311

a Nicole with a VCR and an icemaker instead of social connections and smart Palm Beach dinner parties.

She leaned forward to instruct the driver how to find the cemetery where Elena Duarte was buried and wondered if Gladys ever lay in her bed next to her Antonio dreaming of all those young men with the wicked eyes and wicked hands who raced like a hot wind on the fastest of motorcycles . . . Or was it the boy with the sexy Latino eyes who was as "sweet as sugar" that she dreamed of?

Jonathan had been in his office for an hour — he'd come in a little before seven, eager to make up for all the lost time — when his secretary arrived for the day. "Coffee, Mr. West?"

"No, thanks. I put the pot up when I came in, and I'm already over-caffeinated. Would you please get Paul Banks for me on the phone and tell Bob Halpern I want to see him in ten minutes?"

"Will do." Patti consulted her watch. "But you do know the man from *Time* will be here in about fifteen minutes?"

"No, damn it, I didn't know. It's *your* job to make sure I do."

Patti stiffened. "Yes, it is, sir, and I left your schedule on your desk yesterday in case you came in last night and also left messages with your housekeeper *and* on your answering machine."

"Oh." Jonathan was chagrined. When he'd finally arrived home Wednesday evening he'd been utterly exhausted, despite the fact that jet lag rarely took a toll on him. So he'd ignored the neatly piled notes from Sarah and the blinking light on his machine. "Sorry. So why don't you just get me Banks on the phone and we'll let Halpern go until later, after the man from *Time* leaves."

"Yes, Mr. West. And by the way, how was your trip on the *QE2?* All it's cracked up to be?"

"It was great. Just great."

312

"Why do you *do* it, Mr. West?" Anthony Parks of *Time* asked. "You've already got half a billion dollars, more money than most men can spend in the course of a lifetime even if they're really trying. Some men do it for their progeny—a sense of dynasty—but as yet you don't even have a family."

"That's not to say I won't have a family. I am only in my thirties."

"Well, would you say that's why you do it? Because you *do* have a sense of dynasty? You want to build a fortune that will live on after you, like the Rockefellers, for instance?"

Jonathan shrugged. "Even the Rockefeller fortune has been diminished as a whole. They're a big family, and the fortune's been split at every generational level. And there's always estate taxes. Frankly, Mr. Parks, I haven't thought about it all that much."

"Then why *do* you do it, Mr. West?"

"I do it just to do it. For the fun of doing it. If you've got a million, you want two million . . . for the pleasure of it and for the spending of it. It makes sense at that level. That if you've got a million to spend, it's twice as much fun to spend two million. But after that you do it just to do it. To see how big this pile you've earned can be. In a way it's a measure of the man, of his achievement in a world that values money above all else."

"And in a world that doesn't value money above all else?"

Jonathan smiled. "I'll have to wait until that happens to make a judgment."

Jonathan answered by rote as the interviewer proceeded with the remaining four of the five Ws from Journalism 101—who, what, when, and where—but thought a little harder when Parks finally got to *How?*

He started in on his "checking your back" spiel and then

added something new: "No distractions." *At least not from now on.* Then, glancing pointedly at his watch, he announced abruptly that the interview was over and rang for Patti to escort the slightly miffed Mr. Parks to the door.

Andrianna rested her hand on the cool marble gravestone and squeezed her eyes shut against the flow of tears. *Tell me, Mama, was it worth it? Just before you died, did you still think it was golden sex in the afternoon? Were you still happy with your choice—your gringo who never married you? Or would you have been happier maybe, lived a longer, more fruitful life with an Antonio Garcia, who would have taken better care of you, given you lots of babies with real names?*

Or maybe a Jerry Hern, who would have loved you so much he would have even changed his name for you? Then you could have lived forever maybe . . . . for an eternity, at least until the end of time . . .

Oh, Mama, did you ever even think about how life might have been for you if you had loved another kind of man? A man who would have loved you more? If you had taken a chance on finding him? Maybe even a man like Jonathan West? . . .

But there was no voice to respond, no words of reassurance. Still Andrianna thought she knew the answer. Elena *had* gambled, *had* taken a chance on life and love. The only problem was that she had taken a chance on the wrong man. And that was always the risk of the game.

And what did you die of, Mama? I have to know. Was it SLE? Or was it chagrin d'amour?

But there was no answer. The gravestone was not Elena but only marble. Still, Andrianna blew a kiss toward that rectangle of northern California earth. All these years it had been her birthright, her only claim to the land where she'd been born and where all dreams were supposed to come true. Maybe now it was her turn at the dream . . .

Tomorrow she would talk to Dr. Jerry Hern, and hopefully she would learn more about her chances, about

314

whether she had the right to gamble on Jonathan West.

"How did it go?" Patti asked, closing the draperies of Jonathan's paneled office against the afternoon sun. "Was it a good interview?"

"Fine, I guess, though he didn't ask me anything a dozen other interviewers haven't already asked . . . and I'm not sure I came up with any new answers."

"Oh, I'm sure it'll be great. That one that was in *Los Angeles* a few months ago? You came across as a real killer."

He laughed. "Really? I suppose that's what they like to read . . ."

"Of course. It makes people envy or respect you—or both. That's what counts, isn't it?"

"I don't know, Patti. I'm not sure I know what really counts anymore."

"Oh, Mr. West. If you, of all people, can say that, you really must be suffering from jet lag. But I bet by tomorrow you'll be fine. Now, shall I call Bob Halpern in? Or do you want to see a list of your calls first? Hugh Lansing said he really has to talk to you immediately about that zoning on the Oceanic project, and Jane Perkins from accounting said that—"

"What time is it?"

"Almost one."

"Look, I have a lot to catch up on, and I need some uninterrupted time to review this pile you've left on my desk. We'll put everything else on hold until after lunch."

"Fine. But I do want to remind you about that celebrity polo match at the Equidome tonight. You're playing for the March of Dimes, remember?"

"Oh, God, is that tonight?"

Patti sighed. "I'm afraid so. Are you up to it?"

"Of course I'm up to it. Why do you ask?"

"Well, if you'll pardon my saying so, Mr. West, you really *don't* seem yourself. Maybe you can get someone to substitute for you? After all, you haven't had a chance to practice in a—"

"I'll do fine. What's the worst that can happen? I'll break a leg or a few ribs or my nose."

"It's no joking matter, Mr. West."

"Who's joking? At least there's one thing you can't break playing polo."

"What's that?"

"Your heart. Now, that's no joke."

Twenty-three

Friday

"Good morning, Mr. West," Patti chirped brightly when Jonathan arrived at his office a bit later than usual.

"Is it?"

"Oh, dear. Did the game go badly last night?"

"We lost, if that's what you mean."

"That's a shame. At least I don't see anything broken," she offered cheerfully.

"Not so it shows . . ."

"Well, good," she said with a sigh as she picked up a stack of papers and followed him into his office. "Jason Watts is waiting in reception, and these are the papers on—"

"What does he want?"

"Mr. Watts? He has a nine o'clock appointment . . . *had,* that is—it's ten past nine." With a slightly indignant glance she added, "Everything *is* marked on your calendar. You always consult it before you leave the day before."

"But why didn't you remind me yesterday anyway?" he reproached her.

"It was never necessary before, Mr. West," Patti said stiffly, hurt. "I'll certainly do so in the future if you wish . . ."

"Oh, hell . . . I'm sorry. I guess I *am* suffering from jet lag . . . You don't have any more surprises in store for me today, do you?"

"Not that I know of. There *is* the benefit for Shelter the Homeless tonight at the Hilton . . ."

"Did I buy tickets?"

"Yes, sir."

"Fine. Then I've done my part. I don't have to actually attend."

"I'm afraid you do. I believe you told Merv Griffin, who's one of the hosts, that you'd be there. And you bought a table for ten and invited people as your guests. And just in case you've forgotten, which evidently you have, you're taking Staci Whitley."

He looked at her blankly. "Staci Whitley. Who's she?"

"Really, Mr. West. She's in that sitcom, 'Are These Really My Children?' She plays the daughter who always has these nerds as boyfriends. Anyway, you promised your friend Peter Darwin, who's her publicist, that you'd take her." She was losing patience. "Do you want me to get Mr. Darwin on the phone so that you can explain to him that you can't or won't take her?"

"No." Jonathan sighed, resigned. "A promise is a promise. Would you please make arrangements to have Miss Whitley picked up? I'll meet her there. What time is this thing?"

"The invitation is right there on your desk, Mr. West, with all the necessary information. I'll go get Mr. Watts. You know, they say jet lag can last for several days."

"Is that a fact?"

Andrianna had called the preceding day to make sure Dr. Hern would have the time to see her and that she wouldn't be a surprise when she showed up at his office.

But *he* was the surprise. Jerry Hern could have been cast as a doctor in the flicks of the thirties, his handsome image implanted on the silver screen for young women to moan for and lust over. So romantic were Dr. Hern's looks and so classic his profile, he could have been a Tyrone Power or a Laurence Olivier or even a Valentino. He was not only handsome but *lushly* so, with high cheekbones, a strong,

318

firm chin, a chiseled nose, full sensual lips.

And then there were Jerry Hern's eyes — the hot, sexy eyes Gladys Garcia had described. Who could resist them? No wonder his wife, the cool, blond Melissa, had fallen for him, had wanted him so much she had thrown all discretion to the winds, possibly ignoring even the objections of her family.

And given half a chance at him, *would* Gladys have been able to resist? Given a *real* choice, provided Jerry Hern wanted *her*, would she have really eschewed him for the safety of Tony Garcia? It was too incredible to believe.

Jerry Hern came from behind his desk to greet her, both hands extended in warm welcome. "Andrianna Duarte! I remember you! You were the little girl with the lovely yellow cat eyes. But of course you weren't a cat then, only a kitten. And now you're all grown up, and I see that you and your eyes are as lovely as ever, though I think that maybe they're more orange than yellow. I'll have to study them some more before I make a final decision."

Handsome and charming.

Dr. Hern apparently had a way with words too, Andrianna thought, but having met such men before, she was wary.

He held out a chair for her, and she sat down, saying, "I wish I could say that I remember you, but the truth is I don't. I suspect that I was a very self-centered little girl who paid no attention to anyone but myself . . ."

"I'd say being self-centered is a pretty normal state of affairs for kids, and why not? It's probably the only time in their lives when they have that option."

"But *you* weren't so self-centered that as a big fifth-grader you didn't take notice of a little second-grader."

"Oh, but that doesn't mean I wasn't as self-absorbed as any other kid — it just shows that even then I had an eye for a pretty girl."

They both laughed, and she wondered if that was how Jerry Hern always dealt with his female patients, disarming them with all his dazzling charms and pretty words. Was that, then, all there was to the man?

As if reading her mind, he smiled at her in a way that reassured her, as if he had said, "It's okay, you can trust me."

And while the smile was no less charming than everything else about him, there was something else, and she struggled to define it. Then it came to her. It had to do with how the smile traveled up to those hot, intense eyes and seemed to come from deeper within. Jerry Hern was for real!

"So, as I understand it," he said, "you've just returned to La Paz after being away for something like thirty years?"

"Yes. A long time."

"Well, then, either you liked living abroad very much or you disliked the Napa Valley to the extreme." He laughed.

"Neither of those is the case exactly. It's been more a matter of circumstance. Which brings me to why I am here, taking up your valuable time."

"Not at all. Today is the day I usually don't have any appointments so that I can catch up on my reading . . . you know, keeping up with what's new in medicine. Now, what can I do for you? How may I be of help?"

"I can understand your wanting to know specifically what your mother died of, since there *does* seem to be a propensity for SLE to be passed on in the genes, but I'm not at all sure that your decision to marry or have babies should be based on that possibility. Right now lupus is something of a mystery, as I'm sure has been explained to you by doctors far more expert than I in the area, but medical science *will* eventually learn the answers, and if lupus does show up in a child you bear, by that time it might well be a snap to cure. Even now, underresearched as the disease is, it's more easily diagnosed than ever before and can usually be controlled if doctor and patient are diligent.

"The real problem, of course, is that the sickness is so underresearched, but that too is bound to change. And short of finding a cure, they might well learn how to control these periods of remission so that they can extend them until . . . well, till the end of time."

"God, I hope so, and I would hope that all doctors would be as enthusiastic and optimistic as you. But right now my immediate problem, Doctor, *is* my mother's records. I *must* know what my mother died of. *Are* they available?"

She was so afraid he was going to say no she could scarcely breathe.

"There is a bit of a problem," he said, and Andrianna's heart sank. "Space being something of a problem, my father's old records are in storage, so it's going to take a little digging to find them."

Andrianna was so relieved she laughed aloud. "Thank God. I thought you were going to say they were lost forever."

He laughed too. "Hardly. Old medical files are medical history, and research was my first love. What is research without history? What I propose to do is send my assistant over to the storage company right now to start digging while you let me take you to lunch so that I can talk your ear off telling you all about myself . . . what I'm doing here in La Paz and why. Does that sound fair?"

"More than fair. It sounds like I get the best of the deal."

They talked over succulent oysters and meltingly sweet John Dory and a bottle of local wine, and at first she mostly listened.

"I took my residency in pediatrics and planned on going into research. My dream was to find the cures for all the diseases that afflict kids who have no real line of defense. I guess I wanted to be the big hero who would save them. And so when my dad begged me to come into his practice, telling me that there were lots of poor, really deprived kids in La Paz and the surrounding towns who needed a doctor trained in pediatrics, I told him no. I was too noble to settle for the general practitioner's daily grind. I had bigger fish to fry.

321

Remember I told you *all* kids were self-centered? Well, that was me, even though I was a kid in my twenties by that time."

"But you *did* have a noble purpose," Andrianna protested.

His smile was bittersweet. "Did I? Was I really so much into research, or was it self-gratification? And what about my father and what I owed him? He'd been just another dirt-poor Mexican kid who became a doctor against terrific odds, practically starving getting through medical school, and then he *made* me a doctor—handed it to me on a silver platter with no pain and lots of gravy. He sent me to Stanford, and all he wanted back was for me to join him here in his practice, and not just to fulfill his own dream but because he knew I was needed here. And I refused him, probably broke his heart, not to mention that I had even rejected his good name. By that time, you see, Geraldo Hernandez, Jr., was Jerry Hern."

Andrianna thought of his wife, the woman Gladys Garcia said he had changed his name for. Well, he had to please her too. Her happiness was his responsibility as much as, or maybe more than, any other. He owed it to her to try to give her what she needed. That was what marriage meant, didn't it? Each partner giving the other what he or she needed aside from love and sex.

"I'm sure you had good reasons to do that," she murmured.

"I *thought* I did. I changed my name when I was still in medical school. I told myself I was doing it because of all the prejudice against Chicanos, that as Geraldo Hernandez I'd never get into a really good research situation. And how was I going to do all the good I planned to do unless I did get into the best?"

So he hadn't changed his name for his wife after all, Andrianna thought. "But that makes sense . . . to change your name for that reason."

"Does it? I was going to be a Stanford Med School graduate. One would think that would have been sufficient to get into a fine research project. Maybe all I *really* wanted was to rid myself of what I saw as a stigma."

"I don't believe that. That's ridiculous."

"That's what my wife, Melissa, said. But she was talking about the act of changing my name in the first place. She said that it was ridiculous for me to change my name because that was—" he ducked his head, embarrassed to go on.

"Yes? Tell me, please."

"She said my name was part of the beauty of being me and that whatever I attained would be all the more beautiful if everything about me was the same as when I came into the world—a kind of summation of my parts. That's how Melissa talks," he said, his dark eyes gleaming, and Andrianna thought that in spite of who and what he was, Dr. Hern was prouder of his wife than he was of himself, and that in itself was beautiful. And she knew that Gladys Garcia had been wrong about Melissa Hern.

Overwhelmed, Andrianna lowered her eyes. "I think your wife is a poet."

"Yes, but I didn't listen to her, and I *did* change my name. And in the end I fooled no one. Everyone still knew who I was and what I was. How does it go? 'A man is not known by his name but by his deeds.' I think that was what Melissa had tried to tell me. But by the time I really understood all this I'd been Jerry Hern so long that it was too late to go back—I had already lost part of myself."

"Oh, no!" she cried. "You still are who you are no matter what you call yourself!" She stopped abruptly, startled by the realization that she was protesting on her own behalf as well as his.

"But you still haven't told me how you got from research to *here*. Back to La Paz."

"I didn't come back until after my father died. I was working in a big hospital in San Francisco doing my research, and when my father died it was his funeral that changed my mind. That's when it hit me—when I saw all the people who came to his funeral, hundreds of them, and how they cried

323

and mourned him. They weren't just from La Paz but from all over the valley, and all I could think of was how sorely he was going to be missed.

"These were people who couldn't afford to go to fancy doctors or travel back and forth to San Francisco in the hope of being accepted into some big hospital's clinic without money or any kind of health insurance. And how they mourned! They'd just lost one of their best friends — my father — who'd begun life as one of them and was totally dedicated to their cause.

"And I realized that there was important work to be done. Maybe not *more* important than research, but at least equally important. And you could say that it's research too. Real, live, relevant research in the field rather than in an isolated laboratory. So I made a choice that day, and I've never looked back, never regretted my decision."

He laughed. "Not even when I hear how much money all my old buddies from med school are making . . ."

She smiled at his joke, but really felt like crying. *I've never looked back, never regretted my decision* — oh, what wonderful words they were!

"Well, I think all your patients are most privileged to have you for their doctor and that Melissa is a very lucky woman."

And she thought that she had been privileged to have met Jerry Hern and that, no matter what happened, even if she never saw him again, she would never forget him. Even with the jury still out and the verdict yet to come in, Jerry Hern had given her something of infinite value — the gift of friendship.

He had opened himself up to her, fully revealed himself unashamedly, even with humility, and if he did nothing more for her, he had already shown her that there was hope, that there was a way to go, a way to come back home even if one had changed one's name.

And she found herself telling him far more about herself than she had ever intended, more than she had ever told

324

anyone. It was as if once she started to talk she couldn't stop, starting with the man who was her father and the day her mother died . . .

"But what did you do when you left Gino Forenzi's house?"

"I didn't want to stay in Rome, where Gae and Gino were, so I went to Paris."

"And what did you do there?"

"I knew a few people there, one *real* friend and some acquaintances. And they invited me to parties and things, and I met more people who became friendly acquaintances, and they took me to more parties, and soon I had *many* friendly acquaintances. And then, since I knew a lot of people and a *little* about art and was running out of cash—I was heeding Gino's advice about hoarding what jewelry I had against my personal rainy day—I took a position in an art gallery, which mostly entailed bringing in my rich friendly acquaintances to buy. It wasn't a very fulfilling career, but I became fairly good at it."

"But you had been Gino's executive assistant. Surely you could have gotten a good position—an executive position in the business world. You could have built a real career."

"Maybe, but I couldn't have gotten a job in business without mentioning my experience with Forenzi Motors, and if I had done that, I never would have been sure that I'd gotten the job on my own rather than because Gino had pulled some strings. And I really needed to disassociate myself from him altogether. But most of all, building a career meant thinking of the future—the long term—and I just couldn't face that. If I had made any *real* plans for my life, I would have had to take into account the very real possibility of coming out of remission. So I refused to think more than a couple of days ahead. I considered everything—and everybody—a transitory thing. I *did* become involved with a man in Paris for a time, rather a nice man, but when the relationship showed signs of heating up, with the man demanding a commitment I was unable to give, I was afraid. I decided it was time to move on.

"Besides, I was tiring of my job at the art gallery — it was unpleasant to be using people, especially since I had felt so used myself by Gino, in spite of all he had done for me. So I packed up and went to London, saying good-bye to my special male friend, telling him to forget me but taking along the pieces of jewelry he had given me. You see I still thought Gino was the smartest man in the world, and I never forgot the advice he had given me." She paused and then added dryly, "Of course it wasn't until years later that it occurred to me that in doing that I was guilty of the worst kind of using there is.

"And then, once in London, I didn't want the man from Paris hunting me down, so I started using the name Anna della Rosa. Besides, in London it was more appealing to be Anna della Rosa than Ann Sommer, as it had been to be Ann Sommer in Paris, the exotic always seemingly more attractive to the natives.

"And no longer wanting to be in the art game, I became a dancer since I was fairly good at the flamenco and had had some lessons in dancing. But I wasn't really very successful — as an amateur I was adequate, but as a professional . . . well, there was a lot to be desired.

"But it didn't really matter. There were always a lot of people who were eager to be friendly, especially men. And after that I went to — well, I really don't remember which country came before which. But I tried singing for a while before I turned to acting before I moved on . . . new name, new profession, new acquaintances, new men. Before I decided to come back to the States, I was back in London, acting under the name of Andrianna DeArte . . . and here I am."

"And here you are," Jerry said, smiling, "only a couple of letters away from being beautiful little Andrianna Duarte again."

"No, I don't think so. Not yet, anyway. After all, *you*,

Jerry Hern, are the one who only a little while ago told me that after a while it's too late to really go back—one has already lost part of oneself."

"Well, maybe the name part isn't all that important. Maybe we can reclaim ourselves by dealing with the truth—confronting it, acting on it, *being* who we really are. Doing better, doing more . . ."

Perhaps, she thought, Gino Forenzi wasn't the wisest man she had ever known. Maybe it was Geraldo Hernandez, Jr. As for Jonathan West, she had no idea how really wise he was or what his thinking on this truth business would be, the truth here being that she barely knew him and didn't know how he would react to who she really was and how she had lived her life. Just thinking about it made her nervous and fearful. All that she positively knew about the man was that she loved him and believed that he loved her.

Then, since she had already told Jerry Hern practically everything there was to know about her, she told him about Jonathan West . . .

Jerry pulled into the parking facility that adjoined his office building and gestured at all the parked cars glistening in the afternoon sun. "Look at them. They've got all the best spots—out here in the light and the fresh air—and they're only cars. Someday I hope to see a clinic for kids grow right here in this cement paradise, like grapes growing tender on the vines. But so far I'm afraid that's just a dream."

"Why? What's holding up the dream?"

"What usually holds up a dream. Money, or the lack of it. And time, of course. If I had the time, I might be able to line up some benefactors to get the project going."

"Maybe I can help."

"You? But you're not even planning on living in northern California."

"No, but I told you, I do have some very rich friends."

"Yes, but rich doesn't always mean willing, does it?"

327

No, it didn't. It *was* a debatable question. Who would know better than she that there was rich and then there was rich, and at best they were an unpredictable crew?

Jerry Hern's Rikki was waiting for them with Elena's records in hand. "It was a snap," she told them gleefully. "Everything was still in alphabetical order."

"Great," Jerry said, taking the records and circling Andrianna's shoulders protectively with an arm as he led her into his inner office.

Andrianna sat and waited like a child, hands folded in her lap, as Jerry read through the stack of pages. Every now and then he skipped impatiently, shuffling the pages, knowing the tension was mounting unbearably for her. Every now and then he looked up from the records to smile at her encouragingly.

Finally, his voice filled with relief, "Your mother didn't die from lupus. She had a defective heart."

Her own heart leapt. "Are you sure? You're not lying just to tell me what I want to hear?"

"Andrianna!" he reproached her. "I would never lie to you."

With a jolt she recalled that only a few days before she had heard the very same words from Jonathan.

I didn't lie to you, Andrianna. I would never lie to you.

And then she thought that in so many ways Jerry and Jonathan were alike in spite of the obvious differences of coloring and disparate backgrounds. There was the same steadfast gaze. A kind of honesty, a genuineness both wore like a mantle. And they shared that quality of openness that bespeaks both self-confidence and courage — the confidence that one will be accepted, the courage to face the consequences of one's own actions, one's own convictions.

Obviously both were giants among men — the still-youthful Jonathan, who had already made a fortune to which few men even dared aspire, and Jerry, who practiced the kind of

328

medicine other doctors didn't think they could afford. Both were, in their own way, heroic figures, the big difference between them lying in the nature of their dreams. Jonathan dreamed of making an ever bigger fortune just for the doing of it, the challenge and the winning, while Jerry dreamed of raising money to build a children's clinic. And perhaps it was the nature of the dream—a thin line—that separated the heroic figure from the true hero.

But you didn't love a wonderful man any less because he was only a thin line away from being a true hero. Rather, you loved him for what he already was and what you believed he could eventually be . . .

Oh, Jonathan!

She was one step closer.

But almost immediately she thought of something else, something that transformed the whole picture, and it was a chilling thought. Her mother had died from a defective heart, and wasn't that how lupus eventually killed? By attacking the vital organs, like the kidneys and the heart?

Jerry seemed to know what she was thinking just by watching her face, and he got up and came around the desk to crouch at her chair. "It wasn't the wolf lupus that preyed on her heart. It seems your mother was my father's patient from the time she was very young—he was easily twenty years her senior. She already had a bad heart when they first brought her to see him."

"Oh, Mama! My poor Elena. But why? Was she born with a bad heart?"

"I can't say for sure. But from the records—my father's conclusions—I would say she had had rheumatic fever. In those days rheumatic fever often went undetected and *could* leave a little girl with a severely damaged heart."

"Do you think *anything* could have helped her? Surgery?" She thought of the quality of Andrew Wyatt's love. Elena had loved him so. How hard and how much had he loved her back? "More care? Better care? What?"

"Don't do this to yourself, Andrianna. Don't torture yourself with the possibilities . . . the *ifs*. Your mother died thirty years ago. So many unknowns. Maybe today—a transplant? Who can really say?"

"I was thinking about love."

He smiled at her sorrowfully and shook his head. "Love?" And then he said again, "Who can really say?"

For a few minutes they were both silent as he concentrated on Elena's medical history again, she on trying to make sense of it all. And she realized that in the end it really didn't matter how hard or how much Andrew Wyatt had loved Elena. What was really important was that *she* had loved *him* and that, at least for a while, she had had her golden moments stolen from eternity. For her it had been until the end of time . . .

And for that Andrianna was grateful.

Finally Jerry put the file down.

"At least you know there's no evidence that your mother suffered from lupus. And that's what you really wanted to know, wasn't it?"

"Yes. But—" Now she smiled. "I'm not through with you. You're not off the hook yet, Dr. Hern."

"Oh?" He smiled. "What can I do for you now? Tell me and I'm yours."

"I have a plan in mind, and if it turns out . . . well, if things go my way, I'll be living in L.A., which is not all that far from here, and I want *you* to be my doctor. I *am* in remission, so you won't have to see me that often, just periodic examinations. And I can fly up here—when and if . . . Please Jerry, you can't refuse me!"

"But I'm not a specialist in the field! And why would you want to have a doctor that you have to take a plane to see? Besides, there are probably more doctors every square inch where you'll be liv—" He broke off to look at her hard. Finally he said, "Andrianna, don't do this!"

"Don't do what? Ask you to be my doctor? Shame on you, Dr. Hern. What about the Hippocratic Oath? Aren't you sworn to help anybody you can?"

"You *know* that's not what I'm talking about. I'm talking about your *not* telling this man you're thinking of marrying the whole truth. Goddamn it, Andrianna, you owe him the truth! If he loves you, he'll accept whatever the facts are. And if you love him, you have to trust him to do that. If you can't, well, what's the point?"

The point was that for the first time in her life she was gambling on love, on life, and not being a true gambler, she needed all the odds she could get.

"When we were at lunch, when we were talking about your having changed your name, you said that when you realized it had been the wrong thing to do it was already too late, that there was no going back. That you had already lost part of yourself.

"Well, I thought you were wrong about that, at least for you. But it's certainly true for me. There's no going back. All I can do is get on with it. Jonathan loves me enough, I think, to accept me on faith. And I will prove my own faithfulness by being the best wife I can possibly be. There can't be anything wrong with that—being the best I can possibly be. Is there?"

"No, not with that. But there is something terribly wrong about living a lie . . . all these lies."

"It's not really a lie if you do it in the name of love . . ."

"Will *he* think so if he finds out the truth?"

She didn't want to think about that, so she said, "Well, so far this discussion is academic since I haven't positively made up my mind what I'm going to do. I just want to know if I can count on you just in case."

"It's not that I'm unwilling to help you, Andrianna, not even that I think what you're doing is wrong, which I most emphatically do. But I'm not qualified. You need a specialist—"

"You're special enough for me. I *am* in remission, and neither one of us knows for how long. And I have a feeling that by the time I might need a doctor informed enough to treat me, you, the great researcher, will know enough about it all to be the right man for the job. All I really need now is to have routine checkups. Nothing you can't handle. I have every faith in you, Dr. Hern. And if and when I do become pregnant . . . well, I'm sure you'll know what to do with a pregnant lady, *n'est-ce pas?*"

He shook his head at her, almost in despair. "Pregnant? There's too much risk for *you* involved."

"All right, Doctor. I promise. I'll get pregnant only if he asks. *If* Jonathan says he wants a child."

Jerry Hern groaned, and Andrianna asked him what the groan meant.

"It means that if I'm going to be your doctor I have to recommend that you think long and hard before you become pregnant, in spite of the baby not being at risk — *if* you can manage to carry to term. As *your* doctor I wouldn't want you to put *yourself* at risk, taking the chance that the pregnancy will trigger flare-ups . . . possibly a massive one."

"Does this mean what I think it means? That you're saying yes, you're willing to be my doctor?"

"I don't think you're giving me any choice in the matter," he said dryly.

"Oh, but this is *all* about choices. And chances. Thank you, Jerry, for giving *me* a choice and a chance."

Oh, Jonathan, we're getting really close.

She threw her arms around Jerry to kiss him in thanks and gratitude, and he bent his head to kiss her back, full on the lips. She found his kiss sweet but not nearly as sweet as Jonathan's, and for that too she was grateful.

"I'll let you know the minute I make the final decision. If the man still wants me after the way I've acted . . ."

"He'll want you, Andrianna. Only the most foolish of men wouldn't want you."

For a moment then she wondered what would have been if Andrianna Duarte had never left the Napa Valley and there'd been no Ann Sommer, no Gae and no Gino, no long line of men with nameless faces. And if, for Geraldo Hernandez, Jr., there'd been no Jerry Hern and no Melissa.

Would the big-shot fifth-grader and the little second-grader with the big yellow eyes have found solace and comfort, and yes, love in each other's arms?

They were looking into each other's eyes, and Andrianna sensed that perhaps he was asking himself the same question. And then she saw him flush before he lowered his eyes. It was a question that would never be answered, and that was only as it should be.

Still, her eyes filled with tears. She felt as close to Jerry Hern as she had ever felt to anyone.

She reached for her snakeskin bag to take out a checkbook.

"What do you think you're doing?"

"Writing a check. Do you have a pen? But I have to write the check on an English bank and in pounds. I haven't had a chance to transfer funds to an American bank."

He shook his head. "You're way out of line. You can't pay me to do what I'm doing out of friendship for an old schoolmate, especially when it's something I think is essentially wrong."

"There you go again, being terribly self-centered," she mocked him. "It was never my intention to pay *you*. What I'm doing is making the first donation to that children's clinic that's going to take root in that parking lot one of these days. Surely you wouldn't deny me that privilege. You see it will not only be the clinic's first donation; it will be the first time in my life that I will be a benefactor. You're officially my doctor now, and as such you have to realize that my doing this is very important to my mental health."

Then she dropped the bantering tone. "Please, Jerry. Let me do this. All I've ever done is take, grabbing everything I could get my hands on so that I could save it all up for my rainy day. Well, this is an act of faith. Faith that rain isn't even in the offing and that, at last, *I* can spread a little sunshine. Be generous. Let me do it.

"Besides, I'm not writing a check for a fortune. This check is only a drop in the bucket for what you have in mind. And

333

I can afford it."

"With or without Jonathan West's money?"

His question was tersely stated, and she thought it was a wee bit mean, hitting somewhere below the belt, but still it was an honest question and she was not offended. She shrugged.

"With or without Jonathan's money. It doesn't matter. It's something *I* need to do."

"Then on behalf of the children of the Napa Valley, I accept your donation . . . and thank you."

"Thank *you*.

He walked her outside where her limousine was waiting for her. "I see you're ready for Los Angeles — the Beverly Hills side of it, that is." He smiled and nodded toward the hired car.

"Well, I'm staying at the Stanford Court in San Francisco. How else would I have gotten here without a car and driver?"

He laughed. "Most people would have rented a car, jumped in, and taken off. That's the California way. The American way, I'd say."

She sighed. "But then I'm not your usual American, and certainly not your usual Angeleno. To tell the truth, I've hardly ever driven a car myself." Then she too broke into a smile. "But you know what? I will do it! I'll do whatever it takes to be a real Californian. And if it means jumping into a car and taking off like a rocket, I'll do that too."

He kissed her again, hard and quickly. "Brava, Andrianna Duarte. I'm betting on you," he whispered. "You'll be leaving for Los Angeles in the morning, then?"

"No. Not quite yet. I still have some unfinished business before I make up my mind for sure."

"Yes?"

"Yes" was all she said. Dr. Jerry Hern already knew far too much about her, almost everything there was to know, and she wasn't used to quite so much disclosure.

She looked around the parking lot. "What will you do with all the cars once the clinic is built?"

"Stick them underground. Save the sunlight for the living. That means you too, Andrianna. I mean it. I'd like to see you come out of the darkness *completely.* Try it, won't you? Who knows? You might even like it."

His words were jaunty, but his voice was intense and his hands gripped her shoulders tightly.

She looked at him for several long seconds as if she were weighing his words. Then she laughed. "Really, Doctor, you should know better than that. The sun can be very bad for one. At any rate, partial sun is all I can possibly take right now. Maybe I'll do better later on."

He closed the car door after her.

"Wish me luck?" she said through the window.

"I can do better than that. I can wish you love . . ."

Staci Whitley was a cute, shapely blonde with a hank of hair pulled to one side and tied with a perky bow that matched her extremely short, sequined party dress, but when Madison Short pulled Jonathan aside, he wasn't particularly reluctant to leave her. "Be back in a few minutes," he said.

"There are four of us who are buying this parcel of land in the Marina. We need a fifth. Interested?" Madison wanted to know.

"What have you got in mind?" Jonathan straightened Madison's black bow tie. "Investment or development?"

"Development. A miniature Century City. I can send over the figures."

"Why don't you do that?"

"You got to give me a quick answer."

"Like a bunny," Jonathan said and went back to Staci Whitley at their table.

"How do you spell your name, Staci?"

335

"With an I . . . Why?" She put her hand on his thigh.

"No reason. I was just wondering why so many young women I meet spell their names like that. With an I instead of a Y. It seems like it's all the rage."

"Well, that's not the point," she pointed out, her hand creeping closer to his crotch. "The point is to be different from everyone else. All the ones who spell their names with a Y. Do you follow?"

"Sort of."

She was massaging him now, under the table. "Your place or mine?" she breathed.

"Well, I'd say mine . . . only there's a problem. Directly after I drop you off, I have to leave for out of town."

"Oh, that's too bad," she pouted. "Do you promise to call me as soon as you get back?"

He tried not to give out his promises lightly. "I promise to give it a try . . . as soon as I can."

Andrianna got into bed with her room-service dinner and the local telephone directory, but she was looking for an address, not a number. It was one thing to call a doctor's office for an appointment and quite another to call a member of the Wyatt family who probably didn't even know that she existed. Besides, what could she say over the phone? Where would she begin? The only possible way to do this was in person.

Since she had no first names to go by, she looked for a business listing in the directory and found Wyatt Associates, Inc., with a whole roster of financial institutions listed under one inclusive address. She felt certain that she had the right place and the right parties, and tomorrow would tell the tale.

Still, after she finished her dinner and clicked on the TV, hoping to find something interesting enough to keep her mind off the next day's mission, or boring enough to put her to sleep so that she wouldn't toss all night, she picked up the phone directory to read once again the listings of those named Wyatt. There was a Dorothea Wyatt who lived on a street called Broadway. Could that be *her* Mrs. Wyatt?

She also found a Bernard and a Mortimer Wyatt. Were *they* Dorothea's sons, her own half-brothers? Was it just possible that they *did* know about her, and had wanted to meet her for a long, long time, would even open their arms to her, their long lost sister, in warm welcome?

Then she scoffed at herself. She was weaving a child's fairy tale and she'd be lucky if the Wyatts were barely civil.

Nonetheless, she fell asleep with a half-smile on her lips as the television played on into the night, and it wasn't until daybreak that she awoke to realize that it was Saturday morning and that she would have to wait until Monday to beard the Wyatts in their den.

Two more days to wait. Two more days before she discovered who . . . what her father had really been. Two more days before she could, like a bird, wing her way south to find the sun. Maybe, just as the doctor had ordered, it *was* time for her to come out of the dark into the daylight, to revel in a lifetime of gloriously golden afternoons . . .

It was very late by the time Jonathan pulled into the driveway of his beach house, very late and very dark. Still, before he went inside, he ran up the back staircase leading from the sand to the deck to look out to sea. The water was calm, which was restful, and then he looked up at the sky and saw stars. It was that kind of night in Malibu. Most nights you could barely see the stars for the fog or the smog or the mist — whatever it was that could get between the viewer and the heavens. . . .

And then he started to count them, one by one. . . .

Twenty-four

Monday

Andrianna rode up to the penthouse floor where the top-level executive suites were located. The marbled and brassed elevator zoomed as fast as lightning but was even more glitzy than that phenomenon of nature.

The Wyatts were no mere millionaires, she mused, recalling what Jonathan West had told her about millionaires becoming quite commonplace in the last few years. The Wyatt Building—a block square and with a marbled lobby filled with crystal chandeliers and paintings and sculpture and thousands of yards of fine carpeting—obviously belonged to a family that were, cumulatively, at least, billionaires.

"Mr. Wyatt, please." Her most cordial tone, her brightest smile.

"Which Mr. Wyatt did you have an appointment with?" Crisp, clipped, basically bored. "Andrew, William, Sinclair? You *do* have an appointment?"

Andrianna felt the intended chill, hugged her lynx coat more tightly to her, drew herself up. "You're to tell Andrew Wyatt that Andrianna Duarte is here to see him," she said imperiously, just guessing that Andrew was the one in charge, the firstborn son named for his father, as she herself was.

But the receptionist was not intimidated by Andrianna's grand lady manner either. "You *don't* have an appointment, then," she said flatly. "I'll inform Mr. Wyatt's secretary that you're here, but I can tell you that without an appointment you're *not* going to get in to see him." This last with a great measure of satisfaction.

Andrianna permitted herself a tight-lipped, icy smile. She hadn't survived all these years by allowing cheeky young women to intimidate *her*. "He'll see me," she said frostily. "Just be sure you get the name straight." She spelled it out slowly, then repeated it, emphasizing the soft Spanish pronunciation.

Eyebrows raised superciliously, the young woman picked up the phone, punched a key hard, and said into the receiver, "There's a woman here to see Mr. Wyatt. She *doesn't* have an appointment, but she insists he'll see her."

She swiveled around so that her back was to Andrianna and what she said inaudible. Then, without looking at Andrianna, "You may take a seat."

"Mr. Wyatt is going to see me now?"

"I was told to ask you to wait. Someone will be out shortly." Then, grudgingly, as if routine courtesy was an afterthought and just in case Andrianna Duarte turned out to be someone to be reckoned with after all: "Would you care for some coffee?"

"I think not," Andrianna said, careful not to add a thank you.

She took a seat, choosing a somewhat uncomfortable chair rather than sinking into one of the downy gray velvet sofas, sitting with her back absolutely erect, deliberately crossing her legs at a precise angle, despite the sickening realization that the tone for what was to follow had already been established, its pattern set, and it wasn't looking too good. So much for fairy tales.

After nearly an hour had passed, a young man with pink cheeks came into the reception room and the receptionist gestured toward Andrianna. He approached her. "Ms. *Do-Arty?*"

Her pulse quickened. Was this Andrew? No, it couldn't be. This man in his conservative dark gray worsted was much too young.

"Yes?"

"Would you please follow me?"

He led her out of the reception room, down a corridor seemingly blocks long, and finally into another reception room where a gray-haired woman sat before a huge desk. He announced "Ms. Do-Arty" before making an exit.

"Please be seated, Ms. Do-Arty. Mr. Wyatt will see you presently," the woman said, scarcely looking at her.

"The name is not Do-Arty but Duarte," Andrianna enunciated sharply.

At exactly sixty minutes to the dot after Andrianna had first entered the room and without so much as the ringing of a phone or a buzz from an intercom, the woman rose and went to one of several closed doors, knocked once before opening it, and told her, "You may go in now."

Four men were seated in the paneled room, decorated in the fashion of a library in an English manor house, and they were all looking at her as if she were a bug under a microscope. The man behind the desk attired in pearl gray and rimless spectacles—Andrianna guessed that he was Andrew—rose and acknowledged her presence with a tight-lipped "Miss Duarte." He, at least, pronounced the name correctly.

"I'm Andrew Wyatt, and this is my brother William." He indicated a balding man in charcoal gray flannel.

William stood up briefly before quickly taking his seat again without offering his hand.

340

"And this is my brother Sinclair."

Sinclair in pin-striped gray was the youngest of the men and resembled Andrew Wyatt as well as Andrianna remembered him. Sinclair half rose from his chair, as if willing to be halfway well mannered but no more.

"And this is Porter Jameson, our sister Hillary's husband," Andrew went on without inflection. "Porter is our chief attorney as well as being an officer of the company."

Porter did not rise or even nod; he merely blinked at her like a pot-bellied toad dressed up in slightly rumpled pale gray gabardine.

Without waiting to be asked, Andrianna sat down in a chair facing the four. If they were willing to be rude, she would not observe the formalities either, standing before them like some unruly child awaiting her headmistress's pleasure.

Once seated, she shrugged off her lynx, crossed her legs to their best advantage, and said, "Gentlemen."

Obviously, they knew exactly who she was. They *had,* after all, gathered here to greet her in Andrew's office like a coven of warlocks after having kept her waiting for at least two hours. Now she would have the small satisfaction of forcing one of them to speak first.

Porter took up the gauntlet. "You didn't bring an attorney with you?"

She flashed a wide smile. "Should I have?"

Porter only blinked again and Andrianna thought that foolish Hillary, her half-sister, had had the poor sense to marry a fat slug.

"What was it exactly you wished to see me about, Miss Duarte?" Andrew asked, a touch impatiently.

"Please, call me Andrianna," she said, displaying the wide smile again. Then, suddenly she was impatient to bring the conference to a head. "After all, we *are* brother and sister, are we not, Andy?" Her yellow eyes turned from Andrew to William to Sinclair. "Are we not, Billy

341

dear and darling Clair? Or does everyone just call you Sin?"

Sinclair giggled nervously, and William stirred uncomfortably while Porter tapped his foot. It was Andrew who said in a monotone, "What do you want? Or should I ask how *much* do you want?"

"How much?" Andrianna repeated after him. And then she laughed. But of course! Naturally they assumed she had come looking for money. Never had it dawned on them that she had come seeking only reassurance . . . that their father and hers had loved her mother, had loved her . . .

Porter bit at a cuticle. "You're right in not answering that question too quickly, Miss Duarte. Before you do, keep in mind that you're only worth so much as nuisance value. While any claims you may *think* you have would be worth *nothing* in a court of law, it still bears some expense for us in terms of manpower hours to go to court. So in the interest of cost efficiency, it's worth something for us to buy you off and get rid of you, but only so much and no more."

In spite of herself his words stung. *Buy you off and get rid of you.* Like she was a bag of trash.

"I'm your sister!" she cried out angrily, looking not at Porter but at Andrew.

Andrew appeared pained, but even in her anguish she could tell it was not because her plaint had touched him but because she was behaving badly—the child who had forgotten the rules of acceptable behavior.

William crossed and uncrossed his legs and spoke for the first time in a voice that managed somehow to be both whispery and loudly ominous. "You have to understand, Miss Duarte, that there've been dozens like you before, would-be heirs crawling out of the woodwork ever since Father died."

"And our mother can testify that there were dozens who

came to her *before* Father died, all kinds of persons claiming they were Father's illegitimate children," Sinclair added disdainfully. "Every wealthy family is subjected to this sort of thing."

Porter shot Sinclair a withering look. "That is beside the point. The question, Miss Duarte, is, what proof do you have that you are Andrew Wyatt's illegitimate daughter?"

"Proof? I'm named for him!" Andrianna shouted, too aroused now to remember to be cool, to watch her words. "And when my mother died, I was almost eight years old and your father was still coming around in his Rolls-Royce. It was a love affair that lasted over nine years, at least. And then when my mother died, he assumed responsibility for me. It was he who arranged for my adoption into an English family . . . who sent money for my support all those years until he died. Does that sound like he didn't accept me as his daughter? And you, you lying hypocrites! You're all here to deal with me, aren't you, even though I came here unannounced this morning, even though you weren't expecting me? Which means you all knew about me before this . . . were *very* much aware of my existence. Otherwise none of you would have bothered to see a woman named Andrianna Duarte at all."

"Of course we were aware of your existence, Miss Duarte," Andrew Wyatt said wearily, flicking a piece of imaginary lint from his lapel. "As soon as Father died, the attorney who was handling your . . . account, shall we say, came to us with the details of the arrangement between Father and that Sommer woman. He handed over all the records, including the checks that had supported you and your mother for years before that. The point is, Miss Duarte, you aren't the only one of dubious parentage. There are at least three others of you whom Father supported up until the time of his death. An admission of fatherhood? Of culpability? Perhaps. But knowing Father, I would say it was just the easiest way of dealing with a difficult and potentially embarrassing situation."

Andrianna was devastated. Her worst suspicion—that all her father had ever wanted was to be rid of her and her embarrassing presence—had been confirmed with one simple phrase.

Porter consulted his notes. "There's an Andrea Hodges in Sonoma and an Andy Cutter living up in Eureka and a—"

"I don't think all the details are necessary, Porter," Andrew said dryly. "If it's any consolation to you, Miss Duarte, the alliance between your mother and our father was the longest-lasting of any of Father's arrangements."

Arrangements! Elena and her golden sex in the afternoon reduced to an arrangement.

"I'm his daughter," Andrianna said dully. "There might have been others for your father, but there was never anyone else for my mother."

William Wyatt uncrossed and recrossed his legs and snorted. "You were only a small child, Miss Duarte. What did you know? And how can you possibly speak for the time period of your conception?" He gave a little laugh. "Your mother could have had a dozen lovers at the time . . ."

"You didn't know my mother or you wouldn't say that—"

Porter rubbed his nose. "Of course we don't expect you to admit anything like that, but the nature of your mother's profession being what it was—"

His meaning was inescapable, and enraged, out of control, Andrianna started to rise from her chair. "Oh, you unspeakable, sleazy bastard! You—"

A door flew open, and all eyes turned toward it as a woman in a wheelchair rolled through the doorway, then expertly maneuvered her chair into position in the middle of the room. She was a still-handsome woman of some seventy years wearing dark blue silk, discreet diamonds and pearls, her hair pulled tightly back into a large chignon dressed with a large dark blue velvet bow.

Andrianna fell back into her chair. She had never imagined that she was going to meet Mrs. Andrew Wyatt in the flesh.

"Mother Babs!" Porter protested her entrance, and Andrew cried, "Mother, you said you wouldn't — that you would allow us to handle this . . ."

"But you weren't handling it," Babs Wyatt snapped. "What should have been disposed of with dispatch and some dignity was turning into a cat-and-dog fight!" She threw Porter a particularly contemptuous look. "Disgusting and counterproductive."

Babs Wyatt's anger was obvious, but Andrianna thought that very possibly the anger was a cover for the elderly woman's humiliation at what she had overheard, for her pain. She thought Mrs. Wyatt's sons and son-in-law would have done everything possible to circumvent her knowing anything about this meeting . . . that they would have tried to spare her, especially since she was apparently an invalid.

Softly she said, "I'm sorry that you overheard —"

"Of course, I overheard!" interrupted Mrs. Wyatt. "I *was* in the next-door office listening on the intercom. Frankly, I was curious after all these years to see what Elena Duarte's daughter had to say for herself."

Porter and Andrew made protesting noises, afraid that she would make an admission that would be compromising, but she dismissed them with a wave of her hand.

"Those others who came forward claiming they were Andy's children didn't really interest me," she continued. "We just paid them off to get rid of them. But you and your mother fascinated me. Yes, I admit it. It was Andy's only affair that lasted . . . and lasted. And you were the only one of his possible heirs he provided for *so* handsomely. Really! You attended such good schools in Europe. And

345

all that expensive traipsing about for your holidays. He really must have had a soft spot for you . . . as much as he could have had for anyone. But I think I already knew that when you were born and he bought that house for your mother and that woman, Rosa."

Andrianna found it incredible that this woman was telling her all this, and from the looks on their faces, so did her sons and son-in-law.

"You mean you knew about me . . . about Mother and me . . . *all* along?"

"Exactly."

"But why didn't you—"

Babs Wyatt smiled tightly. "Why didn't I do something about it? Because by the time your mother came into the picture, Andrew and I had long since come to an understanding. I believe today it might be referred to as an open marriage. All I required of Andrew was discretion. Your mother was hardly the first of Andrew's women and not the only one at the time. And she wasn't *the* woman Andrew and I fought over, which resulted in my spending the rest of my life in this contraption."

She tapped the arm of the wheelchair, and they all stared at her in fresh shock.

"Mother!" Andrew cried out in protest.

"Oh, will you stop doing that, yelling 'Mother' every five seconds? What I'm saying can't be all that much of a shocking revelation to you. None of you are six years old, for God's sake."

"But it *is*, Mother . . . a revelation," William said in his whispery voice. "You never told us before that Father was responsible for your being crippled. We always assumed that it was an accident."

"Oh, I'm not saying your father *deliberately* pushed me down those stairs—but responsible? Yes. We were fighting over what I believed was the very first of his women—who knows anymore?—and I lunged at him, lost my balance. I believe that constitutes responsibility."

"But you never said anything. Why didn't you ever tell us?"

"It's not the sort of thing one goes around advertising, is it? Any more than we advertise the fact that you're a cocaine addict, William, or that Sinclair drinks too much, that Andrew's wife won't sleep with him, or that Porter likes to look at dirty pictures."

"Mother Babs, have you lost your mind?" Porter sputtered.

But the matriarch ignored him. "And you, Elena Duarte's daughter, why are you looking at me like that? Why do you find what I'm saying so shocking? *You're* hardly wet behind the ears."

"I'm sorry. It's just that I find all of this unbelievable . . . that you stayed with him. He was my father, but I had no choice in the matter. He was my mother's lover, but she was a naive, unsophisticated woman who worshiped him blindly and clung to what little she had of him until the end. But you, a woman of substance, with the money and the power and the ability to do whatever it was that had to be done, stayed, living this great lie, living this wasted life. Yes, I find that shocking!"

Suddenly Mrs. Wyatt looked worn, her years showing, her mouth turning down at the corners in bitterness. "What do you know about anything? You've had only yourself to think about, and you never had anything to safeguard. Not a fine old name, no reputation or a family to protect from scandal. I had my parents' good name to think of as well as my children's. And the family's fortune. A great fortune and a great name are a responsibility and an obligation a woman like you is incapable of understanding.

"There was no way that I was going to see that fortune decimated by a divorce or the public's trust in Wyatt Associates destroyed by gossip. Wyatt Associates are *financial* institutions whose officers must be above moral reproach. As you said, Elena Duarte's daughter, I *am* a woman of substance, and a woman of substance always puts responsibilities and obligations first, before personal happiness. That is what I did, and I have never regretted it!"

In spite of her spirited, resounding words Mrs. Wyatt, slumping in her chair now, seemed on the verge of collapse.

"But was it really worth it?" Andrianna demanded. "My Aunt Helene talked about the same thing, and she was hardly happy for it."

"Helene Sommer's happiness was hardly my concern," Mrs. Wyatt retorted, "but she had worse than I to deal with, what with the unspeakable habits her husband so nastily indulged."

Seeing Andrianna's quizzical expression, she went on, "You didn't know? Oh, yes, Alex Sommer's perversions — whips and chains, men and children and the Lord knows who or *what* else — were hardly a secret, despite his wife's efforts."

Andrianna felt the blood drain from her face. Helene had *known* she was telling the truth about Alex when she was only thirteen and had let her go on thinking there was something wrong with *her.* But worse, *far* worse, was that her father must have known what type of man he was turning her — his own *daughter* — over to. And apparently hadn't hesitated to do so.

Andrianna felt completely drained, but still she was glad that she had come. Despite everything, she felt grateful to Babs Wyatt for sharing so much with her, the terrible secrets of a lifetime, and giving her answers to some of the questions that had troubled her for so long. She wasn't *happier* for having come, yet the burden of uncertainty had been lifted from her shoulders.

Then she saw the older woman visibly rallying herself from the edge of collapse, pulling herself together with sheer effort of will, sitting up now ramrod-straight, and Andrianna was filled with a kind of admiration.

Babs Wyatt was a tough old bird with the guts her sons lacked. No wonder she had survived her fall and her husband's infidelities, life in a wheelchair and a loveless marriage, even her children's weaknesses, still managing to keep the reins of control over her empire in her two thin, vein-marked fists.

Then she heard the older woman say irritably that it was high time they finished up with this unsavory business. "For God's sake, Porter, give Elena Duarte's daughter her check and get her out of here."

A check? But she had thought that Andrew Wyatt's widow understood why she had come here, even if the men didn't!

She rose to protest, to tell them that she didn't want their filthy money . . . until she saw the amount of the check Porter was shoving under her nose, along with a statement he told her to sign. Then the words froze on her lips.

She quickly glanced through the document, which declared that in exchange for $50,000 she was surrendering all claims to either the Wyatt name or the family's fortune. Now she knew why they had kept her waiting so long: so they could have this statement drawn up.

She tore the check in half, walked over to Mrs. Wyatt, and let the two pieces flutter into her lap. "If I'm worth anything at all, I'm worth far more than this. I may sell out, but I don't sell out cheap. Besides, you're such a strong woman, I must try to emulate you. When *you* sold out, you did it to keep a real fortune intact. The least I can do is hold out for a hell of a lot more than this."

Mrs. Andrew Wyatt picked up the two halves of the check, looked at them, and shook her head in disgust. "You always were a fool, Porter, and a skinflint. Of course this isn't enough, and I don't blame you for being insulted,

Andrianna Duarte. You *are* worth more than this, certainly. After all, dear Andrew *did* screw your mother for almost ten years, and that's a lot of screwing."

Andrianna managed to keep silent in spite of the widow's shocking choice of words and waited for her to go on.

"How much do *you* think is fair, Andrianna?"

Andrianna considered. "A million dollars."

Actually, she'd been thinking of a half million until the "screwing" bit of rhetoric. But a million dollars was a nice round sum, and *if* she kept the money, and added that to the worth of her jewelry collection, she would be a millionaire two or three times over. An accomplishment of sorts and not at all bad for a girl who had started out life as a fatherless, homeless waif.

"Of course," the widow agreed. "A million dollars. And you shall have it. Andrew, have the check made out."

Andrew adjusted his glasses. "As you wish, mother."

"Have the check made out to the La Paz Children's Clinic, will you please?" Andrianna instructed as he picked up the phone.

Then she turned to Porter, who sat red-faced, rubbing his chin in frustration. "That isn't the official title of the clinic," she confided. "The name hasn't really been decided on as yet, but I imagine that it will do in the meantime, legally speaking. Is that right, Porter? May we have a legal opinion on that?"

Porter didn't answer.

"Well, we'll take our chances." She scratched out the $50,000 figure on the release and wrote in $1,000,000, initialing it, while the others sat watching her in an uneasy silence.

Smiling, she signed Andrianna Duarte at the bottom of the release with a flourish. The amount she had written her own check for had been a trifle by comparison. Now Jerry Hern's children's clinic, while not yet quite ready to bloom where there were only cars and cement, was that much closer to becoming a reality. And thus, out of the ashes of dead dreams, a new dream, a far better dream, rises, bewitching in its beauty, Andrianna recited to herself grandly, feeling slightly delirious with joy at what she had just accomplished.

"Oh, and just to be on the safe side, will you make that a cashier's check since you do have that nice big bank so handy on the ground floor? How convenient, really. The fabulously wealthy certainly know how to do things right."

"You could have been rich too if you had chosen to keep the money for yourself. It's interesting that you didn't." The widow looked at Andrianna thoughtfully for a few seconds before adding, "You should have married Gino Forenzi, you know. It would have been an excellent alliance for you considering your background."

And then it dawned on Andrianna that Mrs. Wyatt had kept tabs on her as she moved through life, even after Andrew Wyatt had died, and she wondered why. Why had she continued with her surveillance of Elena's daughter?

Because this understanding that she and her husband had worked out had not, after all, sat easily on her chest . . . Because, when all was said and done, she had been jealous of Elena, jealous of Andrianna's existence. Perhaps all of her efforts to keep the Wyatt fortune and the Wyatt name intact had *not*, after all, been worth it.

It wasn't until later, when she was already in the air on her way to Los Angeles—still torn with indecision, still not absolutely sure that what her heart cried out for her to do was right—that Andrianna realized her father's widow was, like Gladys Garcia, another Nicole, who had chosen safety and security over a real life, over a chance at love. Gladys had her VCR, Nicole her correct dinner parties, and Babs Wyatt had her reputation and her fortune.

Now she was even less sure that her mother had been

351

wrong. Maybe she hadn't been such a fool after all. However misled, and for too short a time, she, at least, had had her golden afternoons . . .

And Andrianna made her final decision on the matter. Right or wrong, Jonathan willing, she'd take her crack at those golden afternoons . . . at all those moments stolen from eternity, for as long as it lasted . . . till the end of time.

Part Four

Los Angeles
1989-1990

Twenty-five

It was January, but a line from an old song—*it might as well be spring*—kept running through her mind.

Before she'd turned him off, the weatherman on "Today in Los Angeles" had cheerfully advised that it was indeed a great morning, with the temperature at a sanguine seventy-two degrees in Los Angeles (sixty-nine degrees at the beaches, several degrees higher in the desert, and several degrees lower in the mountains), with near-zero humidity and a minimum of smog.

Oh, yes—she breathed the air—it was a rare and perfect day. Today, from the ceiling-to-floor French windows of her lovely new bedroom (almost bare of furnishings save for the huge, lushly canopied bed, the Art Deco mirrored vanity, and the thick carpeting the color of a beautiful pink-blushed peach) in her lovely new house perched high on its hilltop, she could see clear to where the sky met the sea, an unusual occurrence no matter the reckless promises of the real estate people who sold the jewellike, multimillion-dollar properties in Bel-Air.

It was an especially exquisite day for a wedding, and she was sure it meant that Penny and Gae were going to be supremely happy . . . as happy, if it were humanly possible, as she and Jonathan. If nothing else, it meant

355

Penny could have her outdoor ceremony and reception as she'd planned.

But suddenly, despite the balmy day, Andrianna shivered.

Gae! And Gino! She was going to see both of them today for the first time in years, even though she and Gae had made it a practice to speak on the phone every now and then. In fact she'd spoken with him fairly recently when she'd called to tell him how happy she was that he and Penny were getting married. Maybe it hadn't been really necessary, but she had needed to do it—to wish him luck, to wish him love . . . just as she had Penny. And after she'd hung up, she'd been glad she had called. It was a kind of final good-bye to that time when they'd been children playing at love. True, they'd both cried a little, but it was okay. The tears had been good tears.

As for Gino, there hadn't been any phone calls, but there'd been notes every now and then, hers to him just to touch base, his to her to let her know that he was there for her just in case she needed anything. And there'd been cards on birthdays and on Christmas, fairly impersonal the way cards often were. Sometimes it had been months before his cards caught up with her.

But today they'd not only see each other, but all of them—Gae and Gino, Penny and Nicole—would meet the husband they didn't even know existed. She hadn't planned it this way, hadn't meant to keep her marriage a secret, but old habits died hard, and when she'd talked to Penny and Nicole on the phone about the upcoming nuptials she'd always hung up without getting the words out. Besides, this time her secret was such a terrific one, she really wanted to keep it to herself for a while. Keep it and savor it . . .

She hadn't even given either of her friends a number where she could be reached. It was a case of "Don't call

356

me; I'll call you," just the way it had been most of the time in the past.

As always, she'd managed to skirt the whole issue of what *she* was up to, and she knew she hadn't given Penny or Nicole a clue. But would they know, the minute they saw her, that everything had changed?

And although she *was* a little shaky about seeing Gae and Gino, about introducing Jonathan to them, she wasn't really worried about either of them betraying her. Both had kept the secret of her illness all this time, and that was really the only secret she wanted to keep from Jonathan.

Or was it? Jonathan hadn't asked any questions about her past. And for that she had been grateful, because she'd wanted nothing to disrupt the golden bliss of being with him. Yet occasionally, when they weren't making love or laughing together or marveling over their wonderful new home, she found herself wishing that he *had* asked since she couldn't seem to find the right moment to tell him everything on her own.

Still, she'd been glad that all the prenuptial parties had taken place in Dallas rather than in Los Angeles so that she'd had an excuse not to attend . . . a kind of reprieve, putting off the day of execution until today, the day her present met up with her past.

She had even made an excuse to skip last night's dinner party at the hotel for members of the wedding party who had checked in the day before—the bride and her groom, the parents of the bride, the bridesmaids and the ushers, and the groom's best man, his father, Gino.

Today would be better . . . easier . . . for the first meeting when she introduced Jonathan to her past. Today there'd be too much going on for anyone to focus on her—today all the fuss and attention would be on the reigning queen, Penny Lee Hopkins Forenzi, and that was as it should be. And hopefully she would get through the day in one piece.

When Jonathan came up from behind as she stood at the windows, wrapping his arms around her, nuzzling and nipping and kissing, her eyes filled with tears, and when he saw the tears he was upset. "What is it?"

"Nothing." She laughed. "Really. I was just thinking about Penny marrying Gae today, and I got all sentimental. You know—they're both such old, dear friends, Gae as much as Penny. But it's a lovely day, and it's going to be a lovely wedding, and they'll be able to have the ceremony outside just as Penny wanted, with the sun shining, with all the flowers in bloom and the swans swimming in the pond. I think the gardens at the Bel-Air are a really perfect setting for a wedding."

"Are you sorry that we didn't have a big wedding? That we went to Vegas to get married? I guess it wasn't very romantic. But when I saw you walk into my office that day and realized what it meant, when that explosion went off inside me and the bells started ringing in my ears, I knew it was wedding bells I was hearing, and then there was no way I wasn't getting your name on that wedding contract immediately. That's the first rule of being a good businessman, you know. When you see a good thing, you get the name on the dotted line quick, before the person can have a change of heart."

"Oh, Jonathan! I would never have had a change of heart. But I loved eloping . . . flying to Las Vegas to get married. It was the very most romantic thing I can think of! The most romantic wedding anyone could wish for! And just look at all the time we saved! All the extra days we've had being married to one another. I wouldn't trade them for anything, especially not a silly, fancy wedding."

358

"But that twenty-four-hour wedding machine of a chapel with the neon sign flashing outside? With that little justice of the peace yawning in our faces and his wife playing the organ in her flannel bathrobe?"

"But she played so nicely. 'I Love You Truly' and 'Till the End of Time'—my favorite."

"Ten bucks extra for that one."

"But you were such a sport. You handed it over without thinking about it twice."

"And don't forget the extra twenty I forked over for the bouquet."

"Without blinking an eye," she marveled. "Pink carnations."

"Not your favorite flower . . ."

"But my favorite color."

"And that ring. That viper charged me twenty-five dollars for that wedding ring, and it wasn't even solid *brass!*"

"But you bought me another wedding ring the next day." She looked at the circle of diamonds and topazes on her finger. "Such a beautiful ring."

He laughed. "Nobody would believe that I bought my wife her wedding ring in the arcade of shops at Caesar's Palace instead of Cartier on Rodeo. Or, for that matter, that we spent our two-day honeymoon at Caesar's. Now that's a honeymoon for you. Two days at Caesar's Palace. Whoopee!"

"It *was* their very best suite! And it was the two best days of my life . . . up until then. Now it just gets better every day."

"But I should have made time to take you on a real honeymoon. I should have taken you to Paris."

"Paris! What makes you think I would have wanted to go to Paris?"

Oh, God, if she'd told him everything, he would have known how very much she didn't want or need Paris . . .

or London or Marbella or Rome.

"Don't you know that I wouldn't trade two days with you in Las Vegas for a million days with anyone else in any part of the world? Besides, we never left our suite for very long. For all we knew it could have been Paris outside . . ."

She couldn't have been in his office more than five minutes when — without a single preliminary — he yelled, "Las Vegas!"

"What? What about Las Vegas?"

"We can be married there tonight! No waiting period, no nothing!"

She'd been about to protest that she wasn't prepared . . . that they really should talk about this . . . that she wasn't properly dressed to get married — and that she was wearing *black!* — but Jonathan wasn't listening, not to any protests.

Shouting to a startled Patti that he wanted his car waiting outside by the time the elevator hit the lobby, he hustled her out of the office to charge down the corridors, pulling her along by the hand while she tried to keep up with him, taking two steps to his every one.

Even in the elevator he didn't give her a chance to protest or even to talk, pinning her to the wall with his body so tightly, covering her mouth with his so demandingly that she could scarcely breathe. Even in the car . . . on the plane, there seemed to be no time to say all the things she'd planned to say to him. There was only time for hungry lips and champagne kisses, seeking bodies, and the soft, breathy murmurings of love . . .

It was already dark by the time they deplaned, and instead of calling for a car, which would take too long, they jumped into one of the cabs lined up at the curb, Jonathan directing the driver to take them to a marriage chapel on the Strip, the one closest to Caesar's Palace.

For all that, she *was* given some choices. Her pick of any number of standard wedding melodies and a choice of flowers—an orchid corsage or a bouquet of carnations.

She couldn't make up her mind. "What do you think, Jonathan?" She held the orchid up to her black faille suit.

"Hmm . . . try the carnations."

She put the orchid down and held the bouquet in front of her with both hands.

Jonathan cocked his head to one side and then the other. "Wow! This *is* a tough one. Damned if I can make up my mind. How about both? I'll spring for the two."

"Are you sure?" she played along.

She put the bunch of carnations down, pinned the orchid to her shoulder, picked up the bouquet again, and posed before him. "You don't think it's overdoing it a bit?"

"Gee, I just don't know. What do you think?" He turned to the justice of the peace and his wife, who were watching the proceedings solemnly, thinking the couple were in earnest.

"Very pretty," the wife said, and the husband agreed, "Very nice indeed."

"Hmm. I just don't know. Maybe the two together *are* a bit much. Just choose one or the other, dear."

"All right."

She put down the bouquet and unpinned the orchid. "I'll take the carnations. Pink is more weddingish, don't you think?"

"Absolutely." Jonathan beamed.

She hesitated only a moment before signing *Ann Som-*

mer to the license. Jonathan, watching her, appeared bemused.

"What?" she asked, trying to smile. "What is it? I told you Andrianna DeArte was my stage name."

"But you never told me Ann Sommer was your real one."

"Don't you like it?"

"It's fine. It's a wonderful name, but—"

"But what?" she looked away from his eyes, suddenly terrifyingly, electrifyingly blue—afraid of what he was going to say. Afraid that his answer was going to break the spell of incredible enchantment that hovered in the air.

"It's just that you don't *look* like an Ann Sommer."

"Oh? Who *do* I look like?"

"Andrianna DeArte West. I'm afraid you're always going to be Andrianna to me. Is that okay with you?"

Was now the right time to tell him that Ann didn't really exist and that all there really was, was Andrianna? But she speculated for only a split second before she answered, "Andrianna DeArte West is very okay with me."

"Good," he said. "Wonderful! And if I didn't want to be absolutely correct, I would kiss you right now. But I think I'll wait until it's legal."

"Must you?"

"Oh, yes. We don't want to take any chances on doing anything that's not strictly by the book, do we?"

"Absolutely not. Strictly it is."

Then she breathed deeply, sighed happily, picked up her spicy-smelling carnations, and the organ boomed out, the justice of the peace spoke, Jonathan slipped the imitation gold ring on her finger, and they were pronounced man and wife.

"You may kiss your bride," and Jonathan did, a kiss that lingered until the justice of the peace cleared his throat several times.

362

Then, hand in hand, she clutching her carnations tightly to her, they ran the couple of blocks to the hotel.

"Will they give us a room? We don't have any luggage."

"You have your bouquet."

"Yes, but we don't have a reservation—"

"Will you stop worrying and just leave everything to me, lady? Don't you realize whom you married?"

"Whom?"

"The man *who* . . . That's who."

Oh, yes, the man who . . .

And he did take care of everything. They were shown to what was surely the most opulent suite in the house. There were twin bathrooms with sunken tubs, everything marbled and mirrored with lots of gold fittings, the sitting room was a rococo marvel of pastels and gilt, and the bedroom was silk and satin and velvety carpeting with a bed as big as the Ritz.

Andrianna sat down on the bed covered in quilted pink satin, looking up at Jonathan as she bounced up and down. "Lovely," she pronounced. "A wonderful bed."

He sat down beside her, now, after all the rushing, taking his time, bouncing along with her. "Very nice. Springy."

"What are we going to do now?" she asked, her voice all innocence. "Go down to the casino and gamble? I do love the slots."

"I don't think so. I'm really not in the mood. We *could* go shopping for a real wedding ring." He kissed her ring finger. "We don't even have to go outside the hotel. They have super stores right on the premises."

"Oh, that can wait. I love this ring! It's the ring I was married in, you know. But we could go shopping for a nightgown. I don't have anything to sleep in."

He slipped an arm around her shoulder. "Is that a

363

fact? Well, I guess it is. But you really don't need a nightgown. You *can* get through the night without one, can't you?"

"Well, I suppose. We *could* take a bath. There *are* two of them and such lovely tubs. It's a shame to let them go to waste. All those nice gold taps and things . . ."

He kissed her neck. "But we didn't bring any bubble bath with us, and I refuse to take a bath without bubbles."

"But the hotel supplies bubble bath *and* bath salts. I saw jars of them in the bathrooms."

"Really? That was very observant of you." He began to unbutton her jacket. "But I don't feel in the least bit soiled. Do you?"

"*Soiled?* Well, no, not soiled. But—"

He slipped the jacket off her shoulders, leaving them bare but for the slim straps of a black lace teddy.

"Surely there must be *something* we can do to entertain ourselves," she murmured as he pulled down the straps and his lips brushed her breasts. "I know. We can watch the telly."

"No, I don't think so." He gently pushed her shoulders down until all of her was supine. "I checked the guide. There's not a damn thing worth watching."

"But I heard that in these hotels they have special movies on cable . . . *sexy* movies," she said, her breath coming faster as he removed her skirt and then the teddy and then, when she was lying only in hose and pumps, his lips began to trace her body, beginning at her throat and working down. "Very, *very* sexy, they say . . ."

"Boring . . ." He removed her pumps and began to slowly and delicately peel the hose from her legs.

"What's boring?"

"The dirty movies. *This* is sexy." His lips traced her body again, this time beginning at her toes and working their way up.

"What is *this?*"

"What we are doing here . . . you and I."

Now he was very serious, and she knew that playtime was over. "Your sex in the afternoon . . . a sunny, golden surprise . . ."

He stood up to remove his own clothes, and she watched him discard each article of clothing, piece by piece. Then his nude body leaned over her, his head bent to hers, his lips found her lips, and against them he whispered, "I love you."

She whispered back, "I love you."

And then she found the waiting no longer tolerable. "Please, Jonathan, make love to me . . . now!"

But he got to his feet.

"No," she protested, holding her arms out to him. "No more waiting, please."

"No, no more waiting, but first—" He went to the windows, drew open the draperies, and the room was suddenly flooded with neon light from the Strip. Then he started to circle the room, flicking on lights.

"No, Jonathan, you don't have to do that. We don't need the lights. We don't need any sunshine flowing in. No matter what we do, whether it's day or night, it already *is* sex in the afternoon . . . as golden as it can ever be!"

"Still, we should have had more than a two-day honeymoon. I messed up there."

"Oh, you fool, I was much happier shopping for this house than sipping brandy on the Champs Elysées. And now that I'm here, in this house, nothing's going to budge me until I finish buying furniture and decorating and landscaping and doing all the things one does to a house. And I intend to learn how to cook. You know, real California cuisine. Nouvelle and healthy with a southwestern flavor — with a touch of Mexico thrown in, real Tex-Mex."

He laughed, almost mollified but not quite. "I bet your playboy friend, Gae Forenzi, will be taking *his* wife to Paris . . ."

"Believe me, Europe is no treat for Penny either. In spite of all the time she's spent abroad, deep down beneath that jazzy exterior there's a simple Texas gal who longs for home. Dallas and Nieman Marcus." Andrianna giggled.

"What Penny is planning on for a honeymoon, the last I heard anyway, is taking Gae on a tour through the heart of Texas. I think what she has in mind is talking him into buying a big spread there. You know, cows and horses and maybe even oil derricks, à la South Fork on 'Dallas.' And who knows? Maybe they'll even live here in Los Angeles for a while. Penny said her father is planning to make an offer for the Hotel Bel-Air and give it to her and Gae as a wedding present. I forget who she said owns it, but it's a woman from Dallas. A Carol—"

"Caroline Hunt Schoellkopf."

"Right. That's the name. But how did you know?"

"It's hardly a secret, and I *do* deal in real estate. I even own a couple of hotels — remember? But the Bel-Air is in a class of its own. Reputedly it's one of the five greatest hotels in the world. If the hotel were to go on the block, the competition would get really hot, including the foreign buyers. The Beverly Hills Hotel went to the Sultan of Brunei and the Bev Wilshire to a Hong Kong group. And all the interest wouldn't be just from hotel people. Today the name of the game is acquisition and diversification . . .

"But that's really interesting. I mean about your

366

friend Penny's dad wanting to buy the Bel-Air. I wonder if he knows something we here in L.A. don't. That Shoellkopf's ready to sell. It *would* make a very nice wedding present. What about you? Would *you* like it as a wedding present?"

"Me? I already got two wedding presents."

He kissed her, rubbing his lips lingeringly across hers. "Two? Is there one I don't know about?"

"Yes, two. This house and you."

"Me?" He grinned. "I don't count."

"Oh, you count, all right. More than you know . . ."

"Well, there *is* something I know," his voice was muffled as he buried his face between her breasts.

"Yes?"

"I know that if we hurry we'll have just enough time to—"

She put her fingers to his lips. "You're wasting time."

"We really have to start getting dressed this minute," she said, getting out of bed reluctantly. "The ceremony's at noon, and all the guests have been invited for eleven, and since I'm part of the wedding party and there's going to be a rehearsal, I'm supposed to be there at ten. Come on, lazy boy, get up."

"Are you sure you have the schedule right? I thought you said the ceremony's at one. Where's the invitation? I'll check," he said, reaching for his robe.

"We don't have one," she mumbled.

"We don't? How come? Such an elegant wedding and no engraved invitations?"

"Well, I'm sure there *were* invitations, but we never got one. It just wasn't necessary—I've been talking to Penny on the phone at least three times a week."

"Still, you should have had it in writing," he joked.

"Suppose we get there only to find out that she changed her mind about inviting us."

"She *can't* do that, you nutter. *I'm* the maid of honor even if now that I'm married I really should be referred to as a matron. Still honored, of course."

"I still think it's strange we never got an invitation."

"Not really. Penny . . . well, she doesn't have my address."

"Doesn't have your address? How come?"

"Because . . . because I didn't give it to her."

"But why not? You said she was your best friend. You're not ashamed of this address, are you? May I remind you that we're talking prime location here. Is it the house that you're ashamed of? This fine twenty-two-room Mediterranean villa with seven bedrooms and nine-and-a-half baths, not counting the servants' wing or the guest house. And how about the Roman pool and the north/south tennis court?"

Of course he was teasing her now, but why was he going on at such length?

"Jonathan West, you really are daft! I *adore* this house, and you know it! Why would you think I'd be ashamed of it?"

"Well, I know how competitive you women are. I thought that since your girlfriend will have a bigger and better house than you, you might be just a touch—"

"They don't get much better than this house! Anyway, what makes you think she'll have a bigger and better one?"

"Well, for one thing, her main abode will be in Italy, right? And don't the very rich live in palaces there? Besides, she's marrying a much richer man than you did. Or one who has a richer father, at any rate."

Now she was no longer sure that he *was* teasing, and she wished they could drop the whole conversation.

"Really! You're impossible! Rich is rich, and after a certain point, what difference does it make who's a little richer? And you have the gall to say it's women who are so competitive! It's the other way around. It's you men who worry about who has more money."

"I think the truth is that men and women are *both* competitive, only about different things. Men about their businesses *and* how much money they're making, and women — about things like houses and jewelry and the men that they marry."

"Jonathan," Andrianna broke in, "that description *might* fit Penny or Nicole, but not me."

"I'm not so sure . . ."

Andrianna thought she caught a wistful note in his voice but when she turned to look at him the teasing expression was back on his face.

"And then, of course, there are those men who are competitive about the women they're screwing."

"Oh? Is that so?" She tried not to smile.

"Yes. But that's not the case with me."

"Well, good. I'm pleased to hear that."

"Don't you want to know why?"

"You're going to tell me anyway, aren't you?"

"It's because I already know that I'm screwing the best."

"Oh. That's nice." She wrinkled her nose at him. "That's *very* nice. I only wish I could say the same."

And she sprinted for the shower as he ran after her.

He was shaving in his half of the his-and-her bath while she applied makeup in hers. "You still didn't tell me why you never gave out your new address to your friends."

Andrianna sighed inwardly. She thought they'd gotten

past that. What could she say?

I'm not a sharing person or *I never tell anyone anything until I bloody well must!* Or she could make a joke of it and say, *But, darling, that's part of my mystique. If I told all, I wouldn't be Andrianna DeArte West. I'd just be like everyone else . . .*

"I didn't give my friends my address or tell them about my new house because, if I did, we'd both be sorry. You don't know these people. They're used to descending on one another for weeks at a time. Being a houseguest is practically a profession among some people in Europe—a way of life." She sighed. "Actually, if you must know the truth, they don't even know I'm married—"

"Ah! So that's it! It's me you're ashamed of!"

He was teasing again, or was he?

"Oh, Jonny, I just wanted to keep you a secret until they met you. I wanted you to be a surprise . . . a golden surprise."

"What do you think?"

Andrianna stood before Jonathan in the rustling yellow taffeta antebellum gown Penny had chosen at Nieman's in Dallas, which she had then picked up at the branch in Beverly Hills. The dress, with its extremely low-cut neckline and a hooped skirt, fortunately, had needed little alteration. Her satin sandals were dyed to match, and her hair was arranged in a bustle of curls caught up with a huge yellow bow that matched the dress's bustle.

"Well, Ah do declare, Miz Scarlett, if you all don't look right purty!"

"Jonathan, don't you dare tease me. I can't help it if this is the dress Penny picked out." She giggled. "Nicole is wearing the same dress, only in a different color. And if you knew Nicole, you'd know how *really* funny that is.

370

Nicole is always dressed stylishly severe and at the same time ultra-soignée. I wonder what she did with her hair. She usually has the very sleekest, latest cut from Paris."

"Well, I don't know about her hair, but I *would* like to hear what she has to say about that dress. What was your friend Penny thinking of anyway?"

"The idea was for us all to look like old-fashioned flowers in Penny's southern garden of love. That's why I'm wearing jonquil yellow and Nicole is wearing violet, and the bridesmaids are wearing green—for foliage, you understand—and the two flower girls different shades of pink—geranium and peony. I believe Penny's mother is wearing orchid."

"Charming, I'm sure. Now tell me, how do you think I fit into the picture?"

He assumed the exaggerated stance of a bodybuilder even though he was completely dressed in a new double-breasted pale gray silk suit she had chosen for him. She thought he looked lovely, especially with his blond hair slicked back the way she loved, as if he had just stepped out of the shower.

"Hmmm . . . Well, ordinarily I might say you look like a cross between Robert Redford and John Kennedy, but—"

"Hell, I thought you were going to say Arnold Schwarzenegger."

"And as I was saying before you so rudely interrupted me, since you suggested I looked like Scarlett right out of *Gone With the Wind,* and that this *is* supposed to be an old-fashioned, southern-style wedding, I'd have to say you're Ashley Wilkes . . ."

"Ashley Wilkes! Well, I like *that!* In the course of seconds I go from being Bob Redford or JFK or Arnold to that wimp! Would you mind telling me how I managed this?"

"Well, really, Jonathan, look at yourself. You're hardly qualified to be Rhett Butler . . ."

She sat in front of the vanity table, making a last-minute check on her makeup, wondering what jewelry to wear. No matter what she chose, the problem was that all of it reposed in her jewelry case, which sat within the walk-in safe that was part of the dressing room unit in their master bedroom suite. She had placed it there the day they'd moved into the house and hadn't gone near it since. And Jonathan had asked no questions, indifferent to its contents, or at least pretending to be. She wasn't quite sure which. And if she wanted any jewelry, she'd have to march into the safe and retrieve the jewelry case while Jonathan watched.

But is now the right time to open up Pandora's box with Jonathan watching? Isn't it better to leave well enough alone? Or, as Nicole might put it, why tamper with success?

She decided that her wedding band was adornment enough. But then Jonathan came up from behind her and without a word picked up her hand and placed a ring on her finger just in front of her wedding band, and it was the largest stone she had ever seen—bigger even than the emerald Gino had gifted her with so many years before.

"Jonny! What is this?" she practically screamed.

He laughed, gratified by her reaction. "It's pretty obvious, I would think. It's a diamond ring."

"Yes, I think I can recognize a diamond when I see one, but—"

"It's something I overlooked that I'm catching up on. Your engagement ring."

"But we're already married. I didn't need—"

"Need? What kind of word is that? No one really *needs*

anything outside of a crust of bread, a glass of water, and some kind of a roof over his head."

"And love?"

"Of course love! For God's sake, what do you think this is all about? Besides, could I have you go to your friend's wedding where all those Texas women will probably be wearing rings the size of the Taj Mahal and have you looking like some little waif? Andrianna DeArte West? Think of your image, girl!" he joked.

She smiled at him tremulously, confused. What was he thinking of despite the joke? Love or image, and if image, whose? His or hers?

And then, to compound her confusion, he said, "You still seem a little bit naked," and produced a velvet box from van Cleef & Arpels on Rodeo Drive. He opened it and withdrew a diamond and topaz necklace that blazed so fiercely it could have started a fire.

She was speechless as he placed it around her neck and fastened the clasp. "The topazes match the stones in your wedding band and *almost* match your eyes," he said and kissed her.

"Oh, Jonathan, it's beautiful! But why two presents on the same day?"

"Well, the ring is for our engagement, which we didn't have time enough to do properly, and the necklace is a wedding present."

"But, as I said before, this house was my wedding present. And what about the car you just bought me?"

"The house doesn't count because it's for both of us. And a car is only a car . . . transportation, not a real present. Besides, I told you — the topazes *nearly* match your eyes." And then he kissed her again.

Jonathan had ordered Freddy to bring the limousine

373

around, but at the last minute Andrianna begged him to let her drive them to the wedding in her new car.

"But the Rolls is already out of the garage, and I have to warn you that practically everyone else will be arriving in limos. That's the way it is at the Bel-Air. After the hotel's parking lot is filled with stretches, they line Stone Canyon Road with the overflow. Do you really want to show up driving yourself in a plain old car?"

"I don't care how anyone else arrives. I want to show Penny and Nicole and whoever else Penny's invited from Le Rosey that Jonathan West's wife is a real California girl and can whip around the curves and cut people off with the best of them."

"Okay, California girl, go for it!" And he told Freddy to put away the Rolls and bring the Lincoln around.

Before buying her the car, Jonathan had offered her a choice of a Rolls, a Mercedes, a Jag, a Lamborghini, or even a Forenzi, but she'd insisted on the Mark, wanting to drive only an American car.

"Where do you make your money, Jonny? Here or there?"

"Here."

"Well then, doesn't it make financial sense to spend your money on American products?"

First he shook his head in wonder and then he kissed her. "My wife, the financial genius. Tell me, is there anything more I should know about you that I don't know now?"

But that had been only a joke, not a serious question.

She fastened her seat belt and insisted he buckle up too.

"We're going to be there before you can count to ten, but okay, if you insist, I'll buckle up. Anything you

374

want—"

"Okay then. Here goes."

"Hold it a minute. We're not *quite* ready."

A shudder of trepidation ran through her. "We're not?"

"Uh-uh. I think that before we go there are things that have to be said."

Oh, God, no! Not now!

"Now? We *are* running late. Can't it wait?"

"No, it can't. I've been putting it off, and I can't put it off any longer. If there isn't honesty between two people, then there isn't anything at all. Agreed?"

She *didn't* agree, but then she couldn't very well disagree. "Well, if you really think you can't put it off any longer, then perhaps you'd better get on with it," she said with stony resignation.

And then she listened as Jonathan unburdened himself. He had initiated an investigation into her past before calling it off . . . before he'd uncovered anything much more than her name and that she'd been on the London stage. And he had followed her in New York to learn—what? That she'd been registered at the Plaza as Anna della Rosa, staying in Gae Forenzi's suite, and that she had lunched with her friend Penny at the Russian Tea Room, after which they'd visited at Trump Tower.

"Nicole," she said quietly. "We went to see Nicole and stayed the night."

"And I know that the next day you went to see a friend at the medical center uptown, after which you got on a plane for California . . ."

"Is that it?" she asked tremulously. "Is that all you wanted to tell me?"

"Yes, but I had to level with you. What I did—even thinking of starting an investigation, following you—well, it wasn't right. And I—I didn't want anything hidden to stand between us. And I hope you'll forgive me. Will

375

you?"

She nodded, unable to look directly into his eyes, didn't want him to see the tears in *her* eyes—the tears of relief and the tears of regret . . .

This was the right time for her to tell him all there was to tell. He hadn't asked, but he'd certainly handed her the moment. There would never be a better time . . . and yet she knew she was going to miss it. It was a matter of timing, and timing had never been one of her strengths. Not even as an actress, which was probably the reason she had never really made it. The look of her was good, her voice and projection fine, her ability to play a variety of roles even more so . . . but somehow her timing had always been a beat off.

Besides, it was late and they had to go. She only hoped that it wasn't *too* late.

"So do you forgive me?" he asked again.

In answer she gave him a dazzling smile, one of her very, very best, and gunned the engine.

Twenty-six

Sunday afternoon

No sooner had Andrianna and Jonathan stepped from their car in front of the canopied entrance to the hotel than Eloise Hopkins, the mother of the bride, swooped down on them.

Andrianna and Eloise were good friends, Eloise having visited Penny often at Le Rosey, flying in for three or four whirlwind days loaded down with presents and once even a big pot of Texas chili. She would then take Penny, Nicole, and Andrianna out for extravagant dinners or to Lausanne for the weekend, where they'd put up at the best hotel in town. And then Andrianna had seen her since the Le Rosey days too, for whenever Penny had been in Europe, Eloise hadn't been too many flights behind.

Wistfully Andrianna had always thought her the most wonderful of mothers, completely devoted to her daughter, but Penny, who was no less devoted to Eloise than Eloise to her, had another word for her mother. "Controlling," she would sigh. "I do love her dearly, but my mama is easily the most controlling person I have ever met. And manipulative? Actually I wouldn't trust her as far as I could kick Pavarotti, which is saying a lot."

"Annie Sommer, you bad girl, you're late!" Eloise, slightly overwhelming in orchid velvet, shook a finger in Andrianna's face. "They're already rehearsing, and I've been standing here for hours waiting on you. I've been instructed to hustle you over the second you arrive." She kissed the air on each side of Andrianna's face.

"Oh, it's so good to see you, Eloise, and isn't it a beautiful day for Penny's wedding? I worried so that it wouldn't be warm enough to—"

But Eloise wasn't listening. Instead she was staring over Andrianna's head at Jonathan. "My goodness, who do we have here? From the looks of him, I'd say a real California blonde. You don't blondine your hair, do you, whoever you are, you gorgeous creature?"

"Smashing, isn't he?" Andrianna laughed, taking Jonathan's arm.

"Not bad."

"Eloise Hopkins, may I present my husband, Jonathan West?"

"My pleasure, Mrs. Hopkins, and no, I don't blondine my hair."

Jonathan smiled nicely, but now Eloise ignored him. "Your *husband?* So you finally landed yourself a big one, Annie. I always said to Penny, that girl doesn't have any trouble hookin' 'em, but she does seem to have a problem gettin' 'em out of the water. But then I figured it out. It wasn't that you couldn't reel 'em in—it was that you were throwing them back. They were just never big enough for you."

"Eloise!" Andrianna protested, turning beet red. But when she sneaked a look at Jonathan to see how he had taken Eloise's comment, he was grinning widely.

"I better join the others before I miss the whole rehearsal," Andrianna murmured. "Where is everyone?"

"Over by the gazebo"—Eloise pointed—"where we're having the ceremony. But hold on a minute and tell me—when did you all get married? Penny never said a word."

"About six weeks ago, and Penny still doesn't know. No one does. I wanted Jonathan to be a surprise."

"Oh, he'll be one, all right, a right delicious surprise. But didn't anyone ever tell you, Annie, that when you go to another girl's wedding you bring a gift, *not* a surprise?" She smiled acidly. "It's kind of like wearing white satin to the wedding when only the bride's supposed to do that. You know, stealing her thunder, *her* limelight?"

Eloise's implication was clear, and Andrianna was stricken. "That was *never* my intention, believe me! I wouldn't dream of trying to take the limelight away from Penny. Why would you even think such a thing? I *love* Penny."

Eloise looked from Andrianna to Jonathan thoughtfully as he moved to put his arm around his wife protectively in the face of the older woman's obvious hostility. Then, changing expressions, Eloise soothed, "Of course you do, honey. I was just pulling your leg."

She smiled brightly at Jonathan. "This bride of yours never could take a joke. Overly sensitive, I always said. Now my Penny, she's got a hide like a rhinoceros. Nothing makes a dent. I guess that's why she doesn't mind taking Annie's leftovers."

Oh! So that's it! That's what's bugging her! That it was Gae and I before it was Gae and Penny. But what a word to use! Leftovers! And Jonathan! What must he be thinking? And what was I thinking of to bring him here? What ever made me think that I could pull this off? The day's going to be a disaster!

She looked at her husband again, but Jonathan was merely smiling politely at Eloise. "I beg your pardon. I didn't quite catch what you said."

"I said that Penny didn't mind taking Annie's leftovers." And then, "Oh my, I hope I haven't gone and put my big foot in it. Don't tell me you didn't know that Annie here and Gae Forenzi were — Well, I guess you didn't. You really *are* full of surprises, aren't you, Annie darling?"

"I think that's one of the things I love best about my wife," Jonathan told Eloise, winking at Andrianna. "It

379

keeps a guy from getting bored, that ability to surprise."

He took Andrianna's arm. "And now I think we'd better get Andrianna over to that rehearsal before it's all over."

"Yes, I reckon we'd better at that."

Eloise took Jonathan's free arm, and they headed in the direction of the Swan Lake Gazebo.

"Tell me, Jonathan, if you don't mind me asking—I don't believe in pulling my punches and at my age with my money, thank God, I don't have to—how old *are* you? Not that it matters, but to my eye it seems you're a few years younger than our Annie. Is that a fact?"

As Andrianna fervently wished that she could just turn around and leave, Jonathan threw back his head and laughed. "I think what's a fact, Mrs. Hopkins, is that age, like beauty, is all in the eye of the beholder, and to my eyes my wife grows younger and more beautiful by the minute."

Andrianna looked at him gratefully, and he gazed back at her with a smile full of sunshine. Maybe she was wrong about the day. Maybe it was Jonathan who would pull it off.

Andrianna saw the wedding ceremony as if through a soft golden haze.

The guests seated on rows of little white chairs . . . beribboned and beflowered columns—roses and white delphiniums and lilies of the valley—marking the path of the bridal party up to the gazebo overhung with more pink and white flowers and masses of greenery . . . a solitary flute sounding through the sunshine . . . Gae and Gino standing by, Gae in his favorite white, Gino in greige . . . the bevy of bridesmaids in their willow green . . . she and Nicole smiling at one another encouragingly before they walked down the garden path . . . the two flower girls, as sweet as little flowers themselves, scattering rose petals, both pink and white . . . and then "Here Comes the Bride." A radiant Penny in her exquisite virgin's white wedding gown—long tapered sleeves, tight satin bodice, a girdle of orange blossoms, the skirt three tiers of bouffant flounces with an overlay of tulle, a lace train an incredible eighteen feet long, a tiered veil attached to a crown of orange blossoms—had the wedding of her dreams.

And then they all moved to the reception in the South Garden. A dance floor surrounded by a plethora of little round tables covered in pink, on each table a cascade of flowers, artfully designed to appear as nature's own careless arrangement . . . two long bars (silver buckets and sparkling crystal) . . . three buffet tables, each more spectacular than the other with a bewildering array of offerings and an overabundance of yet more flowers and love doves in sculptured ice . . .

After all the champagne toasts were done and over, the bride herself toasted Andrianna and the lucky guy who had won her: ". . . and isn't he the handsomest thing you've seen in ages?" Andrianna, touched by Penny's generosity, began to wonder why she'd been so apprehensive. Except for that first interchange with Eloise, everything was going beautifully . . .

Old friends from her schooldays . . . compliments going back and forth . . . they generously oohing and aahing over her rock of an engagement ring—"Honey, that ring puts Liz Taylor's to shame"—envying her stunning new husband . . . recalling almost-forgotten escapades . . .

Much more meaningful, much more of an emotional scene, reaching to her very core, was Gae, her dear, sweet friend, almost the same as ever, his dark curls still luxuriant, but wearing a moustache now, hugging and kissing her as they stood by themselves at the edge of the festivities as everyone wined and dined and danced by.

"Anna, what do you *really* think?" he asked. "Do Penny and I have a chance?"

"Oh, Gae, of course you do. All you have to do is love each other very hard and not let other people, other things—unimportant, superficial things—get in the way."

"And you? This American that you married, this Jonathan West, do you love him very hard?"

"Yes."

"And he? Does he love you the way you deserve to be loved?"

She started to say that she certainly hoped so, but then she found herself wanting to give Gae a real answer, an honest answer, and she cocked her head to the side. "I think he already loves me far more than I deserve, and I'll have to run very hard just to catch up."

"That's a funny thing to say. I think you are probably the best person I know."

She laughed. "Now, *that's* funny. I think the truth is that you probably don't really know me very well at all. Or perhaps, you're remembering the girl I used to be, and the memory plays tricks. It makes everything and everyone all pleasantly blurred."

"Oh, I *know* you, sweet Anna. And sometimes, even now, every once in a while, I think of you and I can't sleep for the knowing and the remembering . . ."

Those brown velvet-pansy eyes gazed wetly into hers and she was overcome with emotion mixed with a bit of melancholy, and she reached up for a second to touch the black curls suddenly so wrenchingly familiar again, before kissing him once more on the cheek.

Just then Jonathan danced by holding the happy bride in his arms and, without a second glance at the embrace of his wife and her former lover, called out, "Hi, stranger," before he and Penny danced away, Penny waving at her and Gae enthusiastically.

Andrianna turned back to Gae. "You know what, Gae,

I think that you and I should *both* run very hard. And then maybe we'll both catch up."

"Whatever you say, Anna. As I've always said, you were the wiser one."

When Jonathan came back to claim his wife, he patted Gae on the back, congratulating him on his great luck in having won so great a bride. Then, dancing Andrianna away, he grinned ruefully, "Now I know why *I'm* Ashley. Because *he's* Rhett Butler."

But then, when she began to protest, intending to reassure him that he, and not Gae, was *really* the leading man in her life, Jonathan reassured *her.* "I only meant the physical resemblance—the dark hair, the moustache, the white suit. An Italian southern-style rake if I ever saw one."

And then she was positive that Gae had been wrong. *She* wasn't the wise one; her husband was.

Her mind's eye snapped the picture of Nicole actually boogying with Gae! Unbelievable! She was positive that Nicole hadn't danced like this in years.

But then Nicole wasn't, seemingly, at all uptight today. Maybe it was the champagne, or maybe it was the incredibly wonderful vibes in the air. Or was it simply that Nicole's Edward, with a fixed smile on his lips and sitting stiffly at one of the round tables, not moving from it, was encouraging her to "have fun, my dear"?

Nicole, so "loose" today that she actually said of Jonathan as she might have twenty years before, "Oh, Ann! He is so very *ooh ooh, la la* . . . and I am so happy for you."

She'd been moved by Nicole's words, really touched. And then when Nicole said affectionately of Gae's and Penny's union, "Ah, it is a *folie de grandeur*," Andrianna knew that Nicole was *really* loosening up. Only weeks be-

fore, the prospective marriage had been only a plain, old
unadorned folly.

Take the shot . . .

She and Gino, dancing. Gino, still handsome despite his
advancing years, his black hair well mixed with gray, still
compellingly attractive in the same jaded way as a world-
weary, aging Marcello Mastroianni was, the Continental
who had seen it all . . .

"How *are* you, little Anna? Your health? The remission?"

She reassured him. "I'm wonderful, Gino. Remission
still holding . . . still going strong!"

"Good! Wonderful!"

He was holding her close, *too* close as they danced, sending disturbing sensations coursing through her until she
realized that they were only *old* sensations . . . faded memories playing tricks . . .

And she wondered what Gino was thinking, feeling, remembering.

Then Gino said bitterly, "This wedding today . . . it is a
terrible mistake."

"Why do you say that?"

"Your friend . . . this Penny woman. She is not for
Gae."

"She loves him very much, and he loves her. Leave them
alone, Gino."

He raised his eyebrows in the intimidating manner she
remembered. "Do you think I would interfere?"

But now she was older and not intimidated. "Yes, I
think you might."

"I only want Gaetano's happiness and for him to be a
man."

"Then leave him be. Leave them both be, Gino, and
maybe they'll surprise you."

"No." He shook his head vigorously. "The marriage is a
mistake. That father . . . that mother. Texans! All the

care about is how *big* things are! No," he said dolefully. "It should have been you and Gae, little Anna . . ."

And she knew what Gino had been thinking, remembering, and feeling. Still Gaetano and only Gaetano. Gino had aged, but he hadn't changed. He was still the father first and the lover only second, and this time, if not that last time, she was glad for that.

"And you," Gino accused angrily. "Why did you marry this . . . this American, this Jonathan West? Don't you know that Americans and Europeans are like East and West? They do not mix. All Americans are concerned with is their mighty dollar. They care nothing about family . . . about the emotions. They don't even understand what it really means to love!"

He should only know, Andrianna thought, exactly how wrong he was about her. But even if he knew about her American roots, would he speak any differently? Probably not. And how wrong he was about Jonathan. Why, Jonathan could give him lessons in the art of loving a woman . . .

"I married Jonathan because I love him so much and because he loves me so much. Because with *him* I come first!"

And because Gino Forenzi was a clever man, he understood immediately what she was driving at, and he spoke almost coldly. "I hope for your sake that you never have cause to think any differently, Anna, that your Mr. West is never put to the test of who or what comes first . . . especially if you should come *out* of remission. I would not want you to be disappointed in him."

No, I won't let Gino do this to me today. I will not think about what Jonathan would do if I came out of remission, a remission he doesn't even know exists! I won't!

"Oh, Gino! How can you? To talk about my coming out of remission when I am so happy! It's *you* who disappoint me!"

And then, because he was *not* an unkind man, Gino apologized profusely, begging her forgiveness. And because he was not an unemotional man and not really an unloving man, his eyes filled with tears. "Oh, Anna, Anna, I do love you! You must know that I love you. That I want only the best for you. That I think about you often and I worry about you constantly . . . your happiness as well as your health!"

Then she smiled at him through her own tears to reassure him. His kind of love would never have been enough, but now she could forgive him that.

"Oh, Gino, I know you love me. That's why I want you to know that I love a wonderful man and that he loves me very, very much. He loves me so much he accepts me entirely on faith . . . he doesn't even *ask* questions. It's enough for him that I *am*. And I want you to be happy for me and to wish me well without any reservations. Can't you do that, Gino?"

"Oh, Anna, Anna, little Anna, of course I can!"

And he stopped in the middle of the dance floor to put both arms around her, to hug her tightly, as if nothing in the world could tear them apart.

It was then that Jonathan danced by with Nicole and while Nicole looked a little alarmed by what she saw, Jonathan grinned at his wife and quipped, "We really have to stop meeting like this . . ."

Andrianna was searching for a few minutes alone with Jonathan so that she could explain why Gino Forenzi had been holding her like that—old friends and the usual Italian exuberance . . . only a warm and emotional gesture really—but as soon as they sat down together at one of the pink-clothed tables with their selections from the buffets, they were joined by Cole Hopkins holding a Villeroy & Boch flowered plate piled high with barbecued ribs.

"Penny said we *had* to have all the rest of that fancy foreign grub—that people expected it—but there ain't nothing in the world to compare to a mess of Texas ribs, so we brought them with us. Am I right or am I right, Mr. West?"

"I suspect you're right, Mr. Hopkins."

Jonathan was eating shrimp wrapped in swordfish, so he was more or less on neutral ground. But since Andrianna's plate held the fancy foreign grub—the veal noisettes and the lobster ravioloni—she was already compromised and could only say, "You should try the ravioloni, Mr. Hopkins. It's really delicious."

"If it's all the same to you, Annie, I think I'll pass. I don't go in for these foreign dishes. If you must know, I don't go in for foreigners either, including these charming *Eye-talians* . . ."

Oh, God, here we go again, Andrianna thought, worrying how much Cole Hopkins had had to drink.

"Between me and you, West, I can't for the life of me figure out why the hell my daughter wanted to marry up with this *Eye-talian*. It's not like there's any shortage of American fellers around who's got the right stuff and the right brand on their behinds, if you get my meaning."

"I'm sure Gae Forenzi has the right stuff," Jonathan said quickly and diplomatically, and Andrianna hastened to add, "Oh yes, Mr. Hopkins. Gae's a wonderful person."

"If he's so great, Missy, how come *you* didn't marry him?"

"I? . . ." She almost choked on a mouthful of lobster.

"Yeah, you, Annie. You and Forenzi had a good go-round, didn't you? But you were too smart to hook up with him for long. I can see who *you* married, and I like what I see. Here, have a rib, son, and call me Cole."

"Thanks, Cole, don't mind if I do."

Jonathan picked up one of the proffered ribs and dug in. Then, mouth full, he told Andrianna, "Mmmm, this *is*

387

good. You really have to try one, sweetheart."

Jonathan was really going a bit far being agreeable, she thought. "Who knows? Maybe I will."

"See?" Cole pointed with a rib. "I told you she was smart. Smart enough to know the real goods when she sees it. And don't think I haven't heard all about you, son. You got a reputation for having a head on your shoulders. One of my friends from Dallas who's here today says you're a mighty sharp feller. That they put your face on the cover of that *Time* magazine and that you know California property like nobody else and you own more than your share."

Jonathan shrugged modestly. "I try . . ."

"Listen, son, you got a reputation, and I don't believe in a feller being mush-mouthed about his accomplishments. If you don't blow your own horn, who will?"

"You're right, Cole. But from what I hear, you're pretty savvy about California property yourself. The word around town is that you're thinking of buying this hotel. Is it true?" Jonathan sounded both impressed and ingenuous.

Cole Hopkins laughed. "I see they're right about you, boy. You *are* sharp. The news that the hotel might be up for sale got you salivating, has it? Now, don't tell me no. You're a sly young fox, but I'm an old one, and it takes one to know one. But don't go working yourself up into a lather. I already spoke to the Hunt gal, Caroline. Made her one hell of an offer, but it's no go. She ain't interested in selling, boy."

Andrianna noted that Cole Hopkins had gone from calling Jonathan "son" to "boy" within a matter of moments. But Jonathan made his own adjustments.

"Is that a fact, *Mr. Hopkins?* That's too bad. But you're wrong about me panting after the Hotel Bel-Air. Even if I were so inclined, I would never undercut, or should I say attempt to outbid, a friend, and that's what I got you down in my book as—a friend, since I am a guest at your daughter's wedding and my wife is *her* dear friend."

"Sure, you wouldn't go after it if you had a taste for it and if you thought you had a chance in hell of getting it." Cole laughed in disbelief. "Yep, you got yourself a real All-American winner here, Annie, and that makes *you* a winner in *my* book."

After Cole Hopkins moved on to other guests, Jonathan shook his head. "You know, I really don't like the way the Hopkins bunch insist on calling you Annie when Andrianna fits you so perfectly."

She squeezed Jonathan's hand gratefully, just for being . . . her Jonathan.

When Nicole, with plate in hand and Edward in tow, sat down at their table, Jonathan got up to fetch some more champagne himself, insisting Edward come along with him. "I'd like to hear how you feel about the trade deficit, Ed. You know those boys in Washington. What are they really thinking about to let—"

Andrianna noted that the only thing on Nicole's plate was a small portion of salad, its primary ingredient an avocado mousse set on a bed of radicchio and citrus slices, covered with a red sauce flecked with bits of yellow and green, which she tasted and then ignored.

"You're not hungry, Nicole?"

"Well, I do find this salad a bit . . . odd."

"Yes?"

"Yes. When I discussed the menu with the people here and they suggested an avocado mousse, I thought that sounded lovely—elegant but with a California flair—but I had no idea they would dress the mousse with this rather bizarre mixture. Tomatoes, perhaps, but kernels of corn and these bits of—? Frankly, I can't imagine what these little things are."

"They're jalapeños." Andrianna chuckled. "I think you're just not familiar with a certain type of California cooking. The Mexican influence."

"I suppose not." Nicole sounded weary, as if she had exhausted herself all afternoon being "up" and now she was coming down from that high. "But then, it hardly matters, does it?"

"Hardly," Andrianna agreed, depressed that Nicole was depressed.

Then Nicole reached over to finger Andrianna's new diamond and topaz necklace. "Most impressive. This, and the young, sexy Jonathan too. So, Ann, after all this time, you think you finally have it all, don't you? *Everything?*"

Andrianna looked deeply into Nicole's troubled eyes, unsure now in what kind of spirit her question was couched. Was it as mean-spirited as it sounded?

She wet her lips. "Yes, I think I have everything, Nicole. God knows, I hope so. God knows I pray that I do. And I also know that you're my dear friend and that you love me and that you're praying for me too—aren't you?"

It took Nicole a few seconds to react. Then she threw her arms around Andrianna, pressing her lips to each cheek in turn and whispering fervently, "Oh, Ann, you imbecile, you idiot, of course I pray for you! I am not a fool, and I have often suspected how hard it has been for you. Why it has, I do not know, but—Of course I have prayed for you, and now I am so happy for you, there are no words to express what I feel."

Andrianna didn't need words; her cheeks were damp from Nicole's tears.

When Jonathan came back with Edward and a full bottle of Perrier Jouet, he looked from one woman to the other before asking cheerfully, "Nicole, will you and Edward join Andrianna and me in a kind of private toast?"

"But of course. What are we drinking to—?"

"To all of my wife's great friends. It's really been a wonderful day and I hold *you* largely responsible."

"Oh?" Nicole's eyelids fluttered coquettishly, and she dimpled beguilingly, rising to the challenge as easily as the most artful of her French ancestors. "How so?"

"Well, it isn't every day that I meet a beautiful Frenchwoman who can wear a southern belle of a ball gown like you are"—his eyes flirtatiously emphasizing his words—"and put every last woman south of the Mason-Dixon line to shame."

Nicole's laugh pealed out in delight, and she turned to Andrianna. "Oh yes, Ann, he's very much *ooh ooh, la la.*"

Andrianna couldn't have agreed more, and if Edward's dry little laugh was any indication, so did he.

When Jonathan and Andrianna got up to dance, Edward said, "It was a pleasure talking to you, Jonathan. And Ann, my dear, I'm so pleased that you married such a nice, sensible young man. We're both pleased, aren't we, Nicole? I can't tell you how many nights Nicole tossed and turned fretting about you, worrying what would become of you . . . that you would never settle down and make a suitable marriage. Especially during that period when you were living with Gino Forenzi. She was really upset about that; she thought no good would come of it. But all's well that ends well, isn't that so?"

He laughed the dry little laugh again, which turned into a fit of coughing, and Nicole, eyes pleading with Andrianna's apologetically, patted him lightly on the back.

Andrianna wanted to tell her to hit him harder, beat him up while you're at it, the fool. *God! And this man had been a diplomat?*

And then, as she went into Jonathan's arms as the band played, "Falling in Love Is Wonderful," she wondered why on earth she hadn't just gently corrected Edward, said something about how she had *worked* with Gino in his

391

house as well as his office . . . not *lived* with him per se. And that would have been the end of it. Well, she would tell Jonathan that later. Not here, not while they were dancing. Still she wondered what was going through his head, and she decided to risk finding out.

She picked up her head from his shoulder to look up at him. "What are you thinking?"

"Oh, I was just thinking about your friends, Nicole and Ed. I like them. She's cute, and he's a nice old guy. Only I wish they wouldn't keep calling you Ann. I feel like they're talking about some stranger, and I don't care if it is your real name. I think Andrianna is the most beautiful name in the world for *the* most beautiful woman in the world, and therefore they go hand in hand."

"I have to say I admire your thinking, Mr. West."

It was just after Penny and Gae had cut the seven-tiered wedding cake and Andrianna and Penny finally got a few minutes alone together that Penny pinched her arm.

"Ouch! That hurt! Why did you do that? Are you so delirious with happiness that you've lost your mind?"

"Oh, I'm delirious, all right. But *that's* for being such a sly little boots and keeping that man and your news to yourself all these weeks after I've spent virtually my whole life baring my soul to you, you ungrateful wretch! Where did you find him and when?"

"On the *QE2* crossing from Southampton to New York."

"You mean you married him barely knowing him?"

"Oh, I wouldn't say *that*. I know him quite well."

"I just bet you do! And I remember when we were in New York and I asked you if you were there because of a man, and you said in this little mealy-mouthed voice, 'Oh, no, Missy Penny. Would little old me be in New York because of a *man*? I'm just here to see about my little old career.' I mean, butter wouldn't have melted in your mouth."

Andrianna laughed. "See? You're all mixed up as usual. I was telling you the truth. I couldn't have been in New York because of Jonathan because I didn't even *know* him before I started out for New York. On the other hand, I *am* in California because of him since he is my husband and he does make his home here."

"Yes. And speaking of homes, *am* I ever going to get to see yours?"

"Oh, Penny, of course."

"I swear, if Gae and I weren't leaving for Texas tonight, I'd fix you good. We'd just move in on you and spend our honeymoon with you and Jonathan. Wouldn't that be fun? Just like the old days?"

"No, Penny, it wouldn't be like the old days, and we wouldn't really want them to be. Oh, Penny, don't you know? The best days are yet to come!"

"Oh, God! Oh, that's beautiful, Annie." Penny clutched her breast and her eyes teared. She pulled a beautiful lace handkerchief from the tight sleeve of her wedding gown and dabbed at her eyes. "Oh, Annie, do you *promise?* That the best is yet to come?"

"Yes, yes, yes. I promise!" Her own eyes filled, and Penny passed her the lace handkerchief.

A second later Penny screamed, "Oh, I forgot! Oh, my Lord, don't get it dirty! It's my something old and borrowed. From Nicole! It's from France and it's antique and she's going to just about kill me if I don't return it in absolutely pristine condition!"

"Don't worry about it. I'll take it home with me and have it laundered at this special place, and I'll mail it back to her, okay?"

"Registered?"

"Oh, *certainement*. Registered and Federal Express, and whatever else. I swear on your mama's life."

"Oh, Annie, you are a lifesaver, and I love you and I forgive you for not telling me about Jonathan West, and he is a wonderful surprise, and thanks again for everything!"

"What are you thanking me for . . . for washing, ironing, and mailing Nicole's old hankie?"

"No. For not marrying Gae and leaving him free for *me* to love. And for promising me that the best is yet to come for both of us. And don't think that I'm not going to hold you to that promise."

"Oh, what promise?" It was Nicole, coming up from behind, holding a big piece of wedding cake and actually nibbling at it.

Quickly Andrianna whipped the damp lace handkerchief up her sleeve and out of sight before explaining that she'd just promised Penny that their best times were still ahead.

"And aren't you going to include me in that promise?" Nicole pouted. "We used to be a trio."

"Oh, *mais oui,* Nicole, *mais oui.*"

"Then let's have a toast," Nicole proposed. "To the three of us and the best times ahead."

"I'll drink to that and I'm buying," and Penny took them both by the hand to lead them over to one of the bars where the professional photographer took their picture for Penny's album of informal shots — the bride and her two attendants, three maturing attractive women opulently costumed for the day, all saying "cheese."

But for a moment Andrianna saw the three of them through a different lens and had a different picture — a picture of three so young and hopeful schoolgirls, innocently dreaming of a glorious future . . . of a world that was going to treat them like the princesses they really were . . .

And then her home movie camera eye went to work, recording pictures for her to affectionately gaze at in the days to come.

Penny, pulling up all her flounces and net and satin to reveal her blue garter for all to see like any eighteen-year-old bride might . . . Nicole detaching Penny's train from the loop that held it fast to wrap it around the three of them, binding them together, and then clowning, choking Penny with it . . . Penny, grabbing the veil and crown from her own red-topped head to place it on her friend Annie's dark hair, and then she, in turn, snatching it off to try it on Nicole's blond head . . .

Then, giddy with the pleasure of the moment, forgetting that she was no longer a girl, Andrianna picked up her bouffant skirts to break out into—it had been years—a flamenco, stamping her heels and snapping her fingers above her head, while Penny and Nicole squealed in delight.

In a few seconds the band picked up on her dancing to accompany her with the appropriate Spanish music, and then she had more pictures to store away—Gae, remembering, applauding fiercely . . . Gino wiping at his eyes with a red silk handkerchief . . . Jonathan, laughing and proud and kissing her, holding her close, whispering in her ear, "I had no idea that you could dance like that! How could you keep this great secret from me? Aren't you ashamed?"

Finally it was time to clink fluted glasses, to toast those best days yet to come. It was Nicole who wanted the toast to include drinking to their friendship, and Penny agreed enthusiastically. "Yes, we must drink to our friendship too. You make the toast, Annie."

"All right." Andrianna hoisted her glass. "We're drinking, my friends, to a wonderful new era . . . for all three of us . . . to many golden moments . . . to all the very best times yet to come . . . and to our friendship, which will warm and sustain us forever . . . till the end of time . . ."

"That is *very* beautiful, Ann. Isn't it, Penny?"

"Oh, poop! That Annie. She's such a little bitch!" Penny cried. "She does it to me every time, makes me cry and ruin my makeup with all these fucking tears!"

At that moment Andrianna believed that at last her cup was truly running over . . .

* * *

The guests were beginning to take their leave, and Andrianna looked around for Jonathan. And then she saw him . . . talking to Gae and Gino. A chill ran up and down her back, and she realized that the sun was going down and the day was no longer warm. What were they saying to one another and who was questioning whom and what was going to happen to all her golden moments, all her best times yet to come? Would they be snatched from her before she even had a chance to drink from her overflowing cup?

Twenty-seven

Sunday evening and the following week

Andrianna and Jonathan were in their bedroom, preparing for bed even though it was still early, he not taking notice of Andrianna's pensive mood. He was busily hanging up his suit, putting away his cuff links, and all the while singing bits of songs — a mixture of all the tunes they had danced to that afternoon. He mentioned how much he had liked the use of the flute during the ceremony, and then they both had something to say on almost every aspect of the wedding — the officiating clergyman Cole Hopkins had flown in from Dallas, the food, the band, the assorted guests, even the women who'd been at school with her at Le Rosey.

Just listening to them, Andrianna reflected, one would think that they were any average couple — a couple without any secrets between them — who had been married for years, amiably discussing an affair they'd just attended.

Still she felt that the question of her intimate ties to the Forenzis hung in the air like a wall separating them and she needed to tear it down. But how should she begin? Where? And where did she stop after divulging how much? Her relationship with Gae, she supposed, was relatively easy to explain, the one with Gino much more complicated, enormously so. Now, even to her, the whole thing with Gino sounded slightly bizarre . . .

She shook her head as if to clear it. Sometimes she

thought it was she herself who was bizarre and that it came from going over the same old material in her head, again and again.

"I bet you're so exhausted you're ready to drop," Jonathan said, massaging her shoulders with tender fingers as she sat at the vanity table in a thin wisp of a nightgown, brushing her hair.

"I *am* tired," she admitted. "By the way, you know that business about me and Gae . . . you know—what Eloise said—that he was my—"

Jonathan laughed. "Leftovers? A funny word to use. But then again, she's a funny lady. A character. The fact that it *bothers* her that when the three of you were really no more than kids Gae preferred you to Penny is funny in itself. Personally, I don't blame him a bit. If I had had a choice between you and Penny, even as teenagers, it would have been no contest. Gae would have had to have been out of his mind to pick her over you. Even with those big tits . . . if she had had them *then*, which somehow I doubt. Am I right?"

She had to laugh and admit that he was right, that in those days Penny had been quite flat-chested.

"Although I'm not saying Penny isn't a knockout if a guy has a yen for redheads, which personally I don't. Give me a girl with hair the color of midnight every time."

"I'm really glad you feel that way about it. It just goes to show how really smart you are, just like Cole Hopkins said. But *he* wasn't really very funny, was he? Actually, I was very annoyed by every last thing he said. The nerve of that man to cast aspersions on your integrity."

"Forget it. Forget him," Jonathan said goodnaturedly, lifting the hair off her neck to kiss the soft flesh beneath. "He's hardly worth your being annoyed. Nothing is."

She reached around to touch her fingertips to his lips. "Well, to tell the truth, I was *really* annoyed by what Edward

398

Austin said . . . that he and Nicole were worried about me when I was staying with Gino in his house. It so happens that I was working for Gino at the time and it was the easiest thing . . . the most convenient . . . for me to live in that big house. And the way Edward made it sound—I was Gino's special executive assistant and—"

"In his business? You never told me that."

"Yes. And believe me, it was no part-time job; it was an around-the-clock thing."

"That's terrific," Jonathan said, getting into bed. "That you know the car business. I'll keep that in mind in case I want to make a move on General Motors."

A joke!

Didn't Jonathan take anything seriously? Didn't he realize that she was trying to explain matters? No, that wasn't quite accurate. What she was trying to do was explain *away* certain facts the way she always did, with half-truths and evasions. But Jonathan wasn't having any. It was no questions asked, and no explanations of any kind, if you please . . .

"Come to bed, my beautiful business executive. No, I take that back. Come to bed, my beautiful flamenco dancer. Wow! Was that something! Now that I know all about this secret vice of yours, I'm going to buy you a flamenco dress and make you dance for me all the time. But then again, maybe we don't really need the dress. Without might be even better." He considered. "Well, we'll see. Maybe we'll do it both ways. With and without." He patted the space next to him. "Aren't you ready yet?"

"In a minute. I want to put my necklace away in the safe."

"You're going to wear the ring? All the time?"

"Of course I am, along with my wedding ring. That's the way it's done."

"Come to bed," he said again.

"Yes. In a moment."

She went into the safe to get her jewelry case and brought it out, setting it down on the mirrored vanity. She picked up the necklace, searching the tabletop for its velvet case, and then, biting her lip, put it down again.

"By the way, what were you talking about with Gino and Gae for so long? You can't possibly have that much in common with them."

"Why not?" He smiled slightly. "Do you think that they're too rich for my blood? Too international jet set?"

"Oh, stop teasing. You sound just like Cole Hopkins, that boor. You know perfectly well what I mean. You *don't* have that much in common with them, and that's natural enough, considering that—"

"That what? That they're billionaires and I'm only a paltry millionaire?"

Is he teasing again? Why is he talking about money now?

"Will you stop? I mean because they're so typically European and you're so typically American and—"

"I think I resent that 'typical.' I think I'm pretty extraordinary, if you must know."

"Be serious."

"Okay," he said, reasonably. "But what about us? You're English with a Spanish mother, and I'm that same typical American, and we have lots in common. At least we would if you ever came to bed."

"Jonny, I'm warning you. If you don't stop teasing—"

"Okay, I'll tell you what we were talking about. It was the effect the Japanese were having on the American and Italian economies with their *Italian* emphasis centering on the car business, naturally enough, while I, the American businessman, was more concerned with how much real estate they were buying up in California. How's that for something in common? Worrying about the Japanese . . . besides you, of course."

"What is it? That I'm a *thing* all three of you have in common, or that you're all worried about me?"

"Well, I wouldn't put it that way, exactly. Let's say the word is *concerned,* rather than worried. Which is understandable. Naturally *I'm* concerned about you. You're my wife and I love you, and I'm concerned with every square inch of

400

you and concerned that I make you happy. And they are both very fond of you since you are all such good, close friends, and naturally they're concerned that I make you happy, that you're in good hands.

"Actually I was very touched by their concern and how much they thought of you. Gae spoke of what a good friend you'd been to him, what a warm and caring person you were, how you had tried to make a better man of him no matter how hard he fought you, and how for him you idealized everything a woman should be. In a way he made me ashamed . . ."

"Ashamed? Why, for heaven's sake?"

"Well, he spoke of you in such spiritual terms, and my feelings for you are not quite so spiritual, so high-minded. I mean, they *are*, but they're also very . . . well, physical . . . sensual . . . Hell, I have to admit it—*sexual.*"

"Well, thank God for that!"

And thank you, Gae, for the kind words, the right words.

"And Gino Forenzi! Wow! He is tough."

"What do you mean, tough? In what way?"

"Well, the way he went at me he might have been your father. And I don't mean one like Cole Hopkins either. But he asked hard questions, like what was my financial situation and my prospects, and was I prepared to take care of you the way a woman like you deserved? And he kept probing as if he were trying to find out exactly how much, how strongly I loved you . . . as if he wanted to make sure that my regard for you was all it should be. As if I had a very precious treasure entrusted into my care and he wanted to make sure that I was worthy.

"He was really most impressive. He couldn't have acted more like a doting father than if he had been your real father. To tell the truth, I was very proud."

"Proud?" she asked automatically, thinking that Gino too had come through for her, had acted the good father.

"Yeah, proud. That I was married to this magnificent woman who could stir such profound feelings in her friends.

And now that we've got these old friends out of the way, can we get on with things here? In all fairness I must tell you that right now I am feeling anything but spiritual and don't give a hoot about your friends from out of the past. It's only the immediate *present* that interests me."

But he knows. He senses. He feels. He must have doubts. And I have to explain how it was . . .

"But there are things I have to tell you."

"What kind of things?"

Even if you don't care, darling Jonathan, I have to tell you, have to take that step . . .

"About Gae. About Gino. About other—"

"But you don't! You don't have to tell me a thing. Do you think I ever thought a woman like you just popped up out of nowhere into being? Without a past, a blank?

"Hell, Andrianna, I don't *want* a blank, a woman without feelings—a woman who didn't live life as a complete woman, giving and taking and sharing. I accept you as you are since I know exactly who you are and I treasure you, as is. Okay? But there *is* one thing I would like to ask of you just to set things straight—"

Her heart pounded. What was he going to ask? How *big* a question? "Yes?"

"The next time you see the Forenzi boys, would you *please* ask them to stop calling you Anna, or little Anna for that matter? I never did meet a woman before whom everyone called by a different name. It's very confusing, not to say irritating."

He had ended with a joke, but the rest of it had been as serious and sincere as anything anyone had ever told her. He was telling her that he loved her so much and believed in her so much that he was even closing the door on a man's natural enough curiosity about the woman he married . . . an act of faith, a gift of love.

And she? What was she giving him in return? Lies and secrets. And not about the men in her past. They were as if nothing in the grand scheme of things, the totality of her

402

life. And she had to give him something that showed her faith in him, in their future together. Her eyes lighted on her jewelry case sitting on the vanity. Her security blanket. Her ace in the hole just in case it started to rain. If she gave all of it away to him as a gift, a gift of love, it would be a testament to her belief in her future . . . in *their* future . . . in her belief that it wouldn't ever rain again so long as they were together.

She opened the case, picked through it, taking out a few pieces—the bracelet Jonathan had given her on board ship, her mother's jewelry, her beaded baby bracelet, the charm bracelet Gae had once given her, the small gold heart that had been one of Gino's early presents, a silver friendship ring from Penny and another from Nicole, the silver earrings she had worn when she had danced the flamenco in Marbella. The past did have its place, no matter what.

She opened all the velvet boxes, emptying them, and uncovered those pieces wrapped in chamois.

"What are you doing now?" Jonathan asked.

"Preparing your dowry."

"I didn't know I was getting one."

"But you're such a nice man. You deserve one."

"Do I?"

"Yes, you do. And here it is."

She took the box, carried it over to the bed, and turned it upside down, releasing a shower of rings and bracelets and necklaces and brooches, large and small, to cover him. It was a cloudburst of yellow gold and white gold and pink gold, of platinum and diamonds and citrines and amethysts and blue topazes, of emeralds and rubies and sapphires, yellow stones and purple stones and jade, pearls, white and cream and black. They blanketed him like hailstones, a king's ransom.

Jonathan picked up a bracelet, examined it, let it fall. He touched an antique necklace of coral and burnished gold and brushed it aside. He fingered the huge emerald ring Gino had given her and said dispassionately, "*This* has to be worth a couple of hundred thousand all by itself," before he dropped it.

"What's all this about, Andrianna?"

"It's about giving you a present. I told you, it's my dowry. A gift of love."

"You don't have to do this, you know. All of this . . . it doesn't disturb me. It's only . . . a pile of metal and stones, even if they call it all precious. It just isn't necessary for you to do this."

"Oh, but it is. Take my word for it, it *is*."

"All right then. I'll always take both your word and your gifts. And now, what do you think I should do with this gift of love?"

He picked up a handful of the jewelry and let it slide through his fingers.

"I don't know. You don't want to keep it?"

"I don't think so. I *could* save it for you, just in case you should change your mind."

"No, I won't change my mind. And besides, that would ruin my present."

"Yeah, I can see that it would."

She sat down on the bed, pushing all the jewelry aside, some of it spilling to the floor. "We can give it away. I mean, sell it and give away the money."

"It will be a lot of money. Who or what would be the lucky recipient?"

"Well, I think I have just the ticket."

He said nothing, waiting for her to go on.

"Well, I have these friends who live near San Francisco. In the wine country. Napa Valley. They're the ones I went to visit before I came to Los Angeles. Melissa and Jerry Hern. Well, he's a doctor and she's a terrific person, and they're both really into helping people. And they're trying to raise money to build this clinic for the children in the area. Of course they wouldn't turn away any child who needed help, but they're particularly concerned with the poor children. You know, the underprivileged ones . . . the kids of the people who work in the vineyards."

"They're mostly Mexican, aren't they?"

"I suppose. The point is that there's a great need, and I think it would be wonderful if all . . . all this junk . . . could fill that need. What do you think?"

"Well, first of all, I think it would be nice if you didn't refer to *my* present as junk. First it's a gift of love and now it's *junk?* Second of all, I think maybe I ought to match whatever this gift of love brings. Kind of double the love . . ."

"Oh, Jonathan! Will you?"

"I will provided you get this crap off my bed and get yourself into it. What about it?"

"Crap? And you object to the word *junk?* If you really must know, I think that Nicole would object to *your* language. She would say you were *très gauche.*"

"And you know what I would say to that?"

"What?"

"Screw Nicole!"

"Oh, that would be a waste. I'd so much rather screw you. Oh, Jonathan, I would much rather screw you . . ."

When she awoke she saw that Jonathan was already dressed but not in his workaday attire. He was wearing a pair of white jeans and a navy blue sweatshirt.

"Are you going to run this morning or play tennis or something else strenuous before you go to the office?"

"No. I'm going to the beach house. Want to come?"

"What a question! Of course I want to come! But what's the special occasion? This is Monday morning, isn't it? And it's not a holiday. At least I don't think it is, is it? And Mondays you always go to work, don't you?"

"God, but you're difficult."

"I am?"

"You see, another question. That's what I mean. I ask you one simple question. Do you want to go to the beach house? And what happens? You answer me with at least five ques-

405

tions of your own. No, I am not playing tennis, and no, it's not a special occasion, but yes, it is Monday morning, and no, it's not a holiday, and yes, on Mondays I always go to work. Only I'm not this morning. This morning I'm going to the beach."

"Why?"

"There you go again. Why? Because this morning I don't feel like going to work. This morning *I'm* declaring it a holiday."

"So it *is* a holiday, and it *is* a special occasion after all, and I wasn't so far off base when I asked my questions. Isn't that so?"

"Yes, that is *so!*"

And he made a sudden yank, pulling the pale peach sheet and the blush peach comforter off her and the bed and throwing them to the floor, leaving her uncovered and nude.

"And if you don't hurry and get up this second, I will go off, leaving you behind. Or on second thought"—he looked lecherously at her naked body—"I will first rape you and then go off, leaving you behind. Take your chance."

"Rape first, and then I'll hurry so you won't leave me behind."

At her insistence she was driving, taking the curves of Sunset in stride. "So, now that I'm in the driver's seat and you are at my mercy, you'd better tell me—why are we enjoying this special occasion of going to the beach on an ordinary working-day Monday?"

"Because . . ."

"Because what?"

"Because this morning when I woke up I said to myself, 'West, you're a damned fool. Here you have this gorgeous, wonderful wife, and you're wasting all these precious hours working when you and she could be enjoying each other.' And you know how I feel about wasting time."

* * *

It was a wonderful day, Andrianna thought, a day she would always remember, even though nothing really special happened. They spent the day quietly, walking the beach in the morning, hand in hand, Andrianna wearing hat and sunglasses, stopping occasionally to pick up a shell or to marvel over a piece of driftwood, polished by time and sand to a fine sheen.

They lunched on hamburgers and fries from one of the quick food places, sitting on the sand and eating greedily, debating what they'd do next. Just go back to the house and hang out on the deck, spend the afternoon horseback riding in the hills, or hit a few tennis balls back and forth on the court Jonathan owned in conjunction with a few of his Malibu neighbors?

"I know, Jonny. I've been wanting to plant all those pots on the patio. They're just sitting empty. Why don't we go to the nursery and buy some flats and fill those pots full of flowers?"

"I don't know a damned thing about flowers. Why don't we just hire someone to do it, and then we can sit around and do nothing."

"You don't have to know all that much. Only what works in the sun and what works in the shade and what needs a lot of water and what doesn't. *I'll* show you the way."

"You? I don't believe this. Arranging flowers, yes. But what can a sophisticated woman of the world like you know about *planting* flowers?"

"But I do know. Once upon a time I was a little girl before I became this marvelously sophisticated woman of the world you see before you—" She plucked at her oversized sweatshirt and wiggled her ponytail at him. "And when I was this smart little girl, I helped my mother take care of this most beautiful garden . . ."

"Tell me about it." He leaned forward eagerly. "You never talk about your—"

She shook her head. "I really don't like to talk about those days. My mother . . . she died so young . . . and I was so young myself when it happened. It just hurts too much even to think about. But believe me, it's a wonderful feeling to dig your fingers into the soil. A really sensual thing."

"I'm convinced. Come on." He got up from the sand and held out his hand for hers to pull her to her feet. "Let's go see what kind of flowers the nursery has to offer."

"Shall we eat in or out?" Jonathan asked from the depths of a low-slung chaise on the deck, having the drink Andrianna had promised him once they were finished potting.

Andrianna moaned softly from her chaise. "Mmmm, I'm so comfortable now I don't think I want to move. But after a while I'll get up and make us dinner. How about that? We really don't want to go out to a restaurant, do we? We don't get out here that often, and it's such a nice house. And we couldn't ask for a more wonderful view, could we?"

Jonathan looked out at the waves rolling in, breaking high on the sand, and laughed.

"What's so funny?"

"You. All those questions. Everything." Still laughing, he stood up and, with a dramatic flourish, said, "And now *I* will wine and dine *you*, madam, with spaghetti à la West, and how does a nice chocolate milk sound? We happen to have a wonderful vintage in stock."

Andrianna looked at him dubiously.

After they had eaten, Jonathan grinned and said, "Well? Was everything to madam's satisfaction?"

"It was . . . interesting. Dare I ask for the recipe for that spaghetti sauce?"

His grin broadened. "Catsup and melted butter."

"Oh, boy, are you in trouble now! Just you wait until I tell Nicole about this one! Catsup and butter! She'll advise that only one thing will do—divorce!"

"You know something about your friend Nicole?" he

asked. "She may be French, she may have dined at the White House, but she still has a hell of a lot to learn . . ."

The following days were no different. It was clearly Andrianna's week.

On Tuesday morning Jonathan pulled her out of bed to take her out to the Santa Monica airport.

"Are we going someplace?"

"We might. We might go just anyplace you want. Anyplace in the whole wide world. Just name it. What Andrianna wants, Andrianna gets."

But after Santa Monica Airport they went straight home to Bel-Air again and to bed after she saw the jet Jonathan had just bought from an Arab oil magnate who was in need of cash. On the side of the plane in big, amber-colored letters was the name *Andrianna*.

When she asked *why* all Jonathan would say was that it had been such a bargain and he had always wanted his own jet, so why not?

Still she knew that that wasn't what the jet was all about. The jet, or at least the name painted on its side, was about love . . . a gift of love.

On Wednesday Jonathan stayed home from the office again, this time to go shopping with her at the Design Center for things for the house, to have lunch on the patio at the Bistro Gardens in Beverly Hills where he looked around at the lunch bunch crowd to announce that she was easily the most beautiful woman present, stopping in at Tiffany after lunch to buy her a necklace of rubies and antique gold.

"Jonathan, are you sure you have time to do all this?"

"I think I don't have time *not* to do this."

A gift of love.

On Thursday Penny called by way of Jonathan's office since she still didn't have their home number.

"We're in Aspen," Penny said. "Gae got tired of touring Texas and said he was longing for a bit of skiing. We've got a condo here big enough for ten. How about you and Jonathan joining us?"

"On your honeymoon?" Andrianna asked, incredulous. "Anyhow, I don't think so. Jonathan has his business to think of—he has to go to work."

But Jonathan said no, he didn't *have* to do anything except make his wife happy. Besides, it would be fun getting to know her friends better and to get a little skiing in.

And so they went, in their new plane. And it *was* fun. More, it was good—the four of them together—and it was easy. It was as if Jonathan and Gae had been friends all of their lives. But she knew it was Jonathan, making the effort.

A gift of love . . .

Twenty-eight

Andrianna was lying on her bedroom chaise, trying to relax with a copy of *Architectural Digest* before Jonathan arrived home for dinner. It had been another hectic day in a series of hectic days, in the course of several exhausting months. Never in her wildest dreams had she imagined that a woman without gainful employment—if that was what one chose to call it—one who had no children and a household staff of five, could be this busy and this tired!

But she didn't want Jonathan to take notice of how tired she was. For one, she didn't want him to suggest that perhaps she was doing too much, that decorating without the aid of an interior designer, running the house, and taking a course in gourmet cooking as well as a class in screenwriting were enough to keep her busy without the added burden of flying back and forth to northern California to help the Herns acquire the land for the children's clinic.

He might even suggest that they had already done their part for the clinic and that she should devote her charitable energies to Los Angeles organizations instead. Surely they were as worthy, and she knew he would enjoy seeing her name in the L.A. society columns as a sponsor of this charity ball or as co-chairwoman of that fund-raising event.

Even so, he had been generous about the clinic, offering to fly up there personally to help with all the red tape that

411

went along with acquiring the land, this being his area of expertise. He had said jokingly, "After all, I do have a stake in this thing—it's *my* dowry they're using to get the ball rolling."

Of course she had told him that this wasn't necessary. She could hardly allow him to get involved in the La Paz project even though Jerry Hern would have covered for her, and for that matter, so would have Melissa, whom, in the course of her visits to La Paz, she'd gotten to know fairly well.

Melissa Hern was the most giving person Andrianna knew outside of Jerry and, of course, Jonathan, who would give *her* the world if he was able. But of course, that wasn't the same kind of giving.

Andrianna was sure that even if he had the wherewithal, it would never occur to Jerry Hern to give his wife a ring with an emerald as big as a house as Jonathan had just done. But then Jerry wouldn't have had the fresh memory of Gino Forenzi's emerald to deal with—the one piece in her jewelry collection that had brought the most money when they'd sold the collection. That did add another dimension to the overall picture.

When Jonathan brought his own emerald home and placed it on her finger, she had felt that, without asking her any questions about who had given her what, Jonathan had sensed that the huge emerald had been Gino's gift. *How?* She guessed that it was just part of his extraordinary gut instinct.

He had placed the ring on the third finger of her right hand since her gigantic diamond was already on her left hand, and she had asked him if she should wear it all the time as she did her engagement ring. But what she was really asking was whether he *wanted* her to wear it all the time.

His answer had been succinct and to the point. "You damn well better wear it all the time! Why hide all that glory in a dark safe? Let it sparkle in the light."

Jonathan believed that if one had it one might as well flaunt it, and let the critics be damned. But he did ask her a favor, their running joke.

"Will you please *not* consult with Nicole on this matter? Because I must tell you—I do *not* wish to hear her dictum on the appropriate display of flashy jewelry."

She had agreed not to even tell Nicole that she owned anything so vulgar as a twenty-carat emerald, which was at least three carats larger than the one Gino had given her.

Jonathan came rushing into the bedroom. "So here you are! When I didn't see you downstairs, I was worried you hadn't gotten back yet from La Paz. It's a hell of a trip going back and forth in one day. Really too much."

"Don't be silly. It's not more . . . well, not *much* more than an hour away by plane."

To get Jonathan off the topic of her trips to La Paz she showed him the pictures of a lodge a friend of his had recently built in Aspen, which was featured in the magazine.

"It's very attractive, isn't it?"

"Not bad, but it's kind of small, isn't it?"

"I just wanted to ask you if you liked the way it's furnished."

"Okay. Not great. Look at what you've done with our Malibu house. That makes this Aspen place look sick. We really should get *Architectural Digest* to do a layout on our beach house or, when it's finished, this house."

"Would you really like that?"

"Of course I would. Besides, it's good advertising."

"But you're not in the kind of business where you need to advertise."

"It's *all* advertising, Andrianna. Image-building and mentions in columns and write-ups in *Time* and *Architectural Digest*. And besides, I like it," he confessed. "Is that so terrible?"

"Of course not." And it wasn't, she thought. Jonathan was entitled. Who said he had to be that much more altruistic and modest than anyone else?

* * *

"You know, you really do look tired, Andrianna."

"Oh dear, am I showing my age?"

"No fishing for compliments, please. But I was thinking that, instead of going to that benefit tonight, why don't we stay home, have our dinner in bed, and relax? We haven't been able to do that lately. How does that sound? A quiet evening at home, just the two of us?"

It sounded heavenly, but she knew that there would be people—bankers—at the gala tonight with whom Jonathan wanted to make contact and discuss business away from the official boardrooms.

"I'm fine, really. We'll go."

"We won't. Who's the boss in this family, anyway?"

"Oh, you, sir. Absolutely. But weren't there people you wanted to see tonight? Those men from Los Angeles First Trust?"

"Are you crazy? Why would I want to look at bankers all night when I can look at you?"

"All right. Just hold that thought."

The second Jonathan touched the remote control to catch the evening news, Donald Trump appeared on the screen standing in front of an airplane bearing his name. The anchorman, chuckling with his co-anchor about it all, made a big thing out of the fact that the moment Trump's deal for the Eastern Airlines shuttle had gone through he had had the fleet of planes refurbished, down to putting his own name on every last plane.

"You see, Donald isn't squeamish about a little self-advertising. He's put his name on every damn thing he owns, which adds up to a lot of naming. The only thing he owns that he *hasn't* put his name on so far is the Plaza Hotel, but he'll probably get around to that too one of these days."

Jonathan's voice was full of approval. Still, Andrianna suspected that it was also touched with more than a little envy, and that made her feel sad, thinking that somehow

414

envy diminished Jonathan and his own accomplishments.

"Money isn't the only measure of a man, you know."

"I'd bet Ivana Trump thinks Donald's quite a man even if *his* plane isn't named for her, as ours is for you," he said pointedly. "Do you know how she refers to him in public? 'The Don.' That shows what she thinks of him."

Andrianna thought that that was more funny than anything. "And you think that's a compliment?"

"Sure it is."

"And you'd like it if I referred to you like that?"

"Sure I would, *if* my name was Donald."

"Well, your name isn't. It's Jonathan. But I'll tell you what I can do about that. I can call you 'the Jon.' "

Jonathan had the grace to laugh before he said, "Speaking of acquisitions, guess which hotel is on the block?"

She thought for a moment. "The Hotel Bel-Air?"

"Right. And that probably means that Cole Hopkins knew all along that it was going to be, even as he was telling us at the wedding that the owner had no interest in selling."

"But why would he do that? Just flat out lie?"

"Because he is, just like he said, a sly old fox. Or maybe just a plain lying son-of-a-bitch. I guess he thought I might be after it and he wanted one less competitor."

"And are you? After it?"

"I might have been."

"But you're not? Is it too late for you to make a bid?"

"No, but I'm not going to."

"But why not? If you're interested—"

"Because it's not the way I play. I told the man I would never undercut or try to outbid him, not on this hotel anyway, and I won't."

"But if he lied to you, what do you owe him?"

"I owe *myself* not to be the same lying son-of-a-bitch he is."

"You know what, Jonathan? *You're* quite a man."

He grinned at her. "I thought you always knew that."

"I did. But I didn't want to tell you that I knew. I didn't want you to get a swelled head."

Jonathan took the *Architectural Digest* to bed with him to re-study the pages featuring his friend's chalet in Aspen, and Andrianna took a pad and pen.

Jonathan asked her what she was doing.

"Just making a list of things that have to be done. You know how it is. If I don't write things down, I forget half of what I have to do."

"Yeah, well, be sure to put down at the very top not to *overdo,* and remember: first things first."

"Which are?"

"Which *is* pleasing your husband."

"And how do I do that?"

"That is one area where I don't think you require any instructions." And he rubbed his leg against hers.

"I guess I don't at that."

She put aside her pad and he the magazine.

Later that night, unable to sleep, she crept out of bed, careful not to wake Jonathan, went into the study adjoining their bedroom, and sat down at the desk to work on her list.

Even though Jonathan had laughed at her little joke about calling him "the Jon," she wondered how amused he'd really been and whether he admired the attractive Ivana almost as much as he admired her husband. She knew he thought she was the perfect wife for the powerhouse who was "the Don."

She also had to admit to herself that it was hard to find fault with Mrs. Trump. She was not only the perfect wife, the perfect hostess, the perfect keeper of multiple homes, and the perfect mother for their three children but also the manager of one of their casinos and now the Plaza. And to top it all, she also made the charity benefit scene to help "advertise" her husband's proud name.

Didn't Jonathan deserve an Ivana too?

She started to write, and at the top, right after "Please

Jonathan in every way," she wrote: (1) Get more involved in local charities with a high profile. (2) Get more involved in Jonathan's businesses. Offer services wherever needed. Perhaps in one of his hotels. (3) Once house is completely decorated, entertain more. (4) Find out about getting *Architectural Digest* to feature said house or the one in Malibu. (5) Quit cooking class and screenwriting course. No time. (6) Remember to take vitamins. *Very important.* (7) Get more rest.

At the bottom the last notation on the list was: *Think about having a baby.*

She hadn't forgotten her promise to Jerry. She *would* wait until Jonathan asked. Still, she had to make her own decision first.

A week later she had to revise her list. Jonathan surprised her with a chalet in Aspen that bore her name on the deed and on the nameplate in front.

So much for you, Ivana! Do you have a chalet with your name on it?

She added to her list: Decorate Aspen chalet as quickly as possible and get *Architectural Digest* out there even if you have to hijack them. Then she underscored the notation *Think about having a baby.*

She could never really be sure of her future, but one thing she knew—Jonathan, who had given her his love so freely, so trustingly, deserved everything she could possibly give him, deserved the very, very best. He deserved a true, *living* gift of love . . .

Twenty-nine

Fall 1989

"I'll be frank with you, Andrianna." Jerry faced her across his desk. "The tests check out okay, and I have to conclude that you're still in remission, but I don't like what my eyes see. I don't like the way you look."

"Well, how ungallant we are today, Doctor. My husband thinks I look more beautiful than ever. He told me so only this morning."

"Then his eyesight's going on him or he's too busy making money to take a really good look at you. If he did, he'd see how tired you look, how drawn and how pale. He's wearing you out with all these demands on you."

"Don't you dare criticize Jonathan. I won't have it. If you must know, Jonathan makes *no* demands. He's not like that. He's always after me to take it easy, to pamper myself. It's I who's decided he's not going to be shortchanged because he married a woman who—

"Oh, never mind. We've gone through all this before, but believe me, if you met Jonathan you'd see in a minute what a wonderful person he is, almost always good-natured, no matter what's on his mind. And generous. So generous. Do you know I get a present for every holiday, no matter which one it is? For Labor Day, even. And for the Fourth of July he gave me a red, white, and blue bracelet, rubies and sapphires and pearls."

"Sounds pretty gaudy to me."

"And you sound pretty nasty to me. I don't know why I put up with you."

"Oh, I think you do. Because you need me for your own nefarious purposes."

"Oh, Jerry, let's not fight. And really, I must go now."

"Why? Is your husband's private plane waiting for you?" he asked snidely.

"No, it isn't. He doesn't even know I'm here today. And you really are impossible. And so ungrateful. I bet no one has contributed as much as Jonathan has to the clinic, time after time."

"Big deal. It's only money. Besides, it's a tax deduction."

"I'm going. I've really had enough of you for today. And to think that that first time I thought you were a saint, so sweet, so good, so sympathetic, so understanding, and so damn good-looking."

"And now?"

"Now I think you're only so damn good-looking. Really, what's gotten into you?"

He played with a tendril of her hair. "Who knows? Maybe it's just that I'm a little bit jealous," he said, apparently joking.

"You jealous? I don't believe it. What would you be jealous of?"

"It's not a what. It's more like a who."

She didn't ask any more questions. She didn't think she wanted to hear the answer.

"We're having the official groundbreaking in two weeks. Will you come? I think it would only be appropriate if you took part in the ceremony since if it hadn't been for you—"

"No, Jerry, I don't think so."

"Why not?"

"Because you don't need me there. Now that you're really launched and you have most of the money you need, it's better that I remove myself. Besides, if I came to the ceremony, Jonathan might insist on coming along, and I really can't afford to take the chance of having Jonathan in the neighborhood, you know?"

"You still can't tell him the truth about yourself? You keep telling me how wonderful he is, but the truth is you still don't trust him enough to—"

"The truth is that while you're still the one person who knows everything about me, *you* still don't understand. Now good-bye and good luck with the groundbreaking and my best to Melissa."

"Sure. I'll walk you outside." Then he said, as he said each time: "And remember, take your vitamins, and for God's sake, get some rest and don't get yourself pregnant."

She thumbed her nose at him.

Still, the next morning, as she waited in the atrium for Jonathan to come down to breakfast, she kept thinking about what Jerry had said. Did she really look that bad? Tired and pale? Worn out? She *was* feeling more tired more of the time lately, even though she hadn't confessed that to Jerry. Maybe she *had* better ease up a bit. Cut down on the activities. Run around less. And not think of having a baby just yet. Put it off for a while until she was feeling better, more rested.

If her remission should come to an end—if the damn monster was then only "medically controlled"—it might well be the beginning of the end of everything . . . the whole beautiful life she and Jonathan shared.

No, she couldn't bear to lose everything now that she had finally experienced what life could be . . . real love. It was love that made everything she touched, looked at, and felt, beautiful. Every small act. Even the ritual of their eating breakfast in this atrium every morning.

As soon as she had finished decorating the room, she had decided that they would do just that, make a ritual of having breakfast here, putting her hope in the power of ritual, praying that it would prove to be an ally . . . an adhesive that would bind her and Jonathan together tightly, forming a bond so strong nothing could drive them apart.

And Jonathan had agreed that it was indeed a delightful way to start the day, to sit in the middle of the profusion of palms and ficuses and potted orchids—white and yellow and purple—everything blooming gloriously, with the bonus of the special light of morning streaming in from all eight sides of the glass-walled, octagon-shaped room. But then Jonathan always agreed with her about these things, constantly enthralled with what he saw as her golden vision of life, her gift for making even the commonplace seem exciting and enticing.

Jonathan bent down to kiss her before sitting down, his lips lingering on the back of her neck, as sensuously as he had made more extensive love to her earlier. And she shivered with the pleasure of the kiss, relishing it as she relished every minute they were together. And not for the first time she wished for a magic wand with which she could point—at Jonathan, at the day, at their love—and catch the moment as if with a camera and preserve it intact for all the time to come, and then some . . .

As she rang the bell to signal Sylvia that she could start serving, Andrianna made a pointed pretense of studying Jonathan's attire, which was what he wore every day of his working week—dark business suit, white shirt, a not quite bright red tie, with only minor variations from day to day—and drawled, "While I do think you're the best thing I've seen in years, Jonny darling, I thought that since today is such a gorgeous day, you might want to break down and deviate from that uniform of yours just this once. After all, darling, this *is* L.A., and only morticians, lawyers, and theatrical agents wear business suits to do battle in."

She often made similar remarks, that too being part of

their day-to-day ritual.

And he answered her in kind.

"Okay." He nodded solemnly. "One of these days I'll d just that and wear nothing . . . nothing at all. But I war you. You'll be sorry when I'm attacked by hordes of ser starved females fighting to take possession of my grea body. Or I'll go to the office in a tee with the slogan *Sa the California Fruit Flies* or, better yet, *I Believe in Sex, Drug. and Rock 'n' Roll.*"

It was nothing more than another bit of nonsense, running joke between them, and by now another piece ritual.

The first time she'd urged him to dress more informall was soon after they'd been married, and she'd been quit serious, not fully understanding that Jonathan's reserve suit and tie were more than a simple preference for tha kind of attire. But then she'd come to realize that Jona than's look was a studied thing, and she really should hav known that since he rarely did anything he hadn't firs thought out thoroughly, except take up with her, of course

In a town where almost everyone wore casual attire Jonathan in his more formal clothes was different from th rest, his tie and suit and blazingly white shirt nothin more than props, a gimmick, to help him stand out fror the crowd. And, of course, Jonathan believed in being standout. It was part of building the image, and imag was one of the things Jonathan did believe in.

As a matter of fact, Jonathan was in a particularly goo mood this morning because last night Johnny Carson ha made him the subject of one of his jokes, feeling com pletely comfortable about Jonathan West's recognition fac tor. Johnny had cracked on network television that an morning now he expected to wake up at his home in Ma libu to find that his neighbor had erected in the middle the ocean a sky-high sign that proclaimed in huge letters "Jonathan West's Pacific."

And Carson's audience had laughed immediately. There had been no delay while they screwed up their collective faces to wonder: "Who the hell is Jonathan West?"

As Sylvia brought in the oversized balloon glasses of orange juice, frothy and frosty from having been whipped in the blender with ice, the way Jonathan liked it, she also brought in a little white sign and placed it in the center of the table. The sign read, "Jonathan West's Breakfast Table."

Jonathan broke up. "Very funny, Mrs. West."

Andrianna tipped her head in acknowledgment and rose from the table, ostensibly to stand at one of the walls of glass to look out at the grounds. On her back was a sign — "Jonathan West's Wife."

Jonathan broke up again. "Very, *very* funny, Mrs. West."

Then she called him over to the window to look out at the rose garden. "Seriously, Jonathan, I bet you haven't noticed lately how beautiful it's looking these days, you're so busy being the important Mr. West. You really must take time to smell the roses."

Jonathan admitted that he hadn't *really* taken a good look at the roses lately, wasn't even aware that they were in bloom. And then he looked out to see the sign planted squarely in the middle of the beds: "Jonathan West's Rose Garden."

He laughed again but begged, "Please! No more! I surrender, dear. And I promise — no swollen head." Then he shook his head in mock grief. "The poor 'Don.' I bet Ivana doesn't perform this valuable service for him — making sure he keeps everything in perspective. God! That poor man!"

Then Sylvia brought in the day's mail, and Andrianna laughed. Forbidding Jonathan the daily newspapers at the table and allowing no telephone calls, she always hoped the mail wouldn't arrive until *after* breakfast so that they could have a totally relaxed, leisurely meal without distraction from the world outside—just the two of them enjoying each other, talking about nothing of consequence or nothing more stimulating than whether they would go to the beach house for the weekend or make three days of it and fly up to Tahoe or down to the Springs. Bliss!

But not this morning, Josephine, she told herself, as she saw Jonathan's eyes light up at the pile of mail overflowing its square Lucite tray.

"What do you expect to find in that pile of junk beside household bills? A billion dollars?" she teased as he lit into it. "All the important mail goes to your office."

"Ah, but the *fun* mail comes here. Seeing who has invited the most socially eligible Wests to what important charity event or intimate gathering of no more than five hundred close friends, or which gallery has what new show, not to mention looking at all the pretty models in their underwear in these catalogs you're forever getting. And look at all these magazines I never get a chance to see."

"That's not true," she objected. "You read magazines all the time."

"Yeah, sure. The dull stuff. *Business Week*. *Economics Today*. But you've got all the good stuff here. *Vanity Fair*. *People*. *Los Angeles*. I know why you never want me to see any of this. You want to be the *only* one who knows the latest hot gossip. Who's asking for how much settlement money from what poor sucker, or whom Liz Taylor is thinking of marrying, or better yet, whom Sly Stallone is currently banging. All the inside dope on who's doing what to whom. Selfish!"

"Ridiculous," she countered. "It's hardly inside dope once it's in a national magazine."

"Maybe so," he allowed, flipping through the envelopes, occasionally stopping to tear one open to scan its content quickly. "But checking the mail out *before* you do, is my one chance to catch you . . . find out which one of your many secret lovers is sending you covert declarations of undying love."

He bit into a piece of toast, chewing thoroughly, deliberately looking her in the eye, trying to keep a straight face while she laughed.

"You're such an old-fashioned romantic, Jonny, and abysmally ignorant. Didn't anyone ever tell you that no one sends a woman love letters anymore? They call you from airplanes or on their car phones, or if they must write, they send you a fax."

"I suppose that's true," he sighed. "So tell me. Have you gotten any interesting faxes lately?"

Without waiting for an answer he went on flipping until he found a letter from Penny. "Ah, what do we have here? The latest news from Italy hot off the presses."

He tossed her the letter while he went after a magazine—Forbes—and she could see from the cover that it was the issue with the magazine's annual list of the four hundred richest men in the country. And her heart beat faster. Today was the big day, she thought. Today was the day Jonathan waited for all year . . .

Sighing, she tore open Penny's letter. It would be a lot more fun to read than watching Jonathan's expression as he went down the list until he found his own name. She only prayed that it wasn't too close to the bottom. He might try to hide it from her, but he would be disconsolate.

And then she had a pleasant shock. "I am, as they say, preggo," Penny wrote, "and Gae and I are supremely happy, as I think Papa Gino is too. But, sadly, I'm the only one who is also nauseated. I will keep you posted on the progress of both the upcoming event and the nausea."

But before she even had a chance to tell Jonathan the good news, he flung his magazine across the room.

Oh, my poor darling Jonathan!

"What number?" she asked. "And how much do they estimate is your net worth?"

"It doesn't matter. It's only a list and only *their* evaluation of my net worth. Who cares?"

He did, but she wasn't about to call him a liar.

"Besides, they never took into account the biggest part of my fortune."

"Oh? What did they leave out?"

"You."

"Oh . . ." She hoped that it was so—that he really, truly felt that way.

"You know what I'd really like to do today, Andrianna, sweet fortune? Something very dear to my heart?"

"What?" She was almost afraid to hear.

"I think I'd like to take the day off, go down to the beach house, and make love to you all day long. We'd make golden love in the afternoon. What do you say? Will you come with me to the beach house and be my love?"

He sounded so strange, so serious. Somehow it was as if he were asking her to marry him a second time, as if he were asking her to pledge her love once again.

"Of course, Jonny. I'll always go with you—anytime, anywhere, to any place you say, to do whatever you want me to do . . ." It *was* a pledge.

"Do you know what I *really* want to do? My absolute heart's desire? More important than anything?"

"Tell me, Jonny."

"I want to make a baby. I want for *us* to make a baby."

Finally Jonathan had said it. The words were out. He had expressed, as he put it, his absolute heart's desire, more important than anything . . . *More important than being a billionaire?*

She had to believe him. He had said he would never lie to her, and he never had. And in return she had pledged herself not to deny him any gift of love it was in her power to grant . . .

426

He leaned over the table and grasped her hand. "So what do you say?"

"Oh, yes, Jonny, yes!"

She ran upstairs to get ready and tried not to think about what Jerry Hern would say. Anyhow, she couldn't let him — no matter how good a doctor he was or how fine a friend — make this decision for her. This was a matter of the heart and only between her and Jonathan.

Besides, Jerry didn't know everything. He didn't know that sometimes a baby was more than a baby . . . that sometimes a baby was also an act of faith, worth more than any millionaire's dream of being a billionaire . . . easily a billion times more.

Sometimes a baby was the *ultimate* gift of love.

Thirty

Christmas eve! And it was all she could do to keep from telling Jonathan that she was pregnant. He would be so happy, so excited; it would be the best present she could possibly give him. Ever since that day at the beach he had been waiting with such high hopes. But with that high risk of miscarriage hanging over her head like a sword, she didn't dare give him a gift that might soon be snatched away. By the time she showed and he *did* know, the chances of her miscarrying would be that much slimmer.

As for Jerry, she just wouldn't go to see him for a while. After all, she *was* in remission, and it was so early in the pregnancy that it wouldn't matter if she put off seeing him for a couple of months. No one would be hurt by the delay—not she, not Jonathan, and not the baby.

She couldn't bear to listen now to Jerry's gloomy words and dire warnings. The problem with Jerry was that he didn't have enough faith, didn't really believe in the miracle of birth like she did. But he would find out! She would teach even the good doctor a lesson!

Jonathan's Christmas gift to her was a brooch in the form of what appeared to be a house. Its roof was fash-

oned of red rubies, like so many clay tiles, its facing—
ink rubies—with diamonds for windows and a trim of
meralds. "I had it made to order," Jonathan told her
roudly. "I designed it myself."

"It's lovely. I can see that it's a true California house,
ink with green trim, but is it a *particular* house?"

"It's not a house at all. It's a hotel."

"Oh," she said, puzzled.

He laughed. "You don't know which hotel it is, do you?"

"I have to confess, I don't."

"It's the Beverly Hills Gardens on Sunset."

Now she was even more mystified. "But—"

"It's the latest of L.A.'s trophy hotels to be put on the
uction block. But this time I intend to be the boy that
ets her—I don't intend to be outbid—and when I do, it's
oing to push me over the line from millionaire to billion-
ire."

So he still hasn't given up on the dream. Hasn't really traded his
ld dream for a new one.

"But how can buying the Beverly Hills Gardens do that
or you? Push you over the line? When the Hotel Bel-Air
inally sold to the Japanese, you told me that they paid far
more for it than it was worth in terms of what they could
xpect in earned revenues. But that they were willing to
verpay because of the prestige involved in owning the tro-
hy hotel.

"So if you're determined to get the Beverly Hills Gar-
lens, you're going to have to overpay too. If you want the
otel for its prestige and the pride of ownership, that's one
hing. But if you're overpaying, how can that possibly in-
rease your net worth? Am I making sense?"

"Perfect sense. But I have a secret weapon."

This time she laughed. Supermen always had secret
veapons.

"It's called selling off *part* of the assets for more than the
um of the whole. The Beverly Hills Gardens is on the

north side of Sunset, right?"

"Right."

"The land directly north of Sunset there is probably worth, acre for acre, foot for foot, more than any other parcel of land in the country, and the hotel is sitting on more acres than any hotel in a cosmopolitan city can possibly need or financially justify. It's not a country club, but it has its own golf course, which is a mere convenience for guests, certainly not a money-maker in any real sense. Acres of gardens that don't bring in a cent of revenue. Bridle paths that belong someplace out in the country where land isn't at such a premium. A lobby bigger than the Waldorf's for a hotel not even a fifth its size. A world famous lounge in its own building on more land surrounded by more gardens.

"I'll take the lounge, move it into the lobby, and free up more land to sell. I'll sell it *all* except for the hotel itself and the bungalows directly behind the main building. And when I'm done trimming it down to size and refurbishing, I'll have a much more efficient hotel—one that's easier to run and therefore more profitable per room—and I won't really have sacrificed any of its beauty. And in addition, I will have—I haven't got it all worked out yet—somewhere between three and four hundred million dollars that I didn't have *before!*"

He was so excited, so *ecstatic*, she could almost feel the electricity emanating from him, almost see the adrenaline pumping through his veins, and she wondered if anything else in the world could possibly mean this much to him. The baby? Even she herself?

"When will all this be settled?"

"Well, they're accepting bids now, but in a couple of months—February fourteenth to be precise—they're going to let the three top bidders slug it out face to face."

"I see."

"Is that all you can say?"

430

She smiled tremulously. "I don't know what to say. I'm speechless."

"Say *something*. Anything."

"Okay. February the fourteenth is Saint Valentine's Day."

"Good! Then the hotel will be my Valentine present to you. Don't you have anything else to say? I know . . . say you love me."

That was a joke, wasn't it?

"You already know that, but all right, I'll say it. I love you, Jonathan West, more than life itself. And I'm *very* happy for you. I'm happy that you will finally have your dream."

Even if it is not my dream.

"Why the funny look, Jonny? Don't you believe me?"

"Of course I believe you. I would never *not* believe you. I was just thinking how much I love you. If anything ever happened to you—Oh, God, Andrianna, you mean more to me than anything. More than anything in the world!"

"More than a billion dollars?" she teased.

"Of course more than a billion dollars. A billion dollars is only money."

No, sometimes a billion dollars is more than money. Sometimes it's a dream, the most precious of dreams.

"Now *you're* looking at me funny, Andrianna. As if you don't believe *me* . . ."

"Of course I believe you. You once told me that you would never lie to me, and I believed *that*."

That was what love was all about, wasn't it? Belief and trust and taking chances . . . acts of faith, just like their baby growing inside her. And she wished that she could tell Jonathan about the baby this very second, but she couldn't . . . any more than she had been able to tell him who and what she had been from the very beginning.

That night she couldn't sleep. At first it was because she

was too excited to sleep, thinking about the baby and about Jonathan's dream, the acquisition of the hotel. Worrying whether it would work out for him. She prayed that it did.

At first she'd been jealous of that dream because it meant so much to him, and she wanted . . . *needed* . . . to come first. But gradually she'd come to see that the dream *was* the man. Realizing that, how could she deny him it, even in the secret recesses of her heart?

Then she was too tired to sleep, her body exhausted, aching for sleep, but her mind perverse and unwilling. Next came the stage in which one just lay there and all the dark thoughts subjugated by the light of day came back to torture the victim in the black of night.

Most of all she agonized about Jonathan's finding out the truth about her, more frightening now that their baby was growing inside her. If Jonathan should find out the truth now at this stage of the game—that she was not only an impostor but a very sick one—would he still want her, trust her, love her? Would he ever forgive her for not trusting in him enough to tell him the truth?

Rather than just lie there being miserable, she crept out of bed to go into the study. She closed the door and turned on the television. Maybe a middle-of-the-night film would distract her or even lull her to sleep. She flicked the remote until she found an oldie in black and white when she really would have preferred something in color, cheerful and bright, but *Wuthering Heights* was just beginning, and she had never seen it and had read the book years and years before . . .

Jonathan found her there, curled up in the big leather chair and sobbing, just as the film was in its last few minutes.

"Andrianna, darling, what is it?"

"It's *Wuthering Heights*. Cathy is dying. See, Heathcliff is holding her in his arms by the window so she can see the heather on the moors for the last time."

"But Andrianna, it's just a movie."

She continued to sob, and he looked at the screen. "Look, I've seen this movie, and they're going to get together later on," he said, trying to comfort her. "Their spirits, anyway. See, Laurence Olivier is telling Merle that they'll be reunited. That he's going to be waiting for her on those goddamned moors until she comes back to find him and then they're going to make love in the heather. That's not so terrible, is it? Come on, sweetheart, come back to bed."

"Jonathan, you don't understand. It's a wonderful love story, but it's the most *terrible* love story. Cathy's dying, but Heathcliff comes to her deathbed only to curse her. He damns her soul for eternity."

"Well, can you blame him? They swore eternal love, but then when he's forced to leave her to go earn his fortune, she gets tired of waiting for him, the faithless little baggage, and ups and marries the rich neighbor and destroys everybody's life. Even if Heathcliff is a moody and surly bastard, you have to admit he had a right to curse her for that."

"No, you don't understand. He doesn't curse her for her faithlessness. He curses her for *dying*, for cheating *him* by dying."

"No, sweetheart. He loved her too much to curse her for dying. For faithlessness, yes. For dying, no. Now come to bed. It *is* only a movie, and in the end their spirits are going to get together. For them it's going to be sex in the afternoon, romping in the heather for eternity. What could be better than that?" He clicked off the TV.

Dutifully she allowed Jonathan to take her to bed, but she remained unconvinced. She would never forget Heathcliff's terrible words. And the most terrible part was that he hadn't cursed only Cathy; at the same time he had put a

433

curse on himself . . .

Catherine Earnshaw, may you not rest as long as I am living! . . . May your soul haunt me! . . . Be with me always! . . . Take any form! . . . Drive me mad! . . . Just don't leave me where I cannot find you! . . . You are my life, and I cannot live without my life! . . . You are my soul, and I cannot live without my soul! . . .

Not sex in the afternoon but a curse! For herself she could bear it, but not for Jonathan. He was the golden boy . . . too golden to bear the brunt of so terrible a curse . . .

Thirty-one

Cedars-Sinai
February 15, 1990

When Andrianna first opened her eyes, she was confused. There were two men standing over her, one darkly
handsome and one beautifully fair. They were both scowling and she had to struggle to get them into perspective.
The darkly handsome one was a proper Heathcliff for
sure, but the fair one—*he* was her Heathcliff, wasn't he?
Both her Heathcliff and her Jonathan, and both sworn to
love her for all the time to come. But Heathcliff didn't really exist—he was only a character in a book, a movie. So
he really didn't count.

And that left only Jonathan . . . her Jonathan . . . who
had once loved her . . . before he knew that she was not to
be trusted. Still, even if he wasn't really Heathcliff—if he
hadn't already damned her—he was going to do that now.
Wasn't that why he was here?

The darkly handsome one was, of course, Jerry Hern.
But why was *he* here? He who had not sworn to love her
forever but who *had* promised to keep her secrets until the
end of time.

And then she looked around at the windowless room
and remembered where she was and what had brought her
here. "Our baby!" she cried. "Did I lose the baby?"

Jonathan just shook his head, unable to speak. It was

435

Jerry who huskily answered her. "No, you didn't lose the baby and your condition is stabilized for now, no thanks to you. Andrianna, how could you *not* tell me you were pregnant?"

And the funny thing was that she reached for Jerry's hand and begged *him* to forgive her when of course it was Jonathan whose forgiveness she should ask, beg for . . . Jonathan, whom she had deceived so badly.

She tried not to look at Jonathan, so afraid of what she would see in his face. So, instead she looked at Jerry, asking him, "But how did they find you, Jerry? How did you get here?"

"Your husband brought me here in his own fancy plane, the *Andrianna*."

Then she *had* to look at Jonathan. "But how did you know that Jerry was my doctor?"

"Because I'm the boy wonder, don't you remember?" His tone was just a touch ironical. Or was it bitter? "And I was able to add up one and one and get two."

"So you told him everything, Jerry?" she said, not looking at Jonathan once again.

"Yes, I did, and I'm not going to apologize for it either. And if you don't like it, Andrianna Duarte, then it's just too bad. Don't use me for your doctor, okay? And now I'm getting out of here to leave you two alone. But I'll be back. I'm hanging around for the next couple of days just to be checking in on you, but after that, lady, I'm history and you're getting yourself a bunch of new doctors."

But in spite of his angry tone he picked up her hand and kissed it, and she began to cry. "I love you, Jerry."

"I know. And I you. I'll see you later. I'll see you both later."

And then they were alone, she and her Jonathan, and she didn't know what he was thinking or what she could possibly say that would make things right between them. She didn't even know where to begin, but he spoke first.

436

"You missed Saint Valentine's Day, you know."

"It was when?" She had lost all track of time.

"Yesterday. And I promised you a present. The hotel. But you're not getting it now."

"Oh, I know. I don't *deserve* a present."

"No, you sure as hell don't," he said ruefully. "But—"

"Ivana didn't get a Valentine Day's present either, you know?" she interrupted him. "The Don didn't give her one this year."

"What?" he smiled slightly. "Andrianna, why are we talking about the Trumps at a time like this? Are you trying to change the subject? Up to your old tricks, is that it?"

He sounded like he was only teasing but she wasn't sure.

"Oh, no! It's just that we were talking about Valentine presents and it's so sad. Instead of a present, Ivana got— splitsville!"

"*Splitsville!*" Jonathan laughed. "Where did that come from? I never heard you use that word before."

"But that's what the headline said. The one I read just before—" She broke off and shook her head. "Poor Ivana. I knew she was in trouble. That she never really came first with the Don."

"Oh? And how did you know that?"

"Because he never put *her* name on anything. Not on their yacht, not on their plane, like you did . . ." Her voice trailed off. Jonathan would probably want to change the name on the jet now and she could scarcely blame him considering . . .

"Well, that had to mean *something*, didn't it?" she asked solemnly. "It was always Donald's this and Donald's that and now it doesn't look like her name was officially . . . legally, that is . . . on *anything*, except of course, that prenuptial agreement. Even the Plaza Hotel . . . even though she ran it. It was always Donald's Plaza Hotel and now I guess it always will be—"

She broke off suddenly, stricken with embarrassment as

she realized how she must sound. Of all things to be talking about now! Whether or not Ivana owned the Don's trophy hotel legally and officially! Her own Valentine present—the one she didn't deserve and the one Jonathan had just told her she wasn't getting—was *Jonathan's* trophy hotel . . . his dream . . . and now . . .

She felt sick just thinking about what he must be thinking—that she was being manipulative and self-serving, trying to get him to give her his hotel in spite of everything . . .

"I . . . I didn't mean . . ." She smiled at him weakly, shrugging her shoulders in a helpless gesture as the tears ran down her cheeks. "Splitsville . . ." She shook her head.

"Oh, Andrianna! Andrianna!" he whispered. "Don't you cry! Don't you cry for anyone! Besides, they might reconcile, you know. They very well might still have a future together and next year . . . well, who knows? Valentine's Day comes around every year. So, here, let me dry your tears." Tenderly, he patted at her cheeks with his handkerchief.

"But, Jonathan, you don't understand. I—"

"Hold on a second. You didn't let me finish before. What I was going to say was that while you *weren't* getting the hotel as your Valentine gift it wasn't really because you didn't deserve a present but only because I don't have it to deliver."

"Oh, Jonathan, you *didn't* get the hotel then? Because of me . . . You had to leave before the bargaining was finished. You lost your dream because of me!" And the tears started to flow again.

"I'd like to say that that was the truth so you could feel really guilty. You deserve to feel guilty, believe me. But since I swore to a certain Andrianna DeArte, the woman I *thought* I married, that I would always tell her the truth—I must confess that, no, I didn't lose the hotel because of you. As a matter of fact I had the deal all wrapped up when the call came through that you were in trouble. All I had to do was give the very last bid before I tore out of that room. I knew the other guys were through and it was all over . . . if I wanted it to be . . ."

If I wanted it to be!

"But Jonathan, didn't you want it to be? It was your big chance to become a billionaire. It was your dream."

And finally, instead of cursing her, he *really* smiled at her—that big Jonathan West golden-boy smile.

"Nah. It wasn't my dream. A guy can be a billionaire any old day. All he needs is the right mathematical formula, and I was the mathematical formula champ of my school. Didn't I ever tell you that story?"

As he spoke, he again wiped away at her tear-stained cheeks, and her pulse was racing as fast as it had ever raced when he was making love to her.

"Jonathan, you're the guy who never tells lies. Remember? So stop playing with me. Why didn't you make that last bid before you left?"

"Because it was more important for me to walk away from it than not. Because I had something to prove to myself, if not to you."

"What?"

"That being a billionaire doesn't mean a thing. All it means, when you come down to it, is having another couple of hundred million to fool around with, and to tell you the truth, I'd rather fool around with you. You're a hell of a lot sexier, even if you are a lying fool."

"Oh, Jonathan. Can you ever forgive me?"

"I think so. The way I look at it is that if you couldn't trust me enough to tell me all about Andrianna Duarte, the little girl with the big yellow cat eyes from the wine country, then part of the fault has to be with me. So if you will forgive me, I'll forgive you, and then our baby—our Valentine to each other—will have a lot to be happy about. The only one who isn't going to be all that happy is Dr.

Hern, and somehow I don't feel so bad about that. He's a little too good-looking and a little too smug for my taste."

"Oh, Jonathan, Jerry was never more than a wonderful friend . . ."

"Oh, Andrianna, do you think you have to tell me that?" And this time *his* eyes filled. "And I *am* grateful to him."

"Then what is it? Why isn't Jerry going to be happy?"

"Because his children's clinic isn't going to get all the gravy. Some, but not all of it. Most of it will be going into SLE research."

"Oh, Jonathan, I have a feeling Jerry won't mind at all."

He grinned at her, that old black magic golden-boy grin. "I have the same feeling. And it's a good thing I didn't buy the Beverly Hills Gardens. I think I'm going to be too busy with our new foundation to have bothered with it much. You know, once I take a project over, things happen! They didn't put me on the cover of *Time* for nothing. Before you know it, you're going from 'medically controlled' back into remission and then, hah! A complete cure will be next. Just a matter of time. You know me — I'm the guy who doesn't take no for an answer. Right?"

"Oh, yes, right!"

And then finally he bent to her, his arms encircling her, his lips reaching for hers. It was then that a nurse appeared.

"I'm sorry, Mr. West, but you're going to have to leave now. Ordinarily a visitor is allowed only five minutes in ICU, and you've already been here much longer than that."

"It's OK. Mrs. West is doing fine. When are they transferring her up to the eighth floor? She's a woman who needs a room with a view. She likes to look out and see the sunlight."

The nurse smiled. "I'm afraid that's not up to me. You'll have to speak to the doctors."

"It's all right, Jonathan. I can wait."

"But I don't *want* you to wait. I know how much you

440

love the sunlight."

"It's all right, Jonathan, really. I don't need the sun when I have you."

She remembered when she had played the role of Juliet at Le Rosey when she had been young and untutored in the ways of life, still the innocent. And she had always treasured some of the lines . . . lines that had caught her imagination and held her in thrall. They were written about Romeo, but they could have been written about Jonathan, he who had passed over a thin line. Not from millionaire to billionaire, but from a heroic figure to a true hero.

And he will make the face of heaven so fine
That all the world will be in love with night,
And pay no worship to the garish sun.

But then, of course, she was no Juliet and he no Romeo, thank God, because after all, Romeo and Juliet were star-crossed lovers. And neither were they—she and Jonathan—Cathy and Heathcliff, because they too were star-crossed. And they most certainly weren't Ivana and the Don . . .

She and Jonathan? They were only lovers, not crossed but *kissed*, by both the sun and the stars. And wherever they were and no matter what time it was, it would always be afternoon for them . . . an eternity of golden afternoons. She was so sure of it, she would stake her life on it!

Epilogue

Malibu

1990

August 1990

She sat on the deck with the baby to her breast while a nurse hovered over her. "It's all right, Maria; you can go do something else. I promise, as soon as the baby is through feeding, I'll call you."

Maria was reluctant to leave but she did.

Andrianna kept insisting she didn't need a baby nurse, but both Jonathan and Jerry were adamant.

Now, as the baby fed at her breast, she kissed the sweet-smelling head and breathed in the air, looking out at the water and watching the parade of humanity passing below on the beach. How wonderful it was, she thought, to be in Malibu with Jonathan constantly at her side.

Now he came out on the deck with the mail, wearing only a pair of shorts, and she thought for the millionth time how beautiful he was, as beautiful as baby Elena.

He kissed both of them, first the mother and then the baby. "How's our daughter doing?"

"She's doing fine. Look how hungry she is, how she sucks . . ."

"I don't blame her."

"Oh, Jonathan, isn't life wonderful?"

"Wonderful," he agreed. "But you just remember, you're not to overdo. Jerry says you're—"

"Oh, what does Jerry know? He's not even my doctor anymore."

"He's *more* than your doctor, and you're to listen to everything he says."

"Okay, boss. But if I had listened too well to Jerry, there wouldn't even be an Elena."

"Come on, Andrianna. It was only that he was so concerned about you."

"Oh, I know . . ."

Jonathan was flipping through the pile of mail quickly. "Ah, look here. A copy of *Business Today.*"

"Jonathan!" she squealed. "Your picture's on the cover! You didn't even tell me. And what does it say there?" She peered over Elena's head. " 'Jonathan West, Making a Business Out of Philanthropy.' Oh, Jonny! How wonderful!"

Under the caption it quoted him: "It doesn't matter what game I play—I play to win!"

"Oh, I like your quote, Mr. West."

"I do too. But it is a game, you know, funding research . . . as much fun as business. And searching for answers is easily as interesting—more—as making money. And besides, look how nicely I can live this way . . . without going into the office . . . spending the time with you and Elena. Though I wish you had let me have my way and called her Andrianna."

"It was very important to me, Jonathan, that I—"

"I know."

"Besides, since Jonathan West, the golden boy of

444

philanthropy, is on the case, who knows how many babies we'll get to name?"

"No, Andrianna—we've been lucky, and we're not pushing our luck."

She smiled secretively. "Whatever you say, Jonathan. Whatever you say . . ."

After all, she was Andrianna Duarte West, and she wasn't known for telling the truth—at least not the *absolute* truth.

Maria came out on the deck again, and Andrianna handed her the baby while Jonathan watched her face. "What are you thinking, Andrianna? What's that little smile for?"

"Ah, ask me no questions and I'll tell you no lies."

"Andrianna—!"

She ran for the staircase that led down to the sand, and he ran after her. "Hurry, Jonathan, hurry!" she called over her shoulder. "Let's catch the last few rays before the sun goes down . . ."

FEEL THE FIRE IN CAROL FINCH'S ROMANCES!

BELOVED BETRAYAL   (2346, $3.95)

Sabrina Spencer donned a gray wig and veiled hat before blackmailing rugged Ridge Tanner into guiding her to Fort Canby. But the costume soon became her prison—the beauty had fallen head over heels in love!

LOVE'S HIDDEN TREASURE   (2980, $4.50)

Shandra d'Evereux felt her heart throb beneath the stolen map she'd hidden in her bodice when Nolan Elliot swept her out onto the veranda. It was hard to concentrate on her mission with that wily rogue around!

MONTANA MOONFIRE   (3263, $4.95)

Just as debutante Victoria Flemming-Cassidy was about to marry an oh-so-suitable mate, the towering preacher, Dru Sullivan flung her over his shoulder and headed West! Suddenly, Tori realized she had been given the best present for a bride: a night of passion with a real man!

THUNDER'S TENDER TOUCH   (2809, $4.50)

Refined Piper Malone needed bounty-hunter, Vince Logan to recover her swindled inheritance. She thought she could coolly dismiss him after he did the job, but she never counted on the hot flood of desire she felt whenever he was near!

CONTEMPORARY FICTION
BY KATHERINE STONE